CW01663415

CONOR RENNICK

# Electric Blue, Plague Green

*First edition*

*This book was professionally typeset on Reedsy.*
*Find out more at reedsy.com*

# Acknowledgments

To Yvonne Cullen, for her years of support and feedback, as well as to John, Feargal, Monica, Brenda, and all the others at our writing circle for indulging the one arsehole with 1500+ words a week to read.

To Susie Murphy, for answering some nobody's questions about self-publishing. And to my non-writer friends for humouring my delusional ramblings.

And reluctantly, to my parents, for always badgering me about how I was *so creative* as a child and *really ought to write some of these ideas down someday.*

Well guess what? I did it now. Happy?

# Chapter 1

You think the strangest things when you're chasing a UFO in the arse-end of nowhere.

For instance, if it weren't for human imagination, we'd have froze to death in caves millennia ago. But just as human imagination has given birth to angels and unicorns, it has created far more monsters.

This is a problem if, like me, your job is hunting down the monsters.

Which, incidentally, was why I was spending my Friday night driving speedily down a dark road, looking for aliens.

I was jolted as the car ran over a pothole. In the seat next to me, Dawkes glowered in my direction.

'Jesus, Reilly!', she hissed. 'We'll be dead before the Visitors even notice we're here!'

'You know as well as I do, that they won't target us if we look too cautious.' I responded, drumming my fingers on the wheel, 'If you can't handle a little turbulence, you'll be buggered when they take us up anyway.'

Dawkes' eyes narrowed, then a voice cut in between us.

'Ah, will the pair of ye give over?', Boyle said, adjusting an old ham radio, lifted straight from the 60s. 'Sure, I won't even be able to find the feckin' signal with the two of ye giving out.'

Dawkes, slumped back in her seat with a sigh at our superior's words, her dark hair and complexion blending with the darks of her suit and the night. Despite joining up roughly the same time, we hadn't really spoken before this mission, but the frustration in her eyes was clear even to me.

It was hard to blame her for being on edge, given that we'd been driving for over an hour with no sign of paranormal activity. With the recent kidnappings weighing on the Enlightenment, heads would roll if this tip turned out to be a wild goose chase.

If any of this bothered Boyle, you wouldn't have guessed, as he continued fiddling with the radio, the darkness stark against his pale skin, outlining the furrowed wrinkles on his forehead, where his hairline had made a rapid retreat halfway up his scalp. One of the few field veterans of the Enlightenment who'd stuck around in Ireland despite its reputation for being quiet and boring on the paranormal front, Boyle was naturally the one calling the shots on this mission. I didn't know what was funnier, that he was using such outdated tech, or that it'd probably work if only because he was using it.

After a brief, blessed moment of silence, interrupted only by the rumbling of the car and the whine of the ham radio, Dawkes spoke up.

'Don't suppose it'd too much to hope that those druids just had a bad trip?'

I fidgeted in my seat. The Ciorcal Darach, (Oak Circle if you don't understand Irish) were the ones who reported the sightings of Visitor craft in the area. While they were known to use psychedelics in some of their rites, I doubted they would've called us down here if they weren't sure of what they saw.

'You really think they'd be thick enough to call the Order on a hunch?'

Dawkes rolled her eyes, the tension leaving her shoulders.

'Guess not. Just wish we weren't leaving our beats exposed while we're out playing X-Files.'

I shrugged. 'It's not ideal, but we work with what we have. With the pacts in place with the native paranormals, Ireland's a fairly low-priority for the Order. No sense assigning more agents than needed to maintain stability.'

'Oh, come on, Reilly. You're really giving me the canned line on this?' Dawkes responded, her tone rising slightly. 'What about the Dingle Incident? Maybe if we'd had more people back then, that cabal wouldn't have gotten as strong as it did! And twelve years later, the number of field agents in Ireland's barely risen at all!'

My breath hitched, and I struggled to keep my hands steady. Dammit, why'd she mention Dingle? I tried to get my breathing under control, memories bubbled to the surface, the fingers on my right-hand drumming frantically against the wheel.

No. Reilly, focus. Remember what you were taught. Send them to the vault, lock the door, don't let them out.

I repeated the mantra in my head as I banished the memories to the same place the rest of my old life went. That person doesn't matter now, you're Agent Reilly now, proud foot soldier of the Order of the Enlightenment, the first and last defence between humanity and the madness of the paranormal. Act like it.

I peeked over at Dawkes and Boyle. Boyle was still absorbed in his work, while Dawkes was regarding me with a single raised eyebrow. Good, I think I managed to keep a lid on it.

'That Inci...event was certainly unfortunate.' I began. 'However, there are many places in the world where events like that would be commonplace if not for the greater presence of the Enlightenment in those areas. Besides, our manpower is limited worldwide. We might be spread thin here, but better here, where most of the paranormals already toe the line, than in America or China.'

Dawkes stared at me for a moment, her expression unreadable. 'I'd heard you were a bit of a company man. Guess that was understated, huh?'

''Article 1 of the Agent code of ethics. It is the duty and honour of all agents to protect the human race from the horrors of the paranormal.' I shot back. 'Just because it's hard doesn't mean it's not worth doing.'

Luckily, I was spared from having to justify myself further when Boyle cut across, voice giddy.

'Here, quiet up over there, I'm getting something!', He said, pressing a headphone to his ear, a grin growing, 'Ah, we got 'em now, lads! Reilly, slow the car to 50, and Dawkes, keep an eye out for any lights!'

We sprang into action. Dropping the car's speed, I didn't bother looking for any signs of UFO activity myself. Visitor ships are nearly impossible to spot in broad daylight, the chances of me seeing one in the middle of the night, rain splattering the windshield all the while, was impossible.

Besides, we had our own tools to bring to bear.

Dawkes put a finger to the side of her green-tinted glasses, whispering a word in a language I didn't recognise. I felt the surge of power as her spell took effect, the glasses shimmering for a second. Dawkes looked out, her eyes showing no strain from the piss poor visibility.

'Got a visual, sir. Northeast. A bit over a mile up.'

Boyle began working at his radio again. Even over the sound of the engine, I could hear he'd starting whispering a chant, and the flicking and twisting of the knobs and switches took on a ritualistic rhythm. After a moment, the squeal of the radio itself seemed to take on a lyrical note, the kind that catches your attention and stays in the back of your mind hours afterwards

'Suggestion's deployed.' Boyle said, putting down the radio and reaching for something in his jacket. 'They'll be on us any moment now. Reilly, you ready for when they take us up?'

'Yes, sir.' I responded, already reaching into my own jacket. 'I'll fry their systems the second we're on the ship.'

'Good lad, so.' Boyle responded, the shadows along his face giving his grin a feral quality. He patted me on the shoulder, sending an unpleasant jolt down my body, before sitting back to regard both Dawkes and I.

'All right now. Remember the plan. We're going for the captives first. Then, we take out the command structure. Once the aliens are dealt with, we force them to land the ship. All goes as planned, we'll come back with the hostages and a new shiny UFO for the techies to lose their shite over. Understood?'

'Understood', Dawkes and I both responded, Dawkes flicking an absent-minded salute while I gripped my weapon with one hand and the wheel with the other.

Boyle shifted to look at Dawkes, his mouth turned up at the side, 'Dawkes, I trust you'll be able to restrain yourself until then?'

'Oh, I'll try my hardest sir.' Dawkes responded, matching Boyle's teasing expression with a similar smirk. 'But I might just take a quick peek around once we're done.'

The two quietly chuckled. For the next couple of moments, the only sounds were the rain and engine.

After a few tense seconds of driving, harsh light filled the road, the brightness straining my eyes worse. Dawkes hissed in pain, hurriedly removing her glasses, while in the back I swore I heard Boyle let out a laugh which morphed into a scoff.

As I managed to adapt to the light, I felt my eyes start to grow heavy and I struggled to remember what was happening. I could feel my hand loosen on the wheel, and even though part of me knew something was wrong, all the rest of me wanted was to lay back and rest my eyes.

Just before slipping away, I was brought back by the sound of the old radio squealing once again, the sound striking me like a slap to the face. All at once, the pressure evaporated, as if the radio's whine was a hot flame held directly to an ice cube.

Shaking myself, I shot my head around. Everything looked the same. Dawkes was also looking around, her eyes wide and shoulders tight, while Boyle was regarding us like he was a disappointed teacher.

'Ah, here. I know the two of ye are still new to this, but you can't expect me to give you a dig out every time.'

'Apologies, sir. I promise that's the last time that'll be a problem.' I responded, embarrassed. Of course, the Visitors would try to disable us telepathically before the abduction, but I'd made the mistake of assuming Boyle would cover that. While I was correct, the idea that someone else would always be on hand to take care of a problem wasn't something I could count on.

'Consider it a learning experience, you need to be prepared

for anything in this job.' Boyle flicked his eyes upward. 'Like how we're gonna be face to face with those light-bulb headed feckers any second.'

Dawkes and I shared a confused glance, before looking out and seeing, all the clearer thanks to the light, that we were now suspended high in the air. Above us, a large, disc shaped shadow, big enough it took up our entire vision, was emitting the light from directly on its underside, which we were being drawn into.

'Bleedin' Hell.' Dawkes whispered, the native London slipping out, her eyes wide as the saucer above us, and I felt the same sentiment. I'd seen images of flying saucers before (real images, mind), but the scale up close and personal carried a weight that, for a moment, made me question if we weren't out of our league.

'Admire it when we're done, lads!' Boyle's voice cut across; his tone stern. 'It's showtime!'

For a moment, the light became all-consuming. I shut my eyes, but the light crept in through the cracks. The experience was short-lived, and after a few seconds, I could feel the light receding.

Boyle's radio had already started up again, only this time, the warbling sound frequency quickly rose above my ability to hear it. Around us, however, I suddenly heard hoarse screams. I risked opening my eyes and could see Dawkes had already pulled up her sleeve, revealing a smart glove emblazon with Cyrillic script along the sides, and seemed braced to pounce the moment the light cleared entirely.

As it did, we got our first proper look at our surroundings. The car, which still felt like it was floating, was in the middle of a large, circular room lifted straight from 60s sci fi, back when everyone thought the future was shiny metal, flashing lights and featureless chrome walls. The closest thing to decoration were a few shiny gurneys, with restraints for both wrists and ankles. Standing around the car were five, very tall spindly creatures, clutching their heads and writhing in pain.

When I say the creatures were tall and spindly, I mean they ranged from 6 to 7ft tall and so thin even the chunkiest one looked emaciated. They wore strange, shiny jumpsuits that covered most of their bodies, but what skin I could see was a pale grey, and their heads were bald and wrinkled. The creatures' features were similar to humans, except the eyes, two, empty black orbs, with a shine that made it seem like those eyes were reflecting the void of space itself.

In UFO lore, they're known as Greys, but those I worked for, knew them as the Visitors.

The moment I felt the car wheels touch a solid surface, I yanked out my own weapon, a black-handled athame knife, consecrated for channelling energy. While the Visitors were still distracted by Boyle's radio, I pulled myself out of the car, swiping the blade through the air as I reached out with my senses.

As the athame swayed and cut at the space around me, I felt the tingle of energy brimming on all sides, great, thick currents of electricity pumping through the ship like veins and arteries, the rhythmic pulse of whatever monstrous engine was powering this thing.

Even knowing what to expect, feeling so much energy in such proximity was enough to send trembles down my arms and spine, the same mix of trepidation and the bizarre, self-destructive curiosity you'd feel holding your hand over an electrified railway track.

And here I was about to cut it all up with a knife.

I set the blade into a reverse grip and spun, slashing at the biggest flow of energy I could sense, bellowing out 'Tin-treach!'.

Both the word and tool gave substance to my will behind the spell, and I cut at the area of the current. I felt the electrical flow stutter and redirect, leaving the wiring technically unharmed, while the electricity that was powering it ran rampant across the delicate systems around it.

A few things happened right after I did that. First, all the lights filling the chrome room died. Immediately after, the ship took an unhealthy lurch and I had to grab one of the gurneys to stay upright, the crashes and cries of several voices indicating I was the exception there.

While the ship definitely had some redundant systems that kept the whole thing from falling out of the sky, I'd dealt the internals of the saucer a nasty blow that hopefully left the Visitors reeling with most of their none essential systems offline.

So, there we were, in a dark room, surrounded by paranormal lifeforms with powers beyond mere humans, no doubt less than impressed with us disrupting their operation, inside a large, airborne flying saucer that was having noticeable trouble staying that way.

We had them right where we wanted them.

# Chapter 2

Whatever feelings of triumph I felt quickly unravelled.

I heard a shrill, inhuman shriek and immediately dropped down and rolled to the side, an instinct justified when the outline of the gurney I had grabbed onto earlier flew through the space I was just standing in, smashing into a wall. Looking back, I could see one of the taller Visitors seemed to have resisted Boyle's assault, risen to its full height and levelling a hand in my direction.

Suddenly, the ground disappeared from under me, and I had maybe just enough time to realise I was flying, before I collided with something solid, which made a distinctly Boyle-like cry of pain as we both tumbled to the ground. I heard a crash as what was likely Boyle's radio landed hard against the floor, clattering away with a lethal abruptness.

I scrambled to my feet, my back screaming. Already, I could make out in the shadows of the room that, with Boyle no longer maintaining his spell, the Visitors were starting to recover, some pulling themselves up while others had already risen to stare down our little rescue party.

However, while me and Boyle were busy playing human bowling, Dawkes had been plotting her next move.

Before the tallest Visitor could do anything else, I heard

Dawkes shout out another foreign word, followed by the sensation of a wave passing over me, towards the Visitor. The wave struck it, and the Visitor's body went stiff, then started jerking its limbs in bizarre contortions, collapsing to the floor with a distressed rasp, stuck in a yoga pose by way of Picasso.

'Cover me!' Boyle shouted out, his voice strained as he broke across the room towards the radio. One of the Visitors began to make some gesture at him, cut short when Boyle punched it in its tiny jaw, his broad, portly frame sending it spiralling, with a crunch. The alien fell to the floor and stayed there.

Two down, three standing, and maybe another couple of seconds before they paste us.

I yanked my left sleeve up, exposing tattooed lines, streaks through each line indicated a word. Ogham writing, the alphabet of Old Irish, and once closely guarded by the druids who codified it. The writing on my arm translated roughly out to strength or force, and was a potent symbol of kinetic energy. Course, channelling kinetic energy straight out of my arm like I was planning, would've been dangerous and could rip my arm to pieces if I wasn't careful.

Or, like most magi, I could cheat and use another tool to aid it. Like one specifically designed to channel and redirect energy.

Concentrating my will, I felt the tattoos on my left arm burn, transforming my will into energy. I sprinted towards the remaining Visitors, shifting my athame to my left hand. A couple had already shaken off the remnants of Boyle's magic, ready to retaliate.

I didn't give them the chance. With a bound, I thrust my athame straight into the floor between the Visitors, the growing energy flowing from my arm into the athame giving it enough force to pierce an inch into the metal.

With a roar, I sent the power billowing out of me, through the athame and into the floor below. An invisible dome of force blasted out from around me and I heard a chorus of shrieks, followed by the sound of tearing metal.

I tensed up when the noise died down, expecting to feel myself get tossed about again or have my brain turned inside out now that Boyle's radio wasn't screwing with their telepathy. When neither happened, I risked looking up.

It was still hard to make out, with the lights out, but the fight was done. The Visitors I'd struck now lay crumpled like broken dolls against the walls, heavy dents indicated where they'd become closely acquainted with the surfaces. Boyle had recollected his radio, and once again the air was filled with psychic static. Dawkes was checking the bodies, making sure none of them were planning any last-minute surprises.

The whole encounter had taken only a few seconds.

I picked myself up, suppressing a gasp as my arm flared with pain, throbbing fingers almost losing their grip on my knife. Dammit, I should've known better. Using the athame and tattoos together might have reduced the strain from using magic, but I'd still slammed my fist into solid metal.

'Looks like we're all clear here.' Dawkes remarked. She rose, turning to Boyle.

Boyle nodded. His posture was still slouched and loose, even after having me thrown into him. I wasn't sure whether to envy his pain tolerance, or his acting. 'Well, could have gone worse, could have gone better. Fair play, the two of ye there, keeping things from going titsup.'

His head shifted in my direction, 'Are you alright, there?

You took a couple of spills during that scuffle.'

'I'm fine.' I responded. 'Just a couple of bruises. I can keep going.'

'Are you sure?' Dawkes' voice cut across. 'You're holding yourself a bit stiffly. If you're hurt, maybe we can get some first aid from the car.'

I was grateful for the darkness then, which hopefully hid any tension in my face, 'The suit absorbed most of the hits, and everything else is just bruises. Do we really have time to worry about this right now?'

Dawkes made to take a step forward at first, before Boyle interjected.

'Suit yerself. Let's just hope a few bumps' the worst we have to deal with tonight.'

Dawkes stopped at this, and I thought she was going to press the matter, but she didn't, instead softly shaking her head and readdressing Boyle.

'Well, sir. What's our next move?'

'Now...' Boyle began, reaching into his pocket, producing a tuning fork. 'We get a proper lay of the land.'

He struck the nearest wall with the fork. The hum took a moment to reach me, but when it did, the vibration penetrated my entire body, reverberating against my bones. Boyle moved the fork back and forth, his head leaned back. The hum echoed throughout the room, and beyond, into the rest of the ship.

I like to think of myself as fairly skilled in magic for my age, but there's nothing quite as humbling as watching someone perform a skill you take pride in with greater finesse than you ever had.

After a minute, Boyle's head straightened, and he pressed the fork against his leg, instantly silencing the hum. Or, I think it did anyway, my ears were still ringing.

'That's a bit odd, so.' Boyle said, putting the fork away. 'The sound picked up a large number of bodies, but in two groups, both a short distance for here, and up near the centre of the craft.'

'Doesn't sound that strange.' Dawkes said, 'Presumably one group's our prisoners and the others the remaining Visitors running the ship.'

'Aye, that'd likely be right. The odd bit's that neither groups coming towards us right now.'

'Huh? Why?' I said. 'Shouldn't the other Visitors be aware we've taken down their crewmates?'

'Ye'd think so, but seems they've got something else keeping them occupied.' Boyle's brow furrowed. 'Very strange, indeed.'

'Good news for us, though!' Dawkes said, cracking her knuckles. 'While they're distracted, we should be able to swoop in, secure our hostages and catch them off-guard!'

'Oh, we'll certainly be taking advantage of this.' Boyle responded, his expression still pensive, 'Just keep your wits about ye, alright? Whatever's distracting them, must be pretty attention-grabbing if they're ignoring us.'

With that, our intrepid group made its way to the doorway. Course, when I say doorway, I was referring to a flat, shiny piece of wall otherwise identical to the rest of the room except for it being set into a doorway. Technologically advanced they may be, the Visitors didn't have much flair for aesthetics.

As I came up to the doorway, I caught a glimpse of a wide shouldered, blond man, his freshly pressed black business suit, neat hair and clean shave doing nothing to hide the dark shadows under his eyes, or the flat, dead expression that seemed to be his default. I winced at the sight of my reflection.

The door stuttered for a second, before opening fully, light shooting out from the hallway ahead.

The light was coming from a fixture running along the ceiling, which flickered erratically in a way that brought back unsettling memories of the last time I'd watched Alien. The hallway differed further from the last room by having vents set into the floor, and on the wall opposite us, a couple of windows showed the dark sky outside, clouds trailing below the UFO like large balls of fluff caught in the wind.

We stepped out into the hallway, Boyle taking point. We moved quickly but quietly, our backs up to the wall as we reached a large curve in the hallway. Boyle slowed to a snail's pace before he rounded the curve, and we did likewise, only to stop when Boyle shoved a hand up in air.

'Hold it. There's a door here. Think it's where they're keeping our lot.'

I craned my neck around Boyle to get a look, and could see there was another doorway, similar to the one we just left a few minutes ago, except much thicker.

Boyle assessed the door briefly, then huffed. 'Right, Dawkes, can you handle this? I'd do it myself, but I never got the hang of door busting without making a great clatter.'

Dawkes nodded, then stepped closer to the door, fingers dancing in the air. In the seconds it took for her to close the distance, I could already see both her glove and glasses take on an ethereal, blue glow, the two digital devices interfacing with each other. The door slid smoothly open.

I admit, I was impressed. I could have maybe done something similar by manipulating the electricity powering the door, but it wouldn't have been quiet, and wouldn't have looked as easy as Dawkes made it look.

Dawkes stepped through the doorway, Boyle and I following. On first glance, it seemed very similar to the room where we met our little welcome party, large, shiny and flat, only now with the addition of multiple openings spread out across the room, all projecting some kind of orange, translucent barrier over the opening, and a large, circular desk, with multiple monitors build into it, some still glowing.

None of us said a word as we made a circuit of the room. Every cell had one or two humans, sitting. None reacted when we moved past, their expressions blank, staring at nothing. I suppressed a shudder when one of them slowly tipped over into a limp heap on the floor. It felt like we were looking at a bunch of dolls.

Psychic lobotomies. The Visitors must have used their telepathic powers to shut off the prisoners' conscious minds, so they wouldn't resist whatever procedures the aliens had in mind. We could fix them, but not now. Not until the ship was under control. I tried not to think about how that was probably what that psychic attack during our abduction was, and how if it weren't for Boyle, I'd probably be in one of those cells.

Article 2 of the Agent code of ethics. Innocence is the bedrock of reality. An agent maintains it at all costs. But what was the cost when we'd already failed?

Boyle recovered from the shock first, his face grim as he turned to Dawkes and I.

'Dawkes, check those consoles. Reilly, see if ye can find a way to get these barriers down. Sooner we get them loose, the sooner we can deal with the rest of the Visitors.'

It took a second to register, but I shook off my unease, and stepped towards one of the cells, athame drawn at the ready.

I didn't get far before I heard a yelp behind me. Spinning around, I saw a figure had scuttled out from under the desk as Dawkes approached it, now defensively curled in on itself on the far end of the room, close to the door. The figure had long black hair, and seemed somehow feminine in it's build, it's body shaking.

'Hello? Are you hurt?' Dawkes' voice was soft as she approached the girl deliberately. The figure didn't respond, but her shoulders went still when Dawkes got closer. All the while, Boyle and I kept our stances guarded. If it was someone who needed help, we'd do what we could, but that was no reason to be idiots about it.

As the girl rose, I felt a chill when I recognised the same, pale skin and dark black eyes, her build slimmer than any human should be. There was a flurry of movement as each of us reached for whatever weapon we had to hand, but the creature was quicker.

The strange girl thrust her hand out, and Dawkes let out a cry before she lifted a few feet off the ground, clutching at her throat. Cursing, I tried to level my athame at the creature, but had to stop when Dawkes lurched unevenly between me and the girl.

'Stay back!' At first, I thought the strange girl had spoke, her voice strained. Only her voice seemed to echo telepathically inside my head.

We stood frozen in that stand-off, Dawkes still hovering shakily between us as the girl moved to the door, keeping either me or Boyle from getting a clear shot. When she got beyond the doorframe, Dawkes suddenly lurched to one side, hitting off one of the walls with a pained gasp. The woman then ran out the door.

Boyle and I both sprinted the moment Dawkes dropped. Boyle checked on Dawkes while I ran to the doorway. The woman was quick, I'd already lost sight of her, her footsteps echoing round the curve to my left.

'Don't.' Boyle's voice stopped me mid-step. 'We can't afford to get separated.'

Dammit, he was right! We'd only gotten this far because Boyle was providing interference with his radio. If I went out too far, there'd be nothing stopping the big-eyed pricks from turning my brain into cauliflower. I stepped back, keeping one eye on the door.

'What the hell was that?!' Dawkes shouted, her eyes wide as Boyle helped her up.

'Hybrid.' Boyle said, his jaw clenched, 'Sometimes, the Visitors like to use our genetic material to clone hybrids between us and them. Buggered if I know why.'

'Is that why she wasn't affected by your radio static? Because she's a hybrid?'

Boyle shook his head and sighed. 'Maybe, maybe not. Only heard about them. Never saw one on a scout ship before.'

'We've found the abductees.' I spoke up after a moment. 'How're we going to handle the remaining Visitors?'

Boyle readjusted his grip on the radio, 'This mission's thrown us for a few loops, but the plan stays the same. Now the prisoners are safe, we'll head to the bridge, take down the pilots, and try to get this thing to land.'

He looked out to the doorway. 'Watch yourselves. Still haven't a clue what's been keeping all of the crew busy, but if that hybrid's gone running to them, they might get their shite together to send a few down.

'Could you check again if they're still in the same place?' Dawkes said. 'Even if they're on the move, we can maybe set up a defensive perimeter to meet them.'

'Good notion, Dawkes. Was just thinking that, myself.' Boyle removed the same tuning fork from his pocket and again struck it against a nearby wall. As the vibrations rung throughout the room and beyond, Boyle's face shifted through a few different expressions, before finally his eyes widened.

'We need to get down to the bridge, now.' He said, his legs already in motion.

'Why?' I asked, following him out, Dawkes taking up the rear.

'Because something's killing them, and we're still a couple of miles up in the air.'

I was about to ask him to elaborate, but was cut off when the ship lurched unpleasantly, wavering back and forth like a spinning plate. My stomach threatened to reintroduce me to my dinner as I planted my hands against the wall. Looking over, I saw both Boyle and Dawkes gripping whatever was close and even then, just barely staying upright.

The shudders continued, just long enough to make me contemplate what I wanted my last thoughts to be, before coming to a halt. It was pretty clear, from the way my gut was still halfway up my chest, that we were still falling, albeit slower.

Dawkes looked over at Boyle.

'Run?'

'Run.'

We ran.

All the while I tried to stem the uneasiness in my gut. This didn't make sense, we'd expected resistance from the Visitors, but they'd barely put up a token effort. What on earth could be going on in the bridge that was more important than active intruders?

If it wasn't obvious already something was wrong, it would've become apparent when we reached the large doors that led to the command bridge, and a truly awful stench stung my nostrils.

Imagine what you'd get if you mixed chlorine and spoiled milk, then threw in a durian fruit, and you're somewhere close.

The smell hit me head on, and between my eyes watering and gag reflex going into overdrive, my run turned into a shamble. Judging from the sounds of coughing next to me, Dawkes and Boyle weren't coping too well either, but before any of us could even get our breathes back, the doors slid open at our approach.

What we saw after the doors parted seemed like something out of a nightmare.

The bridge was a mess, in every sense of the word. The shiny metallic walls and floor were stained with the blue of Visitor blood and a myriad of browns, yellows and beige splattered together. Collapsed amid this toxic slurry were the remaining Visitors, their frail bodies strewn about, some of them still making weak, garbled wails and chokes.

In my shock, I felt a wet, warm substance splash on one of my shoes. I stumbled back, looking down to see more of that foul liquid collected in one large splat on my shoe, slowly trickling down the sides with a viscous slowness. A couple of steps ahead of me, the Visitor previously at my feet coughed out another mouthful of vomit before collapsing.

'Oh, God.' Dawkes said, her dark skin unusually pale as she

swallowed. 'What the hell happened?'

'There's no one piloting the ship.' I responded, still struggling to process it myself. 'And judging from the last few spills; this thing probably doesn't have an autopilot.'

Indeed, from the view I could see from the parts of the large window not smeared in alien puck, the ship was descending at an uneven angle, the ground visible from the window. If I hadn't already been stunned from seeing the Visitors, I'd probably have been terrified.

'It must be some kind of toxin or pathogen.' Dawkes' eyes darted over the scene while she murmured; with no indication she'd heard me. 'I can't see any wounds, so it couldn't be spread through injury. They were caught off guard, in the middle of an operation, so it's likely incredibly fast-acting. Maybe- '

'Dawkes, go back to the brig. Do whatever you can to make sure the prisoners are safe. Now.' Boyle's voice cut Doyle off, his face carefully neutral.

'Sir...' Dawkes began, before Boyle interrupted her again.

'I didn't ask for a debate; I gave you a feckin order! Now, go!'

Dawkes sprinted out the bridge, and I felt a tinge of envy. Boyle turned to me next.

'Reilly, I might be able to control our fall here, but I need your help. Can you try and direct some power out of the ship and into me?'

It took a second for the words to register, but when they did, I was stunned, 'Pardon? Sir, that's insane. The strain on the systems would probab-'

'You just let me worry about the strain, lad. You worry about moving that energy.' Boyle shot back, his tone final.

I froze, still in disbelief. Moving that kind of power was possible, even using it for magic was straightforward enough, but there was no telling what ripping that energy out of an alien mainframe would do the system. It was a dangerous gamble.

Yet, as the ground got closer out the corner of my eye, I realised there our other option was even more so. I readied my athame while Boyle moved to the centre of the room. Focusing my senses, I found the nexus of power in the bridge, which, predictably, was the elaborate setup of screens, switches and other machinery making up the command centre of the ship.

'Ready when you are, sir.' I said, breathing deeply, trying to keep my eyes off the window showing our imminent fate.

Boyle nodded, placing his radio on one of the few parts of the floor not stained with alien bodily fluids, while gripping his tuning fork. He turned to me, and struck the fork against the console, the vibrations ringing.

'Hit me.'

I thrust my blade into one of the gaps of the console, where the circuitry lay just underneath. Instantly, I felt the electricity that would have normally fried me at that point build up at the point of my knife, as I forced it to bend to my will. My face started to sweat, as I struggled to keep the energy focused, to persuade it to empower rather than destroy its target. Then, with a cry of 'Tintreach!', I pulled the knife loose and aimed it towards Boyle.

Following my blade, electricity flew across the room and struck Boyle head on, who caught it on his tuning fork. Instantly, his knees buckled and he let out a pained groan as he started converting the electricity into fuel for the slapdash spell he was undertaking. With visible effort, Boyle reached his tuning fork into the air, still vibrating, and with a defiant cry, smashed it into the ground.

The ground shook as the sound vibrations passed through it, and I covered my ears, the sound grinding against my eardrums. Despite the pain, I was still able to feel the same vibrations suspend and buoy the ship, forcing it upwards.

Looking over to the window, I could that the ship's descent had slowed. We were still falling, but we'd gone from a crash to a semi-controlled landing.

While Boyle was doing this, I focused on the power I was drawing from the ship, trying to keep the spell going, when I saw it. Just a bit behind Boyle, I saw the doors to the bridge open.

I stared at the doors for a second, confused, then my blood ran cold. I caught sight of a couple of bloody footprints emerging with wet slaps from the mess leading up to the doors. Bloody footprints with no accompanying body. The footprints stopped, and I felt a shot of fear as I sensed whatever was standing there return my gaze.

In that moment, my will wavered, and I lost control of the spell.

Immediately, the power current cut out, the energy snapping back into the console. On impulse, I tried to reach for it again, but the energy roiled and warped in response. Several machines burst and popped, some bursting into flames, while the monitors cracked and sparked.

But the worst was the one next to Boyle, which exploded, engulfing him in a ball of fire and metal.

I shouted his name, but before I could cross to help, the ship quaked one last time, careening with all the grace of a drunk seagull into the field, sending detritus, alien bodies and both of us, hurtling. I tripped, falling over and sliding until my back flashed with pain again as I smacked into another wall, now covered with the sickly warmth of the unsavoury fluids slopped about.

Despite wanting nothing more than to close my eyes and drift off, I peeled myself off the ground and tried to take stock.

The ship was stranded in some field next to a motorway, the aliens were all dead under suspicious circumstances, I couldn't see where Boyle had landed and I didn't even know what the story with Dawkes and the people we'd come to save was.

Oh yeah, and there was an invisible creature on the ship.

This mission just got a lot more complicated.

# Chapter 3

Article 5 of the Agent code of ethics. Fear is death. An agent must never panic. We are the bulwark that separates humanity from the chaos of the paranormal.

I reminded myself of this a few times to still the pounding in my chest, trying not to think about how I was covered in blood and vomit, surrounded by bodies.

Don't panic. Focus on what to do next.

Boyle!

I bolted over to the bridge and looked around for any sign of him. The smell of burnt meat not helping my anxiety. The source of the smell turned out to be a prone body sprawled awkwardly at the foot of the console.

Boyle.

I went over to check the body, my initial panic giving way to something numb. Gone was the paranoid fear of danger, replaced with dread.

The reek of burnt flesh grew pungent a second before I caught sight of the blistered, red wounds decorating Boyle's face and hands. Reaching for the less burnt of his hands, I checked for his heartbeat.

A weak pulse.

I swallowed my revulsion and lifted Boyle's unconscious

form up by the arms, dragging him out of the bridge, figuring that I shouldn't leave him marinating in every unpleasant substance that could come out of a Visitor. Given it looked like the Visitors were suffering from some disease, odds were good both me and Boyle could be infected.

I banished that thought. It didn't help me to worry about a disease right now. Besides, this was my fault. I'd lost control at a critical moment, and Boyle paid for it. I needed to get him out of here.

Pulling him up onto my shoulders as delicately as possible, I doubled back to the brig. Dawkes should be there, guarding the prisoners. I prayed that our invisible friend was either unconscious or legging it, not waiting to pick us off.

That prayer stopped dead when I caught sight of the doors. The previously uniform chrome doors now sported a large dented split between the two from the inside.

'Dawkes? Are you in there?'

'Reilly?' A familiar face appeared in the small gap between the doors, and Dawkes let out a breath when she saw me, then immediately tensed . 'Is that Boyle?'

'Unfortunately. He caught a lot of backlash from the spell we used to stop the ship.'

'Backlash?'

'Had to pull something drastic to stop the crash. Couldn't hold it. Hit him bad.' I gestured with my free hand towards my ruined suit, 'We got taken for a spin in that room, so if what the Visitors had is contagious, we probably have it. Incidentally, there's something invisible on board and it wasn't bothered by what killed the Visitors.'

What cautious optimism in Dawkes' face slipped away, 'Oh, God. And I thought I'd be the one with bad news.'

My eyes traced the damage along the doors, 'Complications?'

Dawkes let out a bitter laugh, 'Just a bit. When I got here, the power outages had just gotten to the cells, and the abductees got out. I'm not sure if it was a side-effect of the mind control or regular hysteria, but they came at me when I got in. I had to fight them off.'

She then gestured at the doors. 'It got out of hand.'

'Are any dead or dying?'

'No? But I think a few of them have broken bones and-'

'Then it's best not to worry about them now. Boyle needs medical attention first, and we're gonna need to call a coverup team for this anyway. Let them worry about the civilians.'

Dawkes rocked back, 'You're all heart, aren't you, Reilly?'

I felt a surge of heat rise to my face, and was about to open my mouth before a flash of pain from my injured hand clenching shook me out of it. Taking the chance to gather my thoughts, I returned Dawkes' stare. 'Believe me, I'm glad there's no serious casualties, but given that, we need to prioritise our wounded and maintaining Innocence. If you have a better idea, I'm open.'

Dawkes took a step back, quietly mouthing something inaudible, before turning her attention back to me, 'Ok, I'll call HQ and get them to send a cover-up team, then see if I can do anything for Boyle. I know a bit of medical magic, so I should at least be able to stabilise him. I probably already have whatever disease was on this ship anyway.'

'Sounds good. I'll go set up a perimeter. Call me if anything comes up.'

I gently set down Boyle, turned and left the brig, trusting Dawkes to do her part, and frankly glad to leave the conversation.

I had bigger priorities. It's the duty of an agent of the Enlightenment to ensure no humans see evidence of the paranormal, and that required a magical perimeter. Besides, invisible monster or not, any time whatever was on board was pursuing me, was time it wasn't picking off anyone else.

Rounding the corner, I dived into the room where we were first abducted. Reaching the car, I ran over the boot, fumbling with the keys.

The boot had a slew of equipment, meant to cover a variety of scenarios, most of which got pushed out of the way. Naturally, I had to reach the bottom of the boot before I found the required gear, a garda stab vest and a roll of police tape.

The equipment gathered, I bolted out through one of the broken windows, into the field outside.

Throwing on the stab vest, I moved as fast as I could through the clammy mud. The moisture of the mud soaked into my shoes, drenching my feet. Luckily, I had enough left-over adrenaline that my fatigue still hadn't caught up to me when I reached the first tree. I began peeling off crime scene tape and attaching it to the tree, before running the tape along to another tree.

The thing about magic, is that it is fundamentally based on symbolism. Anything you want to do with magic, you need to find some kind of meaningful symbol for the magic to act on. For instance, the reason I use an athame is because it has a long-accepted association in occult traditions with moving and directing energy of all forms, giving me a good bit of leeway for anything related to your standard elemental forces. Similarly, the whole reason I was able to use electricity to power Boyle's spell was because I could tap into the universally accepted association of electricity with fuel for pretty all modern technology.

Think of it like trying to trick the universe into thinking the meaning we put into these symbols translated to reality. It's technically possible to do all this through force of will, without any tools to focus your magic, but doing so tends to lead to backlash, since our fragile mortal frames weren't made to warp the fabric of reality alone.

That's why I needed the police vest and the cordon tape. Magically speaking, they served exactly the same purpose as any pentacle or mystic circle. By draping myself in the apparel of law enforcement, and cordoning off the area with tape, I was setting up an area of 'police business' that, assuming I did everything correctly, would stop any passers-by from investigating the area. It wouldn't help much, with the UFO still out in the opening, but once backup got here and we're able to get it out of direct sight, my ritual would give us carte blanche to hang around as long as we needed without attracting mundane attention.

Once I'd set up a cordoned off square around the ship, I began the ritual. Taking a deep breath to gather myself, I stood dead centre between the tape and the ship, thrust out one hand in a stopping motion and recited the famous line to my imaginary onlookers, 'Nothing to see here, move alone.'

I repeated the whole process three times, moving to each side of the cordoned off square in turn. I put as much force as I could behind the words, imagining a crowd that I needed to disperse from the scene. Upon finishing the last side, I had to step back and take a couple more breaths, the ritual had taken a toll on what little reserves I had left, and all I wanted to do to collapse somewhere dry and pass out.

I stood out in that field for what felt like hours, trying my best to concentrate on something other than how tired and sore I felt. I wasn't jumped by any invisible monster, nor were there any sounds of a struggle inside the ship, so I could only assume it'd taken off. It was maybe after the third or fourth time I'd gone over the events of the mission in my head that I saw lights in the distance.

A black car, identical to ours, parked next to the fence leading to the field, followed by four more. A set of maybe a dozen figures, dressed in dark suits, got out.

I hailed them and the group spread out across the perimeter, while one, a middle-aged, tired looking Asian man stepped to me.

'Agent Reilly' He said blandly, a slight trace of a Hong Kong accent following his speech.

'Captain Hu.' I saluted him. 'I'd advise keeping your distance. This ship, and the people therein, may be a biohazard.'

'Yes, yes. Agent Dawkes explained the situation.' Hu nodded to one of the other agents, who stepped over to me, clasping a small, bronze caduceus in one hand, which he passed over me in a way that reminded me of airport staff using a metal detector.

'Not picking up any contaminants on him, sir.' The agent gagged when the odour from my suit hit him, 'Err, no diseases, regular or paranormal, anyway. Just some light bruising on his back and heavy bruising on his left hand.'

'Good.' Captain Hu turned to address the entire team. 'Fan out through the ship and lock it down. I'll be out here setting up the illusion. Reilly, stay here.'

The group of agents trundled past me into the ship, a couple shooting me glares as if I personally pulled them out of bed.

When I'd first started a year ago, that likely would've got to me, but by now I was used to being unpopular.

Once they left, Captain Hu ordered me to give my report of the mission, and I did so, sparing no detail. While I did, the captain walked in a slow circle around the ship, methodically pouring salt from a large, plastic flask.

In the middle of this, a couple of the other agents came out and gave their prognosis of the situation. The good news was that the civilians were mostly fine, and they should only need basic medical attention, followed by the standard memory editing spells that'd keep them from asking awkward questions later.

Bad news was that not only was Boyle in a critical state, but while they could see plenty of evidence of some kind of disease among the Visitors, there were no traces of the virus itself. As for the invisible creature, it was unaccounted for, but the other agents were planning to send out additional forces to search the area.

The captain acknowledged this with a short nod and an order to get Boyle into care right away. Once I'd completed my report, sparing no detail, the captain stayed silent for a moment, exhaling heavily through his nose.

'This outcome is not ideal, Agent Reilly. I had hoped your team would be capable of capturing this vessel without quite so much damage to either the mystical technology inside or yourselves.'

Before I could attempt to blurt out an apology, he continued. 'No need. You acted under Boyle's orders, and he understood the risk. That said, I would be very interested in hearing more about this 'virus', you and Agent Dawkes both claimed to have encountered.

I shook my head, working to swallow down the guilt from getting Boyle injured. 'I'm afraid I've already told you everything I know about it. In all honesty, I only call it a virus because I didn't have any better way to describe the effects I observed.'

The captain stroked his chin. 'Well, assuming our analysis bears out that observation, anything we could learn about this virus could be critical soon. Very soon.'

I blinked. 'How do you mean, sir?'

Captain Hu looked into the distance. 'This case, assuming your descriptions are accurate, match up with other reports some of our agents have been picking up in Dublin over the last couple of months.'

The captain continued speaking, even while he began pouring out salt in the shape of some Chinese character. 'Intel suggests that some of the paranormal communities in Dublin have come under very similar attacks, a disease-based sorcery that only seems to target paranormal entities.'

'Why only paranormal entities?'

'I imagine both to avoid collateral and drawing our attention. So long as these attacks didn't endanger human life or Innocence of the paranormal, the Enlightenment's not inclined to get involved.' The captain said as he continued his methodical salt pouring. 'This situation changes that.'

'Are you sure, sir? Like you said, the virus only seemed to target the Visitors. If none of the humans were infected, what's changed?'

'What has changed, agent Reilly, is that this is the first time one of these attacks had presented a threat to the preservation of Innocence.'

He then gestured at the crashed ship, his mouth twisting in

distaste. 'Even once we take care of the prisoners and ensure their silence, it is going to take shutting down this entire road to ensure this stays hidden from the public eye. And that's not even accounting for the fact we'll likely need to disassemble the entire ship to move it. This represents an unacceptable escalation.'

Right, that made sense. The Enlightenment tried not to get too involved in the squabbles that went on between the paranormal factions that didn't conflict with our interests. Our manpower was limited enough, without trying to make enemies of every fairy or monster in a region, especially if we can just leave them to tear into each other. Whoever had dropped this virus on the spaceship though, just like the Visitors themselves, had caused far too much damage to be ignored.

'I understand, sir. You wish to avoid any similar incidents threatening our work.'

The captain turned away, focusing on laying out the salt symbols. 'I'm glad you appreciate the gravity of the situation, Reilly. Hopefully, you can continue to apply your understanding to your investigation.'

I was taken aback. 'My investigation, sir?'

Captain Hu kept working, back turned to me. 'That's correct. I'll also be assigning Dawkes to inspecting the ship for any remaining traces, but I expect you to make discovering the source of this disease and putting a stop to it, your top priority.'

This was unexpected. On one hand, I was thrilled that I had finally been assigned my own case, which was a big step up from patrolling the docklands in the middle of the night, making sure no one was being eaten by ghosts.

On the other hand, though, from how the captain was describing it, this seemed a bit beyond a rookie. 'While I certainly have no objections to taking on this task, sir, why are you assigning me to it?'

'To be blunt, Reilly, my first choice for this job is lying in a pool of blood and vomit in that infernal machine over there.' The captain gestured roughly at the crashed ship.

I sharply inhaled, images of Boyle's burnt form refuelling my shame from losing control. The captain continued, unaware of my internal guilt.

'I was already planning on having Boyle lead this investigation, but even accounting for magical treatment, he'll likely be in recovery for weeks. Not to mention, with all the people we're going to have to get on board to make sure not a word of this ship gets out of this field, most of our more experienced agents are going to be tied up either with this, or another task we can't afford to reassign them from.'

Having finished scrawling his last symbol, Captain Hu turned to face me directly. 'Finally, the agents with the most direct experience dealing with this particular brand of magic, are you and Dawkes. Right now, you two know more about this than anyone else available. Does that answer your question?'

An embarrassed flush rose to my face. Of course, we were stretched to our limit. Aside from Boyle, the number of experienced field agents in Ireland has never been high, and most get reassigned to more important locations anyway.

If the captain saw fit to put an agent with just over a year's experience on this case, it was obvious there really was no one else to do it. This was my time to step up, and I shouldn't be wasting it second-guessing my commanding officer.

'Yes sir, apologies. I swear to get to the bottom of this

matter.'

'Excellent.' The shadow of a tired smile stretched the corners of the captain's mouth. 'There're a few angles you could start. The reports we've been able to get of this type of magic beforehand have been localised around Aes Sidhe and Seventh Wave territory, so I'd recommend you inspect those areas. In the meantime, Dawkes can figure out how the Visitors played into this, or any clues into the identity of the being you saw. I expect the two of you to co-ordinate.'

My brow furrowed. 'If I may sir, I'd like to start by looking into the Seventh Wave angle.'

'Any specific reason?'

'I have a contact among them, sir. I believe I could use him to get a start on investigating them.'

'A contact, hm?' The captain frowned. 'That would be your friend at the dojo, I take it?'

I felt a twinge of nerves. The Enlightenment took a fairly dim view of 'fraternising' with the paranormal. They tolerated it when it gave them vital resources or information, but involving them any more than necessary was frowned on.

Article 6 of the Agent code of ethics. The paranormal is not inherently evil, but is inherently dangerous. I could tell that exact article was on the captain's mind.

'I can assure you sir, that my contact's discretion has been ironclad in our dealings.'

The captain gave me a long look, his dark eyes scanning me. 'This being. It isn't a familiar, is it?'

I shook my head. 'Absolutely not, sir. I know better than to magically bind myself to a paranormal entity.

The captain shrugged, seemingly satisfied. 'Very well, but I will insist on all the details of your arrangement be outlined in your next report, is that understood?'

'Yes sir.'

Captain Hu nodded. 'Good. You're dismissed for the evening, Agent Reilly. The car over there will bring you home.'

I saluted the captain, then made my way over to the waiting car. Already I could see a pair of dark vans pulling up, one likely meant to collect Boyle. The other dispensed a small number of men in body armour, soldiers on the Enlightenment's payroll, there to scout the area.

I stepped into the car, the guard slamming the door closed. As we drove away, I looked back in time to see the captain gesture, both he and the ship then disappeared from sight, rendered completely invisible. Between that and my ritual, no one would notice anything amiss.

The ride was uneventful, as the driver exchanged conversation with the guards while I sat in silence. Since my injuries weren't life-threatening, I was provided with the standard Enlightenment medical treatment. That is to say, one of the guards shoved a couple of green vials into my hand.

Still, the drive back gave me time to think about the factions possibly at play here.

The Seventh Wave, sometimes called the 'Wavers', wasn't really a unified faction, more a loose coalition of various paranormal entities native outside Ireland, mostly Eastern Europe and China, who followed new immigrants into Ireland over the last couple of decades, when people actually started moving to Ireland, as opposed to leaving and splattering the Irish diaspora across the planet.

From what I've heard, even the name was coined by the local sidhe and cabals, in a rather blatant play of trying to tie them into the mythological 'waves' of invaders that conquered

Ireland one after the other.

Being recent additions to the local ecosystem, these groups are localised in the bigger cities of Ireland, especially Dublin, being the closest thing to an international melting pot our country had. Clashes between them and the local sidhe, probably upset about having actual competition, was nothing unheard of, but either side resorting to biological warfare seemed an alarming development.

As for which side was responsible, the fair folk always had a knack for working with life sorcery that others lacked, but who knows what secret weapons a grab bag of international paranormals could pull together if they felt threatened. And that wasn't even addressing the question of how that virus got on an alien spacecraft in the first bloody place.

If it wasn't obvious, the Visitors don't get sighted on Earth much. Like a lot of the newer generations of paranormals, they tended to keep a low profile, so unless they had contact with another group, there was no way of telling how they got infected. If I were to guess though, the invisible figure I saw surely played into all this somehow.

My thoughts were interrupted when I was dropped outside my north-side apartment block. By the time I'd finally reached my apartment, I was practically dead on my feet. Opening the door, I shambled into the dark apartment. I didn't bother turning on the light, a year of late nights had given me plenty of time to familiarise myself with my apartment's layout.

I pushed through to the bedroom, stripping off my stained clothes along the way, throwing them in the basket near the door I always chucked my ruined clothing into. The clothes were enchanted to repair and clean themselves over time, but

I'd have to go plain-clothes tomorrow.

Routine falling into place, I sat down on the bed and poured some of the foul-smelling potion onto my wounds from the evening. I hissed, the pain flaring up, why the hell did they have to be so bloody unpleasant?

Once the worst of the stinging subsided, I yanked the covers back and pulled my weary body into bed. No sooner did my head hit the pillow, I felt the fatigue of the last few hours come down on me, as I let my mind slip away, the stinging of my rapidly healing wounds the only stimulus.

Before drifting off, I promised myself Boyle would be the last to pay for my weakness.

# Chapter 4

I woke up and immediately regretted it.

Harsh light shot through the gaps in my eyelids. Some of the pain from last night still lingered, which hardly helped. When I managed to pull my eyes open, I saw my small digital clock read 10:45.

5 hours then. Better than I was expecting.

I forced myself up and into the bathroom. Once business was taken care of, I threw on some of the little clothing I owned aside from the suit, in this case jeans, a t-shirt and a thin, hooded coat.

I rummaged through my still ruined suit for my athame, then made for the drawer where I kept a handgun, useless against telekinetic aliens though effective on most other things, transferring both to my coat's pockets. Hopefully I wouldn't need either, but you never really knew. Everything else in order, I pulled out some leftover bacon and an apple from the fridge and ate them on my way out.

The sun was high in the sky. I hissed, shielding my eyes with my arm. Christ, was the sun always this bright? Guess this is what happens when you work nights for almost a year. Unfortunately, my contact worked during the day, so I needed to endure the great, flaming tyrant.

Before that however, I needed to collect the payment my contact would request. Acquiring said payment was depressing, undignified and repulsed me to my core, but was thankfully short work, and I was soon making my way, a paper bag in one hand carrying my filthy pay off.

I soon found myself outside a small building, cramped in one of the busier parts of Dublin, with only the small sign, 'Bhajan's Dojo', on the window distinguishing it.

I peeked in through the window. Inside, I saw the man I was looking for. A short, somewhat unkempt Indian man, wearing similarly unkempt robes was leading a class through some wrestling stances. Excellent, looks like he was just finishing up a class.

I loitered outside, waiting for the students to file out. A few glanced my way, but none questioned as I lightly pushed my way in.

Inside, the Indian man, 'Master' Bhajan, had just put the last floor mats away when he caught sight of me. He blinked in surprise, before a wide grin spread across his face.

'Mr Reilly! Many moons have passed since you last darkened my doorstep!

He reached out his hand and I met it with mine. His grip was as incredibly tight and borderline crushing as always. Up close, the shabby robes Bhajan wore left just enough view of his chest and arms to reveal the tight, compact muscle that came from fighting, not weightlifting.

Bhajan was my chief contact in the paranormal community. We'd met when I was starting out, and hashed out a deal where Bhajan would keep me abreast of recent events among the paranormals in Dublin. His help had been vital in some crucial cases.

Which was why I was even able to consider his price.

Mercifully, Bhajan let go quickly enough, then placed both palms together in a monk-like pose. 'So, how can the great sage, Bhajan, be of help to you this auspicious day?'

I crossed my arms. 'Start by dropping the 'sage' act, Bhajan. I've seen enough of you to know better. I need to talk to you in private.'

Bhajan snorted, 'Bah, it seems humour is dead in all countries. No matter.'

Striding to the other side of the room, he opened a door and beckoned me. 'Shall we discuss this in my office?'

I walked into Bhajan's 'office'. The centre of the room was dominated by a low table, covered in a thin layer of loose papers, empty paper bags and coffee stains. Around the table were a couple of floor cushions as seats. Much of the detritus had spread to other parts of the room, except, ironically enough, a small filing cabinet, which stood half-open and three-quarters empty.

When the door was shut, I exhaled, pushing my will against Bhajan's human disguise. Among mundane humans, it was flawless, but it faltered under the superhuman will of a magi. In the blink of an eye, the Indian man was replaced with what looked like the missing link between humans and apes, if he did Crossfit.

Coated in white fur, save for his face, which had a curious mix of human and ape features, I could now perceive Bhajan's true form, a Vanara, a paranormal being from India, allegedly originally created by the Hindu god Brahma. I wondered if Brahma might've reconsidered if he knew he'd create someone like Bhajan.

Bhajan stepped forward, and then let loose a string of

very unmonk-like curses as he stubbed his toe on the small table, accompanied by a few very monkey-like shrieks. Then, evidently remembering he had company, Bhajan's shrieks abruptly cut off, and he straightened out, brushing himself down casually.

I waited a moment for him to regain some composure before speaking, 'I'll get right down to business with you, I need-'

'Hoh-oh, not so fast, soldier of Enlightenment.' Bhajan cut me off, wagging his finger. 'You know full well Master Bhajan's services are available only to those willing to indulge his profane appetites.'

He pointed at the paper bag in my hand. 'I assume your payment lies within that bag?'

I sighed, then, with great reluctance, forced myself to open the bag. Bhajan's eyes widened and his mouth split into a grotesque grin, revealing sharp teeth. I reached in and clasped the damp and meaty tribute.

I removed the payment, wrapped completely in paper and roughly the size of my fist. A whoop of glee and the package was snatched from my hands. Bhajan held the thing in his hands, lips quivering in anticipation, then ripped the paper away and sunk his teeth in.

'Ohhh, sweet blasphemy.' Bhajan moaned, bits of beef falling from his mouth.

I watched the scene with disgusted fascination. 'For someone bent on indulging his primal desires, you've got low standards.'

Still groaning in delight, Bhajan took another bite of burger. 'My friend, you simply don't understand the decadent pleasure this offers me, one that my homeland denied.'

He paused, then extended the Big Mac to me. 'Wanna bite?'

I restrained myself from pulling back, revolted. 'No thanks. I prefer to eat food; not whatever processed rubbish McDonalds puts out.'

'Suit yourself.' Bhajan responded blandly, then reached into the bag and retrieved the chips, chewing on a couple as he sat back down. 'What wisdom do you seek from this old sage, wayward soldier?'

'Information. How tight are you with the immigrant paranormals these days? Last I remember, you were getting in pretty close with the Chinese and Russians, right?'

Bhajan paused in his eating. 'Enough that I'd be deep shit if I told you anything sensitive. You've bought my ear, but I made no promise to endanger myself.'

'Then let's just talk about some recent news.' I hunkered down on one of the dirt-encrusted cushions, running my fingers idly along the table. 'Say, for instance, the rumours off the grapevine that the skirmishes between your lot and the Aes Sidhe may have escalated recently?'

Bhajan started choking on a piece of burger, hacking and spluttering until he managed to grab the coke from the bag and take a large slurp.

'Fuck a duck sideways!' He gasped out. 'That's not exactly water cooler talk, you know?'

Bhajan's outburst wasn't surprising. The relationship between the Aes Sidhe and the slew of immigrant paranormals coming to Ireland over the last few decades were frosty at the best of times, with neither side being too keen in involve outsiders. 'I do, but I'd still be interested in anything you could tell me.'

Bhajan's jaw set, then he threw his head back in exasperation. 'Gah! Fine! But only because I haven't had beef all month!'

Setting his meal on the table, Bhajan sat opposite me, slumped like a grouchy teen. 'Ok, I may have heard that some of the immigrants having been getting into shit with local sidhe troops. Fairly scattered stuff, you understand. Some troop takes issue with where some newcomers have set up shop, that kind of stuff.'

'That's hardly anything new. You paranormal types clash all the time.'

'That's a very narrow-minded statement. Anyway, this is different. Anyone who's been having this sort of trouble with the sidhe in the last month or so aren't just getting to scuffles. They're turning up dead.'

This got my attention. 'Turning up dead how?'

'You read the news? You hear about that Pakistani family found dead in their own home under 'mysterious circumstances'?' Bhajan asked, finger quoting the words.

I nodded, my stomach churning.

'Djinns. A family friend comes to my classes. Said the father had got into it with a Leprechaun about his troop squatting near their neighbourhood.'

Bhajan shuddered. 'Their home was coated in blood and vomit, but the bodies had no injuries.'

Alarm bells rang in my head. If that wasn't a lead to my current case, I didn't know what was.

'Has there been any other developments? Anything that would indicate why the sidhe could be escalating things?'

Bhajan took another bite of burger, bouncing the rest of it in his hand. 'Maybe. A rumour has made the rounds recently, gaining strength in light of these tragedies. Some say the local sidhe are mobilising, that some of them have found a new–'

Bhajan was cut off by the sound of the dojo's door opening, and a couple of voices calling out for him.

Bhajan's eyes widened, and I distinctly heard him utter something under his breath that probably wasn't appropriate for Indian children. He pulled himself to his feet.

I opened my mouth to ask what was going on, then Bhajan whirled on me, clamping a pungent hand over my mouth.

'No, not a word. Stay here. I'll try to get rid of them.' Then Bhajan bounded over me and slid out the door.

I sat there for a stunned moment, caught between confusion and disgust, the taste of Bhajan's burger lingering on my mouth. I shook both sensations off and quietly shifted over to the door. Luckily, the door was made from the thinnest wood possible, so hearing presented little issue.

'Ahhah, my friends!' Bhajan's voice cried out, high and nervous. 'You're here earlier than expected! I'd not even prepared the floor for your lessons!'

Another voice, with an Asian accent I didn't recognise, responded. 'Apologies, Master Bhajan. We were already in the area and decided to drop by.'

'I see, I see.' Bhajan said quickly, 'Well, as you can see, the place is a mess right now. If you could simply wait outside a moment, I shall have the floor prepared post-haste!' Bhajan then let out a nervous laugh.

'What's up, Bhajan?' A thick Russian accent presumably connected to a person spoke up. 'You seem stressed. That Order prick giving you trouble again?'

Bhajan's laughter, still a bit too loud to be natural, echoed out. 'Oho, no, nothing like that, Vasily! My relationship with our resident Man in Black in the height of civility!'

I slapped my palm to my face. Bhajan couldn't lie to save

his life, or mine for that matter.

The silence was broken by the Russian voice, now sceptical. 'Master Bhajan, if the Order of the Enlightenment is sniffing around, it could be bad for all of us. Last thing we need is both them and the Sidhe Army closing in on us.'

The statement was so strange I was sure I'd misheard it. Did they think the Sidhe were planning to go to war? The mention of a 'Sidhe Army' seemed to suggest that, but the idea was absurd. The Sidhe had honoured their pacts with the Order for centuries now.

'Oh, I know! Very much so! That's why I've not talked to a single Enlightenment agent in the last month!' Bhajan shrilly responded, digging both of us deeper by the second.

'Maybe we should check your back room, Master Bhajan. Make sure no one is harassing you' There was a loud, cracking noise, like the cracking of a very large set of knuckles. 'Or that if they are, they'll regret it.'

I pushed away from the door when I heard footsteps coming closer, Bhajan's loud complaints going ignored. Crap, if these were Seventh Wave, they'd take finding me talking to Bhajan very badly. Best case scenario, they'd probably rough me up on principle, assuming they didn't just kill me and ditch my body in the Liffey.

I could fight, but that could end badly too. For one thing, I didn't know what possible paranormal entities I was about to match up with, and secondly, I didn't know where Bhajan would fall on that fight. We'd had a fairly cordial relationship, but I doubted he side with me over his fellow paranormals.

No, I needed a different plan.

I yanked my athame out of my coat pocket and focused on the energy in the room. More precisely, I reached out to the light filling the room. I was still learning the finer aspects of creating energy for my purposes, but I'd already made great headway on manipulating existing energy, whether that be directing it somewhere, or, in this case, away.

Channelling my will through the athame, I swiped the blade in slow, steady circles around myself, directing the light away from my body. My vision rapidly went dark, the downside of this method of invisibility.

Quietly as possible, almost tripping on one of the cushions, I shuffled to the far corner of the room. I pressed my back to the wall, straining my eyes to see through the darkness when the door was thrust open.

A large head, quickly followed by shoulders bulky enough to balance a fridge on, poked through. I couldn't make out any features, but I could see the head swivel back and forth, and then move into the room. I held my breath, slowly slinking my way past the large mass as it moved further into the office.

Suddenly, the form froze, and I heard a loud sniffing sound. I froze, fear gripping me as the figure started sniffing the air. Only then did I notice the scent of Bhajan's burger was still lingering around my face. My spell hadn't stopped me smelling of cheap beef.

Just as it seemed I was cornered, there was a sudden crack, and the form dropped to it's knees, yelping in pain as another form, what looked like Bhajan, seemed to appear out of thin air.

'Listen closely, Vasily.' Bhajan said, his voice now a low growl. 'Your concern for my safety is noted and appreciated. But regardless of your good motives, I will not tolerate such a base intrusion into my private quarters, especially not on paranoia.'

Bhajan then did something with his arm that provoked a moan from the other figure. ‘Now, please wait outside with your friends while I prepare the floor. In the meantime, reflect on how you can better regard the boundaries of those you claim to protect.’

The Russian let out a quick series of flustered apologies even while Bhajan threw him out, shutting the door behind him. We stood in quiet for a few seconds, before we heard the outside door shut, then Bhajan looked out at the office.

‘Forgetting to conceal your scent? Rather clumsy for a secret agent.’ He said, a wry grin I clocked even with my obstructed vision.

‘Bite me Bhajan. They wouldn’t have checked at all if you weren’t squealing like a feckin’ lost pig.’ I shot back.

‘My word! Has my teasing provoked a reaction, stone-faced agent of secrecy?’ He let out another laugh, this one natural. ‘The rumours are true; the agents of the Order are human!’

I ground my teeth, but I didn’t retort. It wasn’t because I didn’t have a comeback, I was just letting that git have his moment after he came through for me.

My humiliation was thankfully short, as Bhajan regained his composure, and walked over to the window, opening it. ‘Out here. Best of luck in your endeavours, Mr Reilly.’

Still invisible, I made my way to the window and was halfway out when I remembered something.

‘Hey, Bhajan? What was that your friends were saying about a Sidhe Army?’

Bhajan stopped and stared at my rough location. ‘It was what I was about to mention before they arrived. Word is some noble fae from the mounds has been making the rounds, gathering up troops to ‘defend their homeland’ or some shit like that.' Bhajan then shrugged. 'I'd say more, but I fear our chat has been cut short.'

'Good point. We'll speak later.' I responded, then, quietly, just under my breath, 'Thanks for the help.'

I dived out the window, so I didn't have to see the look on Bhajan's face. I walked quickly away from the dojo until I could find a nearby alley to drop my invisibility, my vision quickly clearing in the process while I digested what I'd heard.

A noble fae setting up some anti-Waver movement? The idea wasn't impossible, but it was bizarre. The only beings you could call fae nobility in Ireland were the Daoine Sidhe, proclaimed descendants of the old gods of Ireland. But unlike the Aes Sidhe, the Daoine were reclusive, rarely venturing into the mortal plane for anything, let alone organising radical movements.

And how'd I hear nothing about it until now?

I might not know how this happened, but I knew who would.

Time to have a chat with the Ciorcal Darach.

# Chapter 5

You probably wouldn't think that agents of the Order of the Enlightened would travel by Luas.

As was the case in Ireland however, the attention and resources demanded by other branches in other countries meant the Irish Enlightenment was always a few steps behind the rest of the world.

Black cars couldn't be assigned to individual agents, so I was having to take the Luas, crushed in-between a haggard mother soothing a wailing child and a spaced-out kid who smelled of weed.

When I'd finally pulled myself loose from the moving sardine tin, I was heavily considering whether preventing mass death among humanity was really that great a notion.

I took the few minutes I needed to walk to my destination to breath and remember all the good things about the human race, and once I stopped outside the small building, I'd come up with maybe three.

The building I stood in front of was a modest affair, tucked away down a quiet street, away from the main roads. It looked like one of the many pubs you would come across if you picked any direction in this country and walked long enough.

The outside was dominated by windows showing a warm,

cosy interior. At the top, a small plaque, read 'The Silver Arm'. When I got closer, I felt it as I always did, an ache in my jaws and teeth. The slow, steady flowing of power, drawn up from the earth and suffusing the building.

This was the local home of the Ciorcal Darach. To the average person, they seemed like typical neo-pagans. Of course; only a small few were brought into the true inner circle.

In reality, they were what the Order classified as a cabal. A small group of magi bound together by common cause or philosophy. Compared to the Enlightenment, these cabals are weak, not least because most people with any substantial magic talent tend to get snapped up by the Order, our access to superior knowledge and global influence usually enough to sway most prospective magi.

Part of our duties was making sure that cabals like this were protected from outside threats, and forbidden knowledge they weren't equipped to handle. Of course, most of these cabals like to fixate on the bit where we occasionally step in when we catch them dealing with forces they can't control, and not the bit where we stop demons from eating their faces.

Unless they needed something of course, in which case out came the plastic smiles.

It'd been them who'd tipped the Enlightenment off regarding the UFO abductions, so I had the perfect excuse to drop by, to announce our success. More importantly, in the past, the Ciorcal Darach had dealings with the Sidhe, despite Enlightenment protests, which made them the best group to ask about any so-called 'Sidhe Army'.

You know, so long as they didn't pick up on the blatant hypocrisy.

I was not looking forward to the next few minutes.

The atmosphere was lively when I entered, considering it was still fairly early in the afternoon. Most of the tables were empty, but the seats up by the bar were taken up by regulars, in quiet, yet enthusiastic conversation. The interior was decked out in wood panelling, a few bulbs hanging from the ceiling giving off a warm light, such that even the shadows it cast seemed welcoming.

Along the walls, images of the Celtic Tree of Life, looping Eternity Knots and the smiling visage of the Green Man, were carved at regular intervals , the steady lines of power reaching up from the ground to the symbols, webbing off into an interconnected lattice of magical wards, individually weak but collectively powerful.

As I crossed the floor, the conversation died down a bit, a couple of the regulars inspected me over their glasses, probably trying to figure out if I was a lost tourist. Ignoring them, I walked up to the bar. The bartender, a middle-aged, woman with short dark hair, wearing a football jersey, gave me a welcoming smile that didn't quite reach her eyes.

'Afternoon, love. What can I get you, there?'

'Can you let the Hierophant know that someone's here to see him?'

The smile vanished as her eyes took on a probing aspect. 'I could. Who should I tell him is here?'

'Just let him know that it concerns an earlier conversation between him and my employers, he'll understand what it means.'

'Ah, Enlightenment, then?' The bartender responded, a note of challenge in her voice. 'Where's your suit? At the cleaners?'

A murmur of chuckles bubbled up from the customers. I felt my teeth grit as the mocking laughter bit into me. With a flash of anger, I felt a surge of power rush through me. Above me, one of the ceiling lights burst with a violent pop, cutting the laughter off.

'Yes, actually. It got covered in blood saving more than a dozen people from alien abduction. Now kindly tell the Hierophant I wish to speak with him, now.'

The woman took a cautious step back, before fast walking away from the counter.

I slid into the nearest chair, feeling the gazes of the entire room. As I settled in, I was pretty sure I heard someone mutter 'fucking fascist'. I drummed my fingers along the bar, the frustration building. I didn't come here looking for a fight, but seems I can't do anything these days without pissing someone off.

The initial anger passing, I felt my eyes move to the now burst light, its absence covering me in a dark blanket. Dammit, I needed to keep a better lid on my powers. What was the point of all the years of learning to control my magic if that was enough to set me off? It'd been a rough couple of days, but I was supposed to be better.

Article 4 of the Agent code of ethics. An agent does what is necessary for the task. No more. No less. I forced myself to look away from the light and repeat that mantra to myself. Times like this, reflecting on the code was the only thing that could settle me.

As Sod's Law dictates of course, right as the ball of anxiety in my chest started to unwind, my attention was jolted by the sound of a deep clearing of a throat. I looked up sharply, irritation tightening my jaw, quickly forced away when I caught sight of the man I'd come to see.

Calling Calatin large would've been an understatement. Up close, he easily cleared 6 feet, with a few inches to spare, and stood as wide and barrel-chested as a professional weightlifter, a thick beard covering his face, like Brian Blessed's stunt double. He was wearing a woollen jumper, with a flat cap concealing thinning hair.

But beyond the superficial, the moment my eyes fell on him, I felt his presence grow and sharpen into focus, everything else fading into the background. Even if I didn't already know who he was, the power I was sensing now would have been clue enough. For a hedge witch, Calatin was exceptionally strong.

The giant grinned, wrinkles from old smiles and laughter erupting around his face as he offered his hand. 'Good afternoon, Arbiter. Susan here told me you wished to speak?'

Unconsciously, I found myself grasping the hand and shaking it, Calatin's use of the old name of my position catching me by surprise. 'That is correct, Hierophant Calatin. I come on behalf of my employers. Might we take this somewhere private?'

Calatin's smile stayed the same, though his eyes narrowed. 'Ay, I suppose we'd better had.'

He turned to the bartender, who still seemed concerned. 'Thank you, Susan. That'll be all for now.'

He turned and I got up to follow. Looking around the room as I went, I saw the onlookers still watching, a couple looking frustrated, presumably hoping that Calatin would throw me out. No chance. Whatever this bunch of hedge witches thought, from what I'd heard of him, Calatin was loyal to our cause.

Calatin opened a door, leading into a small office, occupied by a dark, wooden desk and a couple of chairs. On the walls, more symbols and pictures: depicting scenes from Irish mythology. On the desk, a few papers had been meticulously organised in one corner, whilst the chair had a green cloak draped across it, ogham lines stitched along where the shoulders would be.

Calatin reached under the desk, retrieving a bottle of whiskey, along with two glasses. 'Well, make yourself comfortable there, Arbiter. Anything I can get ye? A drink, maybe?'

'Thank you, but I'm fine. I'm here to discuss the UFO your cabal reported to us.'

'Ah.' Filling up one glass, Calatin took a seat, the chair creaking a little. 'Well then, I'd be happy to help anyway I can. All I ask is that this not take too long. I've a ceremony to lead in an hour and a half.'

'I'll get to the point then. You needn't worry about that UFO. It's been disabled and the crew liquidated.'

Tension drained out of Calatin, and the smile returned. 'Excellent. The less of those foul creatures taking advantage of innocent folk, the better.'

'Indeed. However, I also want to talk about the recent clashes between the local Sidhe troops and the Seventh Wave.'

The tension returned instantly. Calatin threw back the whiskey and reached for the bottle again. 'And what, pray tell, would you want to ask about?'

'Well, sources have reported some 'Sidhe Army' has been organising at the behest of one of their nobility against the Wavers. Apparently this has been going on for a while–'

Calatin suddenly rose to his full height, his eyes burning.

'I have heard about that, and frankly I'm amazed it took the Order so long to act on this. That bastard's been building support for months, now! What's the fecking point of you Order types if you don't even notice this shite?!'

A surge of nerves gripped me. 'I can't speak for my superiors' awareness regarding this matter. I can only act on what I personally know. So, I would be grateful if you could share what you know, and I shall my best to investigate why the Order had not yet acted on this information.'

Calatin stared me down, casting a dark shadow across the room, then fell back in his seat with a groan. 'How much do you already know?'

'Only that clashes between the Sidhe and the Wavers are escalated, apparently at the behest of some noble Sidhe rallying the local troops. And that some of them may be using viral magic designed to kill rival paranormals.'

Leaning across his desk, Calatin raised one large finger. 'First, you need to understand, Arbiter, that the Ciorcal Darach does not maintain relations with the Sidhe as we used to. I've been doing all I can to steer my brothers and sisters away from consorting with those untrustworthy creatures, so we don't know as much about their affairs as we used to.'

I nodded along, all this familiar news. From what I'd heard, over the last decade, Calatin, as local Hierophant, had made great efforts to distance the Dublin branch of the Ciorcal Darach from their longstanding dealings with the Sidhe, whilst bringing the cabal closer to the Enlightenment, including cutting a few deals with us to get hold of arcane knowledge they would've otherwise sought out the fae for.

The Order had Calatin tagged as a useful asset for this reason, but the idea that the Ciorcal had no dealings left with the Sidhe didn't sound right. You don't undo centuries of tradition in a decade.

'I understand the situation, Hierophant, but nevertheless, I'm confident that any information you may have could be put to good use.'

Calatin leaned back and ran his hand down his beard for a few seconds. 'The Sidhe you speak of is named Lord Nechtan, and he is among that most dangerous breed of the fair folk. The one that takes an active interest in mortal affairs.'

'Why? The Daoine Sidhe as a whole are content to stay in their burrows. What interest does one of them have trying to stir up trouble like this?'

The druid gave a shrug. 'Who can guess why the inhuman do anything, Arbiter? By their nature, these creatures' thoughts and motives are alien to us. A lesson I myself learned all too harshly.'

Calatin went quiet, a glimmer of some distant emotion on his face. I waited a moment, giving him a chance to recover, when he spoke again.

'Do you remember Dingle, Arbiter?'

Flashes of memories bubbled up. The smell of ozone, the roars of alien beasts. Cries of terror and pain filled my ears.

'I hadn't been recruited at the time.' I responded blandly, strangling the memories and shoving them in the vault. 'But I'm aware of the broad strokes.'

Calatin snorted, 'Glad to know the Order hasn't let the whole mess slide under the rug at least.'

He threw back another shot of whiskey. 'I'd just made the rank of hierophant among the Ciorcal Darach when it happened. I had a wife, Saoirse. More beautiful than any flower and with a mind as keen as the sharpest blade. She'd only given birth to our young lad, Finn, five months ago, a more handsome boy you'll never see.'

Calatin paused, taking a steadying breath. 'We were in Dingle, working with some of the druids there, researching a disturbance in the Shroud, when those damn warlocks tore a hole between it and our world. Beasts from mankind's worst nightmares rampaged across the town, spearheaded by those madmen. I found one of them, a Sidhe, in my own home, having just finished taking a sword to my wife and son for no reason.'

He reached for the whiskey again, then stopped himself with a reluctant sigh. 'I got my revenge, but it did nothing to help the pain. That's why I've tried to steer the Ciorcal Darach away from dealing with the Sidhe, Arbiter. Because I've seen first-hand that those fickle monsters are capable of.'

I had trouble keeping my expression neutral. When I'd gotten the chance to join the Order of the Enlightenment, I thought I would be able to put Dingle behind me. I'd given up everything for that chance, even my identity and name, but Dingle's shadow cast much further than I thought.

Looking at Calatin, his eyes tinged just a little red, I spoke before my reservations could get to me.

'You have my sincerest condolences, Hierophant Calatin. The Dingle Incident was a tragedy for all involved, and I will do all in my power to prevent any similar events. But to do that, I'll need your help.'

Calatin stared in surprise, whether at my words or the expression on my face, I didn't know. His eyes reassessing.

I continued. 'If this Lord Nechtan is trying to incite conflict between the Sidhe and the Wavers, that has the potential to be on par with Dingle, and in the centre of Dublin, at that. I need to know anything you can tell me about him.'

Calatin held his stare for a few seconds, before responding. 'My apologies, Arbiter, but while I'm willing to help, I've already gone to great lengths to cut ties with the Sidhe, so any knowledge I might have would be second-hand at best. All I've been able to get over the last few months was that this Nechtan has been making the rounds with the local troops, bringing more and more of them under his influence. To what end, I do not know.'

I nodded and started to get up, when Calatin continued. 'However, despite my better efforts, members of the cabal do still have the odd Sidhe contact here and there. I can try to find out where Nechtan might be meeting his followers.'

'Thank you, Hierophant. I will see to it that any help you provide us is not put to waste.'

Calatin smiled tiredly, getting up and roughly shaking my hand. 'What'd you call yourself these days, lad? I know you Arbiters use aliases, but nevertheless...'

'Reilly. I go by Reilly now.' I responded, repeated my alias to him.

'Reilly.' Calatin said it slowly, tasting the name. 'You're a good sort, Reilly. If you need anything else, my doors will be open to you.'

As he released my hand, I nodded back. 'I'll bear that in mind, Hierophant.'

I turned and left the office, closing the door behind me. I was surprised at how well the meeting had gone. Even if he wasn't able to tell me much, Calatin was able to confirm the rumours and put a name to this elusive fae ringleader.

However, this meeting had raised more than a few questions. I still had no clue where this 'Nechtan' was or how he played into the events on the scout ship. More concerning, Calatin had said he'd already brought this budding Sidhe movement to the Enlightenment's attention, but if so, why hadn't they acted on it? I wasn't naïve enough to assume I was privy to everything the Order's resources were being devoted to, but it was troubling.

Walking to the exit, I saw the regulars still in their seats, their eyes firmly looking at anything but me. I spotted the broken lightbulb again and winced. The bartender had to have told Calatin that was my doing, but he'd been open and friendly regardless. That didn't happen enough for me to take it for granted. I made a mental note to apologise next time I saw him.

Outside, I saw the sun had started its descent, the bright light from earlier now similar to the warm, orange light of the pub, if a bit further in the distance, I saw the conga line of cars just beginning their long commute home.

For those drivers, the hard toil of the day was over. But for me, the real work was just about to start.

# Chapter 6

If you want to hide something, the best way is in plain sight.

Present it in such a way that people walk past it every day without paying any mind. This is why cabals like the Ciorcal Darach can assemble the way they do. People would get excited if they heard about an order of druids in the wilderness, but don't give a second thought about a neo-pagan group that meets up in a pub.

As long as anything outright magical is out of sight, it's amazing how much of our work is done by human apathy.

When you consider where the local headquarters of a global conspiracy would be located, thoughts typically go straight to the local seat of power, or some historically significant building, with a hidden entrance to the conspiracy's true meeting place, where we stand around cackling and discussing plans of world domination.

Cute, but wrong. Conspiracies require secrecy, which is rarely accomplished by having everyone important hanging around recognisable landmarks.

I contemplated this, having just endured another godawful forty minutes on public transport to get to that point.

The building was one of those more modern office blocks, all smooth, white brickwork and large shiny glass windows just tinted enough that you can't see inside. It was large, but not so large it stood out amongst the buildings around it. There were no logos, no names on the front of the building.

Every day, hundreds walked past the local headquarters of the Enlightenment completely oblivious.

Even to my eyes, the solid, utilitarian lines of potent magical energies that lined the building's outer walls, seemed bland and uniform compared to the almost organic wards of the Silver Arm, despite the fact these wards were capable of withstanding anything short of a nuke.

I walked up to the large double-doors, and felt a familiar rush of power flow over me as the wards analysed my body to determine if I was a paranormal imposter. I knew well it's next move, scanning my surface thoughts for ill intentions, whilst also readying a potent curse for the situation where I didn't pass either test.

When I didn't collapse unconscious or die from a sudden brain aneurism, the doors opened and I passed through. The inside of the building was as unassuming as outside, and offered no surprises as I took the lift to the second floor, the main offices.

I stepped out of the lift and continued onward down the lines of cubicles, miscellaneous bits and pieces like photos or little figurines taking up space on desks. I saw only a few other agents, typing away at their desks.

I turned into one of the cubicles, bare of all the pointless clutter of the other desks. I sat down and logged into the computer.

I typed up my report for the day's events. I could have done this from my personal laptop, but I preferred being able to print off and deliver my report in person where possible. It goes without saying that an organisation build on secrecy would take security seriously, so the basic process of submitting any information to the captain follows a rigorous process of giving him a hard copy, along with a USB containing a digital copy, then ruthlessly purging any hint of a paper trail, digital or otherwise.

Anyone who's even a little lax in not deleting everything once the relevant information's been passed on can usually expect to get sat down for an extended outlining of why hackers have such easy time of getting hold of private documents. A PowerPoint may be included depending on how vindictive the captain's feeling.

However, I had another reason for wanting to come in, and after I'd printed off the report and was en-route to grab it, I saw my chance.

Agent Dawkes was standing a bit off to the side, having a conversation with a couple of other agents. She said something and the two laughed loudly, then one of them said something that made her quietly laugh.

I was tempted to wait until the conversation finished before approaching her, but I rejected that thought. Dawkes was popular with our colleagues, so either she'd be stuck in that conversation for the next twenty minutes, or someone else will come along and start flapping their gums at her too.

So, the moment I snatched my report from the printer, I turned around and walked straight up to her. 'Agent Dawkes. Do you have a minute?'

Dawkes and the other agents jumped at the sound of my voice, and for a change, I understood why. Unlike Dawkes, outside of joint assignments, I've probably shared less than a dozen conversations with any of the other agents.

Dawkes didn't look as put out as the others, but did fix me with a dubious look. 'Uh, well, I suppose so. Is this relevant to our case?'

'It is. I want to compare notes before we give our reports to the captain. See if there's any connections yet.'

Dawkes visibly relaxed, the prospect of talking to me about work apparently reassuring. 'Right, yes. One second.'

She turned to the others, the bright smile returning. 'Sorry guys, duty calls! I catch up with you two later!'

The two agents mumbled vague agreements and walked off, though not before fixing me with surly looks as they left.

Giving them one last look, Dawkes sighed and turned back to me. 'Can I at least get some coffee before we start? I'm probably two minutes away from falling flat on my face.'

'If you must. I'll start while you're drinking.'

Dawkes rolled her eyes and started down towards the cafeteria, me following. Neither of us said a word while Dawkes got to the coffee maker.

Once she got her mug of crushed bean juice, I relayed to her the events of the day, including what I'd heard about the aggression between the Wavers and the Sidhe, everything I'd heard about this Lord Nechtan and the rumoured Sidhe bioweapon.

'It's not much to go on.' Dawkes said once I'd finished, leaning idly against the counter.

She took another draft from her mug, before wincing and raising one hand to massage her temple. 'I mean, this doesn't add up to me. If some fairy prince's been building a personal army, how come we're only hearing about this now? Wouldn't something like have gotten to us months ago?'

'It's possible that it did, but since we're stretched pretty far, the whole thing may have simply gone done as a rumour and fallen down the priority hole. I'm planning to check the past records of reported paranormal sightings.' I responded.

'Not to mention, while our access to mundane information is top notch, paranormals still tend to be harder to spy on, what with many of them keeping away from digital technology or knowing how to avoid being spied on through it. Somehow, I doubt Nechtan's recruiting via Twitter.'

Dawkes let out a mirthless laugh. 'Guess even Big Brother has his limits, huh?'

I managed to stop myself sighing. Working for what was basically the Men in Black did invite certain comparisons, but I'd personally stopped finding them amusing pretty fast. What we're doing is no worse than what mundane governments do anyway.

Dawkes continued. 'So, let's say some Daoine Sidhe is behind this virus. How the hell did a fairy sneak onto a Visitor ship? And why?'

'I imagine you'd be in a better position to figure that out than me. Have you managed to identify the invisible entity I encountered on the ship?'

Dawkes let out a groan, rolling her neck. 'Nope, whatever that was must have fled the ship before the coverup team arrived. No trace aside from some bloody footprints near one of the broken windows.'

'A bloody footprint sounds like a big trace to me.'

'It would be if the blood actually came from the suspect instead of twelve different aliens. Maybe if the entire ship hadn't been contaminated in every possible way, I could've got something useful.' Dawkes said, idly swirled her mug.

'As it is, all I've got is the entity's shoe size, so watch for any size 10's!' She continued, throwing her free hand up, frustration clear on her face.

'What about the bioweapon? Any leads there?'

Turned out Dawkes' investigation was about as productive as mine was. Whatever spell was holding the bioweapon together dissipated before any analysis could be done, turning it back into the assorted bacteria it'd been modified from.

It made sense. Having the spell be temporary would both keep a low profile and stop whoever's behind the bioweapon poisoning themselves after unleashing it. Course, just because it was expected didn't make it any less aggravating.

'But it does tell us a couple of things.' Dawkes noted when I mentioned this.

'For instance?'

'To start, whoever's producing this bioweapon must be incredibly skilled in biomancy. No amateur could take a completely mundane virus and create a new, more virulent illness that's deadly for paranormals, but completely harmless to humans.'

I nodded along. Might not sound like much, given we already knew plenty of Sidhe had a knack for manipulating life via magic, but at the very least, we could establish this was the work of a big player, not a couple of pixies playing a sadistic prank.

'Also, I doubt whoever delivered the disease to the Visitors specifically planned to do so.' Dawkes continued.

'What's your reasoning?'

Dawkes shrugged. 'Like you said, whoever created the bioweapon must have wanted to keep it from catching our attention. So, it's a little strange they chose to attack a ship that we were on, don't you think?'

Ok, now that I'd thought about it, that was weird. If our assumption that the virus was specifically designed to go unnoticed by humanity, then dropping it on an alien ship that was not only going to crash and attract a lot of attention, but had three agents of the Enlightenment on it at the time was either a deliberate act to draw attention or incredibly stupid.

'That's a good point.' I responded. 'Still, maybe there was a motive we don't know about yet. Hell, maybe they wanted to get our attention for some reason. We'll need to dig a bit more.'

'Fair enough. I'm looking into seeing if the Order can spare any clairvoyants to take a look at what happened leading up to the crash. But I think I've actually got better odds of my fairy godmother showing up than the Order's bureaucracy having a clairvoyant spare.'

I turned my head sharply towards Dawkes. 'Whatever para-normal connections you have outside of work, it's imperative they not be made aware of our operations, Dawkes. This Sidhe familiar of yours could be terminated if she's found intruding on an internal matter without sanction.'

'A joke, Reilly! It was a bloody joke!' Dawkes cried out, slamming her mug on the counter. 'Lord, it's like talking to a Vulcan.'

A hole opened up in my gut. A joke, obviously. Stupid to assume otherwise. I suffocated the feeling of embarrassment. 'Understood, sorry for misinterpreting. If I could suggest something, while you're waiting on that, it might be useful to go through whatever data you can scavenge off the ship. It could tell us a bit about what the Visitors were doing leading up to the incident.'

Dawkes gave me another of those strange looks, before

letting out a breath. 'Yeah, I was already thinking of that.'

Pausing, she seemed to consider something. 'It ever bother you how our biggest obstacle seems to be our own organisation, sometimes? We're supposed to be the big scary Illuminati, but we can't even get the proper tools for our jobs.'

'I prefer to be proactive about problems than waste time ruminating on them. Anyway, if we're done here, I've got to hand this report in before I go on patrol.' I responded, keen to finish this conversation.

'Wait. Patrol?'

I stopped mid-step, looking back to regard Dawkes dubiously. 'Yes, obviously. What else would I be doing right now?'

Dawkes stared at me with a flat expression, before a corner of her mouth twitched upwards, and she burst into laughter. 'Come on, Reilly! I know they work us like dogs here, but even the Order has some standards! They assigned a couple of free agents to our patrols for now.'

I didn't respond, taking in the new information. For the last year, I'd spend almost every evening patrolling the streets, making sure the local paranormals were toeing the line. Even though I probably should've been glad for the break, I couldn't shake a feeling of discomfort.

'I see. That changes my plans. If that's the case, then I'd best get my report filed before I head back. Might as well take advantage of this to get a bit of sleep.'

Dawkes' now weak laughter cut off. 'Wait, were you actually about to go out on patrol after yesterday? I'm pretty certain you only got as much sleep as I did.'

'Tomorrow, I'll go with my original plan, but I'll also try and find an opportunity to get a live sample of the bioweapon for examination. Contact me if anything develops.' I responded, turning and walking away, hoping she'd drop it if I left quickly enough.

Naturally, I couldn't see Dawkes' reaction, but I felt her eyes on me for a few seconds. 'Sure thing. I hope you get something useful out of that.'

Yeah, she wasn't the only one.

It was dark by the time I'd stumbled off the Luas, the street lamps turning everything the colour of cheap beer. As the tram trundled away, I caught sight of the River Liffey to my right, the waters now a black void.

After spending the day navigating the city, the streets had become quiet, not a soul to be seen. I'd probably walked this path over a hundred times by this point, and so I allowed my mind to wander as muscle memory carried me along, allowing myself to enjoy the blissful silence after an unusually trying day of dealing with people, the time slipping away.

Then, a surge of panic and confusion took over my senses. My instincts screamed a warning to my right. I turned and saw an alley between a couple of the buildings, narrow and black, and every part of my body reacted with terror. Bile rose to my throat, my vision started to blur.

When my vision cleared, I was staring at the pavement, shaking arms just barely holding me up, the taste of bile still on my tongue. I pulled myself up and pushed my back to the closest wall, hands going for the athame in my pocket.

I knew a psychic attack when I felt it. I stood there in complete silence for close to a minute, focusing my will in preparation for the next attack. When no follow-up came, I was puzzled.

I'd been on both sides of an ambush long enough to know

that if you were exposed for long, it's game over. Whatever had just hit me would not have had a better opportunity to kill me without literally catching me with my trousers down. I made the effort to parse the conflicting whirl of emotions that had struck me, and I recalled the sense of panic and blind confusion.

I'd assumed it was a psychic attack meant to stun me for an ambush, but what if it wasn't? My eyes were drawn again to the same alleyway the psychic impulse seemed to come from.

Was it an attack? Or a cry of help? Either way, I wasn't going to find out standing out here completely exposed, and if it was an assault, I couldn't let a dangerous paranormal loose on Dublin.

With no better options, I started down the alley.

Passing the once cream walls and vulgar graffiti around me, I began swaying my athame back and forth, gently deflecting the light around me, my figure melting into the shadows. At the end of the alleyway, the path branched off in two directions, one down a much wider path, completely empty, while the other went straight under a bridge.

I paused, uncertain, when I heard approaching footsteps, and my eyes fell upon a group of people making their way out from under the bridge.

There were six of them, hunched over, dressed in business casual, save for one, a tall but slim woman, being carried by two of the others, her head down, her dark hair falling over her face in a way that recalled long-haired ghost girls in Japanese horror movies.

One could be forgiven for passing this off as a bunch of work friends after a night out, assuming of course, you ignored the woman being carried by the others making a weak attempt to struggle out of their grasps, or if you didn't notice that one of them, likely the ringleader, was surveying his surroundings with flat eyes, whilst his little posse, for all their laughter and conversation, were moving with a noticeable hustle.

Even if I'd ignored all that though, I couldn't miss the tell-tale crackle of power surrounding all of them, marking them as paranormal. Once I saw them go around the corner, I waited a moment, then pursued.

A precaution that turned out to be very well-timed, as seconds after, I heard what sounded oddly like galloping. Emerging from the tunnel, a group of six figures, covered head to toe in dirty coats and cast-off rags, took off down the same path. The figures weren't running, but hopping, like kangaroos. In the dark, it was hard to tell what was wrong with the group, aside from them all looking like some rogue pack of rabid marsupials.

Once I took a closer look, though, the illusion faltered, and I saw, despite the heavy folds of the clothing, I could only make out at most one arm on any of the group. My suspicions were confirmed when one stopped and barked a harsh 'Faster!' to a couple of stragglers, letting me catch a glimpse of a single beady eye poking out from the folds of it's hood.

One arm, one leg, one eye. Super. I'd just blundered into a troop of fachan, a particularly nasty breed of Sidhe, the kind that get it's kicks by chasing down people at night and beating them to death.

Don't ask me why, maybe they're just jealous of the rest of us not having to hop everywhere.

Under normal circumstances, this was the part where I needed to get involved, seeing as the Sidhe seemed to be in hot pursuit of a group of humans. This time however, something bothered me.

Maybe it knowing that the scraps between the Sidhe troops and other paranormals had been getting more vicious, or perhaps it was simply the predatory look in that man's eyes as he led his group off, but I couldn't shake the feeling there was more going on than I could see.

I took off after the fachan, hoping to God that fachan couldn't smell as well as that Russian at the dojo did. Whatever was going on, I'd learn nothing just standing there. I allowed my focus on maintaining my invisibility slip a little, allowing more light to reach my eyes so I could actually see where I was going.

A chorus of snarls bounced off the walls, followed by the sounds of a scuffle. I quickened my pace, moving down the wider path and around the corner, where I caught sight of the two groups, hurriedly separating from each other.

By the time I'd managed to duck behind a large industrial bin, the situation had escalated. Peeking around, I saw the stringy-haired woman was now in the grips of a couple of the fachan, one of them training a knife close to her pale neck. The humans, assuming what's what they were, were standing off with the fae, the two groups staring each other down.

'Perhaps there's a way to resolve this without fighting.' The well-dressed man spoke. 'We simply desire the girl dead. If she has caused you offence as well, by all means cut her throat now. My brethren and I will be content to observe.'

A wave of hoarse laughter echoed from the fachan. 'Oh, is that so? Done something to upset you lot, 'as she? This little slip of a t'ing learn something she shouldn't't've? Or maybe taken something of worth?'

The fachan holding the knife to the woman squeezed her

neck slightly, provoking a pained moan. 'Makes me wonder what's so important ye need her dead so bad? Maybe we ought to go have a little chat wit' her. See what she might cough up.'

'You're making a very poor decision.' The man continued; his voice icy. 'That girl is the property of some of our close associates, and they've entrusted resolving the matter to us. Continue to interfere, and we will be forced to butcher you.'

'Here, would ya look at this?! The overgrown iguana t'inks we're scared of it!' One of the other fachan sneered in response. 'Why don't ya just tuck yer tail in and run back to yer cozy penthouse? S'not like you lot have the balls to back up any of that shite!'

'On the contrary.' The man's voice took on a strange hiss, his flat eyes taking on a feral gleam. 'My brethren have become rather restless of late. Ripping apart a collection of dusty old fae relics will be an excellent way to relieve some stress.'

At once, the men and women shuddered, and their bodies twisted, once regular nails growing long and sharp, eyes developing reptilian slits, their teeth turning needle-like.

So, not human, then.

Whatever they were, it didn't shock the fachan. The knife wielder's single eye went hard. 'You shut yer fuckin' gob. We're sick of you invaders swanning in to our home, taking all the good shit and actin' like you own the place! She was hiding in our turf, where she don't belong! She fucked wit' the fae, and she's gonna pay by fae rules!'

I froze, weighing my options. If this was just between paranormals, there wasn't any need for me to intervene. Agents are only required to step in when paranormal events run the risk of making contact with normal humans. If the only lives at risk were non-humans, then, frankly, the Order only required me to make sure the bodies weren't found, and most paranormal corpses tended to vanish after death anyway.

If anything, sitting back and watching might actually be a good opportunity to further my investigation. Given the Fachans' rhetoric, this troop might well be part of this 'Sidhe Army' that'd been poisoning their rivals. If I was lucky, the troop might have a sample of the bioweapon, which would let me see it in action again, or even give me a shot at getting an active sample.

All I needed to do was sit back and pick my moment.

As I rose from my hiding spot, and starting creeping closer, I wondered why I was doing so. It didn't make a lot of sense. Sure, the girl was a non-combatant, but she was also clearly not human, which meant I had no reason to get involved.

Then, one of the fachan holding her let loose a snarl, and yanked the woman back, while the other got it's knife at the ready.

My feet were already in motion, running straight into the stand-off.

# Chapter 7

It isn't the policy of Enlightenment agents to charge straight into a fight.

We prefer to pick our battles, and when we can't, we get backup. Our role is somewhere between covert agents and special forces. What I was doing right now was formally known as 'Undergoing a solo tactical gamble', and informally known as 'Suicide'. The fachans alone could easily turn me into blood pudding, and I didn't even know what the other group were, let along how exactly they could horribly kill me.

Fortunately, I still had the element of surprise. My lingering invisibility held as I flicked out my athame, sending out whispers of my will across the alleyway.

I could have sent out a wave of force similar to how I'd tackled the Visitors yesterday but I knew enough about fachan to know all I'd achieve with that was a bunch of angry fae who wouldn't take long to make me a member of the one-limb club. This wasn't a fight I would win.

But I didn't need to fight. I just needed to save the woman.

My will focused upon the ambient water in the air. With a whispered word and a flick of the blade, a thick fog materialised in the middle of the stand-off, the sudden absence of heat cooling the air. A chorus of surprised growls came out of the fog, both sides sensing the magic at work.

I sped over to the fachan holding the hostage. With only a couple of seconds before the fachan recovered, I focused my will on the ogham tattoos lining my limbs. I felt the tattoos heat up, channelling energy and power to my limbs. I saw the world around me grind to a crawl, the fachan's knife now moving so slowly I had time to notice the muscles strain under the skin of it's hand as it tensed around the blade.

As I closed in, the fachan's eye fell on me and widened. I gripped my athame and slammed the blade into the fae's collar. The knife sunk in like I was cutting through a steak.

The fachan let out an agonised cry, letting go of it's hostage. I yanked the blade loose and sent a magically-empowered kick into it's side, sending the Sidhe tumbling into the fog, spraying blood.

Barely a second after, my instincts screamed a warning, and the second fachan threw the woman down, bounding towards me with a feral howl. Even with my tattoos enhancing my reflexes, I still felt a flash of pain as a couple of the fae's nails sliced my cheek.

I focused my will on my athame, converting kinetic energy given off by my movements into electricity, sparking along the blade. The fachan lunged once more, going wide, and I seized the chance.

Switching my blade into a reverse grip, I swung it at the fachan, sending a bolt of lightning coursing out and striking the fachan straight in the chest. It dropped to the ground, spasming from electrical feedback.

Knowing I didn't have much time before the one I stabbed returned, I sprinted over to the woman, turning her over.

My jaw dropped as I got my first proper look at the woman

I was trying to save.

Under the long dark hair: familiar dull grey skin and incredibly thin build; eyes closed, still much larger than any human eye. I flashed back to the ship, and recognised the Visitor hybrid.

An animalistic hissing started cutting through the fog. I pulled the hybrid up over my shoulders and bolted.

Before I could get far, more dark forms hopped from the dense fog. Another trio of fachan, heads turning left and right as they attempted to make sense of their surroundings. At the head of the trio, the first fachan I'd attacked a moment ago, the front of it's hoodie stained dark red from the stab wound, glowered at the fog. Crap, I knew fachan were tough enough that I hadn't killed it, but I'd hoped I'd at least stunned the prick.

My teeth clenched, my hopes dashed, when the leading fachan turned in my direction, his eye trained on me.

Caught in that gaze, I was halfway through frantically trying to balance both the Visitor and my weapon when a pair of the rival paranormals skulked out of the fog. They still wore the same suits as before, but their skin was scaly, and their faces were an unsettling mix of human and lizard-like features, most startlingly being the slits they had for nostrils and the sharp, bestial irises in their eyes.

Before the fachan could close the distance, the lizards pounced on him. The fae went down screaming. His two friends rushed to collide with the lizards, tearing and pummelling. The lizards were giving as good as they got, however, and more of them started to pull out of the fog, joining the melee.

After a brief second of shock, I turned and ran. The way

I came from was now thoroughly cut off by a supernatural street fight, so I was forced to jog blindly through my own fog, silently praying to whatever deity had just saved me to just do me one more favour. A few frantic seconds passed before I pulled free of the fog, out onto the main road, the sounds of combat still echoing down the alleyway.

I kept running, aware that any second, one of them could realise that the whole reason they were fighting had disappeared. That fear made it easier to ignore the pounding in my chest as I ducked down multiple corners and sharp turns, relying on my enhanced speed to shake any pursuers. Thank God my passenger was light.

Eventually, my hoarse breathing was reduced to a pained wheeze as I reluctantly came to a stop down a street just out of sight of the main drag. The short burst of my spells wearing off, my arms and legs sagged with fatigue as I propped the Visitor against the wall.

She was out cold, and had probably flinched her natty clothing from either a bin or a particularly low standard thrift shop. I identified multiple wounds, some were superficial scraps and cuts, but I also spotted deeper wounds, notably some parallel claw slashes which bled the same dark blue blood I'd seen only a day ago. Not lethal, but they'd need treatment.

My stomach churned as memories from the ship re-emerged, but I pushed them aside and sat back, finally having the chance to figure out what the hell I'd do now.

Going by protocol, I'd captured an enemy asset, one with relevant information to an ongoing case. Following from that, I was obliged to contact headquarters, whereupon a car would be along quickly enough to spirit the Visitor off, treat her just enough to keep her stable, then interrogate her.

The Enlightenment didn't practice torture, but we weren't necessary bound by any code of conduct, either.

Interrogators would use whatever means they would need to get her to talk, even using magic to directly pull the memories out of her skull. The process would be drawn out, possibly taking a week or more if she proved resilient, and afterwards, she would probably be held responsible in part for the events on the UFO and killed, her death one more example to paranormals who preyed on humans.

Something about that nagged at me more than I'd have liked to admit. I hadn't captured her, after all, I was trying to save her after receiving what I was now certain was a telepathic distress call.

Helping someone only to send them to their death left a bad taste in my mouth.

Maybe there was another way to do this. I could take her back to my apartment instead, treat her wounds, and, when she woke, get her to cooperate in exchange for a pardon. There was precedence for dealing with paranormals this way, if they were only accessories to whatever act caught our attention, but it was far from common.

At the best of times, paranormal beings operate on their own unique brand of logic. Some would be grateful for the rescue, but another could easily interpret your help as an insult to their pride, or would simply feel no obligation from your aid.

In the case of this Visitor, I didn't even really know how she'd react upon waking, and if she managed to escape or I was forced to kill her, I would be in deep trouble.

At the same time, if she understood gratitude or debts, then learning what she knew would go a lot smoother for me than if she woke up in an interrogation cell. Sure, it wasn't technically my job to do anything for paranormal beings, but if I could help her, then maybe-

No, stop that, Reilly.

Whether or not she called for help, that wasn't your responsibility. Your responsibility is to the Enlightenment, and this Visitor was complicit in a direct attack on Enlightenment interests.

Even assuming she would cooperate, it was more efficient to simply hand her over to specialists and let the system do its work.

Article 4 of the Agent code of ethics. An agent does what is necessary for the task. No more. No less.

Decision made, I reached for my phone to call headquarters.

As I was fishing out my phone from my coat pocket, my eyes fell again on the unconscious Visitor, blue blood splattered down her ragged clothing, her almost human face twisted with fear and pain. Like a lost child.

My hand paused.

...

Shit.

Getting back to my apartment block was a tense process. Putting aside that I was carrying an alien on my back, I was also carrying what would look to any prospective good Samaritans like an unconscious woman. Suspect enough, even if I myself looked less like a rescuer, and more like one of the meathead goons Batman hunts for sport.

While it was the middle of the night, Dublin still had a few people wandering around, either coming to or from late shifts or out on the lash. I had more than a few close calls over the walk to my apartment, but you don't last long as an agent if you can't hide from a few drunks, and I managed to make my way back to the apartment block unseen.

I pushed through the door, taking care not to smack the Visitor against the frame. The head desk was empty, but I picked up my speed regardless, not wanting to take the chance that someone might pop out of their apartment.

After taking one look at the staircase and deciding that wasn't happening, I went around to the lifts, just about managing to press the button. When the doors opened, I stepped forward, but stopped dead when I saw a short, balding man with a beer gut on the other side. Dermot Walsh, my landlord.

Far as I knew, he had no knowledge of the paranormal, but the Enlightenment had clearly been able to exert some influence on him somehow, seeing as I'd hadn't had to pay rent since I arrived, and he'd always seemed somewhat nervous around me.

If Walsh had been nervous before though, I didn't even have a word for the look he gave me when he saw me carrying an unconscious woman on my back, streaks of a strange blue liquid running down my coat. We stared at each in silence.

'Ah, Reilly.' He spoke first, his voice pitched a bit high, pointedly not looking at the woman on my back. 'Busy day at work?'

'Yes.' I responded flatly, nerves strangling me from speaking further.

The deathly silence held for a while longer before Walsh spoke again. 'Alright, alright. Well, I've just finished up for the evening, so the lift's all yours.'

He then got out of the lift slowly, eyes fixed on me. I didn't respond, not sure what I could say in this situation.

'I'lljustgetoutyourwaytheregoodevening.' The sentence fell out of Walsh's mouth before he turned and left, visibly forcing himself not to run.

I watched him scurry off before trundling into the lift. Whatever strings the Enlightenment had pulled with Walsh, they were strong enough to keep him from showing concern about what must have seemed an incredibly troubling situation.

I try not to think about why the Enlightenment might need that level of hold over someone.

When I'd finally gotten inside my apartment and slammed the door shut, I sped over to the sofa, letting the hybrid down onto it. Spots of blue dotted my carpet as I reassessed her condition.

My knowledge of alien biology is not the best, but I was not reassured by the odd darkish tint her skin had taken, or the laboured breathing. I ran for the wardrobe in my room, shoving my meagre collection of clothing aside to reach for an old shoebox at the back.

Yanking the box out, I tore the top off to reveal the four gently glowing green, plastic vials, all containing the same healing elixir I'd been given last night. Snatching one, I stumbled back to the Visitor.

Cracking the seal, I applied the elixir to all the wounds I could see. I'd had to pull aside some of the rags covering the Visitor to expose her body fully, leaving me with a sense of apologetic shame while I worked.

The last drop of the elixir dribbled out, and I stepped back to review. Several of her injuries had shown improvement, bloodied slashes now thin scratches, and the bruise on her head shrunk to a fraction of its original size. She still had some healing to go, but with the elixir doing its work, my guest should be stable by morning.

As that thought hit me, I paused, my tired brain taking longer than it should have to work through the implications, at which point I turned and pulled a cabinet open at my kitchenette, producing from inside a large bottle of low-sodium salt.

Salt had been one of the luckier symbolic associations as far as magi were concerned. Long connected with concepts such as purity and repelling evil spirits, while being so common you could buy it in bulk, salt was a mainstay for any attempts to prepare a ritual circle or, in my case, to entrap a paranormal.

I didn't know if a lack of sodium would have any profound effect, but I decided to risk it.

Pulling the top off the container, I spilled the salt in a rough circle around the sofa. I gestured out towards the circle, reciting a chant in Old Irish that druids once used to bind troublesome fae. I felt my will pour into the circle, and sensed the protective circle emerge, blocking the unconscious Visitor in. Normally, I would have had to match wills with her to get that to work, but, being passed out, the Visitor offered no resistance.

Article 6 of the Agent code of ethics. The paranormal is not inherently evil. But it is inherently dangerous. I couldn't afford to forget that, even now.

My body felt incredibly heavy, and I collapsed into the nearby armchair.

There it was. I'd been wondering when all the energy I'd spent casting spells and running across Dublin would take its toll. I tried to grab for my phone to update headquarters, but my fingers felt like overstuffed sausages.

I gave up, slumping back, promising myself I'd try again once I'd rested my eyes for a moment.

Just a moment.

# Chapter 8

I woke to a dull ache across my back. I'd almost drifted back off, when I remembered my houseguest. My eyes shot open and I looked over at the sofa.

Fortunately, the Visitor was still lying where I'd left her. Now assured that I wasn't in immediate danger, I took the chance to stretch, the continued pain in my back reminding me why sleeping in a chair was a bad idea.

Retrieving my phone, I checked the time, and was surprised to see it was still reasonably early. Looked like I might have the chance to talk to her before contacting the Order.

I settled in for a wait, holding my blade in one hand, my gun sitting on the armrest.

It took longer than anticipated for the Visitor to wake, but as I was weighing up bashing some pots together, I heard a quiet groan.

My guest had started to pull herself up, eyelids pulling apart to reveal the familiar pools of pitch black. She looked around the room, until her head turned towards me.

The Visitor jerked back, falling off of the sofa and attempting to scramble away, stopping when her head bumped against the invisible force of my ward. Her hands went down to the salt circle, and I could sense her trying to force her will against it.

'Wouldn't recommend that. That ward's for both our safeties.' I said. 'Break that ward, and I'll have to assume you're a threat.'

I ran a finger down my athame, letting her see the blade.

The Visitor didn't respond, staring at me with those unnerving, dark eyes, her skinny form curling as she looked around, trying her best to look uncomprehending.

'Cut the bloody act; I know you understand English.' I rolled my eyes. 'I remember you from that ship, and I recall you telling us to 'stay back'. I doubt a species as intelligent as yours would have no understanding of human language.'

The Visitor's body tensed. She was silent for a few more seconds before she responded, voice hoarse. 'Why confined?'

'Good question. By all rights you should've woke up in one of our state-of-the-art paranormal containment cells. But I figured you might appreciate the chance to avoid winding up in one of them. Or would you've preferred I left you to the tender mercies of the lot chasing you last night?'

The Visitor glanced away, arms wrapping around her legs. Good. As long as she feared being caught by her pursuers more than me, she'd be more inclined to co-operate.

The Visitor immediately tried to straighten herself back up and regard me defiantly. 'How long intend confine?'

'Until I'm confident you don't represent a danger to any humans and when I've gotten information that I can work on. If you co-operate, I can see my way to getting you off the hook for what went down two days ago. Otherwise, I'll have to take you to my leaders, and they're not nearly as friendly as me.'

'No reason to trust. Could still kill.'

I scoffed. 'Please. If I wanted to kill you, I could've just left those other paranormals to do it. If you deal with me in good faith, I'm willing to return the favour.'

The Visitor dropped her head down, taking a sudden interest in the floor. In the silence, I leaned back in my chair, winching as the pains from last night resurfaced. I also noticed a pit of hunger in my gut, reminding me the last thing I ate was those few scraps of bacon.

I pulled myself to my feet. 'Alright, breakfast.'

'Breakfast?' The Visitor looked up, her head tilting like a dog.

'I haven't had a decent meal for a day now, I'm bloody starved. Willing to bet you haven't eaten anything either.'

Her stomach didn't quite growl on cue, but the Visitor placed a hand on her gut.

'Consider this a show of hospitality. So long as you behave yourself, I'll be a good host. That means feeding you and keeping anyone that wants to kill you out. Sound good?'

The Visitor fidgeted with her hands, large eyes narrowing. 'Our diet. Different from Human.'

I shrugged. 'True, I don't know what you eat, but you're half-human, right? Between that and you not bursting into flames in our atmosphere, I'm willing to bet you can at least digest anything I could cook. At least you can trust I've no interest in poisoning you.'

The Visitor opened her mouth to speak again, then closed it and sat back on the sofa. Satisfied, I turned to the kitchenette, trusting my ward would give me warning if the Visitor tried anything.

As I pulled out a pot and a bag of oats, a thought occurred. 'So, do you have a name? It's getting to be a pain just calling you the Visitor in my head all the time.'

'Designation. V series. Tenth-generation hybrid clone. Variation RA.

My brow furrowed, and I busied myself with measuring out milk. 'So, that would make you V-10-RA?'

'Yes.'

'In that case, how about I call you Viora? It makes things easier for both of us if the designation I refer to you as is short and fast to say.'

'Name irrelevant. Placeholder. Nothing more.' The Visitor shot back, but then following up in a quiet, reluctant tone. 'But Viora sounds...acceptable.'

I finished pouring out the oats and milk into the pot and put the heat on. It seemed Viora had managed to regain a bit of composure, but I could tell she was off-balance, more confused than frightened.

That was my plan. Playing good cop, bad cop by yourself wouldn't have really worked on any human, but I was willing to bet that, for all my concerns earlier regarding her behaviour being unpredictable, she was very much of the same mind regarding me.

As long as I kept her off-balance by alternating between civil host and sinister spook, Viora would probably keep talking, if only because I wasn't giving her a chance to clam up without me shifting gear.

Speaking of, time to go on the attack again. 'You got lucky with that telepathic distress call of yours, managing to get my attention and not someone else's. Should I be worried that you might have given everyone in that part of Dublin seizures or something?'

'No. Captors too close to attack without retaliation. But was able to reach out mind. For individual who could help.'

She looked back at me, somehow managing to look indignant. 'Did not consider who would respond.'

A brief flash of curiosity struck me at how exactly her telepathy was able to search for someone like that, before I shook it off. 'Let's put it this way. There are over a million people in this city, and of that population, less than two percent could be considered paranormal in some fashion. So how, in a place with that many people, did you just happen in be in walking distance of one of the very small number of people in this city that not only knows what you are, but in my case, had a vested interest in tracking you down and taking you alive?'

I took a couple of steps forward and rested my arms on the chair, staring her down. 'Seems unlikely, don't you think?'

Either Viora had a good poker face, or my intimidation fell flat. 'If expecting answer, don't have. Repeat. Was not aware that Human was Enlightenment. Would have affected decision.'

I decided not to push it, mostly because I got the sense Viora wasn't lying. If I were in her position, I'd be hard pressed to think of any reason I'd want to get the attention of one of the guys who might've killed all her co-workers had a magic virus not done it first.

It still bothered me though. Sure, it was technically possible me and her running into each other was pure coincidence, but when you work in a job where magic is an occupational hazard, it pays to be suspicious.

As I focused on getting the porridge to the boil, I could feel Viora watching me intently as I cooked. Carefully, I measured out a few spoonsful of cocoa powder, followed by some honey. Once the consistency had thickened, I poured the resulting porridge into a pair of bowls.

After setting mine down on the armchair, I walked over the salt circle dividing me from Viora. Since the barrier was formed of my will, I was able to reach the hand holding the bowl over the circle, the ward registering only as a static-like sensation along my arm as it passed through. As long as I didn't break the circle itself, it would hold, though it did leave me stretching awkwardly out towards Viora, the bowl wobbling precariously.

Slowly, Viora reached out and took it, eying the food like I'd dropped a dead budgie in front of her.

I pushed down my indignation, took a seat on the chair, and began eating. Viora watched me while I took the first couple of bites, then, evidently satisfied I hadn't slipped something into the pot, began eating herself.

The porridge was hot and thick, with the cocoa and honey adding a nice aftertaste, like eating a chocolate pudding, without the sugar and fat. I chanced a glance over to Viora and saw her greedily shovelling the food into her mouth, bits of porridge splattering her clothing. Partway through swallowing down another large mouthful, she noticed me staring, stopping mid-chew, before continuing to eat, only much slower, her eyes on the floor. I allowed myself a moment of smug satisfaction.

With the worst of the hunger gone, I decided to continue questioning. 'So, why don't you tell me what happened to you after our little spat in the holding cells? You go running back to the bridge to warn your friends?'

'Yes. Abandoned plan when infection discovered.'

I raised an eyebrow. 'Odd that you didn't seem to catch whatever was down there. Looked pretty damn virulent.'

'The same question. Could easily be reversed.'

I shrugged off the comment. 'We know the pathogen doesn't affect humans. What's your excuse?'

'Was created partially from Human genetic material. May have provided resistance.' Viora scraped her spoon slowly along the bowl. 'Also did not enter. Fled instead.'

'Pretty convenient. Except that I did catch a glimpse of someone under some kind of visual concealment wandering through the bodies at the time of the crash.' I leaned forward slightly. 'Know anything about that?'

Viora tiled her head again. 'Repeat. Was not on the bridge at any point prior to the ship's descent.'

'You're saying you weren't the invisible entity I encountered on the bridge before it crashed?'

'Possess no capacity to conceal. If had that ability, wouldn't have been captured.'

I narrowed my eyes. It seemed much too convenient that Viora had nothing to do with the bioweapon, especially since she was the only being, aside from myself, Dawkes and Boyle, on the bridge who wouldn't be affected by it.

On the other hand, if she could go invisible, the paranormals from earlier who didn't even notice me under a basic camo spell would've been hard pressed to chase down someone who was actually invisible.

'So how did you get out then?'

'Went out broken window and slipped away. Guard outside. Bad at spotting.' She said it blandly, so blandly I couldn't tell if she knew it'd been me or not.

I clenched a fist, letting the tension out. 'Duly noted. So why don't you tell me what you know about the bioweapon and the events that transpired on the ship.'

Viora began to speak, only to let out a pained cough. A look of irritation crossed her face as she felt her throat. 'No knowledge of bioweapon. Can only speak about individual part of mission. Was to watch those taken to ensure restraint held.'

'Uh-huh.' I drew the word out. 'And what was your mission?'

Viora let out a sigh. 'Collect those individuals. Satisfy arrangement commander made with natives.'

I stand bolt upright. 'Natives? You mean to Earth? Who are they?'

Viora gave me a quizzical look. 'Didn't know? The shapeshifters. That were attacking earlier.'

I bit down to suppress the irritated groan that rose up my throat. 'Ok, but what exactly were they? Those shapeshifters?'

'Don't know Human term. Identified as Lemurians in prior dealings.'

Lemurians, bugger me, I should have noticed. I leaned back in my seat.

Lemurians, or to give them their common name, the Reptilians, are the ultimate conspiracy nut's wet dream, literal shape-shifting lizard people who have a preference for inserting themselves into positions of power. I'd heard about them in passing, mostly from other countries where they have a strong foothold, but I'd no idea there were any in Ireland. Even if this wasn't related to the case, this was fairly big info by itself.

I responded levelly, 'Right. So, what are these Lemurians to you lot anyway? Allies?'

Viora put down her empty bowl. 'Trading partners. Aid

allowed scout ships to perform much longer missions planetside. Also gave access to much information about world's geopolitics and resources.'

'Right. And what did you give them in return?'

Viora idly toyed with her spoon. 'Varies. Could involve trading technology, resources, or–'

'Or people.' I interrupted, disgust leaking into my voice. 'That's what those people on the ship were for. You weren't planning to do whatever it is you lot usually do to abductees, you were planning on selling them to the Lemurians.'

Viora looked away from me. 'Correct. When Enlightenment launched attack, a representative of Lemurians was already on board. Discussing terms with commander.'

'Didn't see any Lemurians while I was down there.' I said through my teeth.

Viora wrapped her arms defensively around her legs. 'Do not know. Perhaps invisible being Enlightenment encountered?'

That would be convenient, which was all the more reason to remain sceptical. 'If that's the case, why were the Lemurians trying to kill you back there. Hell, how'd you manage to piss off two separate groups after only a day in the city?'

Viora's face twisted. 'Unknown. Were in full cooperation beforehand. Attitude shifted very quickly.'

I took a deep breath, letting some anger out. 'Then tell me what happened between the ship crashing and now.'

'Went to city while dark, acquired clothing to blend in. Slept behind waste receptacle during light. Once dark again, sought out the headquarters of Lemurians for assistance.'

'I'm guessing the meeting didn't go too well.'

Viora nodded. 'Anticipated they would contact scouts from another ship to collect. Apparently different intentions. Able to briefly repel them and flee, but they pursued, despite multiple hours of continuous movement, including branching paths.'

'At which point, you bumped into the Fachan.'

'Correct. Fachan considered movements territorial encroachment. Attempted to explain intention was sanctuary. Fachan insulted, assumed deception. Issue escalated, and in attempt to flee, intercepted by Lemurians.'

Viora broke out into a coughing fit, her vocal cords likely strained from overuse. In an effort to keep my one source from going mute, I got up and filled a glass of water, passing it through the ward. Viora snatched up the glass and began taking small sips.

As she did, I thought through what I'd learned.

While I didn't have any specific reason to think Viora was lying, my gut told me she was holding something back. Her limited speech wasn't doing any favours, but I was certain she was holding something back.

Already she'd handed me a pile of information and possible leads the Enlightenment could chase down, but there was still something amiss. Sure, the invisible figure I saw being a Lemurian made sense, but why, if that figure set off the virus, would you poison your own allies, and with a bioweapon that, until now, seemed to be a strictly fae weapon, not one of Lemurian use. There was more going on here, assuming Viora was being straight with me.

I was jolted when I felt a vibration in my pocket. Pulling my phone out, I saw Bhajan's name on screen. I bit down a curse and walked a few feet from Viora, keeping her in my line of sight as I answered.

'Reilly speaking.'

A loud and exuberant voice blasted my ear. 'Reilly, my good friend! It's been only a day, but it feels like years!'

'Bhajan? What's the problem?' I replied.

A loud gasp burst out of my phone. 'You wound me! Can I not simply be checking in on a dear friend?'

'No.' I shot back. 'Now please get to the point. I'm in the middle of something.'

'Fine, fine.' Bhajan's voice responded airily. 'There's been a development in our little dispute with the Sidhe.'

'I'm listening.'

As Bhajan explained what he'd found, I felt my eyes widen as a mix of excitement, yet exasperation. Of course, after spending yesterday looking desperately for any lead, today's barely started and I already have too many. As much as I wanted to keep grilling Viora, I couldn't let this chance slide.

'Understood. I'll need to take care of some business first, but I'll be there, with backup.' I hung up, turning my attention back to the alien on my sofa.

'We're going to have to continue this conversation later. Can I trust that your fear of the Lemurians outweighs any distrust you have of me?'

'Lemurians perform treachery last night. Enlightenment didn't.' She responded dryly.

'Excellent. In that case, I'll keep the ward up until I can be sure you can be trusted. You could probably breach it eventually, but I'm sure you understand why co-operating with us will end better for you.'

I held my stare, letting the implication hang. If she escaped, she wouldn't only have the Lemurians and Sidhe to worry about. I could only hope that my next interaction with Viora wouldn't be killing her. Viora seemed to think through my words for a moment, before flinching as realisation dawned.

I straightened up and made my way to the bedroom door, pausing briefly, 'Glad you understand the situation.'

I could see her still working up the nerve to respond as I pulled the door shut.

# Chapter 9

'I'm sorry. Could you explain this one more time?'

Dawkes and I were sitting in a Starbucks along Parnell Street East, her nursing an overpriced coffee, me nibbling at a Danish, while we waited for Bhajan to show up.

I was wearing my suit again, the enchantments on it cleaning away the soup of contaminants that previously decorated it, as well as repairing any damage. It felt reassuring to have it back, like being in my proper skin again.

It'd been a few hours since I'd left the apartment. I'd made contact with headquarters to report my latest progress. The captain hadn't been over the moon that I'd put Viora under my protection, but revealing the Lemurian angle helped mollify him. Course, I still had to spend a good chunk of my day writing up a report detailing everything that happened last night.

Rest of the day, I'd spent trawling through Enlightenment databases, in an effort to find out anything about Lord Nechtan, only to come up empty. Either Calatin had been lying about warning us about him, or it hadn't been recorded. Why was another question.

I let out an exhale. 'I thought I was clear. I got a call from Bhajan indicating a meeting is to take place between representatives of the Seventh Wave communities to address the Sidhe attacks on them. Bhajan claims he'll be able to help us infiltrate the meeting.'

Dawkes let out a snort. 'Not that. I'm talking you keeping one of the aliens in your living room.'

'It's all laid out in the report. When I encountered the Visitor, I had to make a judgement call between treating her potentially lethal injuries immediately or waiting for backup and potentially losing our one lead. I weighed up the pros and cons of processing her through the usual procedures and decided those would be inefficient in her case, when a simple deal could get the same information faster.'

Dawkes stared at me blankly. 'I don't get you, Reilly.'

I blinked, puzzled. 'What do you mean?'

'One moment, you have the biggest stick up your arse regarding Enlightenment protocol, and barely reacted when civilians got hurt.' Dawkes threw back a swig of coffee before ploughing on. 'Then the next thing, I find out your best friend's a monkey man, ignoring all protocol on para fraternisation, and you're sheltering one of aliens we'd hunted, risking your own position to do it.'

I waved off the comment. 'Bhajan and I are not friends.'

Dawkes' brow furrowed, and she leaned a little closer. 'Could've fooled me. Not like I've met anyone else you'd call a friend. Heck, back at the office, do you even talk to anyone about anything other than work?'

Once again, the question threw me. I shrugged. 'Why would I? We're there to work.'

Something about my answer seemed to unsettle Dawkes. Her expression now looked almost suspicious. 'Right. What about outside? Any friends?'

Where was this even going? 'I'm an agent, not a socialite.'

'And, as rude as this is, I'm assuming no girlfriend or boyfriend?'

I paused, mulling over the right wording. 'Which one's the sexuality where you're not interested in sex?'

'Asexual?' Dawkes replied, head cocked.

'I'm that one.' I said, with a nod.

'Ok, that point's fair.' Dawkes conceded with a sigh. 'But come on. You don't talk to anyone, ever, except for work. You've no friends, at least by your own words. But now, out of nowhere, you're making deals with aliens and inviting them into your home! Forgive me if that seems a bit odd!'

My fingers drummed along the table, the rhythm soothing the unease in my gut. She wasn't wrong, exactly, but I'd had a perfectly good reason for taking the Visitor in. Or at least I thought I did.

'Do you object to the decision I made with the Visitor?'

'Kind of? I get the rationale, but I don't see why you're going to all this trouble rather than just letting the mind probers dig around.'

She set down her coffee, regarding me seriously. 'You do realise it'd be on your head if it escapes, right?'

I matched her stare. 'Would've thought you'd figured it out by now. Visitors are telepathic, right? Does it not occur that any entity with those abilities would probably be resistant to psychic interrogation?'

Dawkes leaned back. 'I suppose. Still, you're also taking a huge risk hoping that ward will hold. What's stopping it from just knocking that down, then getting into your head the second you're through the door?'

'Nothing yet. I'm preparing a countermeasure before our

next interaction. I've already done some thinking, and I believe I've found a symbol I can use.'

'Yeah? Do tell.'

I told her. Her expression moved from curious, to confused, then incredulous.

'That's got to be one of stupidest things I've ever heard.'

'You know the importance of association. Can you honestly say you can't see it working?'

Dawkes lifted a hand up to her forehead, her expression tensing. She let out an aggravated moan. 'Dammit, yes, it probably could. Just, drop a call to HQ before you try it, so we'll know if something goes wrong.'

'Understood.' Taking another bite of my danish, a thought occurred to me. 'What about you? Any progress investigating the ship's data banks?'

Dawkes ran her hand through her hair. 'About as much as I expected. Most of it is garbled nonsense, and what isn't is built on an operating system with no human parallel. Honestly, magic's the only way you could get anything useful out of that.'

'Well, what have you found?' I responded.

'What little I could get looks like it bears out what your Visitor's saying. I found a few scraps of footage showing our little grey friends chatting with some guy in a suit on the bridge, and them giving him a quick tour of the cells. That's about it.'

'So we know the Visitor's at least partially honest with us.' I said, secretly glad I was able to justify my decision so quickly.

Dawkes hissed through her teeth. 'I'd still take anything it says with a grain of salt. Hopefully I can pick out some more data that will give us a better idea of what happened.'

I nodded. 'I'll try not to disturb your work unless it's necessary.'

Dawkes let out a tired laugh. 'Honestly, Reilly? If it means we're getting somewhere, disturb me all you want.'

She pointed at the small plastic bag at my feet. 'That said, should I be concerned about that 'payment' for your friend?'

I felt my lip curl. 'Don't worry, it's nothing illicit. Just undignified.'

'Riiiight.' Dawkes drew the word out. 'And you're sure this Bhajan character's trustworthy?'

'Bhajan's a perverse, deviant individual with no standards I've seen. But he hasn't screwed me yet, and he's had the chance to.' I finished off the last of my danish and looked around. 'He'll show up disguised as a human, so keep your eyes peeled.'

'Alright. Well, how will we know which one's-' Dawkes paused, interrupted by the sound of a door slamming open behind me, followed by a whoop of glee. Her eyes flicked past my shoulder, then back to me, a gesture I returned with a sad nod, before turning to face the new arrival.

'Ah, there you are!' Bhajan cried out, taking a seat next to us, in his human guise. 'Many apologies for my lateness. Traffic was a horrid bitch!'

I forced my face to stay static. 'Hello Bhajan. This is Agent Dawkes. She's the backup I mentioned.'

'Oh-hoh!' Bhajan's eyes lit up at the sight of Dawkes, whether due to her being particularly attractive, or just them sharing an ethnicity, I couldn't tell, and he offered his hand. 'Well, fondest greetings to you, my dear. I must say, Reilly never told me the Enlightenment contained such visions of beauty among their ranks.'

Dawkes did not take his hand, pulling back. 'Maybe he didn't tell you because of a little thing called discretion. Ever hear of it?'

Bhajan simply laughed in response. 'Ah, they all say that to start with, but the charm always works its magic eventually!'

'If you're quite done.' I cut in. 'I'd appreciate it if we could get done to business.'

'Before that, dear friend, it has been a while since I've allowed myself the luxury of indulgence.' Bhajan turned his lecherous face to me, eyebrows waggling. 'I hope you would be so kind as to provide such a decadence?'

I let out a sigh and reached into the bag, retrieving a pair of cans, both containing the cheapest lager I could find. Bhajan snatched one up and cracked it open, downing the contents with relish.

'That's my side of the bargain, Bhajan. Your turn.'

Finishing the can, Bhajan let out a belch, attracting the offending stares of more than a couple of patrons. 'Calm yourself, noble magi. Master Bhajan may have fallen far from his monastic past, but his word is bound.'

'It's not your word I'm worried about. I'm more concerned how you plan to help us get into this place. Do you have some kind of in with these people?'

'More than that, Reilly.' Bhajan cracked open the other can and leaned back smugly. 'I was invited.'

'You?' I responded. 'I thought this was a gathering of important figures.'

Halfway through chugging down the can, Bhajan suddenly spluttered, pointing a finger furiously at me. 'Hey! I'll have you know that I, the wise Bhajan, am well regarded amongst my fellow migrants for my combat prowess and insight!'

While normally I might have had a snide reply, I held my tongue, the memory of Bhajan instantly disabling another paranormal yesterday still fresh in my mind.

'I'm guessing it's too much to hope we're just your plus-ones?'

Bhajan grunted, wiping his mouth. 'Unfortunately so. But worry not, I have crafted an ingenious method to allow you two to pass through undetected.'

'Alright.' I said, pulling myself up. 'Lead the way.'

Bhajan got up, tossing the empty cans in a nearby bin as he went. I looked over at Dawkes as she too got up.

She stared after Bhajan like he'd crapped on the table.

'Are you sure–'

'Of course not.' I responded. 'At least we know who to blame if this goes sideways.'

The walk down to the meeting point was mostly uneventful, save for Bhajan throwing a couple more passes Dawkes' way, to which she simply responded with a long-suffering stare.

We shortly found ourselves outside a decent sized Chinese restaurant tucked away down a street corner, the name 'The Sichuan Pantry' proudly emblazon at the top. The lights were out and the doors locked, but Bhajan led us around the side of the building, stopping Dawkes and I just before the corner, bidding us to look around.

The turn led to the staff entrance, a single door standing opposite a set of large bins. Standing at the door were what looked like two burly Asian men, well over 6 feet and built like they crushed beer kegs for fun. A more focused look quickly revealed an extra foot of height, hairy hides and tusks. Yaogui, Chinese spirits, if I had to guess. Only thing I was certain of was that they weren't human.

'Well, looks like the place.' I said.

'Could try going invisible.' Dawkes spoke up, her face pensive.

'Possibly. Assuming they were stupid enough to not notice the door opening by itself.' I turned to Bhajan. 'Guessing that's where you come in.'

Dawkes winced, reluctantly looking over at Bhajan. 'All right, smartarse. What's your plan, then?'

'Don't you worry about that.' Bhajan responded, fondly clapping us both on the back. 'Just sit back and let the master ply his art.'

Before either of us could speak, Bhajan had already gotten up and started walking down to the guards with a carefree bounce. As he approached, one of the men stepped forward and held out a hand.

'Welcome, honoured guest.' The man said, his deep voice reverberating. 'Before you enter, I'm afraid we must perform a quick inspection for the sake of security.'

Bhajan let out a mortified cry. 'I'm shocked, Cheng! Do you not recognise your own instructor!'

The burly guard was unfazed. 'Apologies, Master Bhajan. I mean no disrespect, but in light of the recent attacks, we can't afford to be careless. Please co-operate with us.'

'Dah! Very well! But make it fast, or I might take it as a come on.' With an exaggerated huff, Bhajan thrust his arms out, letting the two guards begin frisking him.

When the guard's hands went down to Bhajan's thighs, he leapt up with a surprised yelp, flinging himself backwards and collapsing in a heap on the ground, groaning. The guards watched him with what looked like concern and bafflement, before walking over to help him up.

'There's our chance, move!' I slipped from our hiding spot and sped over to the door, Dawkes following after a second. We reached the door, and opened it slowly, just enough to squeeze through. Our luck ran short, however, as one of the guards started to turn back while Dawkes was only half way through.

'Dear me! A thousand apologies! Allow me to just-' Mid-sentence, Bhajan's foot hooked itself on the guard's ankle, and he let loose another shrill shriek and stumbled forward, collapsing on top of the other guard turning towards us and sending all three to the floor, Bhajan's squirming keeping all attention focused on him.

As much as part of me wanted to see how far Bhajan could push this, I closed the door after Dawkes, muffling the slapstick show outside. We both cast our respective concealment spells, Dawkes simply flexing her gloved hand, her glasses briefly flashing, before her body vanished from sight.

No sooner had we ducked into our hiding spots that the door opened, and Bhajan stumbled through. The door shut again, and Bhajan immediately straightened up, letting out a full body shiver, his illusion falling away and his true form reasserting itself.

Walking down the hallway, he stopped and gave what was clearly supposed to be a knowing wink to a spot nowhere near either of us, before stepping through into the restaurant proper.

The two of us waited thirty seconds, cramped up against the walls, then, I felt a tug on one of my sleeves and a whispered 'Come on.', which was enough to get me moving. We reached the door, me taking one side and Dawkes taking the other. I looked in and was stunned.

Inside, the restaurant was far from quiet. Bright lights lit up the floor with an inviting glow as figures took seats around a grand table assembled from the restaurant tables around the floor. Amongst the energetic chatter, I picked up the sound of sizzling meat and the tantalising smell of fried rice, soy and oyster sauce.

More interesting than the food however, was the clientele.

With the windows shuttered and doors locked, the guests had shed whatever guises let them move among humans. In one corner, a woman with fox ears and tail was bickering with a short, squat man with a beard made of grain stalks. Only a bit away, a Middle-Eastern man with serpent eyes and raven wings was debating something with a pair of Nordic men dressed in wet clothing and carrying fiddles. Further along, a trio of large, grey skinned, bushy haired trolls slurped down bowls of stir-fry, while opposite, several webbed fingered old women gossiped in German over a shared seafood platter.

Watching the scene before me, I felt like I was intruding on a private world, one that might have existed years ago, before humanity's constant encroachment pushed these beings to the outskirts.

Bhajan was certainly not exaggerating about the scale of this meeting. Judging by the sheer variety of beings I was seeing; I was willing to bet they had representatives from most if not all the immigrant paranormal communities in Dublin.

Even though they were eating and conversing, there was an underlying tension throughout the room, much of the conversation sounding like arguments or conspiratorial whispering. They were here out of necessity, but I was still unsure what necessity.

That question was quickly put to the side when I heard approaching footsteps quietly ringing out from the kitchen. The footsteps weren't loud, in fact I was certain I shouldn't have heard them over the commotion around me.

I wasn't the only one. One by one, the conversing entities slowly went quiet. The footsteps grew closer, the entire table silent by the time the creature emerged from the kitchen.

It's head looked like a stag, with long sweeping antlers, and had a large mane. Its body was more similar to a horse's, but covered in shimmering golden scales, which seemed to catch the light in a way that gave the creature an almost celestial glow.

My back went stiff and I heard Dawkes let out a quiet gasp.

'Jesus. A Qilin.' She whispered.

Qilin, cousins to Chinese dragons and familiars of wise sages and rulers, were exactly as rare and noteworthy as that implied. If you believed the stories, they were incredibly powerful and benevolent, but I wouldn't want to bet on the latter assuming the former was true. A Qilin's presence was a sign that this meeting was no joke.

Once the chatter amongst the guests dissipated, the Qilin spoke, a melodious, androgynous voice washing over the restaurant.

'Greetings, fellow travellers. It pleases me deeply that so many of you are arrived in at a time where we all must come together. I am Bǎohùshen, guardian of the Chinese who have sought new life in this city.'

Bǎohùshen stepped forward. 'My dearest brothers and sisters, would that you had been called here during brighter times. Alas, we currently live in a dark period, one where so many of our own live in fear. Fear of both the Aes Sidhe, who even now plot our demise, and of the Lemurians and their disturbing allies.'

I felt my hands tense. Bad enough that it looked like the Qilin was looking to throw some fuel on the Sidhe-Waver conflict, but where did the Lemurians play into this?

Bǎohùshen continued, it's voice the only sound in the hall. 'Whether it be by force of arms or duplicitous plagues, these groups have no interest in co-operating with us. I am by no means blind to the grudges that exist between many of those here, whether they were formed in their homelands or here. However, the threats facing us today are a danger to us all. The same plague that the Sidhe has released freely on Djinn, Trolls and alike will not stop there.'

The Qilin stood tall, it's gaze piercing. 'If the Aes Sidhe, the so-called Enlightenment and others are content to label us all with the brand of the Seventh Wave, I say we embrace it. If they are determined to reduce us all to one group, then let us at least enjoy the benefits of a united front. Instead of squabbling amongst ourselves over the meagre scraps we've been able to wrest from our tormentors, let us instead take what is needed from those who seek our destruction!'

This got a strong reaction from the crowd, who erupted into an overlapping wave of noise, some shouting objections, others cheering.

I'd gone pale. What Bǎohùshen was suggesting was damn close to a declaration of war against the Sidhe, a war we would have to try and keep out of the public eye. It was stretching our resources just keeping the current conflicts under wraps, open fighting between paranormals would be nigh impossible to keep quiet with the limited resources the Enlightenment had given the Irish branch.

One of the ogre's rose and slammed his fists on the table, cracking the wood. 'Cooperation!? You expect my brothers and I to surrender independence to you?! Make ourselves slaves for the faint promise of protection!? I will hear no more of-'

The ogre suddenly cut himself off with a fit of wet coughs, which devolved into equally wet choking. Beside him, his fellow ogres turned to him in concern, and confused whisperings started to move throughout the diners.

'Farrukh, are you well? Do you need assistance?' Bǎohùshen asked, its serene voice tinted with concern.

The ogre yanked back with a scream, his hands clutching at his chest. There was a ripping sound, then the ogre's chest burst open, splattering the other attendees with viscera. Watching in disbelief, I saw large legs, rubbery with octopus-like suckers; extend out of the corpse, something large emerging from the newly made cavity.

It was bright green, with a head that looked like the combination of a parrot and a grasshopper. Though it was initially small enough to pull loose of the chest cavity, I could already see it growing dramatically in size, its thick rubbery skin bulging as muscles developed. By the time the thing had pulled itself onto the table, it was already the size of a small horse. The thing let out a warbling cry and flung itself towards one of the Nordic-looking men, smashing into him, limbs wrapping around his arms.

The crack of bone and cries of pain were quickly accompanied with more spluttering and coughing from the ogre's entourage, not one having more than a few seconds before they too collapsed, and more neon green monsters ripped loose from their bodies. In less than a minute, the room was a scene of chaos and violence.

Crap, looks like I can’t blame Bhajan for this after all.

# Chapter 10

I'd being prepared for any number of things going wrong, Bhajan screwing something up, one of the paras seeing through our concealment, etc.

But this didn't fall under any disaster I'd braced myself for.

I wasn't the only one. The paras spent a few fatal seconds watching the proceedings in shock. That shock didn't last long before the strange beasts descended on the attendees and began ripping into the nearest targets available.

As the more proactive paranormals started to recover, I saw the winged Arabic man lunge at the beast crushing the Nordic man, only to get smashed against the wall by another of the creatures, which then started pummelling him with it's unsettlingly flexible limbs, the impact sounds soon turning wet. Whatever these creatures were, they were powerful, and fast.

The things leaped from person to person, only stopping to brutalise their current prey. It had been less than a minute since they emerged, but there were already three bodies on the ground.

I felt something yank me hard.

'Come on! Let's get out of here!' Dawkes' voice hissed in my ear, her hand pulling me.

I paused, a thought pushing its way to my mind. 'Wait. What if those creatures break out into the streets? We can't afford to have them running about in public.'

'Oh, you can't be-!' Dawkes quietly snarled, before stopping herself. 'Ok, sure, but how about we do the risk assessment from a safe distance?'

I hated the idea, but Dawkes was right. The longer we stuck around, the likelier we'd be discovered, either by the paranormals or the beasts. I stopped fighting Dawkes.

Back at the table, one of the beasts had just finished smashing the Arabic man, its front limbs leaving slick blood trails. Before it could find a new target, Bhajan emerged from amidst the crowd, bounding over to the creature to send a fierce kick down on it's head, the force echoing out like a sledgehammer. The creature let out a gargled snarl, it's limbs scrambled to regain purchase.

Bhajan didn't give it the chance, smashing his foot down on it repeatedly, the monk's face set with a feral expression.

For a moment, I thought Bhajan may have turned this mess around, until I caught sight of another of the beasts, freshly finished yanking the arms off one of the crones, now turned-on Bhajan, emitting a ringing howl before pulling itself up onto the table and wrapping it's front limbs around Bhajan's torso.

Bhajan tried to wrestle loose, head-butting and kicking at the creature even as it pulled him down. Meanwhile, the one Bhajan had been pulverising pulled itself back up, compound eyes fixed on Bhajan. He was putting up a fight, but with two of them, it was only delaying the inevitable.

Article 4 of the Agent code of ethics. An agent does what is necessary for the task. No more. No less.

'Change of plans.' I said over my shoulder. 'You fall back. I'll secure our informant.'

My athame was already out, Dawkes barking out something inaudible as I pulled loose, my attention focused on Bhajan. I stepped out and hopped over the bloody form of the winged man as I got close to the table, both the athame and my tattoos humming with power. I felt my camouflage dissipating, my focus now split between it and the other spell I was preparing. This would need to be a precision strike.

As the tattoos under my suit glowed with heat, I took that energy and channelled it through my blade, pointing at the thing now holding Bhajan.

Sending power through my knife, I imagined that energy taking the form of a long, thin blade, and I thrust my knife at the creature, releasing the power.

I felt the power speed across the room, and the creature let out a sudden spasm, and a pained squall, as its head shot out a spurt of blood, my spell striking home, leaving a new, deep stab wound just above the creature's right eye. The monster thrashed, letting Bhajan wrestle an arm free from its grapple, thrusting his fingers into the wound, before yanking down, his large fingernails tearing down its face, turning what was already a substantial wound into a mess of gore. As the creature let out one final death scream, I had to swallow an influx of bile rising to my throat.

I stumbled, both out of revulsion and in a vain attempt to disappear, when I realised my body was no longer concealed. I looked back up and was greeted not only with the fox tailed woman and the stalk-bearded man, both staring in shock, but also the creature Bhajan had battered moments before, now advancing towards me.

I had just enough time to leap back before the beast slammed down on the spot I'd been standing. Before it'd even fully landed, the thing snapped at me with its beak, and I dropped prone to get clear of it.

I could still hear the sounds of violence around me, as the second of these creatures continued it's rampage, but my attention was focused entirely on the monster five feet from me.

Fear shot down my back. I was stuck in an agent's worst nightmare, alone in close quarters with something much faster and stronger than me. I felt my tattoos heat up again as I forced magical power into my body, giving me just enough speed to dodge another bite from the creature.

Not having enough time or space for a spell, I pulled my gun, firing it at the creature. The bullets struck the creature in the torso, but the thing kept ploughing towards. I cursed, still falling back. No use, it was like trying to shoot down a rhino.

However, as the green-skinned freak tried to close the distance, one of its front limbs shot upwards and smacked it in the face. The monster attempted to move forward again, only for its head to careen forward and crash against the floor, splitting the wood and leaving a splatter of blood. I watched the scene with confusion for a second before I sensed the tell-tale wisps of magic pulling the creature's limbs.

'Don't just stand there!' Dawkes cried out, and as I turned, I saw her furiously pinching and tapping with her gloved hand, power echoing out with each movement. 'Bloody kill it already!'

Knowing Dawkes could probably only keep the thing occupied for a bit, I decided to do something drastic.

Holstering my gun, I readied the athame and advanced on the abomination, until I got within stabbing range, then I thrust the blade into one of its eyes. My body, enhanced with both magic and adrenaline, pushed the knife deep, and the beast screamed, the unpredictable spasms and jerks the only thing keeping it from tearing me apart. Despite the grievous wound, the creature still thrashed angrily.

Inhaling, I grabbed the handle with both hands and muttered 'Tintreach' under my breath as many times as I could, sending the power still brimming in my tattoos down the blade, transforming from kinetic energy into crackling electricity.

With a final cry of 'Tintreach!', the blade exploded with lightning, coursing down the beast's exposed socket deep into its body. The thing went into a seizure, every limb spasming in a different direction. I lost my grip and was sent flying, crashing into the wall, my vision going white.

When my eyes started working again, I saw the creature had dropped on its side, its green hide patched with black burns, my athame still sticking out of its socket, its limbs still twitching from residual electricity.

My attention was then caught by another roar. At the dining tables, the last of those monsters was still up and in the middle of a melee with Bǎohùshen, the Qilin's horns glowing as they delivered strike after strike, each tearing a hefty chunk from their target. Even so, the thing was still moving, and was attempting to wrap one of its front limbs around the Qilin's neck, the resulting grapple sending both careening, knocking tables aside.

Before I could collect myself enough to intervene, I saw Dawkes working her magic once again, now focused on the remaining creature. This time, the monster went suddenly stiff.

The Qilin pulled back, the light gathering along its horns in a visible aura shining enough to light up the room, shot out of the horns straight at the beast. The beams struck the monster head on, burning a pair of basketball-sized holes in the thing's torso. The creature let out a weak gargle, before slumping.

I pulled myself uneasily to my feet, scanning the area. Most of the guests had fled, but a few were still lingering, heads poked out nervously. The once delectable banquet had now been plastered across the room, shattered plates and food stains covering the surfaces, mixing with the blood and broken bodies.

I caught sight of Bhajan storming over towards me, a look of fury on his face. Before I could react, he was inches from me.

'You!' Bhajan's hands grabbed hold of my collar and drew me close to his snarling face, sharp teeth on full display. 'Is it not bad enough that the Enlightenment spies on us and watches our movements, but now you interfere in our private affairs!? By what right do you justify yourself!?'

There was a stunned split second where I stared at Bhajan. Then, something clicked in my mind, and I returned Bhajan's furious glare with a stone-faced expression.

'Unless I'm mistaken, if we hadn't 'interfered', those creatures would have crushed you to death. Perhaps you should consider that before you get indignant with the people who just saved your life.'

Bhajan pulled back with a hiss, all the paras now watching us both intently.

'We would have disposed of these aberrant beasts without your help.' He said, his faux wounded pride so convincing I almost believed it.

Bhajan levelled a finger at me. 'Now explain yourself, magi. Why are agents of the Enlightenment intruding on this meeting? And what do you know of these creatures?'

I could see what Bhajan was doing. By taking the role of the accuser. he was not only covering his own arse from suspicion, but also preventing someone else more hostile taking the lead and picking a fight with me. Around me, I could tell the other paras were hanging back, waiting to see how our argument panned out. I couldn't blame them, after seeing what Bhajan did to that creature grappling him, I was secretly glad this stand-off was an act.

Still, I had my own role to play. 'We got a tip through the grapevine that this meeting was taking place, so the Enlightenment deployed the pair of us to observe. As for those creatures, your guess is as good as mine.'

'So, you admit to spying, then?' Bhajan crossed his arms, his lips curled in a sneer. 'Well, if you have no notion of how those things got in among our compatriots, perhaps you would also be so kind as to explain why you saw need to meddle in our affairs!?'

'We stepped in because you lot were doing a piss poor job of containing them. We weren't going to take the chance of those things getting out of the restaurant and hurting humans just to spare your pride.' I responded, keeping my posture straight. 'As for why we saw fit to observe you, we had a suspicion that this location would become the site of another attack, a suspicion that was clearly right.'

'Oh-ho! So that is how it is, then?' Bhajan shot back, his

laugh mocking. 'You pry into our most private affairs on mere suspicion!'

'First, we hear that we're not doing enough to keep order, now when we're proactive, you get angry at us meddling? You can't have it both ways, either you want us around or not. Which is it?' Despite the act, I still felt my teeth clench as I spoke, this particular question one I'd never gotten a good answer to, no matter who I asked.

I didn't find out what Bhajan's answer was, as the Qilin's voice then cut across the room. 'Enough! Our energy is wasted squabbling with those who've risked their own safety to assist us.'

Both Bhajan and I took a step back, while Bǎohùshen came forward. Despite the welts on it's skin, the stag-like creature strode with a dignified majesty. it's eyes set firmly on me. 'Regardless of your reasons, you both have my gratitude for protecting my guests. However, I warn you now, the Seventh Wave will not ignore this blatant attack.'

'Hang on.' Dawkes said, stepping forward herself. 'That sounds like you're no longer talking about a defensive pact. That sounds more like you're planning to go on the attack.'

'Look about you. Every person you see dead on the ground came here with peaceful intentions, concerned only with protecting themselves and their communities. Fearing, as anyone here would, the plagues and chaos our enemies have brought to our doorsteps.'

Bǎohùshen spun their head round to appeal to the crowd. 'And now, these enemies strike us right at our hearts, targeting leaders come together for mutual co-operation, infiltrating our ranks for the sole purpose of killing all of us in one fell swoop. Tell me, is this how you wish to die!?'

The crowd unleashed a bellow, the individual words lost in the noise, but the anger, the defiance, that came across perfectly.

'Our enemies have made a lethal mistake, my friends. In choosing to unleash these monsters upon us, they have tipped their hand, and revealed their identities.

Dawkes' eyebrows went up. 'You know what those things were?'

'Indeed. I have travelled to many places since I left my homeland and encountered many things in the process.' Bǎohùshen stared into the distance. 'These creatures, I recall hearing of during my brief stay in the New World. Despite these stories, I know their true origin. Born not from the womb, but from alchemy, in labs operated by those scaled demons.'

My head shot up. 'Are you talking about the Lemurians?'

'I am. I spoke earlier of their threat to our safety, but even I did not foresee them acting so brazenly. Regardless, they have caused disruption and chaos in my own household now, and I will not let such an insult pass unpunished.'

The Qilin bowed it's head to us. 'I give credit to your order in its thankless task of protecting the veil of Innocence, but even you can plainly see that we are not the instigators of this. And I feel no obligation to stand idle and put your secrecy first while more of us die.'

Dawkes put her hands out placatingly. 'We can understand your outrage, but more violence only further destabilises the secrecy we all wish to protect. By all means take steps to protect yourselves, but please, surely you can see how open war will benefit no one, least of all you.'

Dawkes' protest was met with jeers from the paras, increasing in volume until Bǎohùshen cast it’s gaze across the attendees, silencing them.

‘I take your argument, Arbiter, but nevertheless, my comrades and I will not let this assault go unpunished. We will do what is necessary to deter our foes and protect our kin, and if they choose to bring war to us, we will respond in kind.’

The Qilin stood to their full height, watching us through narrowed eyes. ‘You see to your obligations, Arbiters, we shall see to ours.’

My senses were almost overwhelmed when Bǎohùshen’s aura struck me full force. I stumbled back, and not just from the power. This wasn’t a debate, the Wavers were out for blood now, and all we could do was hope it wasn’t too late for damage control.

Dawkes had also taken a step back, and we exchanged a single look. Without another word, we made for the exit, the paras watching us. My eyes briefly met with Bhajan’s, and he flashed me an apologetic flinch.

Stepping through the doorway, pausing only to collect my athame from the beast I’d killed, I could still feel the eyes on us, and it wasn’t until both Dawkes and I had managed to get outside, the cool air washing away the tension in my body, that I allowed myself to relax.

Dawkes turned to me, her face grim. ‘That was too bloody close, Reilly. Contact or not, getting involved to save that monkey got us exposed. They could have killed us back there.
’

I winced, shame prickling my skin. I’d let my emotions get the better of me again. ‘I agree. That was rash of me, and I should have waited until you’d fallen back so you weren’t dragged into it.’

Dawkes leaned back, surprise clear on her face. 'Erm, well good then. I guess we came out as best as we could've there, but you probably shouldn't do something like that again. Even if it is one of your friends.'

'Bhajan isn't my friend.' I said. 'Anyway, we have a big problem here. Despite all of that Qilin's posturing on mutual defence, we both know that we just witnessed a declaration of war.'

'Yeah, I guess so.' Dawkes slumped against the wall, hand running through her hair. 'As if the bioweapon wasn't bad enough. Now we have both the Wavers and the Lemurians gunning for each other.'

I joined her against the wall. 'You're telling me. First the Wavers fighting the Sidhe, then the Lemurians weigh in, not long after a Sidhe bioweapon hits a ship piloted by Lemurian allies. Then, one of those allies ends up in a scrap between the Sidhe and Lemurians over who'd get to kill them.'

'Then she wound up on your sofa.' Dawkes remarked dryly.

I shook my head, too tired to even retort. 'It's like the entire Irish para community is falling apart.'

'We need to alert the higher ups.' Dawkes responded. 'Maybe they can pull some strings, cool this mess down.'

'Good idea.' I said, pushing myself off the wall. 'The sooner the Enlightenment steps in, the sooner we can calm these tensions.'

Dawkes stayed against the wall. 'What if this isn't all just normal inter-factional tensions?'

I stopped. 'You'll need to elaborate.'

'Think about it, Reilly. This is all moving so fast, and everything that's happened so far seems almost designed to draw all the major paranormal factions in Ireland into conflict.'

Dawkes fixed me with a gimlet eye. 'What if something bigger's at play here? Could these events be connected?'

Crap, I was really hoping it was my imagination. 'Are you suggesting there's a conspiracy at play?'

Dawkes shrugged, her eyes not quite meeting mine. 'Wouldn't be that shocking in our line of work, would it?'

I'm sure I must have looked like a deer in the headlights. If she was right, we had one of the biggest threats to the Enlightenment in Irish history on our hands.

I managed to force out a response. 'Maybe you're right, Dawkes. Luckily, I happen to know just who to ask about that.'

# Chapter 11

By the time I'd gotten back to my apartment, the sky had started pitching down, and when I pushed through the door, juggling keys in one hand and a bag of groceries in the other, rainwater dribbling down my jacket, I found myself appreciating why so many agents wanted to get away from Ireland.

I shrugged off the jacket, moved to the kitchenette and dropped the bag on the counter. I wish I was surprised that the same day I finally get some time to restock would be the day with the heaviest rain all month, but honestly with my luck, I was thankful I hadn't been struck by lightning.

'Enlightenment has returned.' Viora said, still where I'd left her this morning. I noticed the pitcher of water I'd left her was empty, as was the plate which I'd left a bacon butty on.

I could still feel the buzz of the ward, but it had faded over the day, barely enough to hold back a gnat. I wasn't sure if Viora hadn't noticed she could've broken loose with ease or if she'd chosen to stay put, but either way, it made things easier for me.

'Yeah, hang on. Be with you in a moment.' I responded irritably. Sure, there was an alien behind me, but if I didn't get the groceries packed away now, I'd probably wouldn't have the will to do it for the rest of the evening.

'Why wearing a hat?' Viora spoke up again.

'Well, aren't you bloody chatty tonight?' I said back, taking a moment to readjust the trilby I was now wearing. Not my first choice, but it would do. 'Since you're so talkative, perhaps you'd be willing to talk a bit more about your relationship with those Lemurians.'

'First, release from barrier.' Viora responded.

I looked over, suspiciously. 'On what grounds?'

'Have ingested both water and nutrients and have not had the chance to excrete the waste for nearly a full cycle.' Viora then paused to examine the room. 'Assumed defecating on the floor of Enlightenment's dwelling would be interpreted poorly.'

I paused, now feeling slightly foolish for having provided food and water but not accounting for the logical end point.

'Wait just a moment, there.' I said, dropping a carton of milk into the fridge, then walking up to the threshold of the salt circle surrounding Viora.

'I'm dispelling the ward. Don't think I won't still have my eye on you.' I said, dashing my foot across the circle, breaking it and letting the remaining wisps of power dissipate. I gestured for Viora to stand and she did. I then placed one hand on her shoulder, ignoring her twitch, then began leading my guest to the bathroom.

Before we'd gotten too far, Viora's face tensed, and she looked at me. 'How doing that?'

'Doing what?'

'Suddenly difficult to sense Enlightenment's brain waves.' The Visitor's eyes then fell on my new hat. 'Is hat responsible?'

'Trade secret, you'll find any attempts to attack me psychically similarly hampered.' I lied. My precaution would keep her from invading my mind or ripping up my psyche, but it wouldn't do much if Viora decided to telekinetically chuck furniture around.

Viora seemed to accept this, her eyes fixed on the hat as we walked to the bathroom. I opened the door.

'Be quick, I'll be listening.'

Viora took a few steps in, then stopped. 'Not following?'

It took some effort to keep a straight face.

'That...is unnecessary. There are no exits out of there.' I said once I recovered. Viora stared at me, then nodded and walked further into the bathroom, giving me the chance to close it.

I let out a breath and reached a hand up to steady my hat, feeling the aluminium foil ruffle against my head.

I couldn't blame Dawkes for being sceptical when I told her ritually prepared aluminium hats was how agents in America defended themselves during the initial encounters with the Visitors back in the 60s, I barely believed it myself. But this is where the power of symbolism in magic truly shines.

Even if the idea only caught traction with small groups of conspiracy theorists, the association between the foil and 'blocking out government or alien frequencies' had gotten strong enough that a magi like myself could tap into it.

Belief was the foundation of all magic. Anyone watching would probably call this absurd, and I couldn't disagree, but one of the first things I learned about magic was it was not under any obligation to be reasonable.

Except when it was reasonable, as it often was.

Take Visitors themselves. Despite the external trappings, the Enlightenment was fairly certain they were simply another form of magical life, born from human thought and symbols like every other paranormal being we'd identified over the centuries. Humans dreamed of what lay beyond the stars, and Visitors came to fill that role, taking a convenient shape we'd already provided.

Theories are rampant among more academic types, but all I needed to know was that this meant they had to play by the same metaphysical rules we did, which was why my binding circle and tinfoil hat worked.

I waited outside the bathroom a bit longer, hoping that I wouldn't end up needing to explain to an alien how toilets work. I was saved, thankfully, by the sound of a flush. Once Viora got out, I led her back to the main room, then had her sit on the chair, before returning to the kitchenette.

'Right. I've a few more questions to ask you. I expect them to be answered to the best of your ability.' I said, pulling out a couple tins of chopped tomatoes. 'I'll be cooking in the meantime, so no complaining about only getting one meal today.'

Viora perked up, 'Cooking again? More 'butties' or porridge?'

'Was thinking a ragu, actually.' I responded, pulling a tin open. 'Not used to real food or something?'

'On ship, only sustenance was nutrient paste. Contained required nutritional value, no flavours.' Viora touched a couple of fingers to her mouth thoughtfully.

I should've gotten back on track, but the way she'd answered caught my attention. 'You've never eaten something you could taste before? Do Visitors not eat for pleasure?'

Viora looked down at her fingers. ‘Biological needs exist to be fulfilled. Resources do not allow for luxuries, only essentials.’

Having poured the tins, I turned to chopping up mushrooms. ‘Right, I suppose there’s not much in the way of spices in the middle of space.’

Viora twitched out a shrug. ‘Nor fauna or flora. All sustenance chemically synthesised. Flavour not priority.’

I went quiet, throwing in an extra handful of herbs to the sauce. ‘Doesn’t seem like much of a life, stuck up there without even decent food.’

‘All measures taken necessary to ensure survival of collective. Anything else would-‘ Viora devolving into a coughing fit, the dry, hacking sound sending unpleasant shivers down my back.

Her throat’s getting to her again, which means I can’t afford to get side-tracked. She might have lasted a bit longer just there, but Viora still wasn’t used to extended conversation.

When Dawkes and I split up, my task was to try and get anything actionable out of Viora, while Dawkes reported into the captain and did some digging on what sort of Lemurian presence is in Dublin. I was going to have to make sure that I had something we could work with.

Stifling my curiosity, I forced myself to focus. ‘Well, I’m guessing a lack of good cuisine didn’t help negotiations with that Lemurian diplomat, though possibly poisoning the lot of you with a bioweapon would still be an overreaction.’

Viora straightened, picking up the tone shift. ’If knew reasons for Lemurian actions, would have informed Enlightenment. Is Lemurian current suspect for plague on ship?’

‘You disagree?’ I responded, frying the sausage and mushrooms, the smell wafting through the apartment. 'Seems the most likely culprit, one of their people being in prime position to drop the bioweapon on you and all.'

'No.' Viora's response as blunt as a brick. 'Don't know why Lemurians turn on us, but were not responsible for bioweapon.'

I paused mid-stir. 'I'd be interested in your reasoning.'

'Bioweapon still Sidhe creation. As lethal to Lemurians as to us. Would've killed Lemurian too.' Viora said trivially.

'How'd you know the bioweapon was created by Sidhe magic?'

'Scout ship warned by Lemurians. Told to keep distance from city. Considered possibility of deception, until Enlightenment confirmed properties.'

'But why didn't we find a Lemurian corpse on that ship?' I responded. 'If they weren't involved in the ship going down, the bioweapon should've killed the Lemurian too. Seems much more likely that he was the invisible entity I encountered. What you're saying doesn't add up.'

'Consider different hypothesis. Meeting with Lemurians arranged, but doubts arise if Lemurians made it on ship.' Viora answered, propping herself up on the headrest.

I stopped and looked to Viora. 'You're suggesting whoever met you lot on the ship was an imposter?'

Viora didn't waver, 'Hostility from Lemurians evidence of duplicity. Current hypothesis is that Sidhe manipulated events. Drove wedge between Lemurians and scouts. Lemurian on ship probable double agent.'

I let out a huff, pulling out a packet of pasta. 'That's just speculation. You don't have any evidence that would outweigh the possibility the Lemurians just turned on you and setting up the meeting to kill the lot of you.'

'Enlightenment already proven only Sidhe have access to bioweapon. Implies Sidhe involvement on ship.' Viora tilted her head at me quizzically. 'Suggesting entirely different virus with near-identical qualities?'

I busied myself with the cooking, chewing on what she'd said. What Viora was suggesting didn't gel. If the bioweapon was a Sidhe creation, why didn't we find a dead Lemurian on board? This virus from far from selective.

But given I'd dealt with a Lemurian created parasite only a few hours ago, it didn't seem strange to me that they could've created their own bioweapon. That is, if it was even a real Lemurian we'd encountered there...

As I mixed the pasta into the ragu, I continued to niggle away at the issue. I found myself rethinking my assumptions. If we were dealing with Lemurians, did it make sense that the Lemurians could've gotten a virus like this without having contact with the Sidhe?

Despite calling it a bioweapon, the virus was as much magic as biology, which meant there was likely a specific ritual used in its creation that couldn't be replicated.

Magic isn't like technology, you can't just reverse engineer a magic process without having an intimate understanding of the symbols and first principals the original caster appealed to. It's heritage, if you will...and if the Lemurians were working with the Sidhe on this, that implied exactly the wider conspiracy Dawkes had suggested earlier.

Pouring out two bowls of pasta, I filed the new information away for later. 'Well, that something to consider. But if the Lemurian on the ship was a fake, then why'd the others try to kill you? If the Lemurians weren't the ones responsible for the blast, they shouldn't have any reason to want you dead. Hell, if your groups are allied, they'd have good reason to keep you around, both for information and to stay on the good side of whoever's in charge of your mothership.'

Viora took the bowl. 'Confusing. Unable to deny treachery, but certain Lemurians not responsible for bioweapon.'

Poking my food with my fork, I tried to think of some hole I could poke in her reasoning, but now that Viora had planted the idea in my head, I was doubting myself.

I wasn't quite willing to give up the idea that the Lemurians were connected to the bioweapon somehow, but it was clear I didn't have all the information.

If I assumed instead that the Sidhe were responsible for killing the Visitors, I was still left with no idea of how one got on the ship. Fairies and aliens don't exactly mix regularly.

Neither of us spoke as we ate, but thankfully the same awkward silence that had pervaded our earlier conversations seemed to have faded, and instead the silence now felt oddly comfortable, which was an odd sensation to me. I checked the hat to make sure the tinfoil hadn't been damaged.

It was clear that Viora wasn't going to be much help in determining the nature of this virus. Ultimately, I was sure finding that out would be the key that would start fitting everything together, the rub was finding a sample of the disease that would be stable enough to analyse.

On top of that, if I was going to entertain Sidhe agents being on the ship, I had to figure out how they found out about it. The only way the Enlightenment even learned of its existence was because the Ciorcal Darach told-.

I choked on my food. It took a solid fifteen seconds before I was able to regain any composure, my throat still burning.

Viora looked at me alarmed, but I held my hand up. 'I'm fine, just had a brainwave about where my next step is.'

'Enlightenment knows where find bioweapon?'

'No.' I said, the ache in my throat subsiding. 'But I know who could.'

# Chapter 12

The Silver Arm pub was lively as ever when I pushed through the door.

Or it was.

The atmosphere died fast, the clientele catching sight of me and hushing any newcomers, my dark suit making my allegiance clear. I strode across the room, the familiar weight of my suit giving me a confidence I'd only just realised I was missing.

I made my way to the bar, where the same bartender tensed her shoulders.

'You know who I am.' I spat. 'I need to see the Hierophant.'

The bartender's lip curled. 'Regarding?'

'Classified.' I responded flatly. 'Please tell the Hierophant I wish to speak with him.'

'Nah, can't do that.'

I suppressed a groan. 'Why not?'

Behind me, I heard a glass slamming down on a table, followed by a belligerent voice. 'Cause we don't need you Illuminati shi-!'

Before the drunk could get going, the bartender hushed him. 'He's not in, you'll just have to come back later.'

My fingers scraped against the counter. 'Can you please

inform me where he is? This is urgent.'

The bartender shook her head. 'Nope. Can take a message though, assuming you're willing to talk to me.'

'Did you not hear the part where it's classified?'

'Oh, is it now?' The bartender shot back, sneering. 'Take a look at Mr Enlightenment over 'ere. Far too busy and important to deal with us common rabble!'

I took a couple of steadying breaths. This was even worse than last time. 'I asked you a simple question. If you wish me gone, it's in your best interests to tell me what I want to know, then I'll leave.'

I heard the creak of wood, and a wide-faced man with greying hair, belly visible under his jumper, leaned precariously off his stool to glare at me.

'That's how it starts, isn't it? Then before you know it, we have you lot tramping round our meeting places, dictating to us what to do and who to associate with.'

The man picked himself up and strode in my direction, arms spread. 'So, what'll it be this time, your highness? Gonna put the thumbscrews on our Hierophant till he starts giving you names of Sidhe sympathisers? Maybe put a few of our shrines to the torch so our gods aren't a conflict of interest?!'

I turned to the man. 'I've no intention of doing anything to you. My business with the Hierophant is in as much your interests as-'

'Shove it up your arse, dickhead!' The drunk bellowed in my face. 'You Enlightenment fucks only care about hoarding all the good magic to yourself and keeping us on a leash! If you lot gave even half a shit about regular folk, we wouldn't've had the feckin' Dingle Incident, would we?!'

A cold sweat went down my back, unbidden memories

slamming against my consciousness. My breath caught in my throat, my psyche fighting to block out the memories.

Distantly, I felt my hand reach out to grasp the counter, a faint attempt to steady myself.

Don't show weakness, Reilly, not here.

I mustered up the remaining will inside me to face down the little git, his fat face smug. From the corner of my eye, I saw the others watching with clear interest.

'Tell me, were you there when it happened?' The prick's grin faltering slightly as I spoke. 'Did you see the skies turn dark like the sun had been extinguished? Did you watch innocent people get slaughtered, knowing resistance would only get you butchered too?'

The drunk stared dumbly back. All sound in the bar had evaporated. Eyes burned into me from all angles. I felt my body flush with heat, my skin starting to prickle, power rising to the surface, responding to my desire to fry this piece of crap.

Once I thought that, cold shame settled in my gut. Once I felt the power receding, I mustered up a glare. 'No? Then shut the fuck up about something you know nothing about.'

'Think you're so fuckin' smart, huh, Enlightenment boy!?' The drunk lurched over, eyes flicking briefly over my shoulder, lips splitting into an ugly grin. 'But did you see this com-

I spun on my heels, grabbing the arm of the man sneaking up behind me and squeezing his wrist. The man let out a pained howl, letting me snatch the glass from his hand. With a flick of my wrist, I let go of the man, who tripped over himself and collided with the drunk as he tried to lunge for me. The two hit the floor, one clutching his wrist while the other moaned.

I stared down at the prone men, then across the room. A

few seemed in the middle of rising from their seats but froze as I made eye contact.

'No, but I did hear it coming.' I put the glass back on the counter. 'I feel obligated to inform you that my reasons for wishing to speak to the Hierophant concern a possible traitor in your circle. It would be unwise to give me reason to suspect anyone here.

The bar froze into a stand-off, several patrons sharing shaky looks, some still half risen. All wanting a chance to smash my head in, but not wanting to be the next in line. The stand-off was broken, when the door to the pub swung open.

'Does someone want to tell just what the hell is going on?!' Calatin strode into the middle of the room, positioning himself between the crowd and me. 'Why do you all look ready to pounce on a man who came here with peaceful intent not but two days ago?'

The bartender was the first to speak up. 'We're just defending ourselves, Hierophant! That Enlightenment jackboot was the one to start shit!'

The large druid looked over at the bartender, his expression intense. 'I know for a fact that is a lie, Susan! The wards covering this building would've struck him down had he arrived with ill intent. The truth, now.'

'Bastard, demanded to...see you.' The prone man spluttered out, still holding his wrist as if I'd broken it. 'N-no...fucking... right to be here...making...demands.'

'That is my decision to make, Domhnall! Do you wish to chase away what few allies we have at such a dangerous time?!'

Calatin looked back to the patrons, eyes blazing. 'Do you all forget why we agreed to align closer to the Enlightenment? Do the fighting in the streets and corpses piling up not tell you exactly why we cut ties with the Fae?! Whatever misgivings you may have with the Enlightenment, they are better than giving ourselves over to the same beasts who once stole our children and inflicted curses on entire families!'

The patrons seemed to slowly loose the fire that was fuelling their anger, leaving a sullen silence as the crowd started moving back to their seats. Even the drunk, after a murderous glance my way, stumbled to the bathrooms, his friend scurrying back to his seat.

Calatin looked over at me and jerked his head in the other direction. 'Come with me, Arbiter. We shall discuss this in private.'

Calatin marched back further into the bar, me following. Rather than leading me back to his office, Calatin brought me out the back of the pub, opening the door leading out, pulling a cigarette from his jacket pocket. As the door closed behind us, he turned back to me.

'It appears I owe you an apology for the actions of Domhnall and Fergus. Normally those two keep their opinions of the Enlightenment to themselves, but you know how drink can unshackle a man's temper.'

'No apology necessary; I could tell that he wasn't acting with your approval.' I responded. 'My apologies as well, Hierophant, I concede that I should've handled the situation better myself. Also, sorry about the broken light bulb from my last visit.'

'That actually was you? I'd assumed my acolytes were making a big fuss over a coincidence.' Calatin said, sounding genuinely surprised.

'Yes.' I replied. 'I was under a great deal of stress at the time, and my control slipped. I'm willing to pay for the new bulb.'

Calatin waved his hand dismissively. 'No need. Control is something all magi struggle with, Arbiter, and I can see you have more power than most. Considering that, you've shown respectable discipline for your age. I was certainly not so controlled during my own youth.'

Calatin shook his head gently. 'But judging from the grim look on your face, I'll assume this isn't a simple catch-up.'

He leaned against the wall, his bulk taking up a good chunk of it as he lit up the cigarette. 'Let's have it.'

'I'll cut to the chase. I have strong reason to believe one or more members of the Ciorcal Darach may be passing on information to the Sidhe.'

Calatin's expression turned grim. He took a long drag of the cigarette. 'A heavy accusation, Arbiter, one that must have an excellent justification.'

'It does.' I responded. 'It's become clear it was most likely Sidhe agents that had infiltrated the ship during our mission. Given the Ciorcal Darach informed us of the ship, it would seem very likely one of your own tipped off the Sidhe. Do you have any idea who might have done so?'

Calatin let out a sigh, smoke billowing. 'I certainly entertained the possibility of some of our own still having allegiances to the Fair Folk, but I'll admit, the thought that some would choose those capricious tempters over their own brothers and sisters does not sit well with me.'

'I appreciate how difficult this may be, but unfortunately, that is the most likely theory for how they could've known about the ship.'

'Perhaps, but these are sad days indeed where I'm forced to question the loyalties of men and women I've drunk and worshipped with for years.'

I started to speak, but Calatin raised a hand to stop me. 'Don't misunderstand, Arbiter, I intend to investigate this. However, it will be a delicate process. My authority among my fellows is based on respect, not rank, and the last thing we need is a coup.'

I couldn't help a flash of annoyance at that, wishing that just once, these bloody druids could just act in everyone's' interests and not waste time pussyfooting around their own tribe.

'Understandable, I'll leave that to you. Has anyone told you anything about what the Sidhe might be up to recently?'

Calatin took another long drag. 'Few have admitted any connections to me, and fewer have spoken of them in detail. But among those who have, word has it that there is a rally being planned for many of the local Sidhe troops to show solidarity against the Seventh Wave. If the rumours hold true, then Lord Nechtan himself will be there to stir up his followers.'

'In that case, it would be in our interests to infiltrate this rally. Perhaps if–'

Calatin spoke up before I could continue. 'I'm afraid the task would not be that simple, Arbiter. You see, the rally I speak of will not be taking place in our realm, but beyond the Shroud.'

I let out a frustrated breath. The Shroud, that complicated things. Any journeys through the barrier that separated the prime realm from the mystical worlds that most paranormals were birthed in were far from trivial.

Putting aside the danger of stepping into the lion's den, I'd need to first bloody find what location in the prime corresponded to the correct location beyond the Shroud, unless I wanted to wind up stranded in the seventh layer of Hell or something.

After that, I was going to need to either undertake a complicated and time-consuming ritual to pierce the Shroud or find whatever obscure 'key' might allow me to skip past that speedbump.

I sat there for a moment. 'In that case, would you have any idea where the convergence point might be? Even Sidhe can't just slip between realities on a whim.'

'Therein lies the issue, Arbiter. I do happen to know where the convergence point for the transition is, but it would appear, to my knowledge, that the entrance is under constant guard by Sidhe loyal to Lord Nechtan. Only those who can pass by the guards are allowed entry.'

I hissed through my teeth. The Enlightenment trained it's agents to be capable of infiltrating virtually any paranormal stronghold, but sneaking past a Sidhe was a much trickier proposition than most. Sidhe are no strangers to illusions and shapeshifting and so any guard they would see fit to appoint would have to be able to see through such tricks.

'My apologies if this sounds ungrateful, but that's not much help if there's no way without raising alarm. Can you think of any way it would be possible to slip by?'

'Alas, I'm afraid, as you likely already determined, the Sidhe guarding the entry point will have been selected for their ability to penetrate any common illusion or concealment.' Calatin responded. 'That said, I wouldn't go as far as to claim their defences are unassailable.'

I shook my head. 'No, a direct assault wouldn't be practical. Putting aside the expense, Nechtan will probably just flee the scene with anything of worth.'

Calatin nodded grimly. 'Just so. I'm afraid, aside from an upfront attack, the only thing I can imagine would get you past the guards would be to subvert their minds.'

'Are you talking about mind control?' I replied, taken aback.

Using magic to manipulate the minds of others was one of the greyer areas of magic in the Enlightenment's eyes. Not to say we had no use for it, but just being given the authorisation to learn such magic requires a litany of psychological profiling and loyalty tests, and commissioning one of the resulting neuromancers was only slightly less exhaustive.

Calatin nodded. 'You have misgivings. Good. It's a sign of moral fortitude, Arbiter. Usurping another's mind is certainly a dark act, something I would wish on no human. But the Sidhe are not human. They are capricious, narcissistic beings that toy with mortals for petty amusement. I, for one, would not weep at the thought of the shoe being on the other foot.'

Finding my voice again, I spoke. 'Th...This is all a moot point. I don't have any experience in neuromancy, I wouldn't have a chance on getting inside a squirrel's mind, let alone a Sidhe. And getting access to someone with those capabilities will take time we don't have.'

A mental image of Viora flashed in front of my eyes.

No. No chance. Even putting aside the massive risk that could lose me my one solid source, there was no way I could convince her to go along with it.

Calatin let out another plume of smoke. 'I see. No matter, then. I suppose speed isn't necessarily a priority in your investigation.'

'Hm?' I grunted back.

Calatin glanced back. 'Oh, only that I can understand why

you might want to take a more cautious approach, considering no human lives are currently at stake.'

For some reason, the way he'd phrased that made something inside me wrench. 'Hang on a moment, I never said-'

Calatin cut me off in a relaxed tone. 'It's perfectly alright, Arbiter, we don't need to dance around the point here. The top priority of the Enlightenment is to preserve human life, after all.'

Flicking the last of his cigarette away, a small sneer grew on his face. 'Going above and beyond for the sake of paranormal lives would be a waste. Frankly, the less of them we must bother ourselves with, the better.'

My first instinct was to object, yet I couldn't think of any actual retort.

Technically, he was correct. The Enlightenment's mandate only covers preserving human lives, not paranormals. Hell, the only reason they'd cared about this case was because the ship crash represented a risk to secrecy. I knew my superiors would take issue with me gallivanting off on a dangerous infiltration with little chance of payoff, resorting to paranormal aid to even undertake it.

Article 1 of the Agent code of ethics. It is the duty and honour of all agents to protect the human race from the horrors of the paranormal. To the Order, it wasn't worth the risk when the only lives in danger weren't human.

Still, I wasn't so sure that I could afford to skip this rally. It was risky, but it's also the only shot I had at a breakthrough. Despite my misgivings about Viora, could I afford to miss this chance?'

'Where is the convergence point, Hierophant?'

Calatin seemed surprised. 'Hm? Are you sure, Arbiter?'

'Yes. Tell me.'

Calatin let out a tired breath. 'I see. Very well. The convergence point is located within the old hillfort in Garristown.'

I nodded. Hillforts and Sidhe had a long history together, more than a few having been created by the Sidhe as bases between worlds, back when they didn't have to fear the bite of iron swords.

'Understood. Thank you again, Calatin.' I said, pushing myself off the wall.

Calatin gave me what seemed to be another approving look, then extended his hand. 'You're a braver man than most, Arbiter. I'll pray to the gods that you see this task through.'

I hesitated briefly, before shaking his hand. 'Thank you, if I do, you'll likely see me again.'

I turned down the alleyway, my objective clear. Now all I had to do was convince a prisoner to help me break into a camp filled with beings that would likely want us both dead.

That'll be a fun conversation.

# Chapter 13

'Agreed.'

I was thrown by Viora's response. We both sat in our respective seats, dirtied plates at our sides. I'd barely finished my spiel for what I wanted her to do.

I put a hand out to steady the hat on my head so the tinfoil stayed concealed. 'You're aware I'm asking you to help me infiltrate a stronghold, right?'

'Within interests to learn Sidhe plans, both for safety and informing Network upon return.'

I stared at the alien. Admittedly, I was desperate enough to ask her for help, but this seemed far too straightforward.

'And you also understand that any attempts to escape me during this time will void my protection of you, correct?'

Viora nodded mechanically. 'Not in interests to antagonise Enlightenment. Will co-operate until return to Network possible.'

My attention was caught by that word. 'Network? That your word for the Visitor Mothership or something?'

Viora traced a finger along the rim of her plate pensively. 'Human language insufficient. Best comparison, psychic connections that bind us into greater whole.'

'A hive-mind?' I asked.

Viora's bluish, thin tongue flicked out to lick at the sauce now on her finger, like an iguana drinking from a water bowl. 'Simplistic, but comparable. Connect to others through mind, share information, collaborate, socialise.'

She stopped and let out a small cough, her voice getting strained. 'Also, faster than communicating by squeezing air through meat.'

As she reached for her glass of water, I got up and paced round the small space of my apartment.

Was I really going through with this? It was true that in time it would take for the Enlightenment to get me in touch with someone skilled enough in mental magic to manipulate a Sidhe, the rally would likely be long over.

However, was that enough reason for me to place my trust in a paranormal?

Even disregarding that, with the short time-frame presented to me, I was effectively going to have to give my superiors almost no notice for an unsanctioned infiltration with heavy risks attached.

If I succeeded in finding useful information and a lead on the bioweapon, I might get away with only a very probing debriefing, but failure, assuming I came back alive, could carry harsh consequences.

Our branch of the Enlightenment was more flexible on agents taking initiative if it gave results, given the limits placed on us, but our attitude to failure was grim. Best case scenario, I get my memories scrubbed and dropped on a street corner to live out the rest of my confused life.

Worst case, well, let's just say stupidity was no excuse if your actions actively sabotaged the Enlightenment.

That said, I knew if I didn't take this chance, I had no way of knowing when another opportunity would present itself. Achieving a breakthrough on this case now could not only increase our chances of stopping whatever grand plan the Sidhe might have in store but could also save human lives that could otherwise be endangered. The less conflict between paras, the less risk of it spilling out into the human population.

Despite what some, like Calatin or others in the Enlightenment, might've suggested if they heard this, the lives of paranormal entities weren't a priority to me, it just seemed to turn out that acting to preserve their safety would also prevent risk coming to humans.

That was all there was to it.

I waited until Viora recovered from her latest coughing fit before continuing. 'Are you confident, given sufficient proximity, that you could establish mental control over a strong-willed entity?'

Putting down her drained glass, Viora looked up. 'Psionic capabilities above average for V series. Brief control feasible. Complications could emerge if control prolonged.'

I let out a breath. 'Guess that'll have to do.'

The drive was uneventful, the only sounds being the rumble of the wheels down the M2 motorway, and the radio quietly playing.

I took long, deep breathes through my nose, and I felt the familiar sense of my mind going numb to the world beyond my mission. In the mirror I kept Viora in my peripheral, the large, hooded raincoat and bandana covering her face, concealing her alien features, albeit making her look like a scarecrow.

As messy as it was, it was necessary. Viora didn't have the same gift for impersonating humans most earthborn paras had, which meant her chances of impersonating another type of para without help were nil.

In the time it took to turn into Garristown, all the doubts I'd had were smothered, not to be considered again until after the job. I couldn't afford to second guess myself, not when so much was riding on this task.

It was late afternoon, and as I drove to the outskirts of the town and parked on the quiet, country road, the sky had turned the reddish gold of sunset.

Getting out of the car, I could see atop a small hill, was a small, stone tower, elevated slightly on the remnants of the old ringfort of Rath Esa.

After quickly looking around, I walked over to the back of the car, opening the door. 'Alright, here's the place. Don't speak. I want you in the head of whatever's standing guard before they realise we're not on the list.'

Viora's face was completely hidden under the large hood and bandana, but I could still sense her tension. 'Need time. Distract long as possible.'

'Simple as that, huh?' I muttered, letting Viora out. Keeping the Sidhe from catching even a glimpse of her face was top priority.

The two of us hopped over the wall and made our way to the hillfort, Viora pulling the hood further down her head while I tried my best to look enigmatically inhuman, which isn't quite as hard as you might think.

I mostly just tried to look uncomfortable in my own skin, affecting the slightly shuffling, awkward walk I'd seen disguised paranormals use to look inconspicuous among humans. From the corner of my eye, I saw Viora's head peek in my direction, then start to mimic said walk. Any Sidhe guard worth the name would see through the façade quickly, but we'd only need a moment.

They looked like stereotypical bikers, straight off the first line of pictures if you'd Google imaged 'bikers', but that was where the resemblance ended. The two were standing ramrod stiff, and the shadows cast by the street-lights onto their bodies had an eerily solid quality.

The men were wearing sunglasses, but as we came closer, their heads both turned slowly to regard us, despite the low light. Wonderful, the less human-like they were, the less issue they'd have tearing us apart and eating us.

One stepped forward, lifting a hand.

'Evening. Out on a stroll, are we?' His voice came out a hoarse whisper, with a strange, sing-song quality.

I took a moment to brace myself. 'We heard that there was a meeting close by, concerning recent events.'

'Did you?' The biker responded. I suppressed a shiver as I felt whatever was behind those sunglasses slid across my body. 'I see no illusion concealing your form. How did you hear about this event?'

'Yes, well, I've the good fortune that my features are better able to 'pass' among the...humans.' I twisted my face in faux disgust, spitting out the word. 'Blame my human grandmother. As for this event, well, let's just say one of the circles I move in thought this might sway me to a certain cause.'

'What about that one? Scared to show your face?' This time neither I nor Viora could suppress a jolt as the other sentry stepped from behind us, face close to Viora's. I hadn't even noticed him move. 'Have something to hide?'

I gritted my teeth together to keep my jaw from trembling,

forcing it into a morbid grin. 'If you must know, my dear sister here ran afoul of an iron dagger in the hand of one of those invaders.'

Both sentries let out a flinch, the one approaching Viora stopping short when I came up to stand protectively beside her. 'I sure you'll understand she's a small bit sensitive about it.'

The Sidhe and I stared each other down. Playing on the classic Sidhe aversion to iron had been a good play, but I knew if Viora didn't do her thing soon, the guards were going to press the issue.

Just as I was trying to pre-empt whatever question I'd have to field next, the sentry closest to us, hand still half reaching from Viora, shivered, letting the hand drop to his side. 'Very well, go on through.'

The other biker jerked his head towards the first. 'Our instructions were firm.'

'There is no magecraft obscuring their shapes, no reptile or oni would dare come without such.' The biker reached up to trace the long scar on his face. 'Regardless, I too know what it means for an invader to use our weakness against us. The word to access the way is Friotaíocht. Do no harm upon entering and no harm shall befall you.'

'My gratitude, friend. May all your debts be repaid.' I responded, grasping Viora's arm and leading her past the guards, through the door of the windmill.

Once the door closed, I muttered at Viora. 'Couldn't have done that a bit faster?'

Viora walked a bit further, her back turned to me. 'Influencing minds not simple task. Perhaps Enlightenment can attempt it in future, if so confident.'

I didn't respond, instead breathing the damp air around me, and quietly whispered the word 'Friotaíocht'. When I did, a bizarre sensation washed down me, not unlike pins and needles running throughout my body. I let out a shudder, and I heard Viora emit a small squeak.

When the sensation passed, the inside looked the same, but something was different.

The air, while still damp, had a freshness to it that wasn't there before, and my teeth tingled as I felt magic suffusing the area. Outside, I heard a cacophony of sound, a wild mix of voices and what sounded like enthusiastic Trad music.

I chanced a look at Viora, and saw she'd shifted up against the wall, head swivelling left and right.

I pointed a finger at her. 'Stay focused. However strange you might find this; I can't afford to have to babysit you.'

Viora stared at me, her body still tense. 'Understood. Next step?'

'Stick close unless I say otherwise. Speak to no one and stay inconspicuous.'

I opened the door, which now looked brand new and left a sap-like stickiness on my hand and was assailed by sights and sounds.

It looked like the same field we'd walked up to get here, but the trees were taller, the bushes overgrown and spilling across the field, which was filled with dozens of Sidhe. In the middle of this scene, I saw that an elevated platform, fashioned from a giant tree trunk, sat, no doubt soon to be used whenever Lord Nechtan felt like making his no doubt subdued entrance.

I caught sight of a few of the fae closer to the windmill take note of us, most sparing us no more than a glance, though I noticed a couple lingering on Viora as she stepped out behind me. I didn't return the stares, confidently striding down the hill with Viora trailing behind, giving some of the nearby Sidhe a friendly nod, who absentmindedly returned the gesture.

Any skilled infiltrator would tell you, one of the best ways to pass unnoticed is to simply behave as if you belong there. Your average person isn't looking for spies. Give them no reason to question your presence, and they won't.

That principle applies even among paranormals. Unfortunately, judging by Viora's hands pulling her hood down as far as possible, she'd not received that memo.

Luckily, most of the Sidhe had clearly come with groups, and so most were conversing amongst themselves or taking advantage of the drink and food tents, and I was able to take Viora by the shoulder and lead her to a quiet spot.

'Alright, I'm not expecting any fine detail right now, but can you read any minds out there?'

Viora squinted. 'Thought processes confusing, varied, but surface thoughts simple enough.'

I pointed at her. 'Brilliant, keep scanning for anything interesting. Especially anything regarding a Lord Nechtan and a Sidhe Army. If you get anything, just tug my jacket, don't say anything.'

Viora blinked, then said flatly. 'Understood. What now?'

I cast my eyes back to the platform in the centre. 'We wait for Nechtan to show up. This should be interesting, at least.'

The next few minutes went by without incident, the two of us standing along the outskirts of the crowd, watching as the undercurrent of tension and excitement bubbled up, the chatter getting hushed.

I felt a surge of power close by, as if someone had suddenly turned on a generator, followed by the flaps of the large, colourful tent bursting forward, a tall figure stepping out, all the Sidhe going silent as the figure glided out.

I'd never seen a Daoine Sidhe before, but I'd heard several accounts of their ethereal beauty, inhuman grace and incredible power.

Those accounts had been understated.

The man who stepped out was perfectly proportioned, like a Renaissance statue. He was dressed in the uniform of an early Free State Army general, his hair, concealed largely under a military cap, sheened like burnished gold as he swaggered up the platform, his marble pale skin contrasting his sharp emerald eyes.

As he crossed to the centre of the platform, the old tree trunk seemed to gain new life, roots and shoots sprouting up around his feet, the dead brown of the trunk taking on a richer, slightly greenish tone. I tried to look away to see how the crowd was responding but found myself reluctant to pull away. The mere presence of the man seemed to command attention.

No question, this was Lord Nechtan.

He opened his mouth, and reality fell away.

'My countrymen.' His voice echoed out, smooth and rich. 'I'll not waste your time with idle chat. Our land, our home, is in great peril, from outsiders who threaten our very place in the world.'

I felt an unpleasant jolt down my left arm, and suddenly the fascination snapped away. I spun on my heel, hand on the athame in my pocket, ready to slash. I already had the blade at the ready when my eyes fell on Viora, her hand still holding onto the sleeve of my jacket. Her head looked up as I spun, and when my brain registered who I was looking at, I forced my blade arm down, slamming it against my side.

If Viora noticed, it didn't show in her monotone voice. 'Heard something.'

I returned the blade to my pocket, trying to still the shaking in my hands.

Crap. Don't lose yourself, Reilly.

I shoved the lingering thoughts into the vault in my head, locking them away. Once my emotions levelled off, I wordlessly pushed my way through the crowd, holding Viora's arm.

The moment I pulled free of the crowd, I shuffled the pair of us behind the closest tent and looked over at Viora. 'Alright, talk.'

'Overheard something important. Sidhe on stage just thought about needing to make sure something in personal tent was moved after speech.'

'What kind of something?'

Viora tilted her head slightly. 'Object of some kind. Thought fleeting. Irritated, as if Sidhe wished to remove object quickly.'

My heart pounded in anticipation. If Nechtan had something hidden in his tent, then this was the best chance I had to get some dirt on him.

The guard was going to be trouble, but I couldn't pass this up. As much as part of me wanted to keep listening to Nechtan's speech, I had to act now.

'Interesting. Looks like we know where to go.' I grabbed Viora's shoulder, just in case this was a bluff, and led her through the crowd, pushing past the varying forms around us.

My hand went to my athame again, but I stopped myself. The whole reason I needed to bring Viora was because invisibility would be child's play for many Sidhe to see through. If I were to use it, I'd have to pick a good moment.

Fortunately, Nechtan's speech was having the masses eating out of his hand, so both Viora and I managed to slip between the tents, edging closer to the garishly coloured tent Nechtan had emerged from. As we closed in, I could see the tent didn't appear to be guarded.

I was immediately suspicious. If whatever Nechtan had in the tent was so important, why leave the tent exposed? The most obvious conclusion was that it was guarded, just in a way I couldn't perceive.

Still, whatever precautions Nechtan may've taken, dealing with them was almost certainly simpler than contending with him. I leaned closer to Viora.

'Can you sense any minds inside that tent?'

'None.'

Alright, time for a gamble.

Slowly, I reached up and took my hat off, tinfoil and all, then held it up to Viora. 'Alright, I've removed what was blocking your telepathy. If you see anyone coming up to this tent, telepathically alert me. Don't forget, without me, you've no way to getting out of this rally without being discovered, it's within your interests to make sure I get out of this alive.'

Viora stared quietly back. 'Understood. Enlightenment will be warned of any coming towards tent.'

I reluctantly shoved the hat inside the hood of my jacket, praying I wouldn't lose it. It wasn't exactly hard to come by tinfoil, but Viora would only need seconds if she decided this arrangement no longer worked for her.

I slinked closer to the tent, watching for any observers.

Nope, all eyes were on Nechtan as he continued to speak,

and I had to remind myself not to listen.

Before my attention could be seized, I slipped through the flaps, hoping I hadn't made a fatal mistake.

# Chapter 14

The first thing that struck me was the scent. A rich, smoky smell, like beech wood, filled the tent as I stepped inside.

The inside was large enough for furniture, and Nechtan had taken full advantage of that. A table, upon which incense holders slowly emitted smoke, had been set up, with four wooden chairs, all of which looked hand-crafted, a couple more near a lit fireplace, connected to a bleedin' chimney of all things leading up to the top of the tent.

All this, on top of a wooden floor, with a doorway leading to another room. This one room was bigger than any in my apartment.

Absurd luxury aside, nothing appeared unusual as I made my way over to the other room. Passing through the doorway, I found myself looking at a bedroom, with a queen-sized bed dominating the room, a couple of cabinets arranged neatly in their respective corners.

For pity's sake, did Nechtan know what the point of a tent was?

Shaking my head, I turned around, confident I'd find nothing else of interest.

However, before I could leave, my head lit up with a migraine along my temples, before rapidly fading.

Hang on, that wasn't right, why was I leaving when I hadn't found anything yet?

Looking back, I re-examined the bedroom, trying to figure out what set off my instincts just now, sliding the athame out.

As I channelled my senses through the swinging blade, something about the way the magic seemed to weave about the room seemed off to me, as if my eyes kept trying to glaze over the interplay when it hit me. There was something concealed by a ward of disinterest, very similar to the one I'd cast on the Visitor ship, but what?

Now knowing what I was dealing with, I forced myself to look at the room, straining against mounting boredom as I tried to focus on the lines of energy traced throughout. After what felt like an hour, my eyes fell upon one of the cabinets.

Stepping closer to it, I saw the wispy strands formed into a lattice of potent spells, likely the ward of disinterest. Fortunately for me, disabling hostile wards was something I had a talent for. I focused on the delicate interplay of the energies protecting the case, then began slashing at the air.

As I brought the blade back and forth, I sensed the wards fall apart, the magic coming apart in shreds and, once I was confident they were gone, I snatched the pot.

I turned the pot in my hands, noticing a tight seal, and more concerning, a distinct magical aura swirling inside. I focused my senses and was suddenly struck by a series of sharp memories.

Memories of vomit, blood, bodies scattered about a gore-splattered alien ship. My teeth clattered as I forced the memories back, letting out a gasp.

'Bugger me.' I whispered. 'The bioweapon.'

'Indeed.' A voice hissed behind me. I felt the tip of

something sharp trace along my neck. 'Thank you for finding it for me.'

I froze. I hadn't seen anyone when I entered the tent, and I certainly didn't hear anything moving behind me. I felt my grip tighten on my athame.

'Ah, ah.' The voice mocked. 'Drop the blade, place the jar on the ground.'

I bit down on a curse but obliged. I had an idea, but this was going to get complicated fast. I kept thinking.

'On your feet.'

I slowly stood up, the sword following my neck, then turned around.

The figure standing in front of me was dressed in closely fitted armour, worn under a brown cloak, the hood covering his head, but I was more focused on the face. He looked human, but up close, I could see the tell-tale second eyelids as the man blinked, appearing vertically under the first set.

'How'd a Lemurian get in here?' I asked. 'The guards would see through your shapeshifting.'

The Lemurian smiled, revealing a set of needle-sharp teeth. 'Very cute, agent. You may be about to die, but I'm not so dim as to spill secrets where any could hear.'

Needle-Teeth let out a sharp whistle, and a second man emerged from the other room, dressed identically, who reached down to snatch the jar from the ground. I gritted my teeth and kept thinking, trying not to let the fear of death cloud my mind, even as I noted the additional Lemurian and theorised about how many others there could be.

Needle-Teeth nodded at his compatriot before looking back to me. 'Now, one last loose end, agent. The location of your little Visitor friend.'

I didn't bother wondering if he knew she was at the rally or not. 'Not much point telling you that. The second she sensed your minds; she'll have already bolted.'

The Lemurian let out a laugh, pulling up his hood slightly to reveal the glimmer of tinfoil wrapped around his head. 'We've taken precautions, now enough stalling. I can at least promise a swift death if you co-operate.'

'Fine, I'll tell you. She's-' I slammed my foot into the ground, forcing will through my tattoos, causing the wooden floor to explode in shrapnel, raw force ripping it apart.

Needle-Teeth let out a squall as he was thrown back, smacking against the ground. His partner stayed standing, unfortunately, though stumbling from the shockwave. I snarled as my leg erupted in pain, reaching down to snatch up my athame. I bounded toward the standing Lemurian, slamming into him and sending us to the floor.

What followed was a flurry of limbs. I felt the Lemurian's nails slash across my face, blood running down my nose and lips, while I clamped one hand on the arm guarding the jar. I lashed out with the blade, cutting deep along the Lemurian's arm.

Then, I was stunned as something heavy slammed against the side of my head, my vision flashing as I tumbled to the side. I then felt myself being roughly pulled up.

When my vision cleared, I saw Needle-Teeth, face set in anger as he placed the blade at my throat. Behind him, I saw another, female Lemurian had shown up, now pulling the third up, still holding the jar.

Needle-Teeth hissed. 'Did you really think that would work?'

I shrugged. 'Not really, but I only needed to keep you damn

lizards distracted for a moment.'

The Lemurian's eyes narrowed, and I thought he would cut my throat there and then.

He might've, if we weren't interrupted by the sound of something large smashing, along with the cries of pain of his partners. The Lemurian whirled around.

The scene was in disarray. The table from the other room now lay in several chunks, having been launched towards the pair of Lemurians, both had been knocked to the other side of the room, one stumbling uneasily to her feet, blood running profusely down her head, whilst the other, bend double over the bed, let out a groan, clutching the jar to his chest.

At the entrance, Viora stood, her dark eyes the only visible part of her face as she stared down the Lemurians.

Needle-Teeth froze for only a second, but I wasn't one to waste seconds.

I yanked my gun out and let off a shot into the git's leg. Needle-Teeth let out a shrill cry and tightened his grip on the blade on my neck, but before he could open my neck, I slammed my foot into the leg, my heel colliding with the bullet hole, sending him to the floor with a scream.

Needle-Teeth might've been stronger than me, but a weak point's a weak point.

I moved away from the Lemurians, holstering my gun and picking my athame off the floor, letting out a gasp as my right leg throbbed again. That backlash was going to be a problem.

I looked to Viora. 'For a moment I wasn't sure you were going to show.'

'Considered ignoring, but mind was very loud.' Viora nonchalantly flicked her wrist, and I saw the female Lemurian tumble into the air and smack off the wardrobe, going limp.

'Be more careful of mind manipulation. Reversing effect was aggravating.'

'So that migraine was you, then? Guess I owe you two, then.' I then pointed at the Lemurian still on the bed. 'Get that jar. It's got the bioweapon in it.'

Viora nodded, then held her hand out, the crippled Lemurian made an effort to hang on, but he'd clearly broken something important, and his face twisted, his fingers slipping from the jar, which floated gently into Viora's hand.

'Object Acquired.' Viora looked up. 'Time to depart?'

'Yep, bad idea to hang ar-'Before I could finish, a small object flew in from nowhere, stabbing into Viora's shoulder. She let out a cry, the force behind the impact throwing her down to the floor, the jar bouncing out her hands and rolling out of sight.

I spun around and saw Needle-Teeth, up on one knee, hand stretched out, before bolting inside his cloak, producing a small knife.

I raised my gun, whilst Needle-Teeth flicked his arm in a blur. Before my finger could pull down the trigger, a sharp pain exploded on my bicep, sending my arm wide as the gun went off. The dagger was stuck a good inch in my forearm, my entire arm flaring, the act of holding my gun running fire down my arm.

Nope, not doing this. I threw myself into a graceless tumble out the doorway, away from the knife throwing lizard, his harsh voice shouting out something I didn't understand.

I lurched over to where Viora was lying, looking around for the jar. After a moment, I caught sight of it, rolled under the table. I gasped out a curse, then staggered over, stowing my weapons as I hunkered down, reaching with my one good arm, wounded arm and leg both screaming. My fingers reached for the jar, only to slide uselessly off it, the jar rolling further away.

Oh, just typical.

Just as I contemplated whether dropping on my knees or resting on my bad arm would be worse, I saw Viora pulling herself along the floor while a shape closed on her.

My head whipped over, and the shape became the female Lemurian, cracking her neck as she advanced, sword scraping across the floor, human skin torn away, leaving the reptilian form underneath. Viora let out a whimper before the Lemurian grabbed hold of her shoulder with a clawed hand, pulling her up.

'Dammit, no!' I growled, fumbling for the athame. I tried to direct it at the Lemurian, only to stop short.

As the Lemurian raised her blade up to the shivering Viora, my mind grasped desperately for any spell that wouldn't catch her in the crossfire. Lighting and force were out, too unpredictable, but moving and transforming energy was my main form of attack. What could I do?

Then I remembered the fireplace.

Pointing the blade towards it, I took a deep breath, blocking out the pain, focusing only on the low, cosy heat.

Ignoring Viora's increasingly distressed cries, I flicked the knife from the fireplace to the Lemurian, whispering out 'Teas'.

The fire went out like a candle as the heat energy was shifted away, latching onto a new object.

The Lemurian's sadistic grin was replaced with confusion, then horror, and she let out a shriek as smoke plumed from her clothing.

Dropping Viora, the Lemurian clawed at her clothing, but only scratching the now red-hot armour. The Lemurian tripped and fell over, her screams becoming gurgles.

The smoke took on the smell of burnt meat.

I turned to Viora, who was watching the twitching form, stunned. 'Hey! What're you waiting for? Get over here!'

My voice seemed to awaken Viora, and she scrambled over to me, dropping down to match my crouch. I could see she still had the knife stuck in her shoulder.

I thrust a finger toward the jar. 'Get it!'.

Viora numbly reached out and pulled the jar towards her, which unevenly teetered to her outstretched hand. As she grabbed the jar, Viora's eyes widened. 'M-more co-coming.'

My mouth went dry. 'Where from?'

'O-other r-room.' Viora stuttered out. 'Bu-but also outside.'

I felt dread creep in. Things were dire already, with the Lemurians getting a second wind, having more show up could be the end.

I rose up, pulling Viora up with me, both of us letting out pained cries, and ran to the nearest wall, pushing it open. My eyes watered from the dull agony my arm and leg were both in, the act of holding my athame straining against the knife still in my arm.

'Arbiter!'

I spun back to see Needle-Teeth standing shakily, blade drawn as he glared at me. 'Hope you enjoy explaining this little outbreak!'

He threw a blade toward Viora, which hit dead centre, sending her flying through the gap with a fatal thud.

My vision turned red.

I roared out a furious 'Tintreach!', my athame sending out a coursing web of lightning, which lashed at Needle-Teeth, who fell back, screaming. I turned back, lurching through the gap, getting clear of the tent.

I ran over to Viora, slumped still on the grass. In the distance I could hear a commotion, as several alarmed voices ran over each other, but the panicking Sidhe faded into the background as I edged closer to Viora, praying I had only imagined the dagger striking her in the chest.

'Viora?' I asked. 'Hey, say something!'

A few dreadful seconds passed, before Viora let out a wheezing gasp. 'D-dislike...political rallies.'

Despite myself, I let out a relieved breath. 'Join the club. That knife hit anything important?'

'Yes.' She responded, lifting the jar up to me.

Needle-Teeth's knife was sticking out of a noticeable crack, exposing the contents to the outside.

Outbreak. The jar was his real target.

That's not ideal.

With the disease out, it was only a matter of time before bodies starting dropping. We had to leave ASAP if we didn't want several dozen dead on our hands. I made to get up, only to hiss as the knife in my arm dug further in.

Worst yet, I could see a thin trail of blood trickling from under the knife, almost dripping into the ground.

Blood. Bollocks.

Blood carried a sympathetic connection to whoever shed it. With any Sidhe got their hands on fresh blood from us, they could theoretically do anything from divine our locations to make our hearts explode out of our chests.

I pulled my athame out, bracing myself for what I had to

do, picking up a particularly chunky looking branch from the ground and stuffing it into my mouth.

Channelling the energy from my tattoos into my athame, I converted the kinetic energy to heat with another 'Teas', then, after a few deep breaths, I yanked the knife out of my arm and twisted my wrist to slam the hot athame against the wound. My vision went white as agony exploded from the wound, and I tasted bark from the branch.

Once my senses returned, I picked myself off the ground, spitting out the branch and glancing at Viora. She was staring at me with shock.

I pulled myself into an awkward crouch, presenting my athame. 'This is gonna hurt, but we can't keep bleeding. They'll track us if they find any blood.'

Viora stared wide-eyed at the athame, then let out a shaky breath and reluctantly presented her shoulder. I passed her the branch, and once she placed it in her mouth, quick as I could, I snatched the knife and plucked it from her shoulder, then with another whisper, pointing the athame at her wound, sending the heat into the wound. Viora fell back, a muffled wail emitting between the branch as the stab wound blackened and cauterised.

I waited for Viora to get the screaming out. Like me, she was gasping, though I also saw that her eyes were watering, her body still shaking with fear. My gut twisted in sympathy, but we couldn't afford to sit around. I shoved my burgeoning knife collection into my jacket, then offered my hand.

'Come on. We need to get gone. Keep your head down and cover that jar.' Viora took my hand, and I gently pulled her up, my own wounds protesting, then started guiding the pair of us towards the windmill.

Even as we did, I could see something was wrong. The Sidhe in attendance were clearly close to panic, the crowd dispersing in different directions, having caught on something was amiss.

Much worse, I could see some of the Sidhe closest to us were behaving strangely. A little behind us, the spitting image of a garden gnome was letting out rough coughs, blood spattering down his lips, whilst to our left, a butterfly-winged pixie had slumped on the ground, clutching her head and moaning. The disease was already getting out.

I tried to ignore the growing dread as we both shuffled along the outskirts of the crowd, but when we scaled the hill up to the windmill, I felt a bolt of terror jumped down my back, and turned back.

Back down by the tents, in the middle of the dispersing crowd, I saw Nechtan, standing next to his tent, staring straight at us.

I felt my heart almost stop dead. Just being in Nechtan's presence was almost overwhelming. If he decided to move against us, we wouldn't have a prayer.

Yet, he didn't. Nechtan gazed in our direction, his lips suddenly parted in what looked like realisation, then twisted into a smirk. Lifting a pair of fingers to his lips, he blew us a kiss, then ducked back inside the tent.

The hell?

'What. Was. That?' Viora croaked out.

'Question later. Run now.' I responded, then pushed through the windmill door, slamming it behind.

Gathering as much of my frayed will remained, I gasped out ''Friotaíocht!', then repressed the urge to vomit when the world lurched, colours losing vibrancy and smells becoming sour in my nose.

I glanced at Viora, who looked queasy, but nodded, then opened the door again.

Barely a moment after we'd both shambled out, I had to pull Viora behind me as both guards turned towards us. One spoke, in the same dead voice as before.

'What is the meaning of this?'

Gesturing wildly behind us, I shouted. 'There's something awful happening in there! I think there's been an attack!'

I bolted forward, dragging Viora behind me, praying our very real panic would sell my bluff. My lungs and wounds burned, and my shoes getting soaked with wet mud as Viora and I forced ourselves through the field to the car. Chancing a look back, I saw the guards were contending with more Sidhe tripping over each other out of the windmill, buying us the time we desperately needed.

I didn't slow down when we got to the gates, agonisingly pulling myself over, my arm feeling about ready to fall off, then helping Viora over, her scrambling only making the process worse.

Yanking my keys loose, I unlocked the car, shoving Viora in, before hopping in myself. The tires screeched as I peeled away onto the road, my heart pounding in my ears even as the windmill faded into the distance.

What had I done?

# Chapter 15

I couldn't recommend driving with a wounded arm and leg.

The car lurched across the road as I struggled to keep my leg responding and arm semi-stable on the wheel, all the while focusing on the small portion of what I could see to avoid crashing.

Despite all this, I didn't even think about stopping until I got back to Garristown, and even then, I held out until I could park on a public road.

I stopped the engine and slumped back, clenching my jaw when another surge of stabbing pains danced across my body.

'That should be coast-clear.' I said, before reaching a hand back to Viora. 'Pass that jar over, would you?'

A few seconds of silence passed. I dug my fingers into the wheel.

It occurred to me that, now having the bioweapon, and me without the tinfoil, Viora might be considering taking her shot at me. I decided to give her one more chance, but if Viora was going to turn now, I was going to at least give her a fight. When I spoke again, I turned around, letting my free hand fall towards my athame.

'Did you not hear me? I need to get a look at-'

I stopped short.

Even in the dark, I could see the oily streaks running down her face, as she curled up in the backseat, her hands clamped over her mouth, arms still pinning the jar to her chest.

Viora was crying.

My hand dropped from my pocket, though inside I was just barely holding together. I already barely had a clue how to talk to my own species, let alone comforting a frightened alien. Same time though, I needed to get that jar, so I couldn't just ignore her until she stopped.

'If you want to talk about what happened, do. I've nowhere to be. If you don't, fine, but you might want to put down the jar.' Even as I said it, I internally grimaced, social instincts rusted from underuse telling me you're not meant to be that blunt.

Viora let out a wet sob. 'I-I-I al-almost died.'

My eyebrows shot up; I was pretty sure that was the first time she'd ever even used the word 'I'.

'That was a close one. But we're safe for now. You don't need to-'

'No!' Viora shouted, looking at me miserably. 'No, don't understand. I almost d-died.'

The emphasis she put on 'I' stood out to me. 'What do you mean?'

Viora didn't look at me, gazing with quivering eyes out the window. 'A-Almost died away from Network. Al-almost got lost.'

Ok, on to something here. 'Lost? What does that mean?'

'When individual dies, Network preserves information, memories. Allows preservation. Let's live on. If died away from Network. Couldn't be preserved.' She let out a wet hiccup. 'W-Would be lost.'

Ah. That's it. Nothing quite like having a definite afterlife that gets taken away to put the fear of death in you.

Unfortunately, just because I could see the problem didn't mean I had a damn clue how to go about calming her down, and I didn't fancy trying to take the jar off her before I could be sure I wouldn't wind up becoming the first human frisbee.

'Why's this hitting you now? You didn't seem that nervous after the Fachan tried to cut yo-,' I interrupted myself. Reminding her about nearly getting her throat slit might not help. '-er, attack you.'

'D-didn't think about it. Enlightenment distracted when awoke.' Viora lifted a shaky hand to her burnt stab wound. 'No distractions now.'

An idea came to mind. 'So, if that's the case, would distracting you help now?'

Viora let out another whimper. 'What c-could possibly di-distract now?

The words struck something in me, and in that moment, I wasn't looking at Viora anymore.

I was looking at some stupid kid, huddled up in the back of a black car, driving away from a still-smouldering village, one that would soon have the last two days wiped from history. He was crying too, ruminating on how things could've gone if he hadn't been such a fucking idiot. That kid asked the men who'd first taken him from that place something similar.

I shook my head. That kid was long dead now, but might as well try what worked on him.

I scratched my chin. 'You mentioned earlier that you're a clone, right? Is that normal for your species.'

Viora tilted her head back, small eyebrows furrowing. 'Correct. All are cloned from pre-created templates designed for specific functions.

'Why?' I replied. 'What's wrong with just reproducing the standard way?'

Viora held the frown. 'Genetic templates, occasionally augmented by other DNA, allows greater variety and control of resulting subjects.'

The conversation continued for a while, me piling on whatever questions I could think to ask, and Viora bemusedly answering each one. It actually became fairly interesting the more I listened.

The Visitors' apparently put a lot of emphasis on integrating genetic flexibility into their species, which explained the hybrid phenomena, born from genetic samples taking from abductees. Viora claimed it was for incorporating the best of other species into their own, but I suspected the Visitors might've been having some problem that led them down this path.

I was curious, but as Viora seemed to slowly relax, I left that aside. I gestured towards the jar still in Viora's grasp.

'Well, the genetic diversity's doing one thing for you. That thing's probably been leaking virus this whole time, but you've not so much as sneezed.'

Viora tilted the jar to stare at the hole. 'Theory appears to match evidence. Still, possible that more intense exposure could still cause infection.'

'I'd thought having it open on your chest would be exposure enough. You do something to block the hole?' I reached out my hand.

Viora handed the jar over, giving me a proper look at it. Thankfully, Viora had thrown something together to block the hole that was exposing the virus. The knife was still stuck in, but Viora had also removed her bandana and used it to plug the hole.

I was worried as I took the jar that we might've lost the bioweapon entirely, but when I touched the thing, I got the same surge of revulsion before I quickly dropped it into the passenger seat with a gag, provoking more pain from the hole in my arm.

This was not a good day.

'Slapdash. But should suffice for time.' Viora said, her tone apologetic.

'As long as it's working, I won't complain.' I responded, breathing heavily out of my nose. 'I'm not up for driving back to Dublin, so I'm going to need to call this in. Stay here.'

Viora made a vague affirmative sound as I opened the car door and limped out, producing my phone. I punched in the number for HQ and waited. When they picked up, I reported in an injured agent and paranormal asset, in possession of evidence important to an ongoing case. After giving my location, the voice on the other end assured me an evac and medical team would be en route.

'Backup should be here soon.' I said when I sat back in the car. 'We just need to sit tight.'

'Understood.' Viora's voice responded. 'Wait. Questions. Intended for distraction?'

'Worked, didn't it?' I responded dryly.

'Used to emotional distress.' The response came matter-of-factly.

'Excuse me?' I asked, shifting in my seat.

'Enlightenment experienced with emotional distress.' Her tone was far less casual now, lower and more cautious. 'Can hear it.'

My hand went up to my head.

'You're reading my mind?!' I shouted.

'Not intentionally!' Viora's hands went up in a gesture of surrender. 'Natural response, evolved for better communication. Can feel emotions.'

She lowered the hands, Viora's clouded face gazing straight at me. 'When talking, felt large increase in distress from Enlightenment before questions.'

Fuck. Fuckfuckfuck.

I didn't want to talk about this, I really didn't want to fucking talk about this. Outside, I could see a nearby streetlight starting to flicker and I felt my skin turn hot.

No, no! Lock it away, lock it away!

I repeated that mantra in my head and took several deep breaths. When my skin cooled, I thrust a finger towards Viora. 'Stay out of my head.'

Viora leaned forward slightly. 'Unfair. For Enlightenment to help emotional distress. Then ignore own.'

I let out a groan, rubbing my temples. 'Look, humans like me don't have that Network fallback you Visitors do. We can't just read each other's minds to find the problem or trust that when we die, we'll just be downloaded into a psychic cloud storage'

I stared up at the ceiling, desperately wishing I was back in my apartment, alone. 'Our mistakes, our fuckups, we have to carry them ourselves. We can't just...offload them on anyone just because they'll listen, that's not how we work. Not how I work anyway.'

Of course, the bloody alien didn't take the hint. 'Psychological studies of humans suggest communication integral to emotional recovery.'

I let out a laugh, shaking my head. 'The last thing that'll help me is talking about the shit I've been through. All I can do is lock it away, make sure it can't hurt me or someone else again.'

'Wrong. Concealing emotion only leads to self-damage. Isolation only contributes to further psychological deterioration.'

I could only shake my head further, unable to even look at Viora. Just figures the member of a collectivised pseudo-hive mind would try to latch on to the only person to not actively try to kill her, no matter how ballsed-up they were.

As the memories of the last hour came back, I couldn't help but think of all the ways I could've done that better alone. How many Sidhe did I kill with that stupid stunt? I should've protected the jar better, not pawned it off to the Visitor who'd only just learned she could die.

Now dozens were likely dead, and judging from Nechtan's face when he saw us, he was probably going to spin it as either an excuse to declare war on the Wavers or call the Enlightenment to task. The only reason he had that chance was because I wasn't good enough.

Never am when it counts.

Viora didn't make any further efforts to talk. The next several minutes passed in complete silence, as I stared blankly out the window. A small eternity elapsed until a pair of bright headlights rounded the corner, glaring straight into my eyes.

The rest was a blur. A small group emerged from the van after it parked, examined both me and Viora and took the jar. A few questions were asked, mostly regarding Viora, and I answered numbly, knowing the real questions would come back at HQ. Stinging green fluid was poured on our open wounds.

Then, I was placed in the back of the van, Viora sitting unrestrained opposite me, though I noticed every member of the evac team was wearing hats, one of them firmly shoving one on my head.

As we drove off, I resumed staring into space, thinking of how I was going to explain my fuck-up, and what hell I'd get for it.

'Well, it certainly sounds like it could've gone much worse.' Captain Hu said after I finished, his eyes flicking back down to the paperwork on his desk.

I felt my face go blank, barely able to understand what I'd just heard.

The Captain's office, spartanly decorated, save for a few neat stacks of paperwork and a single, tall office plant, was quiet with the exception of the Captain's own inaudible murmur as he read through one of the papers.

When I remembered how to speak, I forced the words out. 'I'm sorry, sir. I don't understand.'

Hu glanced up, frowning at me. 'Oh, make no mistake, Reilly, I do think you took a few very careless risks regarding the Visitor, especially removing your sole source of protection from it's powers.'

My brain was stumbling trying to follow, while the Captain continued in the same clipped tone. 'That said, it's apparent that you've sufficiently engendered a degree of psychological attachment from it that it didn't attempt to influence you, so we can cut some slack.'

Hu then picked up a pen, shaking it for emphasis. 'More importantly, this jar you were able to acquire is promising.

We'll need to get a proper analysis done on it.'

'W-what about the Sidhe that were exposed to the virus?!' I spluttered out.

Hu paused. 'As I said, your plan could certainly have been better thought out. At the very least, you were too reliant on an unreliable asset. But you've failed to consider the bigger picture.'

'W-what do you mean, sir?' I replied, crossing my arms, trying to maintain some kind of composure.

Hu then tapped his temple. 'Think. Why would Nechtan be carrying a large amount of the bioweapon, where the only individuals who could be exposed to it were fellow Sidhe?'

Some knee-jerk responses came to me, but I hesitated.

Why had Nechtan brought the virus somewhere he had no reason to expect trouble? I tapped my fingers on the desk as I thought. Sure, both us and the Lemurians were there, but if anything, that was less reason to go out of his way to give us something to find.

It wouldn't make sense as a trap either, since we already knew humans are immune, while the Lemurians would probably only end up spreading it to the Sidhe anyway. The only reason I could think Nechtan would bring the bioweapon with him was if he-

My eyes fell back on Hu, who sat calmly, hands loosely clasped. 'You think Nechtan wanted to expose his own people to the bioweapon? Why?'

Hu spread his hand out. 'Consider. Nechtan wishes to rally the Sidhe against the other paranormals. What better way than to fabricate an attack?'

I grimaced. 'But, the bioweapon's known to be a Sidhe weapon. Practically every paranormal I've talked to confirmed that.'

'Have you spoken to any Sidhe about that theory?' Hu responded, steepling his fingers.

'No, I haven't.' I responded reluctantly.

'Then perhaps that knowledge isn't as common as it seems. Perhaps the Sidhe have their own theories, or believe another group is attempting to frame them.'

Captain Hu spread his hands out. 'And now they have a number of Lemurians, who infiltrated their rally and discovered where the virus appeared to originate, ready to take the blame.'

I cupped the side of my face. 'Wait, but how would Nechtan have even known any of that would happen?'

Hu kept talking in an even tone. 'I'm sure Nechtan had his own plan for how to disseminate the virus among the Sidhe and pin it on another group. But why use a false flag when there's a real one?'

'So, I ended up playing right into his hands.' I said dully. Just when I thought I might've given us the advantage over our opponent, I'd given him what he wanted on a platter.

The Captain stopped writing, his brow wrinkled. 'I wouldn't say that. It's unfortunate that the virus was leaked during your escape, but you did still bring back a useable sample. Had you not done that, odds were he'd have infected the Sidhe there on a wider scale, and we'd been none the wiser. It's was a risky gamble you made, Reilly. But it appears to have paid off. Good job.'

Good job? That?

I swallowed heavily, forcing the bile back down. 'Thank you, sir. But, now that we know he was planning to incite a conflict between the paranormal factions, what do we do now?'

Captain Hu tapped his pen against his jaw. 'We'll need to take steps to neutralise Nechtan. He's established himself as a threat, but how to approach him is still up for detail. Kill him, and we'll create a martyr. Best course right now would be to determine the best method, as well as give the virus over to a trusted biomancer to see if they can get to the root of how it works.'

Despite myself, I let out a quiet snort. 'Don't suppose you know one free right now?'

'As a matter of fact, I do.'

I twitched at the immediate response. 'Really? You already have a biomancer on hand?'

The Captain giving me a tired smirk. 'Yes and no. The old spectre of stretched manpower still haunts us. However, I do happen to know one magus who, while not officially part of the Enlightenment, has done similar work for us as an outside contractor. One you've already come into contact with.'

It took a second to connect the dots. 'You mean Calatin?'

The Captain pointed at me. 'That's right. Hierophant Calatin is probably the most skilled biomancer in Ireland, and the two of you appear to have built something of an accord. I believe it would be best that you be the one to deliver the sample to him. The Enlightenment will cover whatever costs he may ask in exchange.'

Normally, I'd been jumping for the chance to take on such a task, but with my conflicting emotions, I was just hoping this was the end of the conversation. 'I...see. Will there be anything else, sir?'

Hu shook his head quickly. 'No. That'll be all for now, Reilly. Get some rest and set up a meeting with Calatin tomorrow.'

'Thank you, sir.' I got up, only to stop. 'Can you update me on the state of the Visitor?'

'The Visitor is still under custody. I've yet to decide if it's better off remaining there, where it can't cause any trouble.'

I gritted my teeth. It was better to just leave it.

'With respect, sir, the Visitor was made my excursion possible. I personally believe that, accounting for risks, she could still be of use.'

The Captain let out a long exhale through his nose, idly stroking his beard.

It was his call how to treat a paranormal in our custody. If Hu decided that Viora was too dangerous to allowed loose, there wouldn't be anything I could do.

The Captain visibly chewed over what I'd said, before nodding. 'Duly noted. As I said, it appears to have developed an attachment to you, so putting the paranormal to use could be feasible. I'll have them transfer it back into your custody.'

I let out a breath, only for the Captain to keep going. 'That said, don't let your guard down. Keep tinfoil on your person at all times. It is not human, agent. Don't make the mistake of assuming it's harmless.'

My mind flashed back to Viora throwing the Lemurians around like rag dolls. 'I can assure you, sir, I'm in no danger of making that mistake.'

# Chapter 16

'Seriously, Reilly. Is getting yourself in insane danger a new development, or have you had a death wish this whole time?!' Dawkes stomped over, glaring.

I sighed and stepped out of the lift into the main office. I suspected I'd be hearing from Dawkes fairly quickly this morning. 'Good morning, Agent Dawkes. I've no appetite for danger, but like all agents, I'm prepared to place myself in danger wherever necessary.

I began walking past, Dawkes following behind. 'Yeah, we're expected to be prepared for danger, not dive balls-deep into an enemy stronghold completely alone except for a paranormal you're counting on having Stockholm Syndrome!'

Much as I wanted to just get down to business, I knew Dawkes wouldn't let this go. 'I doubt Stockholm Syndrome's a factor. The Visitor's co-operation with me was based on mutual interests. The fact we both came back alive from said raid was proof enough that the Visitor had no interest in seeing me dead.'

Dawkes scoffed, crossing her arms. 'Or that it knew that you dying would seal it's fate too. Why the heck didn't you tell me about this?'

My pace slowed. 'I was given short notice and little time to prepare. I assumed you'd be too busy with matters on your end to help.'

'We're supposed to be working together on this case, remember?! At the very least, you should've called in to tell us you were pulling something bonkers!

The more Dawkes kept on about it, the more the unpleasant weight from last night pressed down on me. I'd already spent a good chunk of last night ruminating on what'd happened, and this was only bringing the sour memories back.

I stopped walking. 'You're right. I made quite a few mistakes last night, and it was only a combination of good luck and the Visitor's aid that let me survive and bring back the virus. To be entirely honest, I'm still not sure why the Captain took the aftermath so well.'

Dawkes' posture and expression softened. 'At least you've got some perspective. Look, there was a whole lot of ways that could've gone wrong, but I get why the Captain wasn't too worried. As far as the higher ups are concerned, since the only ones in danger were you and the Visitor, and you got results, it's not worth punishing you for giving us one of our biggest breaks so far.'

I glanced over, unsure where this conversation was heading, only for Dawkes to carry on. 'The reason I'm upset right now is that you could've died without anyone from the Enlightenment being able to help. You're not helping anyone by getting yourself killed, Reilly, even if you're the only human in danger, we have enough problems with manpower without good agents being reckless.'

I ran a hand through my hair. This conversation was still confusing me. Between her and Viora, I'd had more people nagging me about my safety in two days than in fifteen years.

I put my hands up in surrender. 'Alright. I'll be sure to keep you informed of any future movements. My apologies for any issues my lack of communication may've caused.'

Dawkes kneaded her face with one hand. 'I'll take what I can get. Where's the Visitor even hiding at the moment? Is it still in your apartment?'

'That's where I've been keeping her. She knows it's in her best interests to stay where she's out of sight from paranormals that might still be targeting her.'

Dawkes pulled a face. 'I guess it could've legged it by now if that was the Visitor's plan. So, what's the story with transporting the virus to the Hierophant?'

'Once I'd touched base with you, I was going to check in with the Captain to see if he's managed to set up a meeting with Calatin. If we're done catching up, I say we go and do that now.'

I made to turn around, but Dawkes extended a hand. 'There's something else. I've found something in the ship's data files.'

I looked back. 'Could you elaborate?'

'It'll be easier to show than explain.' Dawkes responded, pulling up her gloved hand and flexing her fingers. I felt the familiar surge of power as Dawkes worked her will, and her glasses glowed blue. The light spilled out onto her palm, forming a small floating, almost holographic image between us.

I realised it was showing a scene back on the ship, prior to the crash. More to the point, it was on the bridge. Numerous Visitors were moving about quickly, most working at the large consoles taking up the room, but a couple seemed to be staring down what looked like a human in a business suit, I assumed the one Dawkes had mentioned last time.

None of them were speaking, though I suspected the three were just communicating telepathically, the man's body language shifting as if in response to unheard speech. Whatever was going on, it was interrupted when one of the Visitors at the consoles froze up, the others looking in his direction.

Then, quick as a flash, the man whipped a hand inside his jacket, then flicked it out, something small flying across the room and landing on the ground, shattering like glass. The two Visitors whirled back towards him, one raising it's hand, but the man flicked his hand again, then took a few steps to the right.

The Visitors continued their motion, now moving to face each other, the one with it's hand raised gesturing up, sending the other flying up, slamming against the ceiling with a crack.

Meanwhile, I saw the Visitors clutch at their throats, coughing, which in seconds gave way to vomiting, the horrific multicoloured vomit I'd almost repressed decorating the bridge. Bodies started dropping, clawing at their throats, some drawing blood as their noses and eyes also bled. In the middle of this carnage, the man watched as the surviving Visitor nearest to him also dropped, smiling serenely.

Then, the man's smile dropped, and he looked over in the direction of the door. All of a sudden, the man backed away from the door, then, looking around the scene he'd created, expression irritated.

Scowling, the man waved his hand again, vanishing from sight, mere moments before the doors opened, revealing three very familiar, queasy looking agents.

The image froze on that moment.

'Guess we found your invisible man, Reilly.' Dawkes said

with a pained grimace.

I shook my head. ‘No, not a man. A para.’

‘You reckon?’ Dawkes responded.

I pointed at the image. ‘Check the gestures as he’s casting. No symbolic action, no tool to act as a symbol. The only way he could do that without backlash is if this figure’s effectively a living symbol to begin with. A paranormal.’

Dawkes bit the inside of her cheek. ‘Could be he’s got tattoos like you.’

‘Possible, but unlikely. Even with my ogham, I still need another symbol if I want to do anything other than reinforce my body. Definitely couldn’t do whatever he did to make those Visitors attack each other without another tool.’

Dawkes scratched her chin pensively. ‘Let’s say he’s a para. What kind? Sure, a Sidhe is the most likely suspect, but how the hell would one get onto that ship, let alone with the Visitors’ permission?’

‘A Lemurian, maybe? The Visitor told me her fellows were meeting with one to trade some of the captured people.’

Dawkes huffed. ‘That just raises more questions. Why would the Lemurians try to kill a bunch of Visitors, with a Sidhe bioweapon, at that?

I crossed my arms. ‘I don’t know, but the more I think about it, the more I’m certain the Lemurians are involved in all this in some deeper way somehow. We just need to figure out how they and the Sidhe are linked.’

Dawkes shrugged. ‘Maybe. But right now, we probably shouldn’t keep the Hierophant waiting. Let’s go check with the Captain.’

Dawkes then fixed me with a serious look. ‘By the way, I’m coming with you. If you’re already planning your next life-threatening disaster, I'd at least like to know it was happening.'

As it turned out, the Captain had managed to set up a meeting with Calatin, at his actual home. I was glad to hear that, more than happy to not even look at the Silver Arm again.

Fitting for a druid, Calatin's home was relatively far from the city itself, down by Portmarnock. Parking the car on a gravel roadway, I got out to examine the humble, one-story house.

There was not much to say about the house on the surface, looking very much the picture of a typical, out of the way cottage. What distinguished it was the slow trickle of power drawn from the earth into the house, very similar to the wards in the Silver Arm, only the lines of energy were thicker, less of a web and more of a honeycomb.

Dawkes let out an appreciative whistle. 'Impressive set up. You think he gets enough trouble to justify it?'

We made our way up the road, gravel crunching under our feet. In one hand, I felt the suitcase holding the virus sample bob forward and back, carrying the thing that had given us so much grief.

I could only hope that Calatin could provide some insight.

Reaching the door, I knocked, the dense wood thudding densely. A few moments passed, while I heard someone move about inside, before the door opened half-way,

Calatin's face peeked out suspiciously, until he caught sight of me, then he let out a relaxed smile and opened the door fully.

'Oh. Greetings again, Arbiter. Fate conspires to keep bringing you to my door.' Calatin then turned to Dawkes, bowing slightly in the process. 'I take it the lovely lady here is another member of your organisation?'

Dawkes, responded with a small bow of her own. 'That's correct, Hierophant. You can call me Dawkes. We're here to handle the transporting of the virus.'

'Yes, yes. Come in, then.'

Calatin waved us in. With a nod, I stepped over the boundary, and felt something heavy wash over me. My skin prickled and the hairs on my neck stood up.

I swallowed carefully. Had Dawkes and I tried to breach Calatin's home without his permission, the honeycomb ward would've killed us both on the spot. Whether it was bursting us into flames, making our gut flora devour us inside out, I wasn't sure, but I knew that there would've been nothing either of us could've done to survive it.

I was already aware of Calatin's power, but the thought of that being turned against me was enough to make me break out in a cold sweat. When I glanced back, Dawkes was clutching the doorframe, her posture hunched and her eyes squeezed shut.

Neither of us said a word, but we both moved a bit more cautiously as we stepped in.

Calatin led us into a cosy looking living room, complete with fireplace, colourful rug and a small selection of ugly, but soft looking armchairs arranged around a large coffee table, gesturing for us to sit down. The both of us sat down, my behind immediately sinking a couple of centimetres into the cushion. Calatin stepped around to address us.

'Would you two like anything? Tea, coffee?'

'With respect, Hierophant, it's probably best we get down to business.' I held the suitcase out. 'We are delivering a dangerous bioweapon to you, after all.'

Calatin gave the suitcase a faintly disgusted look, then sat heavily into his own chair, resting his chin on a broad arm. 'I have some questions regarding this arrangement.'

I lowered the case. 'What part of this is causing you concern?'

'Put simply, the main problem that I'm having here is the question of what I hope to gain from this endeavour.' Calatin responded, his face tense.

Dawkes spoke up. 'We will of course be prepared to compensate you generously for your aid in such trying times. Name your price, and the Enlightenment can provide.'

Calatin glared over at her. 'Let me ask you something, Arbiter. How does money help my people protect themselves from paranormals?'

Dawkes frowned in response. 'What do you mean?'

Calatin let his hands drop into his lap. 'I won't mince words. The Enlightenment has been very lax in how it's been choosing to deal with paranormal threats to humanity, especially in Ireland. All around us, the paranormals lurking in the shadows arm themselves with the goal of warring on each other, a war that would drag us all down to their vile level.'

Dawkes pressed her lips together. 'That's simplifying things a little, Hierophant. Nechtan's army are provoking violence against the other paranormal factions, but the danger to humanity at the moment is low. So long as whatever 'war' is planned doesn't cause harm to humanity or secrecy, our top priority is simply to keep any violence contained.'

Calatin huffed, slapping both hands on the armrests. 'That much is true, but what of the Visitors that see us as chattel or breeding stock? Or the Wavers, who take advantage of good folk coming in search of a better life to sneak into an already paranormal-dense land? What of the Sidhe, who when they aren't claiming territory in the city like common mobsters, are spreading a virus that we can only trust presents no danger to humans?! I trust I've made my point?'

Dawkes leaned forward, hand out placatingly. 'You have, but I'm uncertain what we can do to address your concerns. Our forces in Ireland are already stretched quite far. We can't be everywhere at once, and provoking conflicts with the wider paranormal community would only cause them to rally against us.'

A scowl growing on his face, Calatin continued. 'Then perhaps Ireland requires more Arbiters out in the field to properly counter these threats. I understand of course, that the two of you cannot push for such things yourselves, but if you want my aid, then my price is having my voice heard by someone who can make such a request.'

'That's certainly something we can look into, and we can try to get you an answer as soon as possible. However, if that's the case, then we'd still need you to start studying this virus immediately. Curtailing the Sidhe army's efforts are our top priority, but we can't do that until we have an idea where the source of that virus is. As long as Nechtan has a supply of it, he can continue to push the other factions to the outskirts, giving more territory for him and his movement to act freely in.' Dawkes' tone was still diplomatic, but I could see the tension along her jaw.

Snarling, Calatin rose out his chair, looming over us both. 'If you already know the Sidhe are responsible for it's creation, why on earth do you need to find out which Sidhe exactly first created it? Just call in whatever cavalry you need to put this insurrection down, before it spills out and brings innocent humans into it! Hell, if necessary, place geases on whatever paras you need to keep around to have them serve as sleeper agents to find whatever 'specific' sidhe you need to find!'

I reeled from Calatin's outburst, but Dawkes shot back, her own voice raised. 'Are you serious?! Even if we ignore that geases are incredibly advanced magic, you really expect us to just start snatching paras off the street and having our best magi carving runes into them to force them to obey us?! There's a reason that magic's regulated!'

Even that was understating it. Geases were only a step down from mind control in how invasive they were. By carving or branding sigils into the skin of your victim, forcing to obey your commands no matter how cruel or extreme.

It was the direct opposite of a familiar bond. Rather than magically bonding with a para for mutual protection and sharing power, geases were essentially slave collars. Old druids and irish sorcerers used to abuse them regularly. The only reason the Enlightenment hasn't forbidden the practice outright was as a last resort when dealing with threats too powerful to disable conventionally.

None of which seemed to bother Calatin, who threw his arms up. 'Why not?! It's not as if those damn paras aren't snatching people off the streets! What's wrong with a little turnaround?'

Even knowing Calatin's reasons for saying that, hearing it out loud made me uneasy. 'We're not getting anywhere with this. What exactly do you want Hierophant?

Calatin, whirled to me. 'What I want, is for the Enlightenment to do what it has always claimed to do. Protect the human race from the paranormal. More to the point, stop waiting for a few paranormals to step out of line, slap them down, only to ignore the wider communities that enable this behaviour. In the short term, however, I would settle for your administration taking a more proactive approach to keeping humans like my cabal safe, rather than only reacting to threats.'

'In that case, you have my word that, if you assist us with this task, I'll do everything I can to bring your issues to our Captain and suggest a meeting where you can say your piece. Does that sound reasonable?'

The last of the fire seemed to leave Calatin, and he looked at me, his voice going quiet. 'Your word, Reilly?'

I nodded. 'Absolutely, Calatin.'

Calatin glanced between Dawkes and I, then collapsed back in his seat with a grunt. 'I suppose that is the best I could expect you to do. My apologies for my tone, Arbiters, this topic is a sensitive one to me.'

He glowered at the suitcase. 'I can't promise immediate results, but I do promise to inform you of anything I learn that would be useful for you to know.'

Of course, just when things looked like they were calming down, I heard slow and deliberate knocking at the door.

I tensed up, while Dawkes half rose from her seat, both of us then glancing over at Calatin questioningly. Calatin gave us a confused look of his own, gestured for the two of us to stay still, then walked out of the room.

There was a slight creak.

Calatin's voice spoke up, low and hostile. 'I don't recall inviting you to my home.'

'You did not. But I believe you will want to hear what I have to say, and with circumstances as they are, there would not be another time to have this discussion.' The voice, also low but with a snide note, chilled me to the core.

It couldn't be.

Dawkes looked over at me, her brow wrinkled as she mouthed 'What is it?'. I mouthed the voice's name back, and Dawkes' own mouth dropped slightly.

'Fine. But cause me any grief and you will sorely regret it, Sidhe.'

The door slammed shut, and Calatin stormed back into the room, a look of pure fury set on his face. Calatin's new guest followed, and I gripped my athame when I recognised him.

He looked exactly the same he did at the rally last night, dressed in the same military uniform, the same emerald eyes and golden hair, and the same imposing presence. As Nechtan strode into the room, I saw little sprouts of green pull themselves up from the wood panelling, stretching towards him.

Flanking the Sidhe, were the two bikers that had guarded the entrance, walking in perfect lockstep, their sunglasses still perfectly concealing their eyes. As the three approached, I could sense the bikers take note of my presence, with what felt eerily like recognition.

His mouth quirked up in a sly grin, Nechtan gazed straight at me. 'Here as well? The Enlightenment has certainly been busy this week, hasn't it?'

# Chapter 17

Being in a room with a Daoine Sidhe is like being in a room with a tiger.

Sure, it may not rip you apart right away, but it could turn for any reason from hunger to you edging just a little too close.

And Nechtan was a particularly big tiger.

If Calatin was worried, however, it didn't show. 'Yes, I have business with the Enlightenment. Another reason why your appearance is of particular annoyance.'

'Hierophant Calatin.' Nechtan responded, still grinning. 'You have my sincerest apologies for imposing on you, but recent events have forced me to move sooner than preferred.'

Calatin crossed his arms. 'Whatever your position, Sidhe, I'm currently in an important conversation. This is a bad time to show your face here.'

Nechtan put his hand to his chest. 'Please, trust that I would not disturb you without due cause. This humble servant simply saw fit, bearing in mind our peoples' former bond, to provide fair warning, Hierophant.'

'A warning, or a threat?' Calatin sneered.

The guards flanking Nechtan made to move, stopped short by Nechtan's raised hand.

'Take it how you will. I simply desire to inform you that the time has come. In two days, the Sidhe army will march forth and finally route these invaders on our shores.'

The room went cold. Dawkes pulled herself up. 'Excuse me?'

Nechtan's expression stayed serene. 'I believe I've made myself quite clear. Last night, our rally was viciously assaulted by agents of the Seventh Wave. No less than fifteen Sidhe died as a result. Clearly the Seventh Wave desires our destruction, so we must respond.'

I was speechless. Nechtan had announced a declaration of war with all the ceremony of discussing his latest dentist appointment.

'Oh, wonderful.' Calatin rolled his eyes. 'I suppose then that this is your formal join or die request then?'

Nechtan let out a soft gasp. 'Hierophant, you wound me. I only bring word to you so your cabal can take precautions. After all, others may be in motion as well. The Lemurians, for instance. I fear those evil reptiles may be plotting to make their own advance on us and the Wave. You wouldn't want to get caught in that crossfire.'

Dawkes glared at Nechtan. 'You needn't worry about that. The Hierophant and the Ciorcal Darach are under Enlightenment protection. Any action against them will be considered an attack on us.'

Nechtan nodded at Dawkes, his expression serious. 'Of course. I've no doubt that the Hierophant and his cabal are in good hands. If anything, I'd be more worried for your own sakes, Arbiters. After all, if the Enlightenment were to get drawn into our fighting, it would be you on the front lines.'

'It won't come to that.' Everyone looked to me when I spoke, the attention filling me with unease. 'The Enlightenment won't stand by and let you drag us all into madness. This war will be stopped, whatever it takes.'

Nechtan let out a small chuckle. 'I can only hope that's true. I can assure you the current state of affairs isn't something I care for; it is only factors beyond my control that force me down this path. Believe me, if I could simply return home and put this all behind, I would do so. But, alas, we all have whetstones around our necks, don't we?'

Factors outside his control? Were there other figures at play here that Nechtan was working with. Or...were even the ones pulling his strings?

Calatin cut in, face red. 'Enough, Sidhe! I will not tolerate you taunting guests in my home! Get out and don't come back without my express permission!'

Nechtan shook his head, letting out a sigh worthy of a Romantic poet. 'My apologies then, Arbiters, it seems this conversation must be cut short. I would not want to exhaust the Hierophant's hospitality, and I have preparations to make. Farewell.'

Nechtan spun on his heels, both bikers lumbering after him. Dammit, I'd finally gotten something out of Nechtan and now he was about to slip through my fingers. I jumped to my feet.

'Wait!'

To my surprise, Nechtan actually stopped and looked back, staring patiently. A second passed while I struggled to form the question.

'Why are you doing this? Paranormals from outside Ireland have been coming here for decades. What made you act now, and not back when immigrant paranormals first started showing up? And why jeopardise the lives of your fellow Sidhe to do it?!'

Nechtan went still, gazing at me with such intensity a small part of me thought he'd turned to stone.

His lips curled into another sardonic smile. 'You're wasting your time trying to poke into my motives, Arbiter. You'll find I'm not the cause of the conflicts you see around. I wouldn't have come to this point, where it not for the anger and hatred that permeated those around us long before I became involved.'

'You're no longer welcome, Sidhe.' Calatin cut in, still glaring daggers at Nechtan.

Nechtan returned Calatin's glare with a tight smile. He continued on his way out, the two guards following, slamming the door behind them.

Silence reigned.

In one conversation, Nechtan had rendered moot our efforts up to now. The war was on, and Dublin was going to become its battleground.

Calatin gazed over at us, looking ten years older in that moment. 'Sincerest apologies, Arbiters, but perhaps you'd better leave. The sooner your superiors are aware of this, the better.'

Dawkes waved vaguely at Calatin. 'Right. We'll be in touch. Keep us updated on anything you can uncover regarding the bioweapon. If you can formulate a cure, you can expect some gratitude.'

As the two of us turned to the door, I saw Calatin sneaking a glance at me, but I was too stunned to say anything, Calatin's eyes stayed on our backs up until the door shut.

Back in the car, Dawkes ran her hands down her face, groaning. 'The Captain's not gonna be happy to hear this.'

I didn't answer, quietly starting the car. Inside, my mind

raced.

Dublin was on the brink of war, and I still had no idea how to confront it. With Nechtan's declaration, Calatin might actually get the Enlightenment support he was looking for, at the cost of bringing us into the conflict.

The worst part, however, was that I was suddenly unsure if Nechtan was even the lynchpin.

This feeling did not get better when we returned to HQ. Captain Hu had initially been irritated by our request to speak immediately, but quickly sobered upon receiving our recounting. When we were done, he leaned back, massaging his temples.

'I wish I was surprised that tensions had gotten to this point, but the only surprises here are that Nechtan saw fit to approach Calatin directly and that he fingered the Wavers for the attack.'

'But he had an easy target with the Lemurians. Why accuse the Wavers?' Dawkes responded.

The Captain gave a microscopic shrug. 'Nechtan's Sidhe Army has built most of its support on the threat of the Wavers. Perhaps the Lemurians don't have enough rage directed at them to get the desired response.'

I shook my head. 'That still doesn't make sense. Even if Nechtan's looking for an excuse to pick a fight with the Wavers, why the hell would he ignore the obvious threat of Lemurians interfering in his affairs?'

Hu glanced over at me. 'Wishes to avoid getting drawn into a three-sided war, possibly? Bear in mind he also avoided announcing our presence at the rally, probably for the same reason. However, whatever his reasons for doing this, Nechtan has played his hand. We can probably expect the initial violence to spark off very soon. Which means we're going to have prepare to act ourselves.'

Alarm went up my spine. 'Hold on a moment. Sir, I don't think that rushing headlong into this conflict is the best course. There's more going on here than just the tensions on the surface. We can't risk making things worse by aggravating the conflict.'

Hu's brow creased, his hand reaching under his desk. 'If this were the only concern, I'd be inclined to agree. Unfortunately, that is not the case.'

Hu produced a stack of papers as thick as his arm from under the desk.

'Over the last few days, reports have been coming in of violent outbreaks between the Sidhe and Wavers across Dublin, with enough ferocity that it's beginning to spill out into the public eye. We've been able to keep things under wraps by disseminating a gang warfare narrative, but if these conflicts are going to evolve into paranormal war, then we'll need to take greater measures.'

Just the sight of the stacked papers opened a cold pit in my gut. I already knew they represented dozens of cases, the sort that'd normally happen over two months, not two days.

Still, I felt compelled to keep arguing. 'That may be so, sir, but what are we meant to do? March in and start slaughtering every para we find? Surely that's only going to get us sucked into the war ourselves. If anything, the paras might rally against us.'

Hu exhaled. 'That is a risk, but the fact of the matter is, the Sidhe Army and the Wavers are going to be on the warpath, and innocent people are going to trampled. This is precisely the sort of event the Enlightenment is intended to counter. High Command's already heard of what's going on, and they're made it clear that they want something done.'

Dawkes spluttered for a moment, 'Wait, High Command's weighing in on this?!'

I understood her alarm. Matters that reached the ears of our leadership usually concerned entire continents. Them calling for decisive action in Ireland was like the European Union calling for a crackdown in Andorra.

'Indeed. Seems the last week has been eventful enough by our standards that they've taken notice. Given that Ireland's one of the few places where Enlightenment control is solid, it's logical that they don't want that control to slip.'

Hu leaned back in his chair, somehow looking less comfortable for doing so. 'If we can't find a way to get this under wraps, they will.'

If High Command decided to act themselves, it would definitely be decisive in our favour, once they brought the kind of firepower typically reserved for combating supernatural armies, but such power wouldn't discriminate.

It wouldn't be a war, but a paranormal massacre. All of them. From the genuine threats like Nechtan to relatively harmless paras like Bhajan, any standing in our way would be butchered. Human life came first, of course, but the thought of that happening made me feel like retching.

I couldn't let this happen, but I only had one card I could pull to try and stop it.

I straightened up, trying to still the trembling at the idea of having to challenge the Captain. 'I appreciate the situation we're in, sir, but there is far more going on than just a bunch of paras getting riled up. I'm certain that there's something else pulling the strings here for a larger purpose.'

I saw the Captain straighten in his seat. 'Can you explain what you're referring to, Reilly?'

Right. Now just have to not sound mad. 'When we were speaking to Nechtan, he mentioned that something outside his control was forcing this conflict. There might be other avenues we could shake down for clues.'

Dawkes looked at me sceptically. 'You bought that? I figured that was just a load of revolutionary posturing. Nechtan's trying to paint himself as some grand Sidhe defender, after all.'

I gritted my teeth. 'Normally, I'd agree. Except that we already know there's one other group involved. One who Nechtan has ignored even after they attacked his rally.'

'You suspect the Lemurians and Nechtan are cooperating?' Hu leaned forward.

'At the very least, I suspect Nechtan has some agenda that requires ignoring them. That, with his comments at Calatin's residence, leads me to believe there's a deeper conspiracy at work.'

'He has a point, sir.' Dawkes spoke up. 'We've been theorising that the figure in the ship footage I sent to you earlier was most likely a Lemurian. At the very least, the fact he had a sample of the bioweapon suggests a common supplier with Nechtan.'

Perfect! I'd planned to bring that up, but Dawkes backing me up was much better. 'I request permission to investigate this avenue, sir. It might open another solution that doesn't require such a heavy-handed use of Enlightenment resources.'

The Captain sank back into his chair, stroking his chin. The silence that ensued probably only lasted a few seconds, but each second felt like an hour as I held my breath, praying I'd not overstepped.

I had no right to ask Hu for anything, let alone something that could seriously jeopardise his standing if he signed off on it. I could only hope he would believe the yarn I'd spun him.

The Captain closed his eyes . 'As I've told you both, I have no choice but to react to the threat in front of me. You're right that it's clear the Lemurians have their role, but the Sidhe and Wavers are the ones turning Dublin into a warzone. Those aware of the paranormal are going to expect a response from us.'

The spasming in my limbs went dead, the familiar weight of failure already setting comfortably on my shoulders.

But then Hu spoke again.

'I'll be sending word to the higher-ups to request support from agents outside Ireland. You'll probably have a couple of days before they respond. I recommend you make the most of that time.'

Back in the staff cafeteria, Dawkes smacked her coffee mug on the table.

'I'll give you this, Reilly, I was starting to think this job was boring before I met you. Now we've got a war brewing right on our doorstep, and two days before the Captain starts going on the warpath, so the Order doesn't turn Ireland into it's Iraq war. I hope whatever idea you've got gives us somewhere to start!'

I'm not proud to admit I stalled up for a moment. The Captain's parting comment might've seemed unhelpful, but it was probably the best I could've hoped for.

He was right, he couldn't ignore the brewing conflict on the word of some nobody agent, but he could let me off the leash to chase down this lead myself. I couldn't expect any help, and Hu himself would almost certainly hang me out to dry if things went bad, but I had implicit permission to go ahead.

'Uhhh, Earth to Reilly? You in there?' Dawkes' voice shocked me back to reality.

I cleared my throat. 'It's fairly clear what needs to be done.'

Dawkes watched me dubiously.

'The Lemurians are the key. It's just a matter of tracking down whatever stronghold they have in Dublin, getting in and raiding it for any clues about their role in this war or any connections they might have with Nechtan.'

Dawkes snorted. 'Well, that's grand, Reilly, except we don't have a clue where the Lemurians even are! Those buggers have been able to stay under our radar since this all started!'

I leaned across the table. 'No, someone does know where they can be found.'

Dawkes' eyes narrowed widened. 'Y-you don't mean that alien, do you?'

'She ran to the Lemurians first for help. She trusted and knew them. If anyone knows where they're at, it'd be her. If I can get a steer on where they are from Viora, I could get there before Hu's deadline, bring him the evidence he's looking for that might help us find the real enemy here before Dublin becomes a free-for-all.'

Putting her mug down, Dawkes responded slowly. 'Reilly, think about this. Not only are you talking about relying on the word of a para, but worse, you're talking about charging head-first into a Lemurian stronghold with, what? Your athame and a can-do attitude?!'

I knew she'd make an issue of this. 'Of course not. I'm going to recruit some help and, assuming she does have some info, banking on getting a full rundown of the place from Viora before going ahead.'

'Look, I get that you've got the survival instincts of a snail in a salt mine, but even you can't think you can handle anything like that on your own!'

I got up from my seat, staring Dawkes down. 'I think I have a job to do, Dawkes. You heard the Captain, if I don't find proof that the Lemurians are working to drag all of Ireland into war, one which could easily go global once para communities outside Ireland hear what's happening to their cousins, then not only are a lot of innocents going to die, but the Enlightenment is going to get drawn into a multi-front war. My personal safety is irrelevant, if approaching the Lemurians is the way to stop this, then that's that.'

I turned and started walking away, only for Dawkes to barge into my vision. 'Will you just hold on a bleeding minute?!'

Dawkes jabbed a finger at my chest. 'I told you this morning, that if you're going to go running off by yourself, you're just going to get yourself killed, which isn't going to do crap to help the Enlightenment. Maybe you're right about the Lemurians, but that means nothing if you die. Which is why, when you go wherever the alien points you, I'm going too.'

'That's not necessary, Dawkes. I can han-'

'Can it, you idiot.' Dawkes snapped. 'You don't get to keep indulging your martyr-complex then get shocked when someone wants to stop you killing yourself. I'm coming, end of.'

I just about managed to avoid groaning. Ever since we'd been put on the same job, Dawkes had been hounding me constantly, and I still didn't understand why she cared.

And after today's events, my patience hit it's limit.

'Why are you so fixated on my safety? If I'm as much of a suicidal idiot as you think I am, why on earth are you so intent on following me into gruesome death? Why not just leave me to be an idiot, rather than risking your own life as well?'

Dawkes stared off pensively. 'Good question. Honestly, as much as I'm certain you're crazy, you're also the only person now who I think might be on the right track.'

She then turned her eyes back to me, a determined glint in them. 'That, and, as I have to keep reminding you, we're a team now. And teammates stick together, even when one of them is completely mental.'

I wanted to keep arguing, but I knew I wasn't winning this one. 'I suppose I can't stop you.'

With a satisfied grunt, Dawkes stepped aside and began to walk alongside me. 'Don't thank me just yet. If whatever you've got planned winds up getting us killed, you can bet your arse I will haunt you for it!'

I didn't respond, my mind occupied with considering my next move and internally cursing Dawkes for sticking with me. Things were much simpler when I only had to worry about myself.

Between Dawkes and any others I brought in, I'd have a lot of blood on my hands if this didn't work out.

# Chapter 18

It took longer then I'd liked to get home, but I needed more tinfoil.

'Still can't believe this actually works.' Dawkes said, tentatively adjusting the tinfoil under the hat she was now wearing.

I shrugged. 'Well, you'd better start believing Dawkes, otherwise it might not work.'

'Right. You know, I really hate magic sometimes.' Dawkes muttered, smoothing out her jacket.

I opened the door. Viora was still sitting on the sofa, the new salt circle surrounding it, warding her powers as before. I'd felt somewhat guilty for sticking her back in one the moment we got home, but I couldn't take too many chances, and I was sure Dawkes felt better for it.

Luckily, Viora seemed to have calmed down, and was in the middle of flicking through one of the books I'd left her. At the sound of the door, her head bobbed up, first to me, then to Dawkes.

'More Enlightenment?' She said, tone guarded.

I suppressed a wince, hoping the three hours she'd spent in Enlightenment custody before I came to collect her hadn't soured Viora too much on other agents. 'This is Agent Dawkes, she's been helping me in the investigation.'

'Wasn't aware Enlightenment had partner.' Viora responded, scanning us carefully. 'Extra help would've been helpful during rally.'

'Oh, would it have been?' Dawkes responded, her tone rising. 'Fancy that, Reilly. Looks like me and the Visitor might have some common ground after all.'

'Dawkes was researching the video footage on your ship.' I said quickly. 'I was hoping we'd be able to talk more about the Lemurians you met up with.'

'What questions?'

I paused. 'Remind me, didn't you say that you made contact with them at their base when you first arrived?'

'Yes. Went to local headquarters of Lemurians for assistance with contacting Network. Then Lemurians attempted to kill.'

Dawkes unfolded her arms. 'You know where the Lemurians are hiding? Where?'

'Tall building in city.' Viora responded.

Dawkes and I both waited. Viora didn't elabourate.

Dawkes sent a flat stare my direction. 'Egads Holmes, you've cracked the case.'

I chewed my tongue. 'Don't suppose you can narrow that down?'

'Building also very wide. Had many windows.' Viora said, spreading her arms out. 'Building also had symbol and writing on side, but didn't get good look.'

'What did you manage to see?' I pressed.

Viora scratched the side of her head. 'Symbol looked like sphere with jagged points. Name started with 'L', ended in -tech.'

Dawkes' face turned pensive. 'Keep talking, Reilly, I'm

gonna check something.'

Dawkes tapped the side of her glasses and started tapping on a virtual keyboard with her glove. Meanwhile, I continued grilling Viora.

'Can you tell us anything about the interior?'

Viora shook her head slightly. 'Only saw few rooms before situation deteriorated.'

'Well, how abou-'

Dawkes' voice cut in. 'Hold that thought! Take a look, Reilly.'

She took off her glasses and handed them to me. Putting them on, I saw Dawkes had pulled up a corporate website, a stylised sun gracing the top of the screen over the word 'Lumintech'. A quick scan indicated the corporation was an international one, specialising in biotechnology. Nothing suspicious on the surface, but we were in no position to judge anything by their covers.

I jerked my head towards Viora. Pursing her lips for a moment, Dawkes nodded, letting me pass the glasses to her.

'Does this look like the symbol?'

Viora leaned forward, then nodded. 'Identical.'

'Alright, that's something established. They only have the one building in Dublin too, so now we know where these lizard-freaks have been hiding.' Dawkes took her glasses back and poked at the air a couple more times. 'Just off St. Stephen's Green, at that. They've been sitting right under us this whole time.'

I gritted my teeth. 'If they've been in Dublin this whole time, why're we only noticing them now?'

Dawkes continued flicking through the site. 'Going by what's here, the company only opened it's branch in Dublin about two years ago, not exactly enough time to cause any major stirs. Besides that, the Lemurians probably live in that building, doing normal work during the day, leaving them all the privacy they could want after hours. For all we know, chasing down the alien is the first time this lot have had to leave the building since it was set up.'

I straightened up. 'Well, now we know where they're hiding, we should start digging up any information we can about the building, then make an inflitration plan.'

Dawkes looked over at me. 'Seriously, Reilly. Are you sure this is the best idea? Look, maybe we can still try and talk Hu into giving us a bit more help. But trying to break into this place alone with a small horde of Lemurians crawling around isn't smart.'

'What else can we do? You heard the Captain; any Enlightenment support is going to be tied up keeping order on the streets. This is hardly my first choice either, but it's the only lead we've got.'

Dawkes put her hand to her forehead, her jaw set. 'Let's say, for the sake of argument, that I agree this is anything other than insane. You still can't expect just the two of us to storm a nest of Lemurians by ourselves.'

'Definitely not. As a matter of fact, I have an idea of who might be able to help us.'

'Who?'

I gave Dawkes a look. She seemed to pick up quickly.

'Please tell me you're joking.'

'Do you know anyone else who'd even humour this?'

'Maybe not, but saying that really isn't making me any more confident.'

It didn't take long after I made the call, to hear a knocking at the door. I got up and opened the door, coming face to face with Bhajan in his human guise, looking somehow more haggard than last time, his already shabby robes sporting a couple of new tears, the gabs revealing some small bruises and cuts on his torso and arms.

Haggard as he was, Bhajan still managed a wide grin. 'Agent Reilly. Pleasure to see you again. Apologies for the delay, got a little tied up.'

'Evidently. The hell happened there?' I gestured to Bhajan's injuries.

Bhajan looked down, as if just noticing them, then gave a short laugh. 'Ah, the streets aren't quite so safe these days for humble sages. A trio of leprechauns had a notion of jumping me under a rail bridge. Managed to give them the slip, but things are getting hairy out there. I was this close to getting turned into a monkey-skin rug'

'Doubt it. If they wanted a fur rug, I'm pretty sure they could've found something cleaner rifling through bins.' Dawkes sniped from the armchair she'd sat in.

Bhajan's eyes fell on Dawkes, and bugger me if they didn't twinkle. 'Well, if it isn't the beautiful yet sharp-tongued agent Dawkes! Your radiance has only become more blinding since our last meeting!'

Dawkes' scowl deepened as Bhajan sauntered through the doorway. 'Shame it's not more blinding, otherwise maybe I wouldn't have to look at your sorry mug again.'

With a gasp, Bhajan clutched one hand to his chest and another over his eyes. 'Like a dagger to the heart, my dear! I see the Enlightenment still has not a care for the delicate hearts of poor, vulnerable Vanaran like myself!'

Dawkes rolled her eyes, while Viora, watching the proceedings blankly, looked over at me. 'How talking ape help?'

Bhajan turned, then stopped dead when he caught sight of Viora. With exaggerated slowness, he leaned over to me. 'Reilly, there's an alien sitting on your sofa.'

'I'm aware Bhajan, that's part of why I asked you down here.' I held out a hand to the remaining free chair. 'Mind taking a seat? We've got a bit to go over.'

Bhajan's eyes darted from me, to Viora, before he slowly made his way over to the armchair, slumping down into it, eyes still locked onto Viora. Bhajan allowed a long-suffering stare to fall on me. 'What deep shit have you gotten me into, Reilly?'

It didn't take too long to fill Bhajan in about the last couple of days. During the whole process, Bhajan seemed to shift from baffled, to alarmed, then settled lastly on glowering warily at us.

The moment I finished, Bhajan cut in. 'So, in a couple of days, you've gone and found some kind of mad conspiracy to draw the paranormal factions in Dublin into a war, and you think the Lemurians are behind it. Commendable work, can hardly see what reason you could possibly need my help.'

'Have to agree with the monkey on this, Reilly. You really sure you want him coming along on an infiltration?' Dawkes said, still looking unimpressed.

'Don't be fooled by his cartoonish persona, Dawkes. It's only mostly an act.' I responded. 'If push comes to shove, we can trust Bhajan to pull his weight when he needs to get serious.'

Bhajan jumped up from his seat, teeth bared. 'Hang on! Am I invisible now?! What part of any of that makes you think I would want to put any part of myself near a fucking Lemurian nest?! Those mutant freaks they dropped back at the Sichuan Pantry were nearly enough to punch my ticket to Samsara, and you want me to charge straight into whatever mad labs made those things?!'

'You already know the answer to that, Bhajan. If this war kicks off, none of the sides involved are going to give a shit for neutral parties. Even if the Sidhe don't start targeting you for training Wavers, the Wavers themselves are going to try and press gang you into fighting. Hate to say it, but the only way you have of not getting sucked in is to help us nip it in the bud.'

'Sounds a lot like what you're doing right now, Reilly.' Bhajan responded with a moody glower. 'I don't have any stake in this shit! I came to Ireland so I could get away from causes, not to get dragged into them! If you're right, and I'm fucked no matter which side comes out on top, then I'm going to get the first plane ticket off this sinking ship and go to another country where I can finally get some damn peace and quiet!'

'Yeah? Where to, Bhajan? I'm guessing you've got good reason not to return to Asia, and if anywhere else in Europe appealed to you, you've gone there in the first place.'

'I'll go to the States, then. The yanks love their immigrants.'

I snorted. 'Only when they're rich. And, again, if you considered that an option, you'd have gone there from the beginning. Not that I blame you, if you're worried about having to stick to a clique to get by, America's the worst place you could go.'

I stared Bhajan down, letting him stew on the words. 'Sure, you might not have a war like this across there, but only because the para communities across the US prefer to clash with the Enlightenment instead. Does engaging in guerrilla warfare with one of the most well-funded branches of a worldwide organisation really seem like peace and quiet to you?'

Bhajan squirmed, and I had to restrain some guilt. None of what I'd said had been a lie, but I was strong-arming him. Up until very recently, Bhajan had been the closest thing to any kind of acquaintance I'd had, so I felt inclined to throw him a bone.

'Look, Bhajan. If you don't want to help us, if you want to run off instead, I won't stop you. This whole operation is off the books, so I don't have any clout to force you to help us. I'm not asking you for help because it's convenient, I'm asking because the only people who can help me right now are all in this room. If there's anything I can promise or give you in exchange for your help, name it, and you'll have it, as long as I'm the only one paying, you'll be paid.'

Something in Bhajan seemed to change, his expression twisting into a sinister grin. 'That's a very risky proposition for you, Reilly. You realise such an open-ended offer could be easily taken advantage of, yes?'

Bhajan got up, and walked right up to me, his large, sharp teeth bared, hot breath hitting my neck. 'What if I asked for your head, once this is over, hm? Or perhaps to indulge in the ultimate blasphemy of cannibalism? You've always paid me in small heresies, dear agent, are you now prepared to pay me in a large one?'

Next to us, I could see both Dawkes and Viora frantically get up, but I put out a hand to stop them, keeping my gaze on Bhajan, hoping the sweat I felt on my forehead wasn't visible. The Enlightenment always tried to drill into us the inherently dangerous nature of paranormals, but never had I felt that lesson more than with Bhajan's hot breath on my throat.

For all his friendly trappings, I was distinctly conscious that Bhajan was not human, but a being born from humanity's dreams and nightmares, not beholden to our values. Images flashed of the simple, direct brutality I'd seen from Bhajan over the last week, has well as a few imaginings of my own of what that could mean for me, if I misjudged this.

If my plans for getting into Lumintech were going to work, I was going to need Bhajan's help. Perhaps I could get out the deal someway afterwards, or get some protection from the Enlightenment to get Bhajan off my back, but as it stood now, there was only one response.

'One caveat. If you help us with getting into Lumintech and acquiring any and all intel possible, I will give you whatever you ask for once the investigation is done. But I will be the only one to pay it, no stealing or taking another's life.' I then thrust my hand out. 'Deal?'

The room was dead silent as Bhajan slowly leaned back, eyes still boring into my own, his mouth steadily closed. Then, as if a switch was flicked, Bhajan let out a laugh, grasping my hand with familiar tightness.

'Just when I thought I'd finally managed to rattle you, you still stand firm, Reilly! Very well, in acknowledgement of your unflinching resolve, I, Master Bhajan, agree to your terms. Whatever my price is once all is done, not one hair on anyone outside yourself will be harmed. I swear this upon my honour and soul!'

Dawkes walked up with a fierce glint in her eye. 'Just so we're clear, Reilly's life isn't on the table either for whatever messed up 'repayment' you might want. The Enlightenment doesn't trade agent lives just to get some deviant para's rocks off.'

'Not to worry, not to worry!' Bhajan responded; jovial demeanour re-established. 'Forgive me, my dear Dawkes. I was merely tested Reilly's resolve. Be at ease, whatever price I ask will not endanger his life.'

'Well then, if we're all on board, we should get back to the task at hand.' I took a seat opposite Viora. 'Viora, could you get back to telling us everything you can about Lumintech's interior and the people in it? Don't hold anything back. If we're going to put together any coherent plan for getting in, we need to know about any potential security weaknesses we can exploit.'

'Very well.'

Viora's description matched up with what you'd typically expect of a modern office building, detailing four floors of rooms and cubicles set aside for all the functions needed to run a company.

While you might've thought things would get interesting when she started talking about hearing the thoughts of those inside, Lemurian clerks aren't anymore interesting than human clerks. I was just beginning to lose the struggle to remain enthused, when something Viora said caught my attention.

'Hang on, could you go into more detail on that?'

Viora gave me a puzzled glance. 'Which part?'

'The bit where you mentioned some of these minds you sensed went underground?!' I responded, my voice rising in pitch at the end.

Viora seemed unperturbed. 'Some minds traversed under ground level, but lost contact after roughly 50 metres.'

'The hell?' Dawkes said. 'Do they have a underground complex in there?'

Viora seemed taken aback. 'Minds underground unusual for buildings?'

'A little.' I remarked dryly. 'Anything about those minds stand out?'

'Minds appeared mystically inclined. Some thoughts of study in preparation for research projects.'

Dawkes pressed both palms against her face. 'Bugger me, if those lizards have an actual underground lab in the middle of Dublin, I'm going to flip.'

'One thing's certain.' I replied. 'If the Lemurians are hiding anything of worth in that building, it's down there.'

I got up. 'We have our goal now. We need to gain entrance to the Lumintech building, then make our way down to this underground complex. From there, we will need to find anything that the Lemurians are hiding that could potentially tie into the bioweapon, and prove their involvement in stirring up the violence we're seeing out there. This won't be easy, but we have one advantage. The Lemurians have invested significant effort into hiding themselves, enough that they were prepared to kill Viora to keep this facility hidden. Now that we know they're here, we've already taken their main method of security, secrecy, away. Now we just need to prepare for anything else they might have. Ideas?'

Dawkes stroked her chin. 'Wards will definitely be an issue, if they give even the slightest toss about protecting themselves. I wouldn't be shocked if they had a setup similar to ours back at HQ.'

I nodded at her. 'You're likely right. I could do something about that, but I'll need to get close. There'd still be the matter of getting inside without giving ourselves away.'

Bhajan interjected; his tone oddly contemplative. 'I might actually have something for that.'

Dawkes looked over, her face sceptical. 'It's not playing leapfrog with the guards again, is it?'

With another guffaw, Bhajan waved off her comment. 'Oh, no, no! That was a different situation entirely! Let's just say if any wards are taken off the table, I can handle the physical entry.'

'I'll want more detail, but we can discuss that in a minute.' I said, before I looked to Dawkes. 'Dawkes, once we're in, how well do you think you could handle any digital security?'

'Can't say for certain until I'm in there, but for what's it's worth, I've spent the better part of a week magically cracking an alien computer system, so as long as the Lemurians don't have anything more complex than that, I think I can take a shot.'

'Sounds good.' With a strange excitement now brimming in my chest, I whipped round to Viora. 'In that case, once we're in, could we count of you to keep your mind open for any incoming threats?'

'No.'

'...Sorry?' I responded, Viora's response cutting the momentum from under me.

Viora squirmed in her seat, not making eye contact. 'Too dangerous. Could get killed.'

'Didn't seem to stop you following Reilly to the Sidhe rally last night. Know something we don't?' Dawkes said, a sharp undercurrent in her tone.

Viora seemed to shrink in on herself. 'N-no. Want to survive. No more.'

'Don't we all, E.T? So, you can understand if I was a bit concerned that the para that was working with the paras we're planning on raiding suddenly didn't want to help us with that? Sure you don't still have some agenda you'd like to share?'

As Dawkes spoke, she got up and stepped close to the circle still containing Viora, looming over the Visitor.

'Being honest! J-just don't want to d-die!'

I gave Viora a long look, taking in the small, yet noticeable quiver in her arms as they wrapped themselves around her legs, curling up into a ball. I really did need all the help I could get, but, when I remembered our conversation last night, what resolve I had broke.

'Leave it, Dawkes.'

Dawkes snapped over to me, looking affronted. 'Are you serious right now, Reilly?! You've been going on about us needing all the help we can get, but the second the Visitor starts getting antsy, that's it? What if it's hiding something so when we get killed, it can just waltz out of this apartment?!'

I felt my eyes narrow. 'Last I recall, you weren't comfortable being in the same room as her, and now you're upset we can't take her along? Besides, if she did have divided loyalties, would you want her hovering behind you during this operation?'

Dawkes lifted a finger, a word half-coming out of her mouth before she stopped herself. 'Alright, fine. But if they're prepared for us, I'll know who to blame. That's all.'

The silence was tense, the room heavy, until Bhajan casually interjected. 'Oh well, nothing to be done. We'll just have to get by without a mind-controlling space alien floating behind us the whole time, eh?'

Dawkes and I cast an irritated look at Bhajan, who just

responded with a toothy grin. Dawkes then let out an extended hiss from her teeth, her shoulders untensing.

'Guess so.' As Dawkes spoke, she walked back to the chair and sat down. 'Well, what now, Reilly?'

I took a moment to look over the people in front of me. When I first got back here, I'd no real idea how to even approach tracking down the Lemurians, and, if I could've figured it out by myself, I still wouldn't have had even the slightest notion how I was going to get myself into Lumintech.

Yet, in the span of a few minutes, between the four of us, we'd had already put together the first parts of an actual plan. For the first time since I'd first been put on this investigation, it felt like I was in a position to achieve something meaningful. The feeling was unnerving, and I could feel the familiar voice in the back of my mind telling me of all the ways I could still ruin all of this.

I smothered the voice. Even if I could still fail my part, at least this time I could at least hope the others would do better. I took the last seat available.

'Alright. Time to get to work.'

# Chapter 19

Usually, the infiltration of a guarded building requires weeks to years of preparation, planting spies, acquiring building plans, and working tirelessly to cover as many bases as possible.

In our case, planning took about three hours, one of which was spent talking loudly at each other over dinner, and had culminated in me, Dawkes and Bhajan making our way down to St. Stephen's Green.

The only further preparations consisted of me shoving some of my spare potion stash into my pocket and Dawkes comparing Viora's description of the building against images taken from Google Maps.

There was no way the Lemurians could be prepared for an infiltration quite this rushed.

It's was just starting to get dark when we came up to our target. There, flanked by two smaller, brickwork buildings, was the Lumintech head office, blending in almost perfectly with the surrounding buildings, only the sunburst symbol above the entranceway distinguishing it.

The windows were dark, hopefully signalling most personnel had left for the evening.

Human personnel, at least.

We set off down the street towards Lumintech, or to be more precise, towards a small alley next to it. The sun was setting, casting the street in amber, the only sounds while we strolled being the occasional car lazily trundling past. The city was never really asleep, but this was the best we could've hoped for.

We walked until the last possible moment to turn into the alley, keeping a wide berth from the building itself. Once we'd gotten relatively out of sight, I took out my athame, stepping up to the wall. Letting my eyes close while the blade waved in the air, I felt the thick web of wards on the building dancing in front of me.

Dawkes had been right, the set-up wasn't dissimilar to our HQ, only simplified and less powerful, good enough for direct assaults, but more susceptible to the sabotage I had in mind.

I tried to search for any imperfections, any place where the overlapping efforts of multiple casters working at different times might've left a gap. The search was slow, sweat beading on my brow as I focused.

As a droplet of sweat began working its way down my cheek, in the midst of the complex webbing, I saw a small patch, where some of the lines of protective power lined up in a crooked fashion quite unlike the elegant design around them.

Bingo.

I held the blade level with the imperfection, letting my mind extend to the athame, the same way I'd sliced up the wards I'd encountered around Nechtan's jar.

'Find something?' Bhajan's voice cut into my focus.

'Yes.' I hissed back. 'Now stay quiet. On my word, do whatever you need to.'

I lunged forward, slicing the athame at the imperfection. I

felt the lines fray and tear, resisting my blade for a few seconds before giving way. In that same moment, I sensed the weak point in the building's defences already attempting to reform themselves.

'Now!' I hissed over in Bhajan's direction.

I felt a hairy hand clamp down on my shoulder, then a deep trilling 'Ooooommmm' went down my body.

Then, I felt space twist and my body likewise.

It is impossible to describe the sensation as Bhajan warped space to teleport both Dawkes and I into the building, but imagine you were drugged, shoved in a running washing machine, taken out, and slapped in the face.

But far less pleasant.

Teleportation was a rare skill, and having now experienced it first-hand, I can certainly see why mastering it is infamously difficult.

The moment I felt solid ground, I dropped to my knees, gagging, vision swimming while I tried to get my brain working again. Somewhere far away, I heard Dawkes coughing.

Once I could remember what my name was, I pulled myself up to find her hunched over a toilet cistern, blinking heavily while Bhajan leaned against the wall of the cubicle, visibly trying not to laugh.

'Y-you said we'd o-only feel s-slight discomfort!' Dawkes gasped out, forcing herself up to properly glare at Bhajan.

A chuckle escaped Bhajan's lips. 'Well, that's how it was for me when I first learned the art of recognising the illusion of space. Not this humble sage's fault that a pair of hardened combat wizards have weak stomachs.'

'Remember...the...mission.' The words tumbled from my mouth. 'Move to...next stage.'

The two looked over at me, then Bhajan glanced back towards Dawkes expectantly.

'Right, right. Just hold on a bleeding minute.' Taking another moment to straighten herself, or at least as much as she could inside a cramped toilet cubicle, Dawkes tapped her glasses, opening some kind of app.

I couldn't get a good look at what she was doing, but I could sense the thin strands of magical power extend from her digital setup and worm their way into the walls around, connecting to the security system.

'There. Now the cameras in here shouldn't pick us up. Any alarm sensors should be blind too.'

'Guess that just leaves me then.' I gestured for the others to bunch up.

Now close enough to feel the heat of my teammates, I flicked my athame about, feeling the familiar cool sensation and darkening of my vision as I rendered us near invisible.

I sensed a surge of energy from both my teammates, accompanied in Bhajan's case by what sounded like the soles of his feet scraping and tapping against the ground in quiet patterns that reminded me of Boyle's motion sensing trick with the tuning fork.

'Alright, vision enhancement active. Looks to have countered the visibility loss.' Dawkes whispered.

'No-one immediately outside the bathroom.' Bhajan added distantly. 'But rest assured, if so much as a fly touches the ground close to us, I'll know.'

It abruptly occurred to me that I probably should've thought of some way to counteract the loss of vision myself back when I first figured out this spell. At least my teammates were more competent.

Pushing away my embarrassment, I responded. 'Let's go. Remember, our priority is getting down to the sub-level.'

The three of us squeezed out of the cubicle, before making our way out of the toilets, only having left some of our dignity behind.

My vision was still hazy from my camouflage, but I was able to make out that we were in the main reception, if the large desk in the centre of the hall, currently empty, was any indication.

Everything in my immediate vicinity screamed corporate bland, with the white, featureless walls, broken up by the occasional sign or large glass window, the sunburst symbol planted in the wall above the reception desk the sole concession to individuality.

We continued moving, kept shoulder to shoulder by my spell's range. Following the directions Viora had given us, we walked slowly out of the atrium, skulking down the hall, where the lifts were located.

I pressed the button, the doors opening after a few seconds. Still packed close together, the three of us shifted into the lift, and I looked over to examine the controls.

'Doesn't look like there's any buttons for going below ground.' Dawkes noted next to my shoulder.

'Were you expecting there to be?' I responded.

'No, but a girl can dream. Hang on a tick.'

I heard Dawkes shuffle as she flexed her smart glove again and began the next step, hijacking the lift with magic to get us down. Just like with the cameras.

Or at least that was the idea, until Dawkes let out a growl. 'Sod.'

'What?' I asked, my already frayed nerves jittering.

'They've warded the lift; it's blocking me out.'

I spun around, searching for any energy in the air. 'I don't sense any wards covering this area.'

Dawkes let out a hiss. 'Figures. It must be some kind of sympathetic connection to something else in the building.'

I repressed a hiss of my own. Sympathetic magic was always a pain, even when it wasn't as bad as the Sidhe getting a hold of our blood this time. By making some symbolic representation of the thing you wanted to magically influence, preferably with something taken from the target itself, you could use that representation to influence the target.

Effectively, the Lemurians had probably made some kind of voodoo doll of the lift and warded that, skipping over having to ward the lift itself. It was a bizarre tactic, given how large and complex most wards have to be. It would've definitely been less work to just ward the lift normally, but damn if this wasn't tripping us up now.

Still, now that I knew what we were dealing with, I had my own response. Refocusing my attention on my athame, I traced along my surroundings again, only this time searching for a different form of energy.

It took a moment, but I soon found it, starting as an odd tickle down my arm before I narrowed in on what felt like a tide of power flowing into the lift, like a stream of water, going out of the lift and further into the building...

'Found it. There's definitely something being used as the conduit for the actual wards to shield this room.'

'Wonderful. Stupendous, in fact. What now?' Bhajan muttered. Even without a clear view, I knew he'd folded his arms like an irritable teen.

'I'm going to need both you and Dawkes to step back for a

moment.'

I could feel the two give me odd looks, followed by the sounds of footsteps as they moved as far back as they could whilst still remaining in my field of invisibility. Good, now for the hard part.

Readying my blade in one hand, I clenched the other, drawing power from the tattoos on that arm.

Most sympathetic magic is one way. You can hurt someone by stabbing a voodoo doll, but the person stabbing themselves doesn't damage the doll. Technically, it's not hard to step up to a two-way connection where one effects the other, hell, with some magic, it's probably easier than having to take steps to make sure that, for instance, the person you're spying on through a crystal ball can't also see you. But almost all of the time, that connection can only travel in one direction.

But you can't prepare for everything.

While the Lemurians went to no small effort to most likely scribe intricate wards on a tiny model of the lift or something similar, they hadn't prepared for someone like me, who specialised in manipulated the flow and form of energy, and has gotten quite adept at directing it where it wouldn't normally go.

As my left arm started to burn from the kinetic energy brimming inside it, I braced myself, then flung my fist towards the wall of the lift. At the same time, I flicked my athame first parallel with my left hand, then, a split second before I'd have put a large dent in the lift, I gestured towards the flow of energy I'd sensed, letting the athame stab through the stream pouring in, with a harshly whispered, 'Droim ar ais!'

My hand burst with pain as it violently collided with solid

metal for the second time this week, followed rapidly by an unnerving sensation of stillness, my knuckles rested gently against the wall, the kinetic energy that was powering the blow now abruptly absent.

At the same time, I felt that same kinetic force run across my shoulders and down the other arm, into the athame, which then dispersed the power into the sympathetic current I'd found, the kinetic energy defying the tide to speed up the connection, like a salmon scaling a waterfall.

I waited tensely, hoping I'd timed it right.

Then I felt it. Somewhere, at the other end of the connection, I felt the kinetic energy I'd sent upstream make contact with something, which then shattered when the force hit straight into it. The current that was suffusing the lift petered out into a trickle, before vanishing completely. I let my arms drop with a wince.

'Reilly?' I heard Dawkes cautiously step close.

'Try it again.'

A moment of quiet, then...

'I'm in! Great job, Reilly, we're good to go!'

I waved off Dawkes' praise. Hardly that impressive, once you knew the trick.

I stepped aside, letting Bhajan's and Dawkes' footsteps move past me. I then got an unpleasant jolt at what felt like a hand smacking against my back, followed by Bhajan's voice. 'Not bad, dear companions. Heading down then?'

Shaking off the discomfort, I responded. 'Yeah. Remember, we're looking for anything for how the Lemurians connect to the bioweapon. Any information is good, but that's our priority.'

'Got it. Sending us down now.' Dawkes replied.

The lift doors closed, and we descended. We'd gotten this far, but we'd still had no idea what might possibly be waiting at the bottom.

I figured good odds that the lack of personnel or security up top could mean that anyone here was waiting at the bottom. Sure, heading here late at night was a good call, but I didn't believe for a second that we were alone.

The doors gave way with a quiet hiss, revealing a dimly lit hallway. Dull, yellowish lights casting the hall in the sickly colour of urine. When we stepped out, things only became more surreal as, now that I could look closer, I could see this wasn't a normal hallway. The walls were metal, but looked rough and uneven, like the hallway had been carved rather than built.

I remained tense. You don't leave the lights on if no one's home.

'Oh, sod off. It is a bloody underground lab.' Dawkes moaned quietly.

'We planned for this, Dawkes.' I responded.

'Yeah, yeah, just hang on.'

Dawkes worked her magic again, this time, as far as she explained it during planning, using her glasses as a divination tool. It wouldn't tell us anything about possible threats, since the result will be more like a map of the area, but it would still give us a way to navigate this place without stumbling blindly about.

'Now we're in business. Got a few points of interest here worth checking out. I think I even got visual on a lab-.' Her voice paused, before continuing, cautious. 'Guys, we're gonna need to be real careful from here on.'

'Why now specifically?' I responded.

'Because from what I'm getting here, this place has both a sleeping area and an armoury.'

I hated being right.

'Ah. Wonderful. So glad I agreed to step into the lion's den with the pair of you. I feel better about this decision every second.' Bhajan dryly remarked.

'Looks like we'll be following you, then.' I replied, shifting to let Dawkes take the lead. It didn't actually change anything, so I chose not to fixate.

The halls didn't become any less strange as we moved through them, if anything the sounds of movement that seemed to constantly get closer only added a sense of unease to their already surreal quality.

Much as I was sure understanding the nature of how this facility was constructed would give us some insight into the Lemurians, there simply wasn't time to think on it. Instead, my focus was spent solely on maintaining our camouflage and staying one step ahead of the patrols, trusting Dawkes to lead us in the right direction.

After what felt like hours of skulking, Dawkes was just about to lead us around another corner when I felt a hand grab my shoulder.

'Company round the corner.' Bhajan growled. 'Just sensed them move in.'

'Typical. The labs are just down there.' Dawkes muttered.

'Then we'll need to assess the situation.' I said, checking round the corner.

Standing at the hallway intersection were three figures. Two of them were Lemurians, in all their lizardy glory, standing stiffly at attention, wearing dark blue uniforms, the design making them look like discount Soviets, though I doubted the holstered guns were similarly outdated.

When my eyes went to the third figure, my breath caught in my throat.

'You mean to tell me you haven't found any signs of disturbance?' The man said, still wearing the same suit and with the same cocky gleam in his eye that even a damaged camera had been able to pick up.

It was the same guy we'd seen on the Visitor ship, the one that had poisoned the Visitors and set this whole mess into motion, now watching the guards in front of him sweat.

And sweat they did, as the one on the right managed, after some hesitation to hiss out, 'No, Mr Thoun, this sector is locked down. Nothing strange has happened all night.'

'Is that so? I suppose you'd better make sure it stays that way, shouldn't you?' He jerked a finger down our direction. 'Such as down there, perhaps? Unless you think any potential intruders are going to emerge from the ground, instead of the actual entrance?'

'But, sir, the labs-'

'Are hardly going to be any safer if you give any intruders space to get their bearings! Now move, before I have you both shipped back to the tunnels!'

Whatever the 'tunnels' were, mention of them was enough to get the guards moving, scrambling in our direction, missing our group by inches. Thoun watched the two leave contemptuously, watching the hallway for a few moments after they'd already rounded the corner, before letting out a sharp exhale and spinning on his heel, heading in the opposite direction.

A few seconds after, Bhajan's voice whispered out. 'Well... that was fortuitous. Might as well have just handed us the keys to the labs.'

Bhajan wasn't wrong, but staring after Thoun, I couldn't shake the thought that I wasn't going to check another chance. 'Change of plans. We need to follow him.'

'Hang on, hang on. I thought this whole shindig was to raid their labs. Why do you care about some prick in a suit?' Bhajan responded.

'No, that guy's a key suspect. Learning more about him is as important as investigating their labs.' Dawkes cut in. 'That said, we can't exactly ignore the lab either.'

'Then you two can get check out the lab. I'm following him.' I responded, legs still tensed.

Dawkes spluttered in response. 'Wha-Reilly, no! We can't afford to get separated now! Did you forget you're the one keeping us invisible?!'

I paused, clenching my teeth as precious seconds passed. 'Bhajan can teleport the pair of you into the lab once you're close enough, and they just said there's no-one there. You won't need to be invisible. But we do need to figure out who this 'Mr Thoun' is, and we're not gonna get another chance.'

'Alright, fine! But you're taking this with you!' Dawkes shoved something into my hand, which turned out to be a small transceiver.

'The moment, no, the second something goes wrong, you let us know. And if we get in touch with you, I don't care if he's detailing his entire evil plan, you get your arse back to us, clear?!'

'Yes. Good luck.'

I turned and started following where Thoun had gone, keeping my concealment active as I kept moving. Thankfully, without having to split my focus on covering two others, I felt my own, indistinct form blur into near-invisibility.

As I rounded the corner, I caught sight of him again, just about to turn down another path, and I pursued, only to stop short when more Lemurians, dressed in lab coats and talking animatedly, came down the same path. I pressed myself to the wall, trying not to breath too hard while the three walked past, unaware.

Too close. I was getting into the heart of the facility now.

In my pursuit, I had to stop to avoid another small group of Lemurians, a mix of guards and researchers, going about their business. Aside from the worry of having more lizards to keep track of, it made keeping my target in my sights all the harder.

Still, I managed to just about stay a hallway away from him until I saw the man stop outside a door next to a waiting researcher, nodding then opening said door.

Once I got closer, I couldn't believe my luck that the door was still ajar, giving me a chance to look in, the man now seated at his desk while the Lemurian researcher fumbled through some notes.

'-And that should cover our recent movements, sir.' The researcher finished, his tone nebbishly bland.

Thoun leaned back for a moment. 'Indulge me a moment, Rauk, do you recall how I managed to gain command of this nest?'

Thoun's assistant looked up from his tablet, clearly thrown. 'Ah, well, if I recall correctly sir, it was after the Sidhe assault three years back. You were promoted in recognition of your valour and cunning in seeing the threat off.'

Thoun let out a laugh. 'That's technically true, but ultimately, I got this far because I survived. I survived the physical threat of our enemies, the social threat of my rivals and the constant threat of discovery.'

'Why do you tell me this?' Rauk responded, still looking apprehensive.

My heart pounded as I slid into the room, not wanting to miss a second.

Thoun continued. 'Because one does not survive as long as I do without developing a keen sense of potential threats. And right now, my intuition's telling me that this nest has finally been compromised.'

'You mean we might have intruders!?' Rauk just barely managed to keep his grip on the tablet as he stiffened.

I slid behind Thoun, trying to ignore the sudden dryness in my throat.

'As a matter of fact, I do. Not only do I think that our location has been discovered, I believe it is already being infiltrated.'

'You seem rather calm about that, sir.' Rauk said slowly.

Thoun looked up, his voice pensive. 'Do I? I suppose I must. After all, I know one thing our infiltrators don't.'

'What's that sir?' I leaned forward after Rauk asked that question, a nervous tension building in my spine.

'Illusions only work when your quarry hasn't spent years dealing with fae.'

The pounding in my chest stopped. A tiny voice in my head told me to run, but I was rooted to the ground.

Thoun turned around and looked straight at me, a smile on his face.

I bolted, only for what felt like a bolt of lightning to strike in the back of my right leg,, sending me to the ground.

I screamed, the pain swallowing up any coherent thought or action. I could only clutch the bloody wound as I wailed, my body becoming visible as my focus shattered completely.

Through squinted eyes, I was just about able to make out Thoun, casually holding a gun, strolling over, his smile parting slightly to reveal serrated teeth when he spoke.

'Well now. Isn't this an unfortunate situation?'

# Chapter 20

I wish I could say that I answered Thoun with defiance, but the truth was I could barely even see through the tears in my eyes, let alone muster any resistance.

As the Lemurian loomed over me, I tried to gather my will, only for another fresh surge of agony to scatter my thoughts, leaving me gasping on the floor.

The other Lemurian let out a shrill, shocked cry. 'Wha-an intruder! Hold on, sir! I'll alert the guards!'

'No need, Rauk. This one's disabled. Tell them that we have more interlopers running amok that they should watch for. Probably near the labs, if I were to guess.' Thoun responded, voice relaxed.

Now my eyes had stopped swimming, I was able to catch Rauk pause, looking at Thoun fearfully. 'Are you certain, Sir? If he's an Arbiter, he might still be dangerous.'

Thoun made a dismissive sound. 'Don't insult me. I've dealt with far worse than a crippled Enlightenment spy. Doesn't even have the will to work magic through his bullet wound.'

I immediately tried to reach for my will again, only for the sharp pain to tear down my leg once more. Shit. If I couldn't gather my willpower, I was about as magical as a stage magician.

'Very well. I'll tell them to prioritise finding any conspirators.' Rauk responded, his voice warbling with uncertainty.

Thoun nodded in satisfaction. The reedy Lemurian ran out the door. Thoun's eyes went back to me, a predatory gleam shining in them.

'Alone at last. Now, shall we discuss what brings you down to our humble abode?'

'Eat shit!' I barked back.

Not the best response, but you try being witty with a hole in your leg.

Thoun smirked. 'Forgive me, but somehow I doubt you came down here to do that.'

When I didn't respond, Thoun then sighed. 'Allow me to guess, obviously the Enlightenment has finally discovered our hiding space, was that enough reason to attempt to infiltrate us?'

Thoun continued. 'No, too simple. You must have a specific reason for coming down here. Something to find out. Is that any closer to the mark?'

'Why don't you tell me?!' I shot back, the pain making my voice come out strained. While I doubted he'd take the bait, I took the chance to slip my hand inside my pocket, pressing on the transceiver. Assuming Dawkes was still there, at least she'd be able to hear what was going on.

To my surprise, Thoun shrugged. 'Well, if you insist. It's clear that you've come down here to try to find evidence linking us to the bioweapon the Sidhe army have been throwing around, perhaps in the hope of finding some way to link us and the Sidhe as co-conspirators. A brazen move, though I can't imagine what you expected to find.'

Despite the pain, I was still able to muster up a sneer. 'Nice try, but we already know what happened on the Visitor ship. Tell me, did the Visitors do something to deserve that, or did you just need some test subjects?'

Thoun's posture stiffened, and for a second my heart pounded with fear that he'd pull the trigger. 'Ah, in that case, I'll dispense with the ambiguity. Yes, I did kill them, and no, it was not for anything they did. Rather, I needed them to die to ensure our work got the attention of the Enlightenment.'

'You killed your own allies just so we'd notice what you were doing?!' I regretted raising my voice, but I couldn't help it. What master plan could possibly require tipping off the one group of people who could stop you?!

Thoun just kept smiling that damn smirk. 'Of course. After all, with the bioweapon not effecting humans, I had to get creative if I wanted your masters to care about what I was doing. Though I take issue with you calling the Visitors our allies. That relationship was purely transactional, and, in fact, terminating that relationship seems to have done far more to help me than expected.'

'What do you mean?' I asked, it taking everything I had to keep the pain and confusion from showing in my voice.

Thoun let out a tired sigh, shaking his head. 'Is it not plain? I'm dropping as many hints as I can, for pity's sake. Think, young one, what possible reason, given what you've learned investigating this sorry mess, could we possibly have for trying to get the attention of the Enlightenment?'

Despite the pain, I tried to engage my brain.

Thinking about it, everything I'd seen from the Lemurians up to now, from the attack on the ship to the ambush at the rally seemed almost intentionally built to get attention from the Order.

But that didn't make any sense, Thoun had to realise that if High Command was threatened by the tensions in Ireland, they'd just order-

The thought stopped, the pain in my leg paling in comparison to my horror. 'Yo-you want the Enlightenment to purge the paranormals?!'

'Want? Certainly not. But that is the goal I'm working towards.' Thoun responded, looking only mildly put out.

'Why?! Even if you really thought the Lemurians could ride the bloodshed out without being found, we know where you're hiding now. Our men will come for you like everyone else!' I shouted, terrified. I couldn't believe this was happening, the Lemurians were going to drag all of Ireland into a bloody war, one that could go global, and I still couldn't understand why!

Thoun's only response was a click of the tongue. 'Disappointing. I'd hoped you might've put the last pieces together by now. Alas, I've delayed as much as I'm able. The rabble down here will no doubt start to ask questions if I've not dealt with you by now.'

He raised the gun to my head, the gesture resigned. 'Farewell, Agent Reilly. My congratulations on making it as far as you did.'

Even if I wanted to speculate on why Thoun had been spilling his guts to me, it was impossible.

I was going to die. I was going to die and it would've meant nothing. Even if Bhajan and Dawkes somehow manage to make it out with something worthwhile, it'll be despite my efforts, not because of them. At least I'd given them some warning, but that was cold comfort.

As Thoun readied the shot, I desperately tried to think of anything to do. I didn't want to die, and I couldn't let myself fail again, but as my heart pounded against my chest, every slight movement setting off another wave of agony from my leg, every effort to get a coherent idea together fell apart.

I couldn't do it. It was pointless. I was too weak to fight off the pain.

I was going to die like a dog, like I should've back in Dingle. Just like then, every mistake I'd made up to that point flashed in front of me. If only I'd stayed with the team, if only I'd hadn't played loner, if only I wasn't so damn repressed and pathetic–

–Because that's exactly what I was.

I'd spent years trying to fight my emotions, numbing myself so I could work magic without falling down the same pit I'd been down before. But that wasn't going to work anymore.

In that moment where adrenaline made the simple act of Thoun pulling the trigger last a lifetime, something clicked. I had a way out after all, even as I wished there was any other way. Now, staring down the gun barrel, a strange determination set inside me.

I won't fail again.

I reached deep into my consciousness, plunging down into my mind as I searched for the one thing that could save me, the very thing I'd been avoiding.

I found it, the part of my mind where I kept the vault, the one I locked so much of myself away in. The same place I'd stuck my past, and the emotions that always threatened to lash out at the world.

I'd thrown so many pieces of myself into that vault, because I knew what would happen if I let them out again, and because

I didn't want to be that person again.

But the world isn't fair. It doesn't let us hide the parts of ourselves we fear. Sooner or later, you must face what you really are.

I flung the vault open, and it was like a dam breaking. Raw emotion flooded my body as memories flashed before my eyes, memories I'd promised myself I would never let out from that dark place burned my insides.

For a split second I saw it all, the family, never very loving to begin with, looking with fear and hatred at the child who couldn't explain the strange powers he had. I remembered the woman who found that boy, who promised him purpose if he turned those gifts to her burgeoning cabal. The joy as he unleashed that power on any who crossed him, revelling in finally, finally having control in his sorry life.

And then, the shame, as I once again saw Dingle, the town in chaos as I released, with horror, what I'd helped bring about, the power I'd once saw as my salvation now tasting bitter.

Magic is powered fundamentally by will. And I had wasted a lot of willpower holding this maelstrom back. This time, I took the pain, the fear and the anger, and rather than repress them, I seized hold. I channelled them into one solid purpose.

Not again.

It was child's play to reach my mind towards my tattoos, drawing raw energy throughout my body. Opening my eyes, I could see Thoun had pulled the trigger, but as raw power enhanced me to superhuman levels, the bullet moved slowly, my perception easily keeping track of it.

I smirked, relishing the crackle under my skin, then flicked my hand out. Blade in hand, I let a whisper of the power flutter up the knife.

Time started moving again as I unleashed a wave of force directly at Thoun, sending him flying across the room. The bastard never even had a chance to react before he crashed into the wall.

Around us the furniture shattered, the walls cracked and the lights exploded, casting us both into near darkness.

I took my time getting up, the pain in my leg dulled by my tattoos reinforcing my limbs. I strolled over to where Thoun was lying, coughing painfully while he got his legs back under himself, looking up at me with a new expression.

He looked impressed.

'Now where were you hiding that?'

'Behind ten years of repression.' I responded. I'd started smiling, my skin hummed with power. 'You're not done already, are you?'

'Sorry to disappoint, Agent Reilly, but I've no intention of throwing away the opportunity you've just given me.' I saw Thoun rip his dress shirt open, revealing both intricate symbols on his skin and an inner pocket on the inside of the shirt.

He pulled out a small glass sphere from the pocket. 'Well done, perhaps you might beat him, after all.'

Thoun readied to throw the sphere to the ground, and, while I was planning on laying on more pain, the symbols on his skin caught my attention. I hadn't seen them many times before, but I recognised Geas-marks when I saw them.

With a half-second to react, I lashed out with my athame at Thoun just before the sphere hit the ground, releasing a sparkling cloud of dust that rose up, whisking Thoun up into itself, his body quickly discorporating.

Instead of slicing at him, I brought the knife through the

energy flow connecting the geas to their source. Thoun was just a puppet, so I focused my anger into finding whoever the real master was. If I could find out anything about who branded those geas into Thoun, I might finally have our culprit-

-Huh, well that was interesting.

The revelation probably would've been more a shock, but between the sheer power coursing through me and the need to use it, I barely registered it, as the last of Thoun vanished from sight, somewhere far away now.

No matter. I strode to the door, swinging it open.

On the other side, I saw two guards running in the opposite direction, only to pirouette at the door slamming, pausing when they caught sight of me.

I paused myself, then smiled. A little warmup wouldn't hurt.

The closer of the two readied his gun.

Through the Ogham, I sent boiling anger into my muscles and bones, time slowing to a crawl once again as I sprinted down the hall towards the Lemurian.

When I'd closed the distance, he'd not even fully raised the gun, and in one swift movement, I jammed my athame into the bastard's throat, the meat giving way like thick bread.

Then, I pulled back, and kicked him centre mass, the rib cage shattering under my shoe before the lizard was sent flying in slow motion, blood trailing through the air.

A heartbeat later, the Lemurian's body suddenly jetted across the hall as my burst of speed wore off, a loud crack and the sound of glass shattering echoing behind me from where I broke the sound barrier, then a meaty splat when the corpse smacked into the floor, a couple of metres away from the second guard.

He jolted back from the body, staring back at me, wide-eyed. I couldn't help a laugh escaping my lips. I'd almost forgotten what being feared felt like.

The guard raised his own gun. He might as well have shoved the barrel down his throat. Flicking the blood off my knife, I reached out to the area around me for power, feeling the erratic lines of electrical currents under walls and floor.

Perfect.

I pointed the blade towards the thickest of these currents in the floor, then thrust it towards the guard, who had just levelled his rifle only to meet with a tide of electricity erupting from the ground, spilling out like a net, which wrapped itself around the piece of crap.

His agonised screams melded with the crackling electricity, his body burning under the net as it squeezed, crushing the guard to the ground.

The lights went out. I heard the alarms fall quiet, their energy drained, the only electricity left in the area sparking along my body, eagerly licking out at the air, kept in check only by my command.

I was tempted to try and track down Thoun, in case the prick was still close by. But then I remembered the labs. Most of the security were probably already down there, hunting Dawkes and Bhajan.

'We'll see who's crippled now.' The thought sent trickles of hate through my limbs, giving me focus I hadn't felt in years. The tattoos glowed hot. Time slowed once more, and I took off, charging down the hall.

At first, I didn't feel like I was running faster, until I noticed the air pressing against the cocoon of force I'd encased my body in, enough to rip an unprotected body to shreds. My hands spread out to absorb any and all energy I could reach.

Electricity ran off the walls, following my charge, biting at my heels like a pack of dogs, until I felt like a lightning rod, drawing the entire complex's power towards myself.

I rounded the last corner and found myself looking down towards the lab doors, a pack of more than a dozen armed guards attempting to breach them. Clever Dawkes, must have locked them from inside. I'll have to thank her for leaving them for me.

I stopped at the end of the hall, letting time speed back up. I'm not sure if it was the sudden rush of wind or the still snapping and buzzing electricity, but the Lemurians turned in my direction.

'Evening Lads!' I called out, a harsh laugh slipping out. 'Having some bother with the door?'

These guards proved far smarter than the last pair, several rifles rising and firing without hesitation.

Had I been still holding back, that would've shredded me there and then, but now, all I felt when the first flurry of bullets struck against the shell of force covering my body was a faint sensation like getting being hit with raindrops, several loud pings echoing as the bullets ricocheted off the walls.

God, to think I was afraid of letting loose.

'Here, let me give you a hand with it.' I continued.

With a flick of the athame, I felt the power I'd been gathering surge to the blade. Both electrical and kinetic power met and mixed while I focused not on the guards, but the steel doors behind them. Ignoring the flying bullets, I pointed the athame towards the door, then outstretched my other hand.

With a whisper of 'Gluaiseacht', I pulled back the outstretched hand, the athame sending the energy towards the doors.

I felt the power seize hold of the doors, the steel bending and screaming before giving way, sending them flying forwards, right into the backs of the guards.

The lucky ones, near the edges of the blast, were send to the ground in a chorus of pained yells, blood splattered the walls as stray shrapnel did it's work.

The unlucky ones were the ones directly in front of the doors, who spent what was, judging from the look on their faces, a very short period of intense pain and confusion, before I thrust my hand towards, sending the two doors smashing face down on the floor with an organic crunch.

I stepped over the doors, my shoes making wet squelches when they briefly contacted some of the, ah, remains under the heavy steel. I saw the remaining guards trying to recover, a couple already pulling themselves up. Pathetic.

Gesturing with my still glowing blade, I channelled more electricity through it, my hairs standing on end. With a smirk, I kneeled to the floor, placing the tip of the athame to the ground and whispered 'Tintreach.'.

With my permission, lightning erupted across the ground in branches, each branch speeding towards a guard. Before the useless bastards could even yell a warning, the lightning set upon them, the screams combining with the odour of burning meat while I watched the lot of them flail, their bodies blackened like overdone steak.

Standing in the middle of that hallway, surrounded by the dead and the gore, I felt something build up inside me. I tried to fight it, as it pressed against my lips and nose, but it was just too much.

I laughed, the loud, unfamiliar noise echoing around me as I laughed more than I'd thought I was able to. I laughed at the bodies around me, for thinking they could stand in my way. I laughed at Thoun, who pushed me to the point where finally let it all out. I laughed at the Enlightenment, for thinking they could stick a living weapon in a suit and trust him to play nice.

And I laughed at myself, for being so delusional, for thinking I could or should ever hold back what I really was. Under all the pretence and self-repression, I was still the same force of destruction I was reared to be. And it was glorious to realise that at last.

'R-reilly?' A voice called out from what felt like miles away, and suddenly I was back in the hallway, lights shattered and alarms blaring. Looking over, I saw, standing slightly hunched in the doorway, Dawkes was looking at me, her expression unreadable.

I tried to stifle the laughter pouring out, clamping my hand over my mouth. 'Hey there, Dawkes. Glad I got here before I missed all the fun.'

Dawkes gave another of her looks. I was beginning to get fed up with those looks. 'Fun? Reilly...what the hell happened to you?'

I scowled, and the alarms nearby started warbling erratically in pitch. 'I got sick of pretending to be weak. That's what happened. You find anything useful in there, or am I going to have to do that for you as well?'

Dawkes' eyes narrowed, before she shook her head. 'J-just about. Not much in there aside from a few tanks where they're growing more of those monsters we saw at the restaurant. But I was able to get into their computer systems. They've been producing samples of the bioweapon here, but according to the system, they got the original sample from another source. There were a few other things as well, but security started kicking at the door before I could get too deep.'

'Speaking of kicking, where's Bhajan at? Don't tell me the hairy bastard went and got the Vanara on the endangered species list while I was gone!' Another laugh burst out of me, feeling slightly giddy.

'Oh no, my friend! Here I be!' Bhajan's grating voice scratched against my ears while he stepped out, sporting a couple new bruises. 'Had a small scuffle with some brigands protecting the inside of the lab, but all-'

He stopped mid-step, taking in the scene I'd left in my wake. '-Ah. A bit more vicious than your normal methods, don't you think?'

'I'm getting sick of this conversation.' I responded, glancing over at Dawkes. 'Fine, doesn't sound like much, but with what I learned from Thoun, it'll do. We're leaving, now.'

Of course, that's when Dawkes chose to start talking again. 'Hang on! We're not done yet! Sure, I was able to get into their systems, but I only scratched the surface. Besides, that wasn't the only thing I found, there was also-'

God, will she just shut her gob, already? I clenched my fists, letting the electrical buzzing across my knuckles sooth me. 'Don't care. I'm leaving, and I'm taking down anyone I find on the way out. You can come with or stay down here. Makes no difference to me.'

I started stalking down the hallway, taking deep breaths as I felt power build up in my body again, hoping I'd soon find an excuse for another bout. After a short bit, I heard footsteps coming up behind, and I glanced over, only to be disappointed by the sight of my tagalongs following me.

I glowered at the pair, then turned my attention back to the corner I was about to turn. Up ahead, I could hear what sounded like more, frantic footsteps. Rounding the corner, I grinned in anticipation for something to really get my teeth into, only to see, scrambling down the hall in the direction of the lift, maybe a dozen Lemurians, dressed in labcoats and clutching small handguns, already raised towards us.

Researchers, ugh. I rolled my eyes as bullets bounced off my invincible frame. Won't be as much fun as the guards, but at least I'd get some payback for all the bioweapon shit I'd had to deal with. Dawkes started to say something, which was quickly drowned out when I thrust out my athame again, this time projecting a blade of force straight through the head of the nearest lizard.

Before he'd even fully dropped, I stabbed the blade into the nearest wall, this time sending the kinetic force through the wall towards the other researchers. A few tried to keep firing, only for the part of the wall they huddled near to suddenly explode outwards like a giant grenade, the force shredding metal and bodies, their screams cut short.

Once the metal had stopped grinding, I stepped forward, moving to the side to avoid some of the more jagged pieces and viscera, making my way to the lift. Pressing the button, I waited a few moments until the doors opened with a light clunk, then turned back to the others.

Dawkes looked a bit pale, her hand cupped to her mouth as she stared at the remnants of the researchers, while Bhajan's eyes flicked between the bodies and me, his posture guarded. Wimps. I knew letting the real me out would have this effect. That's why I spent so long pretending to be someone else.

'Lift's free.' I said, walking in and leaning against the wall, mentally counting down from sixty.

Lucky for them, the chuckleheads found their nerves long enough to step in before I got to twenty. Dawkes pressed a button, and the doors shut closed, the lift going up.

The ride up was mercifully short, neither of the clowns trying to make conversation. Good, I already knew what I needed to do next. The second the doors opened, I pushed past both and marched to the exit of the building, just halfway through the doors before I heard Bhajan's voice rip at my eardrums again.

'Where the hell are you off to now?!'

I took a long moment to remind myself it'd be a waste of energy to fry him, slamming the door open and walking out. 'Feeling pretty sick of pissing about when we know who's the main threat. Figured I'd cut to the chase and track down some Sidhe and fry them until they tell me where Nechtan's hiding, and I'd appreciate not having any hangers-on.'

You'd think slamming a door in someone's face would give them a hint, but neither of my tagalongs were particularly smart. Dawkes immediately opened the door again and sped up behind me, Bhajan a few footsteps behind. 'You're being ridiculous. We supposed to discredit Nechtan, not make him a martyr, remember?'

I felt heat rise across my body. I'd gone years without being able to terrorise some poor bastards, I wasn't wasting another second. Especially not with Little Miss Concerned dancing on my last nerve. 'Piss off. I know what I'm doing. Just shut up and let me crack some damn heads.'

'No!' Dawkes' voice grated shrilly in my ear and a hand clasped my shoulder. My vision went red. 'Listen, Reilly! You're acting like a psychopath right now! If you'd just bloody listen for one sec-'

'I told you to shut the fuck up!' I roared, spinning around, anger spilling out in one glorious moment.

The windows gave with shattering crashes and electricity spilled out from the gaps of my clothing into the air.

Then it came. That fatal second where it strikes you the horrible mistake you've just made, when its too late to stop it. I saw the lightning and force in the air whip out in front of me. Right at Dawkes and Bhajan.

In the split second before it struck, fear erupted in my gut as I reached out with my will, trying to order the power back in line.

When I'd slaughtered my way out of the lab, it'd been with flourish and grandeur, the heady mix of euphoria and rage making me want to experiment with all the ways I could tear apart the ones who'd given me so much grief.

There was none of that in the magic that hit my teammates. A lashing electrical whip struck Dawkes in the face, the wave of kinetic force knocking the wind out her gut and sending her rolling to the ground.

Bhajan threw his arms up in a protective stance, only for them to get torn into by sparking tendrils. He was then too struck by the oncoming wave, sending Bhajan careening back through the doors, the glass shattered when he was thrown though, his limp form collapsing to the floor inside.

It was like a switch was flicked inside my head. All the anger and arrogance evaporated, as horror creeped in. All the power I'd been building up inside faded away, my will to keep it contained slipped, eaten up by terror.

No.

No no no no, please no!

Not again! Why did I have to give in again?! Why did I make the same damn mistake that ruined my life the first time?! I'd lasted ten years, keeping those thoughts, those urges at bay, why had I fallen now?!

Staring at the prone bodies of the two people who'd trusted me to have their backs, there was nothing I could say. I couldn't even open my mouth. My mind was swallowed up by the enormity of how badly I'd fucked up. So, I did the only thing I still could.

I turned and ran. I sprinted away from the Lumintech building, from the pile of corpses I'd left in my wake and the people I'd hurt playing supervillain.

It'd happened again. In that moment, I wasn't an agent of the Enlightenment, an invincible badass or even a man on a mission.

I was just a scared boy running away from the problems he'd caused.

Maybe I never stopped running.

# Chapter 21

I can't remember how long I ran.

When awareness returned, I was sprawled on the ground, lungs and throat burning, the bullet hole in my leg screaming. I couldn't think, the cocktail of pain, exhaustion and sheer depletion of willpower leaving me practically comatose.

All I could do was lay there, stuck in that place where consciousness loses all sense of time, giving way to only flashes pulled out of your subconscious, most often the parts you regret.

That was certainly the case face down on the pavement, the images of Dawkes and Bhajan's faces kept smashing into my mind's eye, the gore and violence I'd been responsible for, the screams of the people I'd killed, not because they were a threat, but because I wanted to kill them.

The articles floated into my mind once, but where they'd once given purpose and stability, was now just more proof of my guilt. An agent does what is necessary for the task. No more. No less. Innocence is the bedrock of reality. An agent must never panic. By all metrics, I'd failed as an agent, and a person.

Thought might've been impossible, but emotion wasn't. Bitter tears ran down my face.

I must have vomited, because I tasted bile. In the state I was in, a car could've run over me, and if I even noticed, it'd would've been to thank the driver. So when I felt something lift me off the ground, I didn't even make a token resistance. Frankly, if the Lemurians or Sidhe caught up to me and killed me for what I'd done, so much the better.

What else are you meant to do to a rabid dog?

I drifted off into unconsciousness. That blissful state of no thought didn't last.

Ice cold water smacked my face. I awoke instantly, spluttered.

Light stabbed at the gaps in my eyelids while I struggled to force them open, a dark figure looming over me. The figure in front of me took proper form, revealing Calatin standing over me, his face grave as he lowered a half-empty bucket.

'Ah, that did the trick.' He said quietly, dropping the bucket to the ground. 'Guessing you've had quite the rough time of it, Arbiter?'

I blinked rapidly and looked around. We were in a sparse room, the only standout details being the wooden walls, a couple of chairs, one of which I was sprawled on, and a coffee table separating the two. I couldn't see any door or windows, the only exit point being some stairs tucked away in a corner behind me.

'W-wha-where are we?' I managed to spit out, the brief clarity the cold water had given me already fading, confusion and fatigue began to cloud my head again.

Calatin put a hand out in a reassuring gesture. 'In a backroom of the Silver Arm. Don't worry. It's just the two of us right now.'

'Alright, alright.' I muttered, trying to will my stream of

consciousness back into a coherent shape. 'Then why...why are we here?'

'Figured it would be a better spot to bring you than the pavement I found you on.' Calatin responded, his tone carrying a somewhat strained attempt at humour. 'Speaking of which, what happened to you?'

'I-I was...' I tried to start, only for another ache from my leg melting my words into a pained gasp.

'Easy, easy there, lad.' A pair of strong hands gripped my shoulders as my eyes watered, then suddenly, the pain in my leg disappeared, and I felt a sudden calm flow across my body. My head, while still feeling like it was full of felt, slowed down the mad stream that was my thought process.

I slumped back in the chair with an exhale, and Calatin hunkered down to look me in the eyes. 'Now, from the top, lad. What happened to you tonight?'

It took me a few seconds, but eventually my mouth started moving by itself. 'I and two others had discovered the location of the Lemurians' nest. We had gone in to try and find proof that they were involved in stirring up the paranormal violence. We discovered a lab in the nest that was reproducing the bioweapon, as well as a Lemurian who we believe was responsible for releasing the bioweapon on the Visitor ship.'

Calatin nodded. 'I see, and were you discovered? Were you attacked?'

'Yes, but we were able to fight them off and escape.'

'Then why were you on the pavement, sobbing into a puddle of vomit?'

'B-' I stopped when another surge of misery fought to get to the surface, taking a gasped breath. 'Because to escape the Lemurians, I had to throw everything I had at them. I...had to let something out I thought I'd locked away, that I'd finally started to move past. A-and during our escape, I l-lashed out at my teammates. Hurt them. I couldn't face them after that.'

'I'd wondered about that. You've gone to great lengths to hide just how much power you actually have, haven't you?' Calatin responded, his eyes taking on a sad quality. 'Being able to corral that much raw will so young, I should've guessed trauma gave you reason to learn that skill.'

My first instinct, as always when my past came up, was to change the topic, but some distant impulse made me speak up. 'W-when I was younger, before I joined the Enlightenment, I struggled with it. Didn't know about magic back then, just that weird things kept happening around me and everyone close to me was afraid or hated it.'

Calatin's eyes glanced away, and he sighed. 'One of the great tragedies of the modern world. Even with all the mass surveillance modern technology gives us, some still slip through the gaps. How'd it start?'

I suppressed a flinch as memories bashed against my skull, but now that'd I'd started, the words fell out of me. 'When I was seven. All the lights and electronics started going haywire when I was in the room, things would just fling themselves off shelves around me. Hell, one time when I got in a fight with a bigger kid, I wound up breaking his jaw with a slap. No one knew what the fuck was going on, but they knew I was the source.'

'Allow me to guess the rest.' Calatin replied, his expression darkening. 'Your family rejected you, scared and hating what they didn't understand. You either got thrown out or ran away, wandered the streets feeling like a monster until the Enlightenment found you, and gave you the tools to control your power, in exchange for being their attack dog.'

'More or less.' I responded, letting my gaze drop to the ground. That wasn't nearly the full story, but even dazed, I didn't want to say any more.

No reaction came, and I chanced looking back up, only for a broad hand to rest itself on my head. 'Poor lad. Doesn't take a genius to see how badly life's treated you. You finally found a purpose worth fighting for, only for monsters to tear at the very foundations of that purpose. Would that you'd been able to purge the whole sorry lot of those lizards, but at least we've found our culprits.'

'Wait. T-that's not right.' I spoke up, numbly brushing Calatin's hand off. 'The Lemurians were dangerous, yes, but they're not the ones responsible for everything that's happened.'

Calatin gave me a gimlet eye. 'Seems clear-cut to me, lad. They're the ones creating the virus, which they've likely provided to Nechtan to kill off the opposition. Perhaps the Lemurians and Sidhe are even allied. Once they've got their rivals out of the way, the Enlightenment would be their next target.'

'There's more to this. When I confronted Thoun, I saw he'd been branded with Geas marks.'

'Oh?' Calatin leaned away from me.

'I was able to get hold of the sympathetic connection binding the marks to their caster. Get a read on the person that had been manipulating him.' I continued, my words speeding up as the realisation hit that Calatin was exactly who I needed to tell this.

Calatin remained cautious. 'Very interesting. Tell me, what did you find out?'

'I couldn't learn their identity, but I recognised the style and feel of the magic used.' I looked up at Calatin. 'Hierophant, I believe a member of the Ciorcal Darach was responsible for those brands.'

Calatin's lips pursed as he paced across the room. 'A telling clue indeed. One might say that you've all but caught your man.'

'Hierophant, please. I understand I'm asking a lot, but if you know anything about who in your cabal could've cast that geas, it could lead us right to the culprit. We could stop this interparanormal conflict before it has the chance to escalate beyond Dublin.'

Calatin let out a small chuckle. 'That there's the sticking point, isn't it, lad? What if a war's exactly what we need?'

'Hierophant?' I replied.

'Humour me, lad. Wouldn't you agree that one of the biggest issues facing Ireland is the many paranormal entities running about, flouting the established order and constantly tearing into each other and the humans unlucky enough to get caught in the middle?'

I felt my throat go dry. 'T-to some extent, but that's all been squabbling so far in comparison. Outright war would be so much worse, hundreds, thousands would die unless-.'

'Unless the Enlightenment stepped in, aye? Put down all the paras in one fell swoop before they could damage paranormal secrecy and human lives.' Calatin spoke over me, his eyes taking on a feral quality.

I paused, wondering for a moment if Calatin might've had a point. Images of the abductees on the Visitor craft, the Fachan attempting to butcher Viora for trespassing and the beasts the Lemurians unleashed that only just narrowly didn't get into the streets all flashed before me.

Then I remembered the opposite side of the coin. I remembered each time Bhajan took a risk working with me, and Viora's frightened stare into my soul, and I shook my head.

Article 6. The paranormal is not inherently evil. But it is inherently dangerous.

The paranormal is inherently dangerous. But it is not inherently evil.

'No. No, this is all wrong. The paras are an issue but butchering them is just going to make things spiral. Even the Sidhe aren't restricted to Ireland anymore, and when the para communities worldwide learn about it, they'll join forces. Rise up in resistance to the Enlightenment. We'd throw the entire supernatural world into war.'

Calatin's mouth twisted into a sharp grin, not one speck of his previous jovialness left. 'Excellent, I'd hope for nothing less! Think about it, Reilly! How much longer do we have to scrape by, just slapping down the occasional para snatching someone off the streets, when we could tackle the problem at its roots! Think of the human lives that won't be ruined because some supernatural monster decided to turn them into a plaything! An excuse to wipe these filthy beasts out is exactly what we need!'

'You're as-assuming we'd win.' I croaked back.

With a surge, Calatin was on me, our noses practically touched. 'I know we'd win! Why do you think these monsters, once so brazen as to snatch babes from their cribs and devour any who wandered too far into the woods now cower in the shadows?! They're afraid, Reilly! Afraid of the billions of humans, ready to take their revenge on the things that go bump in the night back when we were few and ignorant! Sheer numbers alone would overwhelm them now!'

'At what cost, Calatin! How many lives would have to be lost for humanity to win that war?!' I tried to shout back, despite the now insidious calm trying to push me down.

Calatin's nostrils flared. 'To keep supernatural abominations from ever destroying another life? From killing women and children in their own home? Enough.'

My mouth numbly flapped, my thoughts started to feel like they were moving through sludge. 'Thi-this is about Dingle, isn't it? One Sidhe killed your family and now you want to drag the entire human race into a war of survival!?'

I could see my words hit Calatin, his massive frame went rigid. 'We're already fighting for survival. Every damn day. I learned that in Dingle, but I also learned that the Enlightenment isn't prepared to take the steps necessary to protect humanity. They didn't hunt down the monsters that fled the town after razing it, they didn't follow those monsters to their dens and burn them out. All they did was cut down the cabal that summoned them, wiped a few memories, published a few cover stories and left it at that.'

I felt Calatin's very presence seem to shift, the sheer power radiating off him overwhelming to the point of almost making me vomit. 'I'm only doing this to push the Enlightenment to do what needs to be done. To make sure what happened to my family never happens to anyone else!'

And there it was.

All the chasing down leads, stalking paras and breaking into hideouts had all been pointless. Because the real threat had been one of the first people I'd gone to for help.

'I-it's you.' I whispered hoarsely. 'You created the bioweapon.'

Calatin's red face seemed to lose a bit of colour. He let out a frustrated huff. 'Damn. I always did have a habit of letting things slip when I'm heated. Aye, that was me. I spent years devising that virus, tweaking variables here and there, infusing it with the essence of iron, within a silver chalice, under the light of an eclipse, all to form it into the ultimate weapon for killing paras. After that, it was just a matter of letting it get into the right hands, then watching those monsters kill each other with it.'

Of course, of fucking course it was the one person I knew in all of Dublin who was an expert at life magic. We'd even given him the bioweapon sample because we assumed he'd know how to crack it! All of it, from the Visitor ship, right down to the Lemurians getting their own sample, was all from the same man I'd been using as a confidant.

I wanted to scream, to kick and shout, but more than that, I wanted to put a stop to this bloody madness right now. I surged to my feet, reaching for my athame.

But I only got as far as lifting off the chair, before my legs gave out from under me. My chest slammed against the coffee table; the sensation painless. I sent signals for my arms to move, only for them to twitch lazily in response.

I kept trying to force my body to co-operate, even as each limb started to feel alien and distant, when I heard Calatin's voice. 'I wouldn't bother, lad. You've about as much chance of moving a mountain as you do getting up.'

'Wh-what's happening?' I spat out through numb lips, cold fear managing to break through some of the calm that now pressed down on me.

'That'd be the other iteration of my plague coursing through your veins. I'd hoped not to have to resort to using a virus that could kill humans, but you've thrown one too many wrenches into my plans.' Calatin's voice, now eerily calm, sent a renewed surge of terror through me.

'H-how-?' I wasn't even sure myself what was meant to come after that. How did he create another bioweapon? How'd he manage to infect me with it? How much time did I have left? Each question clamoured for space.

Calatin's voice betrayed no emotion. 'Small sample on my gloves, seeped right through your skin. It's what's numbing your emotions right now. If you'd seen sense, I'd have been able to cure you, leave you none the wiser. A shame. I saw a great deal of potential in you, but seems the best I can do for you is a painless death.'

Had I really been so blind this whole time? Maybe this was fitting. I'd spent my entire life making stupid decisions, getting close to the wrong people while letting down the few who made the mistake of trusting me. Dying, face flat on a coffee table, body unable to so much as twitch, after alienating anyone who'd want to help me.

Perhaps that was exactly the sort of death I deserved, after having played right into Calatin's plans, helped him spark the war he'd been working towards and throwing away years of self-discipline and repression for a brief thrill of power.

A failure's death.

What little resistance my muscles had vanished.

It was pointless. Any willpower I'd left had already been wasted back at the lab, and even if I could somehow force myself up, Calatin would wipe the floor with me.

Besides, I was so damn tired.

Tired of keeping myself under control, tired of the paranormals and their petty bullshit squabbling that Calatin would use to kill them, and tired of knowing that, despite all my efforts, I always wound up in the same place. On the ground, regretting everything.

I deserved this.

My vision began blurring, and I readied myself to accept my overdue punishment, when a single thought interrupted my misery.

Maybe it was a futile gesture, but fuck it.

'J-just tell me what this is all building to, Calatin.' My voice slurred. 'You owe me that much.'

I wasn't sure if Calatin would take the bait, but after what seemed like a contemplative moment, he replied. 'Credit where it's due, Arbiter, you threw me for a few loops. I'd hoped this iteration of the bioweapon would be a last resort, but when you came to me with the sample I'd sent to the Sidhe, I knew it'd only be matter of time before the Enlightenment picked up my scent. The original plan was to simply keep supplying the paras with the tools of their own destruction until the Enlightenment had only a couple of pockets to clean up, but now I'm going to have to escalate this.'

I opened my mouth to ask him to go on, but Calatin was apparently on a roll now. 'I've already been informed by your superiors that reinforcements are due to try and keep the para infighting under control. That's why I'm going to start handing out this new iteration to my catspaws. As much as it disgusts me to take human life, once your command hears of the threat Dublin now presents to them and humanity as a whole, they'll send a proper force to purge this island of its supernatural filth once and for all, and continue the war beyond. Then, only then, will my family finally be avenged.'

'T-then there's something you ought to know, Calatin.'

I mustered up what little control I had left over my mouth. 'You've been assuming that the paranormals that attacked Dingle had used the human cabalists as tools to summon a legion of paras into Dingle, right?'

'What are you getting at?' Though he tried to disguise his tone, I could tell I had Calatin's attention.

'I'm saying that it wasn't the intention of the Sidhe called forth that night to come down on the town...It was the cabalists who called them, who set them on Dingle to destroy everything there.'

In the blink of an eye, Calatin was on me, lifting me up by my collar. 'How do you know that?! How could you possib-'

I don't know why I said what I said next, why I admitted it then after years of pretending it never happened. Maybe it was some attempt at penance, or possibly I just wanted to take one stab at shaking Calatin's resolve before I died.

But ultimately, why I said what I said next wasn't nearly as important as what I said.

'Because I was one of them.'

Even through my darkened vision, I could see Calatin's face go slack with shock, his eyes widening, before almost as abruptly twisting with rage. With what little control I had left over my own facial muscles, I managed a small smirk.

Before Calatin could react, there was a thunderous crash from, as far as my diminished hearing could tell, a room over. Calatin dropped me in surprise, the impact as I slammed back against the table not even registering.

Calatin looked between the direction of the sound, and my prone form for a second, before snarling out a curse and striding towards the noise, barrelling up the stairs.

I couldn't see what was going on, but what I could hear next sounded like absolute pandemonium. I heard wood shatter and glass smash, multiple voices shouted over and at each other, becoming an indiscernible mess of noise.

Calatin let out a pained scream at one point, followed by what I was sure was the sound of a swarm of angry bees as the other voices yelped and cried out. After that, the noise seemed to die down, but just as I was getting ready to die in peace, I heard footsteps charge down the stairs, then a gasp.

'Reilly!' Dawkes' voice, now sounding miles away, still managed to shock me. What was she doing here? How did she even find me?

As I heard distant footsteps get closer, some small part of me remembered what was currently killing me, and I tried to shout out for Dawkes not to touch me but could only manage a garbled 'Dun tuc muh!'

Then, as if that last effort to speak was the last thing my body was holding on for, I could feel my consciousness start to drift away, everything starting to feel cold. From what was left of my eyesight, I caught a glimpse of two silhouettes standing over me, it didn't matter anymore.

In the split second before unconsciousness took me completely, one thought came to the forefront.

'So it really was painless.'

# Chapter 22

The first thing that hit my senses was the half-pain of a mostly healed wound around my knee.

Next came the sensation of a blanket on top of me, then a mattress. After that, a hoarse moan came from somewhere under my nose, which picked up the scent of something burnt.

With sense after sense returning to me, my mind started to piece itself back together, enough for me to start wondering what the hell was happening. I ventured opening my eyes, both resisting before slowly, jerkily opening, only to instantly close as light stabbed into my retinas.

As I was weighing the pros and cons of never opening my eyes again, I heard something move to my right, ruffling the edges of my blanket.

Normally I would've tried to pull myself into action, but my usual slip into danger mode was hamstrung. I just ended up awkwardly pushing away from the threat, forcing my eyes open as I sprawled across the bed.

Once the initial burst of light was done searing into my brain, the first thing I saw was a tall, spindly figure, it's shape only slightly bulked out with baggy clothing.

Even with clear vision, it took my scrambled head a moment to recognise Viora, her black eyes the only feature I could make out before the rest of her face came into focus, her mouth open in a silent gasp, as a hand reached cautiously towards me.

'Alive. Awake' She said, the words coming out as a faint whisper as Viora stared right into me, completely still. Though her body language was stiff as ever, I got the distinct sense that she was incredibly relieved.

'Believe me, I'm as surprised as you are.' The words struggled past my dry throat. I dared a look around. It was my bedroom, right down to the small collection of piled clothing in the corner I kept meaning to wash at some point.

I suppose I ought to have felt relieved, but as my memories start reforming, I was anything but.

I shouldn't be alive right now, I was inches from death when I passed out, and from what Calatin had told me, there was no way my rescuers could've just removed the virus, not unless Calatin just happened to leave a cure sitting out in the open.

I tried worrying at the questions for maybe half a second, before I realised I'd have no chance of figuring any of it out without asking some questions. Turning my attention back to Viora, I saw that she was still on top of me, still staring intently, I don't think she'd moved at all while I was thinking. I must have gotten better at reading her, because I could tell that she had let some worry creep back into her mind.

'Don't suppose you're planning on filling me in? Also, I don't think I'm going to start puking blood or anything, so you can get off now.' I remarked.

Viora blinked, then pulled back quickly, stumbling back to her feet.

'Monkey and other Enlightenment came back. Claimed Enlightenment had fled in panic and wanted help tracking down. Other Enlightenment found location using communication device to track audio transceiver. Went, returned two hours later with unconscious Enlightenment, claimed found Enlightenment at 'Silver Arm' with what other Enlightenment called 'Calatin' and what Monkey called 'Crazy Druid Motherfucker', who escaped after turning wooden furniture and floor into animate hostiles.'

I pulled myself into a sitting position as Viora relayed all that, more confused than ever. Dawkes being able to track me through the transceiver wasn't a surprise, I'd have been more shocked if she couldn't do that, given her literal tech wizardry.

But why? Did she and Bhajan want payback? To turn me over to Enlightenment custody for assaulting another agent? I couldn't be sure, but those questions paled in comparison to the big one.

'Why am I still alive?' I said. 'Calatin infected me. I was moments from death when I blacked out. We still don't even know how to cure the first bioweapon, so why hasn't this one killed me yet?'

Viora didn't say anything, but I could practically feel the whirl of emotions that seemed to come out of her. A thick cocktail of apprehension and anxiety came off her in a way I hadn't realised I was even capable of noticing.

'Need to get others. Explain better.'

My face went cold as she walked to the door, knocking on it a couple of times. My mouth opened to try and stop her, only to be cut off by another voice from outside.

'Yeah? Everything alright in there?' Dawkes spoke through the door. God, she was here? Was she keeping an eye on me, in case I went rabid again?

'Awake. Needs explanation for survival.' Viora replied.

'Right. One sec, I'll get Bhajan to go in.' Dawkes' own voice hurriedly replied, followed by the sound of movement.

Wish I could've mustered any shock at the notion she wouldn't want to be near me.

The door swung open, Bhajan strolling in, his arms spread wide as he grinned with all his sharp teeth on display.

'As I live and breathe, so do you!' He bellowed in my direction, Viora noticeably wincing as he closed, leaning against the wall on his elbow. 'Should've known it would take more than a supervirus to put you down, eh?'

I made to speak, to ask him what was going on, and in doing so, caught my first proper sight of his arms. The fur along each of Bhajan's forearms was visibly blackened and burnt from where he'd thrown up his arms to defend himself from my outburst, a few patches scorched away completely, showing red, blistered skin. The pattern repeated in a few patches on his chest, enough to show that he was still hurting from what I did to him.

I was suddenly back outside Lumintech, staring down at Bhajan and Dawkes, Bhajan still on the ground while Dawkes looked up with fear and pain, clutching her torso. My breath stuck in my throat, the reality of my own monstrousness staring me in the face all over again. I wanted to scream, but I couldn't even move. Tears ran down my cheeks.

The next thing I remember, I was lying flat on the bed again, Viora cradling my head and murmuring something inaudible while Bhajan leaned over, his expression grave. At some point I must've bitten my tongue, judging from the sharp pain and taste of blood.

Viora looked over at Bhajan, a sense of cautious relief coming off her. 'Easy. Was able to relieve the attack, but much trauma still there.'

Bhajan let out a breath though puffed cheeks. 'You certainly weren't exaggerating. Our friend is indeed in a much poorer state than we thought.'

Leaning a bit closer, Bhajan waved a hand in front of my face. 'Agent Reilly. Can you hear me? Do you know where you are?'

'B-Bhajan!' I pulled myself up. 'I-I'm sorry, I didn't mean-it wasn't intenti-that is...'

As I tried to apologise, each effort kept shrivelling up in my mouth. What could I say? What combination of words could I even attempt to force out that would do anything to fix what I'd done?

Bhajan just scratching his chin. 'Naturally. I don't think anyone has panic attacks intentionally. You've given us quite a few scares the last couple of hours, my friend. How're you feeling right now?'

The shock from his response hit me so badly I felt myself freeze up again.

'Am-am I okay?' I finally managed to say. 'Are you okay?! How the fuck can you ask me that while you're still covered in burns?!'

'Oh, these?' Bhajan raised one arm up and turned it back and forth. 'Don't get me wrong, still sting like a bitch. But flesh heals, especially when a certain unconscious friend is kind enough to donate his healing potions. Apologies of that, but given the circumstances, I think we can call it even.'

I was completely thrown.

Dammit, no more dancing around the point. 'You can drop the friendly act, Bhajan. I don't expect us to still be on good terms after what happened.'

Bhajan let out a huff of air. 'I haven't forgotten, friend, and we do need to have words about that. But nothing's ever being achieved by jumping to conclusions without knowing the full story.'

'What's there to know?! I fucking electrocuted you! Why the hell does it matter why I did it?!' I spat the words out as I pulled myself up. I'd turned into a cackling lunatic right in front of him, murdered an entire lab's worth of researchers and fried both him and Dawkes, why the hell hadn't Bhajan snapped my neck already!?

Bhajan lifted a finger. 'For one, a man who was trying to kill us wouldn't have immediately run away and refuse now to make excuses. Which tells me there's a little more going on than you'd like to let on. If you're truly sorry for hurting the lovely lady and myself, the best way to apologise right now would be to explain what exactly happened to you back there.'

'That's certainly what I'd like to know myself.' Another voice cut in, one I shuddered to hear, as I caught sight of Dawkes lingering at the door, holding herself a bit rigid.

'Dawkes?' My voice came out hoarse, the mere sight of her enough to send guilt crashing down on top of me. Bhajan seemed to be making a show of not being that injured, but Dawkes wasn't putting on any act. I couldn't see any visible wounds, save for a couple of cuts along her face from what was probably shattered glass, but her stiff posture alone was enough to remind me I'd made a victim of her too.

Again, for some unfathomable reason, rather than shoot me on the spot, Dawkes instead spoke tiredly. 'Hey, Reilly. Don't take it personally if I hang back here. We still don't know what the exact state of the virus is right now. I could still catch something if I get too close.'

Normally I might've tried to refocus, but right now I jumped at the chance to change the topic. 'I meant to ask about that. The virus was going to kill me in a matter of minutes, at most. What did you do?'

Dawkes' face twisted in discomfort. 'Something pretty radical. Suppose we should go over it quickly. You've probably had an easier time noticing Viora's emotions about now, right?'

'Guess so.' I noted idly, confused for a moment before the pieces suddenly rushed together. 'Wait, are we in some sort of telepathic link right now?!'

Viora flinched slightly. A quick flash of guilt, layered with some offence, echoed across my mind. Bhajan stepped back, scratched his head nervously as Dawkes took a breath.

'Like I said, we had to get unorthodox to save you. You're right that, when we managed to get to you, you were practically on death's door. Only reason we were able to even figure out what was wrong with you was because of the files I got down in the lab.'

'The files?' I replied, only vaguely remembering Dawkes mention something about that in the middle of my killing spree.

Dawkes nodded. 'Yeah, remember how I said I found some other interesting details? One of them was that the Lemurians' virus dealer had introduced them to some variant of the bioweapon exclusive to humans, apparently part of some backup plan. Vague, I know, but they were pretty hush about the whole thing. Still had enough details that I knew what we were looking at when we saw you arse-up on the coffee table.'

'That explains how you knew about the virus, but it still leaves the question: How'd you treat it?'

Dawkes shrugged. 'We didn't exactly treat it. The whole deal with all these viruses flying around is that they're of magical origin, right? Well, I remembered all the screwing around you did with the sympathetic wards on the lift, and it gave me an idea. We've been assuming up to now that the viruses spread like normal diseases, most likely airborne, with magic just enhancing the contagiousness of it, but what if the viruses work on sympathetic magic as well?'

That hadn't even occurred to me. 'You mean, the reason we've never found any traces of them on victims is because the virus uses a magical link to infect its targets? Infecting based on some abstract similarity rather than just conventional disease transmission?'

Dawkes' eyes brightened. 'Exactly! It would also explain how some random virus could be made to easily infect anything paranormal while leaving humans completely untouched, and why we were never able to find any proper traces outside of contained samples! The virus isn't acting like a normal virus; it's been magically altered to latch onto that sympathetic link, only infecting what it's programmed to infect! By using the initial infected as a voodoo doll, it can jump towards anyone else within a certain range who fits the same criteria, which is anything non-human!'

'Then, once it's killed the infected, the spell ends, leaving the virus to vanish without a trace from any corpses it leaves behind.' I mused.

It didn't sound impossible per se, but it was out there. The whole concept of sympathetic magic was about linking like with like so doing something to one target would affect the other. That added up so far, but doing that with a virus implied some seriously precise magic work.

Effectively, the virus' creator would have to enchant the germ itself to be able to establish such links itself, then the ability to act on it independently. Not impossible, but effectively the magical equivalent of brain surgery.

And Calatin had made multiple viruses.

Dawkes continued. 'So, assuming that's the case, I figured, if we could find a way to establish a magical link between you and someone else, we might be able to trick the virus into thinking the other person's an extension of you, so the same magic that was eating your insides could be siphoned off into them, delaying the effects.'

I shook my head. 'But how would you even do that? I'm assuming you didn't snatch some sorry git off the streets to take the bullet, but if you could find a volunteer, you'd still need some way to establish that kind of connection.'

The room went quiet. I looked up, only to see Dawkes' eyes dart briefly between me and somewhere to my left. Bhajan wasn't much more help, just rubbing his chin with a wince.

Eventually, I let my gaze slide over to the only person left.

I saw Viora, still perched on the corner of the bed, returning my stare, the air around her thick with trepidation.

'Wait. Viora? You used Viora?' I asked, not sure if I should be grateful, frightened or outraged.

'No use. Volunteer.' Viora responded quickly, her nervousness now extending to her voice.

'How? Okay, I can see how maybe her telepathy could be used as some kind of link between us, but you'd still need a way to make that connection significant enough to actually count as any sort of bond.'

'Not telepathy.' Viora spoke again before Dawkes could, then continued after a short glance between the two, holding up a bandaged hand, stained dark blue. 'Familiar bond.'

Come again?

I looked back up at the others, only to see Bhajan sinking further into his corner, and Dawkes just nodding.

'We used blood to establish the sympathetic bond. Viora volunteered to provide her own blood and you had plenty to spare from your bullet wound before we got the healing potion into it. We mixed the two lots of blood in a bowl, then Bhajan and I set up a spell to link the two of you together. The only way to do it was to set up a familiar binding, but the virus seemed to take the bait, seeing as how you're still kicking.'

I was speechless. Repetitive, I know, but the hell was I supposed to say to that?! If I was understanding correctly, Viora had agreed to not only mystically bind the two of us as mutual guardians, but for the sole purpose of keeping me alive. No wonder I could sense her emotions, that's how familiars and their magi communicate!

I let out a groan, the questions in my head multiplying by the second, though one kept pushing its way to the front.

'Hang on. If that's all true, then doesn't that mean Viora's-'

'Infected too, yes.' Viora answered without hesitation.

I bolted fully upright. 'So, we're both infected now?! How does that solve anything?!'

Dawkes raised her hands. 'It doesn't, really. Like I said, we couldn't cure it, but we could buy you time. By tricking the virus into trying to split itself between two bodies at once, it's effects should've slowed dramatically. We're still going to need to find some proper fix, but we have time to do that now.'

I looked from Dawkes, back to Viora, who returned my stare with the same bland expression she typically had, only now I could see the concern tensed up along her shoulders and arms. Concern for me, but why?

I was her jailer. Fuck, the first thing I said to her was a death threat after locking her up in this very apartment! What possible reason could she have to risk her own life to protect mine?! I knew she feared death, feared it so much it nearly paralysed her, so why change her tune now?!

Viora, quite possibly reading my mind, placed a hand hesitantly on my shoulder.

'When lost, confused in strange world, Enlightenment provided protection. Gave shelter. Comforting in time of need. Risked own life to ensure safety and made requests when demands could have been enforced. Enlightenment saved me. Why not save Enlightenment?'

That was the most terrifying response I could've possibly gotten.

After all I'd done, kidnapping Viora off the streets, threatening her, forcing her to stay locked up in my apartment, she saw something worth saving? I couldn't even begin to comprehend what alien logic led her to wanting to help me, but the damage had been done. I was alive, for better or worse.

Of course, that could change. 'Ho-how much time have we got, exactly?'

Dawkes flinched. 'We were lucky to catch you when we did. Personally, I think symptoms might start catching up to you two in a few hours, maybe a day.'

Oh, wonderful.

'Dammit. I'd better get moving, then.' I muttered, finally pulling myself out of bed. 'So what's the plan? I take it you got the recordings that transceiver was picking up, right?'

The three shared a confused look before Dawkes began

speaking. 'Well, yeah, but-'

'So, it's clear that Calatin's the one pulling the strings, playing everyone in Dublin off each other in the hopes of dragging all of us into a war. He's got something big planned for when the High Command's military support arrives, so we're going to need to act fast. I suggest we start by-'

Bhajan cut me off with a cough. 'Before any of that. We've answered your questions to the best of our abilities, it's only fair you answer one of ours.'

No. No, I was so close! Why'd he have to bring it up now!?

I opened my mouth, only for Dawkes to interrupt. 'Yeah, he's right. What happened to you back there, Reilly? It was like you'd gotten possessed. And when I checked the transceiver recording, you told Calatin you were responsible for the Dingle Incident. Is that true?'

'I don't see how that's important right now.' I responded, body tensing.

Dawkes sighed. 'Yeah, well, it is. Look, Reilly, I'm sure there's some reason why you lost it back there, but that just makes it more important that we know, so we'll be prepared if something like that happens again.'

'Last I checked; we don't have a lot of time.' I tried one last time to bullrush my way out of the conversation, making my way in the direction of the door.

Dawkes blocked the way, her face pleading. 'Short version then. Sum it up in five or ten minutes. Please, Reilly, we can't help you if we don't know what's going on.'

There it was. I was cornered. In a flash, the familiar instincts for this situation flowed back, only for me to realise that none of my previous tactics would work.

Divert the topic? No, they wouldn't budge. Stonewall? They

would only push. Run? I needed their help.

Sweat formed on my forehead, my heart raced. Why? Why couldn't they just leave me alone?! Why couldn't they be like everyone else, not asking questions, not trying to get into my head? Why did they care so much about the things I wanted to bury?!

That's what I thought, but when I looked up, I didn't see interrogative glares, or threatening stances. I saw furrowed brows, tense shoulders and pleading eyes.

They looked worried. And for some reason, I couldn't stand seeing them like that.

'Alright.' The word came out as a mutter at first, forcing me to say it again. 'Alright, fine! But you'd better listen, because I'm not repeating myself!'

I slumped back onto the bed, turning to face my audience, and prepared myself to tell them everything. What happened in Dingle, why I was such a mess. Everything.

And if they didn't hate me before, they would now.

# Chapter 23

'So, where do I start?' I asked, hoping they'd at least ask me to start as late as possible into the story.

Dawkes rubbed her chin. 'I guess...maybe start from as early as you can?'

I let out a breath. Figures. 'Right. I won't bore you with where I was born, but it's important to note that I was born at midnight on the twenty-first of December to parents with no idea that magic was real.'

I could feel the way Dawkes tensed.

As far as researchers in the field of magic can tell, there's no guaranteed way for anyone to be born a magi, those having the gift more often than not just being lucky enough to beat odds of over one in half a million.

But one of the few consistent ways of having better odds than the majority was to be born at some spiritually or cosmically significant time. In my case, being born during the traditional witching hour at the darkest point of the Winter Solstice was almost as good as being the seventh son of a seventh son.

'When I was a teen, weird things started happening. Things flinging themselves off shelves, rooms going cold when I entered. Small things, really, until the fight.'

I paused briefly. 'In school, couple of the kids singled me out as a target, probably because I never talked to anyone. Had to deal with the tossed wads of paper and regular insults for about a year before the incident. They cornered me during break, and things got violent. I slapped one of them. Next thing I know, kid's on the floor clutching his broken jaw, while I was being dragged off by a teacher. That wasn't pleasant, and my parents weren't too happy when I got suspended over it, but then things only got worse.'

'How'd you mean?' Bhajan asked, his eyes locked on me with that same intensity I'd seen when he had his teeth to my neck.

I shook my head. 'When I got back, my parents ripped into me. I didn't have a clue what happened, but they weren't having it. It got into a screaming match, and one of my screams exploded every electronic in the room. Once my parents figured out things only broke or defied gravity when I was mad, things got tense fast.'

'When they started fearing what they didn't understand?' Dawkes cut in, her tone heavy with resignation.

I suppressed a snort. 'Precisely. Started with them just avoiding me, not even staying in the same room for very long, which was actually pleasant until they started sending me to therapists to pick over my brain, which only gave us an autism diagnosis they didn't know how to handle either.'

My face twisted as the memories trickled back. 'Eventually, they got a priest over to 'test' me for an exorcism, and when that didn't pan out, they started having talks about sending me off to some special school when they thought I couldn't hear. Eventually, I packed a bag and left in the middle of the night.'

Two faces, stiffly terrified and devoid of any affection, flashed in front of my eyes. 'I think I was hoping they'd come find me, post pictures up, that sort of thing, but they never did. Once I figured out no one actually missed me, I spent the last of my spare change on a bus out of my no-name village to the closest actual town. Dingle.'

Dawkes flinched, muttered under her breath. 'Oh, God.'

I nodded. 'We'll get to that. Surviving as a runaway wasn't much easier in Dingle, but at least the place was big enough to hide in. I spent a few weeks actually trying to learn how my 'superpowers' worked. First spell I ever learned was to overload ATMs to spill out cash. Kept me going for a while, bought me a few nights at a hotel with some actual food, until someone knocked at the door.'

'Who?' Viora leaned closer.

I felt myself begin to stare out into space, memories long buried stinging like broken scabs. 'An old homeless woman. I'd seen her a couple of times, but I just figured she was just another beggar. First thing she did when I opened the door was ask how long I'd had magic.'

'I tried denying it, but she just straight said she knew I was the one stealing from the ATMs. Course I know now she probably just sensed the magic off me, but then, her knowing everything about me seemed mysterious and frightening. I remember gearing up for a fight when she said that, but the old woman told me she just wanted to talk. She told me her name was Bodhmall.'

I took another breath, I'd no idea how to even begin explaining the effect of those few minutes, how they shaped me for years to come. 'She...I don't know, she understood, or at least that's how it seemed. Told me my parents didn't deserve to have someone so blessed in their lives, that my powers weren't a curse, but a gift, one that gave me the right to use it however I wanted. It's obvious now she was stoking my ego, but it was the first time anyone had said anything good about me in years, so I ate it all up. And when she offered to take me in, give me the chance to learn to use my gift, why the hell would I say no?'

Bhajan scowled. 'This is starting to sound a lot like some cult recruitment shit.'

I lifted a hand in acknowledgement. 'Called it the Ord na bPór. Claimed she was a druid, collecting those with potential to train them to seize the power the world scorned them for having, to turn it back on those who hated us. I know, but I was angry, confused and this whole deal sounded like the answer to my prayers. We left the hotel that night, and she took me across town to an old derelict house on the outskirts. Mess of a place, and pretty damn cramped once I met the others.'

'More children?' Viora's voice managed to carry a hint of contempt.

'Eight or ten, all roughly the same age as me, that Bodhmall had picked up from one street corner or another. All rejects, thrown out or run away from a home that treated us like shit. But I was different.'

I looked down at my hands. 'I had actual power. The others didn't have enough between them to pull a rabbit out of a hat. Bodhmall taught them how to participate in rituals, add some extra oomph to whatever she wanted to happen, how to steal money or food, or anything else she thought would be useful. But me? She took me under her wing, trained me to harness my abilities, taught me all the occult secrets the other kids wished they could learn. More than that, she taught me how to use my magic to hurt people, how to tattoo myself with ogham so I could channel force though my limbs.'

'Wait, so the other kids didn't get anything out of it?' Dawkes interjected, sounding incredulous.

I shook my head. 'Not exactly. Bodhmall knew how to manipulate kids. She'd give us just enough to get us hooked. Healing a stab wound here, controlling a few rats to steal things there, it didn't happen often, but often enough to make the message clear that what she had was real. I still remember the one kid that tried to convince the rest of us that she was a fraud.'

Bhajan clicked his tongue. 'Ah, inflicted some horrible fate on the naysayer, then.'

I barked out a bitter laugh. Now we were getting into it. 'No. She told me to zap him with the same electricity she'd been teaching me to harness. He fell right back into line after that. Probably the most insidious thing about her, now that I think about. She could've done something about him herself, but why do that when you can use us as an object lesson of why following her was worth your while, and why disobeying her wasn't? Bodhmall had roped us in with a compassionate face and displays of wonder, but really, the main selling point was the hope that one day, we'd all have that kind of power over someone else. Worked on me.'

No one said anything for a moment.

'I spent the next couple of years doing whatever she told me to do. I hurt quite a few people during. Didn't kill anyone, but only because that would've drawn more attention to us. Most of the time it was petty crime, only this time I had people I could lord my power over, rather than hide it.'

'Enjoyed it.' Viora's bland voice undercutting the accusation.

I closed my eyes, distant flashes of delight and the sound of others screaming echoing in my head. 'Course I did. I'd already had people been afraid of me, but only in the way that makes them grab the closest sharp object to hand. The other kids knew that would've been pointless, so they couldn't do anything but take it, and I loved every second of it. Bodhmall never tried to rein me in either, just told the others to get strong enough to stop me. A few did try to stand up to me here and there. I looked forward to those, gave me the excuse to remind them who was in charge.'

Bhajan crossed his arms, brow furrowed. 'Still not seeing how this all connects to the Dingle Incident. It is the Dingle incident you're leading up to?'

I blinked a couple of times. 'Right, guess I do need to get into that. It'd been building for a while, I think. Bodhmall was getting more edgy than normal, got to the point where she broke one of the bigger lad's nose for serving her lukewarm tea. Eventually, she took me aside and told me that she needed to get in touch with the Fair Folk, said she finally had what she needed to settle a deal she'd made. Except she was going to need to perform a ritual, and she needed all of us to help her.'

'What for?' Dawkes stopped leaning against the doorframe, now standing alert.

I leaned back. 'Didn't ask. Didn't care either. Bodhmall was promising more power and that was enough. All I asked was if I needed to 'fry some bitches' I think was how I put it. Like I said, she'd likely been planning it for a while, she already had most of the easy-to-get reagents. Even had the date and time set out, and wouldn't you believe it, it was at the stroke of midnight on Samhain.'

'Oh. That doesn't sound good.' Came Bhajan's quiet reply, hilariously understated given what was common knowledge even among normal people.

That Halloween was the time of year where the boundaries between our world and the Shroud was at its most porous, most fragile.

I turned to Bhajan briefly. 'No, it wasn't. Bodhmall filled me in on some of details when I came back from robbing some health shop. She'd had dug up some old ritual that, according to her, would allow us to summon Sidhe spirits to bind them to our souls, so we'd gain their power.'

'God, you didn't buy that, did you?' Dawkes spoke up again, hand to her forehead. 'Not conjuring nebulous spirits to demand power from them is like, the first thing actual magi learn not to do. You might as well have tried to sell your soul to a demon.'

Shame I had to disappoint her further. 'Oh, yeah. Even back then, it sounded pretty sketchy to me, but Bodhmall was my master, so I went along with it, even when she ordered me not to tell the others what the ritual was meant to do. Not that I would've. Knowing something they didn't was like crack to me.'

I moved on. 'Well, Halloween night rolled around, and we all had our parts to play. Bodhmall and the other kids were to stay in the farmhouse and perform the actual ritual, while I went out and set up the summoning circles.'

'Hang on, did you say multiple circles?!' Dawkes' voice took on a couple more octaves.

I couldn't blame her. Trying to summon and restrain one entity from beyond the Shroud was tricky business. Anyone thick enough to attempt multiple summonings at once was like trying wrangle several angry men with one arm.

All I could do was shrug again. 'We were summoning a whole bunch of Sidhe, remember? And before you start with how we'd have no chance keeping that many Sidhe under control and all that, we were a bunch of idiot kids following whatever our master told us. We weren't overabundant with intelligence.'

'What'd you do?' Dawkes managed to get her voice deliberately neutral.

I sighed, really wishing I could twist any of this to sound better. 'What do you think? I did exactly what she told me to do, and more. The summoning circles Bodhmall wanted had to be drawn in blood, except I wasn't too eager to use my own. So, I'd bullied the other kids into letting me bleed them beforehand. I'd just finished up the last one when I saw headlights coming up to our shack. Next thing I knew, a car was parking outside and a couple of men in black came out, completely silent, and moved straight for the house. One of them did something to unlock the door, then the two went in, guns drawn.'

'Guess things went south when they saw you.' Bhajan interjected, his knuckles tensing and untensing.

'That's the thing, they didn't. I was around the corner of the house when I saw them come out, and I threw up the old invisibility spell when they started coming. Didn't know what their deal was, but I snuck up to the corner, figuring I'd blast them when they had their backs turned. Only that's when the air went rancid in my mouth, and the circles starting steaming. Maybe that was supposed to happen, or the agents interfered with the ritual somehow, either way, I was not prepared for what came out.'

My mouth struggled to form the words, as it came back to me, as vivid as the day it happened. 'I-I thought we were just summoning one Sidhe for each circle, but that wasn't what happened. Those circles erupted into what looked like holes in spacetime, from which I saw maybe a couple dozen things of every size and shape clamber out and spill over into the streets. This was before I knew just how varied Sidhe actually were, mind, so I thought something had gone wrong. I'm still sure if I hadn't made myself invisible already, the ones nearest would've made me their first victim. While the agents rushed into the house, I stumbled out from my hiding place to flank them. That's when I heard the screams.'

I felt my jaw clench. No, can't stop now. 'In the distance, I could see monsters climbing into peoples' windows, bashing down doors, or just jumping a couple of unlucky drunks stumbling around outside.'

I paused as that particular memory hit me again. Unlucky was an understatement, but they didn't need all the grisly details. 'It was madness. I was certain we'd jump started the apocalypse. Definitely didn't help when I started sensing some heavy-duty magic being thrown around inside the houses, including our own, enough to make my eyes water and ears ring. I had never felt that kind of power before.'

If anyone spoke up, I didn't hear them, the past, becoming more real, more painful the more I recalled, was now all I could see. 'I ran. I ran for my life, leaving Bodhmall and the others to face the agents alone. Sometimes I can still hear her cursing me in my dreams. Wish I could say I had a change of conscience that made me turn around, but I was so freaked out that instinct just took over.'

'Didn't have a destination in mind, but I remember what I saw as I ran. The Sidhe hadn't stopped with the houses on our block, but had descended into the streets, breaking into the houses there too. Still don't know what made them so damn rabid. Doesn't matter. What did matter was one of them, a greasy little redcap, stepped in my way, holding a massive scythe. Swung the thing right at my ankles and dropped on my backside. I tried to fire off some lightning in response, but the fecker just kicked me in the face, sending it completely off. Turns out power doesn't mean much when your opponent's faster and smarter. Would've been dead there if he hadn't turned up.'

'He?' Viora's voice managed to break through the haze around me, jolting me back to the bedroom, her face stretched tight as she half-raised a hand towards me.

My hands were shaking. My throat was dry. I could feel the blood had drained from my face. 'One of the agents. Blasted that Sidhe into paste before they'd got within an inch of me. I guess he was probably just protecting what he thought was a civilian until he saw me use magic. Then he had a few questions.'

'How did that go?' Dawkes leaned over.

I looked away. 'I lied. Passed myself off as some self-taught magi who'd learned everything he knew from neo-pagan books. Still not sure he actually believed me, but he didn't press, just told me that the Enlightenment was clearing the area and that I needed to come with him. Wasn't exactly in a position to argue, so I did. He took me to his black car, where from inside I got another front row seat to what 'clearing the area' meant.'

'Once we were all clear, they shuffled me off to a dark room where I was told I was getting the honour of a position within the Enlightenment, in recognition of my 'unusual talent and will. Heard afterwards that they'd managed to take down the rabid Sidhe and Bodhmall herself, though only after she'd sacrificed the other kids as part of the ritual. Guess I was either too useful or too hard to kill. They managed to cover up the incident as a gangland massacre.'

I shivered at that memory. That'd been one of the scarier parts back then. That the Enlightenment had managed to cover up a literal interdimensional assault with barely any questions. 'Skip past about five years of training, where I learned just how badly we'd collectively fucked up in the wider scheme, and one year working in Dublin and we're in the present.'

'So, then, why did you go berserk back in Lumintech?' Bhajan cocked his head, raising an eyebrow.

I blinked. 'Oh, that? Like I said, once I finally got the hang of magic, I used to love having any excuse to unleash on anyone and anything I could. Had to put that part of me away when I joined up. Guess when I finally let my emotions loose back there, it reawakened the old bloodlust. Shit excuse, I know, but it's the only one I've got.'

And that was it. I'd just finished describing, to the only three people I had any trust in, why exactly they shouldn't trust me. How I'd been responsible for inflicting untold pain and death on so many innocent lives, all because I was petty and short-sighted.

That day when the Enlightenment recruited me, I'd just wanted a way out. But then, over the years of training, I learned what was at stake if the paranormal was unpoliced. More importantly, I learned why exactly what I'd done was so much worse than I could've known. I'd sworn to change, to leave that part of me behind.

Judging from the complete silence that filled the air now, as three faces stared back at me with unreadable expressions, it was clear how idiotic that promise was. I didn't deserve to change.

Dawkes' eyes seemed to take an interest in everything except me. 'That's...a lot to take in. Honestly, I'm not sure what to say, except maybe-'

I closed my eyes as she spoke. I think I was actually starting to like the people in front of me. But it was stupid to think I could hide what I actually was, what I was responsible for. I was long past deserving any kind of second chance.

They deserved better than me.

'-I'm sorry you had to go through that, Reilly.'

What? My eyes shot open, and I boggled at Dawkes, who appeared to be wincing with...was that sympathy? That couldn't be right.

'Don't misunderstand. I wasn't any kind of innocent in all that. Even if I wasn't aware of what exactly was going to happen, I still participated in everything that happened.'

Dawkes flicked her hand in a helpless gesture. 'I'm not excusing what you did, Reilly. You directly played a role in the worst paranormal disaster to hit Ireland in decades, that's clear. At the same time, though, from what you're telling us, it sounds like you were exactly the textbook example what happens when a kid becomes the target of manipulation.'

I was on my feet before I realised it. 'Tha-that's no excuse! Didn't you hear me!? I just told you I abused the other kids for fun! That I helped Bodhmall unleash monsters on an innocent town! Bodhmall didn't make me do that, I did it because I wanted to! I was a total bastard!'

It was then that Bhajan rose as well, his face stern. 'Indeed. And yet the man before us is the same one who has thrown himself recklessly into danger for the sake of others, even when pragmaticism would demand he look the other way. Who's spent this entire endeavour putting the needs of others before his own. Do you mean to tell us that man is nothing more than a thin mask for the bullying child to hide behind?'

'Yes! That's exactly what I'm saying!' The words exploded out of me. 'The only reason I act that way is because if I don't, I risk falling right back into what I was before I joined the Enlightenment! You all saw what happened back in Lumintech! I slipped up once, let that part of myself out one time, and I almost killed both of you! What you saw, back there, that giggling lunatic, that's the real me! That's what happens when I don't spend every hour of the day holding back everything I feel! All the hatred, all the resentment just surges right back up and all I want to do is hurt everyone around me! I'm not a good person, a good person wouldn't have to actively force himself not to want to do it again!'

'Also!' I stabbed a finger furiously in the air, my throat straining. 'In case it slipped your collective notice, I've just admitted to being responsible for everything happening now! The only reason Calatin's trying to start this whole damn war is because what happened in Dingle killed his family and he blames the paras for it! If I didn't help tear those rifts open, none of this would've happened!'

I slouched forward, trying to catch my breath. In the oppressive silence that followed my rant, I chanced another glance up at the three faces around me, all visibly startled.

There. Maybe now they'd finally get the picture.

Bhajan scoffed and crossed his arms. 'My word. You're an intelligent man, Reilly, but you truly show immense ignorance at times.'

The sentence hit me like a slap across the face. 'Excuse me?'

Bhajan massaged the bridge of his nose. 'Do you honestly believe that, had you never joined this Ord na bPór, that your old master wouldn't have gone down the same path regardless? You may share responsibility for what happened at Dingle, but assuming all blame for someone else's scheme is not only idiotic, but greedy. Is the guilt of your own actions so insufficient you must flagellate yourself for another's?'

'T-that's uh-' I struggled to come up with a retort. I mean, he wasn't wrong exactly, but I still helped, I was still-

Whatever argument I was trying to form melted away when I felt someone clasp my hand. The sensation so unfamiliar I didn't recognise it at first. I saw Viora had gotten up, both her hands kneading my own.

She spoke, slowly and measured. 'Many words spoken now without context. Here is what is known. When desperate and sending out cry for help, Enlightenment came. When Enlightenment could've imprisoned and tortured for information, Enlightenment instead gave food, promised shelter and protection. When attacked by Sidhe, then later frightened for life, Enlightenment protected, then comforted.'

I could only watch as Viora kept gently stroking my hand, her normally level voice becoming hitched. 'Dingle, Bodhmall, Ord na bPór. All words from a past not seen here. What's seen here is individual who took every opportunity to extend kindness when cruelty would've worked, when callousness would've been efficient. That is the individual I agreed to bind myself to in order to keep them alive.'

I didn't move. I couldn't. Viora's speech made something wrench deep inside me.

Dawkes came up on my left, almost touching me, before hesitating and stepping back. 'Listen, Reilly. None of us are claiming you don't have anything to make up for. What I'm saying, and I'm sure these two will agree, is that you're not the same petty kid from your past. Not only were you manipulated by someone you trusted, you've managed to see that you were being manipulated and have been trying to break away from what happened to you.'

A few gasping, choking sounds were the only things that came out of my mouth.

'You might've had some complicity in the Dingle Incident, but only from a position where you were lied to and manipulated. What you did was wrong, but it's not irredeemable. And I've seen enough of you to know that you're actually trying to do better, which is a hell of a lot more than most people.'

Part of me wanted to weep, while another screamed at me to put my walls back up, put some distance between me and them, because the last time someone talked to me like this, they tricked me into causing a massacre.

Hate, I could handle.

Compassion? After seeing the very worst of me? That I didn't know how to handle.

So, I chickened out. 'Well, uh, thank you for the kind words, I appreciate it. Not gonna have much of chance to do better if Calatin's virus kills me, though.'

Dawkes stared at me for a couple more heartbeats, before pulling back. 'Good point, I guess. Time's getting short, but if we get back to HQ and show them the recording, Calatin's done. They'll know the whole thing's a setup and he'll be on the most wanted list in an hour. We can probably get some help for your infection, as well, at least until Calatin's apprehended.'

Finally getting the chance to pull myself away from the unexpected physical contact, I stepped away from Viora. 'We can try, but if Calatin's just handing out a supervirus to whoever asks, it might not make a difference. Once the paranormals in Dublin are armed with a weapon designed to kill humans, the Enlightenment will have to respond, whether they know Calatin's responsible or not. Besides, putting me into medical care's not gonna help if I'm dead by tomorrow. The only chance me and Viora have now is by tracking down Calatin or one of his crew and hoping they either have a cure or a sample of the virus that can be reverse-engineered into one.'

Dawkes baulked. 'You can't be serious! Reilly, however you feel now, you're still dying. If you drop out there, you'll have no chance to survive!'

I stood my ground. 'We've wasted enough time as is, Dawkes. You really want to waste more arguing about this?'

'You-argh!' Dawkes stalked a few steps away, hand to her face as she muttered what sounded like some very choice words, before turning back to thrust a finger in my direction. 'So help me, if you end up dying out there, I will bind your soul to a bloody ashtray, we clear?!'

I nodded. 'Now, you're going to hate me for saying this, but we'll need to split up. With Calatin, the Enlightenment and probably the Lemurians and Sidhe on the move, we're going to need to cover all bases fast. We know Calatin's trying to spark up a war here, but we still don't know where or when he'll make his move.'

Dawkes emitted an aggrieved groan. 'I do hate you. Especially because you're right. Where do we go, though? Calatin could be anywhere in Dublin right now.'

Dawkes had hit on the main problem. With no way of knowing where exactly Calatin was or who he might have in his pocket, it was going to be difficult to guess at where his next moves are.

Then it hit me. Maybe it was the new sense of purpose or even just having the chance to think, rather than react, but regardless, suddenly it clicked, and I knew exactly what I needed to do next.

'I've got it.' I said, opening my eyes. 'Dawkes, you're right. Get in touch with Enlightenment HQ, tell them everything. Bhajan, I need another favour.'

Bhajan's stony grimace split into a wide grin as he threw his arms up. 'Sure, why not? Not like this hole can get much deeper.'

'Get in touch with your Waver buddies, convince them Calatin's being manipulating the Sidhe and Lemurians behind the scenes and if they don't want to live in a warzone, they'll have to co-operate with the Enlightenment.'

Bhajan ran a hand through his hair as he laughed. 'You don't ask much, do you? I'll see what I can do, but I'll probably need a copy of the recording to make that case.'

Dawkes nodded over. 'Gimmie your number. I'll send it to you once I've finished messaging HQ.'

Bhajan gasped. 'How forward, Ms Dawkes! Have my charms finally broken through?!'

Dawkes' lips pulled up in a sneer, though it didn't quite reach her eyes. 'Keep dreaming, banana breath. I get any weird pics from you, I'll forward them to all of Dublin.'

Still laughing, Bhajan pulled an old phone out from within his robe. 'And kill all mystery so soon? Give me some credit, dear agent.'

The two stood next to each other as Dawkes send the audio over, glancing up at me as she did so. 'Just so we're clear, what exactly are you planning to do, Reilly?'

'I've going to track down Nechtan. He and his army are working with Calatin. If the new virus is going anywhere, they'll be top of the list. We need to get to him before Calatin does.'

Dawkes' head snapped up. 'What exactly do you mean by 'get to him?''

'Let's just say I've put some pieces together that might help us if I can reach him. At the very least, if we know where Nechtan's main forces are hiding out, the Enlightenment will be better prepared when they show up. Trust me, I've got no intention of dying with this much at stake.'

Dawkes pulled that face she always did when I said something she didn't like. 'Just remember what I said, ok? Soul, ashtray.'

I nodded and turned, making only a couple of steps only for someone to grip my arm. Catching myself mid-step, I saw Viora, holding my arm again.

'Going with.'

I froze. My mind went back to the car only a couple nights ago, and my still-fresh guilt ached once more. 'You sure? It's going to be dangerous. I've already asked you to put yourself in harm's way too many times.'

Viora closed her eyes for a moment, her chest swelling then contracting in a long breath. 'Yes. Already risking life by sharing infection in Enlightenment. No logic in hiding now.'

I tried to speak again, to suggest maybe she could help some other way, only to stop short as Viora turned her head up to look straight into my eyes, the dark pits of her own somehow conveying a readiness I hadn't seen in her before. 'Other factor. Enlightenment has protected up to this point. Recompense necessary.'

I sucked in a sharp breath of my own. As much as I wanted to talk Viora out of this, it wasn't like I couldn't use the help.

I looked away, muttering. 'And I thought I was mental. Alright, but stick close. Either of us dying will probably spell doom for the other when the virus doesn't have two people keeping it busy anymore.'

Viora nodded silently, and the two of us began to make for the door, just as Dawkes called out one more time.

'Have you at least thought about how you're supposed to beat Calatin to Nechtan? We don't even know where either of them are!'

'Simple.' I turned back to fix Dawkes with the closest thing to a smirk I was capable. 'We're gonna bring Nechtan to us.'

# Chapter 24

'Clarification?' Viora asked.

'Yeah?' I murmured, still poring low-sodium salt in a circle in front of the door of the old stone tower. Viora, to her credit, hadn't objected to the plan so far, not even when we drove back to Rath Esa.

'Story told earlier contained strong message that summoning powerful Sidhe as a bad idea.' She began, her voice halting as she tried to logic her way through our plan.

'Nearly always.' I replied. I methodically traced a pentacle inside the circle.

Summoning a paranormal entity was almost never worth it. Best case scenario, you bound the creature long enough to try and extract some deal from it, and reading literally any story about genies should tell you enough about how well that can go.

Worst case, you piss off a powerful magical being, who is now standing in front of you with nothing stopping it from turning you into a duck or transforming your eyeballs into oranges.

'Additionally. The act of summoning holds great traumatic weight for Enlightenment, taking into account previous history and nature of the being that is being summoned.'

'Uh-huh.' Having finished the pentacle, I started setting out the cheap scented candles I'd scavenged from my apartment as part of the kit I'd brought with us. Salt, candles and a lighter, not much of a kit, but it'd have to do.

Viora was right on the money. I was scared, terrified even. Even if the whole act of trying to summon something as powerful as a Daoine Sidhe wasn't bringing back bad memories, I was under no illusions that this was going to go well.

'Question remains why attempting to conjure Sidhe leader is a good plan.'

I lit the last candle, then turned to Viora properly. 'Never said it was. Problem is, there's no way we can track down Nechtan before Calatin reaches him with the new virus. We need to draw Nechtan to us. Now.'

Viora's nose wrinkled. She surveyed the setup. 'If summoning so simple. Why haven't Enlightenment superiors already summoning Sidhe and other threats, then overwhelmed with force?'

'One, it's not enough to just know who you want to summon. That's just the bare minimum. You also need to establish some proper link in the ritual to the individual you're trying to call forth, as many links as you can, in fact.'

I gestured out at our surroundings. 'That's why we're here. It's a punt, but I'm willing to bet that what happened here is still fresh enough in Nechtan's mind, that we'll be able to establish that link, maybe bait him into coming voluntarily, just to see what we're at.'

Viora frowned. 'Explanation still lacking on why wider Enlightenment couldn't try something similar.'

I held up two fingers. 'Well, that brings us to my second

point. Even if we've found the perfect lure for Nechtan, he can still resist the call, which will drag things into a contest of wills. Most magi wouldn't have a prayer of holding a Sidhe like him in a binding circle. Hell, I don't even think I'll be able to, which means I'll have no power to stop him from trying to kill us the second he arrives. That, Viora, is why my bosses haven't been in a hurry to try this.'

Viora stiffened. 'Binding Sidhe isn't possible? Why attempt?'

I took a couple of steps closer. I tried to look reassuring. 'Because I'm not trying to bind Nechtan, exactly. I'm just trying to get him over here so I can talk to him. I'm hoping once he understands what I'm trying to do, he'll be willing to talk.'

Viora continued to stand rigid. Time for honesty. 'That said, I suppose the main reason, hell, the whole reason I'm even considering this is because I'm desperate.'

I ran a hand through my hair as I though. 'I won't lie to you, Viora. This is going to be dangerous. I've got a plan if things get violent. I'm really hoping we can solve this diplomatically, but we can't rule out a fight. Nechtan's more than a match for the pair of us. Our best shot is convincing him to hear us out.'

'Very poor plan.'

I let out a wheeze of a laugh. 'I did mention I was desperate, right? I'm going to start the summoning. Last chance to leg it if you've changed your mind.'

As I turned and walked back the circle, Viora called once again. 'Summoning essential to stopping Calatin?'

Standing at the front of the circle, I pondered that question. Truthfully, assuming Dawkes arrived quickly enough to HQ to explain everything, the Enlightenment would know within a couple hours that Calatin was responsible for the bioweapons.

The only problem was that wouldn't much matter if the anti-human virus was already distributed. The Sidhe and probably Lemurians would have a weapon they could deploy with impunity against both the Enlightenment and the normal human population, which the Enlightenment wouldn't be able to ignore. Calatin would have his war.

Article 4. An agent does what is necessary for the task. No more. No less.

I tried to boil it down as best I could. 'Stopping Calatin? No. Stopping Calatin's plan from plunging Dublin, then Ireland, then possibly the planet into a war between magi and paranormals? Yes.'

'Then staying. Debt still owed.' Viora's reply came instantly, though with a slight quaver in her voice, which I think maybe reassured me.

At least I thought she understood the risks.

I glanced back at her, my gut twisting as I saw her thin figure, clearly trying to untense herself. I probably should've said something comforting, but I didn't want to lie. 'Step back, then. Going to need a bit more space for this.'

I heard her shuffle a few steps back, I got out the final part of the ritual, a small bowl and my athame. I placed the bowl in the centre of the circle, then, holding my free hand over it, I ran the blade across my knuckles, hissing at the sharp pain.

I clenched my fist, letting the blood run, then stepped back, checking briefly that the candles were still lit. Satisfied, I reached my hand out and began murmuring the words of summoning in Middle Irish, repeating the words as I willed the circle to reach out beyond the Shroud to my intended target.

Then, I added one last element, the one I was sure would actually let me pull this off. I cast my mind back to Dingle. Resisting the instinct to block the thoughts away again, this time, I let the pain and terror I felt that night bubble back to the surface. I funnelled that emotion into the working, letting it suffuse my efforts to call out to Nechtan.

More importantly than that, though, I focused on the memories of the Sidhe I saw that night, on the chaos, the horror, the blood and the howling. Emotion was already a critical part of any magical working, but if my current theory was right, Nechtan might have particular motivation to answer these memories too.

I felt the air start to pick up, turning from a gentle breeze to a whistling gust, then a howling gale, all within a couple of minutes. I could feel my blood in the circle get hotter and hotter, the wound on my hand mirroring the rising temperature. It was working.

I opened my mouth, raising my voice so it could be heard over the wind screaming in my ears, I shouted. 'Nechtan, Nechtan, Nechtan!'

The wind cracked like a whip, and both blood and wound flashed with such a sudden and fierce heat that I felt the wound cauterise as I instinctively clasped it.

Before I could recover, something pressed against my skull. I let out a scream as the presence drilled through my skull into my mind, and my knees hit the ground as I clutched my head. Gasping from the pain, I forced my eyes open, and was rewarded with a chill of fear.

Standing in the centre of the circle, Nechtan, still clad in his revolutionary uniform, loomed over me. His expression was still and calm, not that that did anything to stop the pounding in my chest as he scanned first me, then his surroundings.

'You.' He began, and that word along carried more than enough anger to counter the stoic mask. 'Have a lot of nerve, Arbiter.'

I pulled myself up, only for Nechtan to flick his hand out.

Instantly, I felt whatever frail barrier still maintained by the circle shatter, as did the circle itself, the salt scattering away. Nechtan blurred in my direction, suddenly standing mere centimetres from me, his teeth gritted, his eyes flinty. As I flinched back, he continued speaking, the heat on his breath burning my jaw.

'I'm not sure what's more insulting. That you've pulled me away from some very urgent matters, or that you've attempted to bind me in perhaps the most pathetic ritual I've ever seen. Honestly, with whatever trick you've managed to concoct that was sufficient to force my answering this summons, I would've expected to least exert some effort in overpowering your will, yet this was like walking into a trap set up by a housefly.'

Shit, I knew summoning Nechtan would be dicey, but I hadn't expected this level of anger. I swallowed the trembling fear in my gut. 'I apologise for calling you here in such a careless fashion, but if you'd just hear me out-'

Whatever I might've said next was cut short with what sounded like a gunshot. Next thing I knew, I was flat on my back, jaw bursting with pain.

From where I was lying, I saw Nechtan sneer as he flexed his fingers on the hand that just slapped me. 'I think not, you flailing ape. You've made a dire mistake. You think me a mere pixie, waiting to be bent to the will of any half-rate dabbler? My kind, just toys you can pull forth at your whim and dismissed when your fun is over?'

As Nechtan's voice got louder and he seemed ready to pounce on me, I still thought it was possible to salvage the situation, perhaps if I grovelled enough, but just as it seemed he'd reached the boiling point, Nechtan paused, then fixed me with a look that was just a little too calm and restrained.

That was when I knew I'd screwed up royally.

'If you truly think us Sidhe so weak and easily conquered, perhaps an education is in order into exactly why your kind used to cower in your homes in centuries past when our processions rode through.'

'Wait! I know that-' I struggled to keep my words clear as I scrambled to get out what I needed to say. If I could only get a chance to tell him, it would still be possible to resolve this peacefully.

But before I could get any further, Nechtan lifted his right hand up, then snapped his fingers, reciting a word I'd heard not too long ago, from the last time I was here. 'Friotaíocht!'

The surge of magic that accompanied the word caused me to cover my head with a gasp, one gesture carrying more power and weight than I'd ever seen in one place before, but things only got worse when I lowered my arms.

We were no longer in the same field, but in a hauntingly familiar one. The trees were taller and the undergrowth more aggressive, with the very sky over us seeming to belong to a different world, dense jagged clouds framing the bright magenta that coloured the sky. The tents were gone, but I still recognised the realm that lay on the other side of the Shroud, a place I'd needed the keyword Friotaíocht and being in the exact right spot to be able to access.

Evidently Nechtan wasn't quite so restricted.

More concerning than our surroundings however, was the wind, which, already howling around us, picked up even more speed, evolving into a furious shriek, to the point where it felt like I was going to be whisked up into the sky.

In the madness that seemed to have caught the whole world around us in its gravity, Nechtan stood as the still, quiet eye of the hurricane, the wind not so much as ruffling his clothes.

I'd made a mistake. While I expected Nechtan to be angry, I'd not even remotely accounted for this level of fury and power. I wasn't facing down an upstart revolutionary, I was standing before a demigod in his home turf.

Lying on the ground, I couldn't even curl up into a ball in a pathetic attempt to shield myself from nature itself turned against me, instead frozen still by Nechtan's stare, his emerald eyes as sharp as the actual gems. There I lay, alone and unprotected, against the sheer might of a being of pure magic, unable to so much as stand.

Except I wasn't actually alone.

Just as my sense of self started to erode away, worn down by Nechtan's presence and consumed by the hungry winds tearing at me, a sharp pain stabbed into my mind, like a migraine that disappeared as soon as it appeared, and as I flinched and clapped a hand to my forehead, it struck me first that I'd thrown off my daze, and that I'd felt that pain before not too long ago, when I'd last needed help breaking out of something effecting my mind.

The savage winds around me suddenly stopped. Completely dead. Replaced with what I could only describe as stale air.

Pulling myself up, I could see Nechtan had stopped staring me down, and seemed to be gazing at a spot somewhere behind. His lips were slightly parted and eyebrows raised maybe half an inch. I heard a hoarse grunt behind me, heavy with strain, and I jerked around as I remembered who I'd brought with me.

From where she'd been half hiding behind me earlier, Viora was now standing tall, arms raised as if she was lifting a tremendous weight over her head, teeth bared and face drawn with effort. All around us, I could still see the trees swaying and ripping in the gale, detritus still flying in every direction.

Except us. All around Viora and I, there seemed to be some kind of bubble, completely invisible yet locking us out from the chaos outside.

Holy crap. She was holding off Nechtan warping reality around us as a weapon. It wasn't by much, but she was holding out. If Nechtan could be resisted, maybe we could pull this off after all.

Nechtan looked no less impressed, wide eyes still fixed on Viora. 'Ah, the lost voyager. I must apologise. I'd forgotten you in my anger at your fool of a master. However he managed to bind someone of your strength, I cannot guess. But don't think this admittedly impressive display will grant you more than a brief reprieve.'

Nechtan flexed his fingers again, and this time, there was a great rumble.

Barely risen, I was almost thrown to the ground again as the earth started quaking, the violence of the vibrations only adding to the intense assault on my senses.

Around us, the greenery shredded and tore as the earth under them split, leaving harsh gashes in the land.

I heard Viora let out a cry, and I saw her stumble. She dropped to the ground as the cracks started creeping into our tiny bubble of protection. For a split-second, I felt the bubble waver. Viora was doing her best to hold, but she didn't have a chance on her own.

I bolted over to Viora, already seeing more tears in the earth creep closer to us. The earthquake continued to grow, threatening to swallow us up. This was going to be risky, but I already knew I had no better options.

As I funnelled as much spare energy as I could afford into the tip of the athame, I felt my tattoos go hot. I extended a hand to Viora. She grabbed hold with one arm. I pulled her up, then, before I could lose my balance, shifted my arm down and wrapping it around her torso.

Then, I pointed the athame down and unleashed all the force I had been able to muster.

Up to now, I'd been using my force magic for breaking things, and people.

This time however, I aimed the force into the ground, to reinforce it.

Another series of quakes hit. But this time, the vibrations smashed against reinforced earth, pain slashing across my skull as Nechtan's will brushed up against mine. My teeth clacked hard against each other.

My head kept erupting in pain, scraping at the thick walls of attention I'd forged inside my mind over a decade of discipline. When the latest wave of vibrations subsided, the simple cessation of pain hit like pure bliss, but I had to remind myself not to let up my focus.

That was only one wave, after all.

I looked back up at the situation around me. Viora, still clutched close to me, continued holding her bubble up around us, making a space Nechtan couldn't get through, but a thin line of blue blood had started trickling out of her nose.

As for Nechtan himself, he remained a lone pillar of order in the chaos, the earthquakes and hurricane-level winds not so much as ruffling his hair. If anything, he had a look of almost faint confusion on his face as the elements kept pummelling us.

There was no chance of beating Nechtan in a fair fight. That was clear. It was time for something I'd scavenged out of one of my drawers back home, bought months ago in case I ever needed it.

I thrust my free hand into my pocket, scrambling as I tried to grab my secret weapon before another set of earthquakes started smashing against my spell.

I hadn't wanted this to be my next resort. There was no way it wouldn't make things tense, but not much point worrying about that when the situation's already pretty damn escalated.

I yanked my new weapon out of my pocket, a small, yet chunky cardboard box, and kept it half hidden in my grasp.

Then, to really make sure I didn't tip Nechtan off, in place of speaking, I thought as loudly as I could. 'Viora, when I give the go-ahead, I need you to open the shield so I can target Nechtan.'

'No! Wind will shred to pieces!' Came the frantic thought response.

'Trust me! I've got an idea, but I can't do it while you're blocking me!' I shot back.

I felt what I was fairly certain was the telepathic equivalent of a groan.

'Careful.' Viora's voice echoed in my head one last time.

Between earthquakes, Nechtan took the chance to speak again.

'You've both distinguished yourselves quite well in surviving as long as you have. But even you must concede that this but a temporary measure'

Nechtan tilted his head at us, looking genuinely puzzled. 'What did you hope to gain by goading me here?'

Well, I wasn't one to turn down a set-up like that one.

'Now!' I mentally screamed and then, in one fluid motion, tore the box open with my knife, furiously shifting my will from the earth below us, which immediately began to weaken, to the large number of small objects inside the box.

That was when the second part of the plan kicked in. Hand already lifted before I even fired, Viora clenched her fist. At this command, the barrier collapsed. The full force of the wind struck us both, the shock of it almost enough to pound me into submission.

Almost.

I followed the motion through into a thrust in Nechtan's direction. The winds raked at my eyes, while I felt the objects in my hand swell with kinetic force.

Out of the box, they launched: seventy small iron nails, the bane of all Sidhe, flying at Nechtan like machine gun fire.

Just before they hit, I twisted the blade in my hand, point down, the gesture letting me ground kinetic power in the nails, holding it, but not quite releasing it.

Nechtan recoiled with a yell, yet the nails whirled around him, stopping mid-air in a very specific pattern. Like a parody of a halo, the nails were now floating in the air, all pointing inwards, ready to stab at a moment's notice.

Nechtan blinked as he saw the nails, then whirled towards us, the calm mask fracturing. 'You would dare-'

This time it was my turn to cut him off. I shouted back, still holding up my athame to keep the nails in place. 'Might want to turn off the wind, Nechtan. Guarantee you want me focused on keeping those nails away from your head.'

Nechtan let out an aggrieved sigh. And just like that, the blitzing gusts died away. The worst attack I'd ever experienced now nothing more than a gentle breeze across the ravaged grove, the shredded plants and torn earth it's only evidence.

I breathed my own sigh of relief. I could see Viora do much the same, visibly dirtied and cut by flying debris. I couldn't believe it'd worked, but it seemed we had Nechtan where we wanted him, the classical bane of iron against all Sidhe hopefully enough to keep him cooperative for what was to come.

Nechtan still managed to look defiant, mind you, staring us down. 'What now, then? Do you plan to skewer me like a cocktail sausage? If you simply wish to kill me, at least have the decency to not make it an iron death.'

I walked towards Nechtan. 'My apologies, Lord Nechtan, but your response to my earlier attempts at diplomacy made it clear that I would need to restrain you to make myself heard. Like you said, I wouldn't have achieved anything by picking a fight I couldn't win.'

I reached out my free hand. 'I also apologise for this, but I need to know.'

I surged towards Nechtan, who recoiled, only to stop as his face brushed against a nail. He clapped a hand to his cheek and wince. I grabbed hold of his shirt and pulled as fiercely as I could.

Slowly, Nechtan removed his hand from his face, both now stained with blood. But what really caught my attention was what I saw on his exposed chest.

Symbols. Nechtan's chest was covered in intricate symbols, lacing across his torso and trailing down to the rest of his body, judging from the brief glance I caught of the marks spiralling along one of his arms.

Symbols. The exact same as the last time I saw them.

On Thoun.

Nechtan raised his hand accusingly towards me.

I spoke up first. 'So, how long has Calatin had you under a geas, then?'

# Chapter 25

Nechtan made a choking sound, his eyes widening.

He took a long, hollow breath, straightened up, his face carefully neutral, even as he found himself mere centimetres from the corona of nails.

'I could not possibly comment.' He responded; his voice completely flat.

'Claim ignorance? Thought Sidhe better liars.' Viora glowered at Nechtan, shaking off the debris caught in her clothing.

I held up a hand. 'You're focused on the wrong word. He didn't say he wouldn't comment, he said he couldn't.'

I then looked back to Nechtan. 'Isn't that right, Nechtan? Did whoever put those geas markings on you command you not to speak about them?'

Nechtan glanced away, his eyes the only part of him moving at all. 'It's not my place to say.'

I drummed my fingers against my leg as I thought. That was almost as good as a yes, but it still left us in a tricky spot.

If Nechtan was forbidden from discussing the geas, it was going to be hard to figure out any way around them.

'Then, indulge me in a hypothetical. If someone were, theoretically, to plot to subdue you and turn you into an agent of their interests, how would they go about doing so?'

Nechtan's eyes narrowed, but when I finished, a smirk started to play on his lips. 'I suppose, if such a thing were ever attempted, it would've had to be done nearly a decade ago, when I was still foolish and inexperienced with the modern world. Such an effort would most likely include an iron forged binding circle to debilitate my ability to resist, accompanied by a most horrible physical assault, where upon the conjurer could begin scribing a geas upon me while I was disabled. Hypothetically, of course.'

'Naturally.' I responded. 'So, on a similar hypothetical note, anyone attempting to bind an entity like you with a geas would almost certainly have some larger plan, considering the effort it would have to take to disable you, correct?'

'In theory. I could only assume any person with enough power and desperation to subvert me into being their servant would have some larger motivation.' Nechtan's smirk grew into a proper smile. 'Being of noble stock, for instance, they could easily use me as a puppet to rally some manner of movement among the commoners, one that suits my 'master's' purposes.'

'And another would be using illusions and shapeshifting to impersonate members of other groups, like a Lemurian?' I ventured, a cautious confidence starting to build.

Nechtan gave a non-committal shrug. 'It's possible. A suitable identity would need to be stolen, but you'd be amazed how easy it is to lure one sheep away from the flock.'

'Such as, say, Thoun, the leader of the local Lemurian nest?' I pressed.

Nechtan raised a hand to his mouth. 'Oh yes, that would be an excellent disguise, provided one disposed of the original long ago while he was still a mere peon and worked up the ranks from there, of course. A time-consuming task, but one that would build more than enough goodwill to allow the occasional absence.'

'Then, if we assume such a replacement did take place-' I forced myself to temper my growing excitement. '-How likely could it be that the same shapeshifter could use connections with a group of Visitors to set up a release of a deadly pathogen onto their ship, and why would they?'

'A very interesting thought experiment.' Nechtan clapped his hands together. 'Certainly, it would seem probable that if such transpired, such an individual would be the most likely culprit. As to why, well, perhaps his puppetmaster wished to draw the attention of larger factions to the use of the pathogen, which would in turn be swiftly seen as connected to other groups aside from the culprit's own, which may be using the same disease for their own purposes. From there, I suppose the use of that and an occasional attack to inflame tensions would greatly encourage said factions to take violent action.'

I was never the type to jump for joy, but I was tempted right there. Everything I'd guessed so far had be confirmed, as much as it could be. Nechtan was Calatin's inside man, for both the Sidhe and the Lemurians.

Even better, that he'd been geased into co-operation, while it meant a lot of dancing around, meant Nechtan would likely try to work with us, if only because Calatin's death might free him from the geas. The breakthrough sent a thrill through me.

That was quickly quelled, unfortunately, as the beginnings of a major headache bump along the inside of my head, as well as a sudden need to still the trembling in my hands.

Dammit, holding these nails was really starting to wear on me, but I couldn't risk that Nechtan wouldn't still try something if I let them go. Need to get to the point.

'Well, perhaps you can fill us in on something else. It would be fair to say that things have been getting fairly tense between your Sidhe Army and the Seventh Wave, right?'

Nechtan nodded once. 'Oh, certainly. Anyone could see that things are getting very heated. Why, it would only take an attack at the right place on the right people to spark the flames of war.'

I nodded, my follow-up question already primed, when my grip around my knife and the spell both loosened, my arm dropping like a lead weight, my other hand just barely catching the athame in time for me to recover the spell.

What the hell? I knew maintained the spell holding the nails would be rough, but I shouldn't be buckling this quickly.

That was what I thought, until I noticed the familiar numbness swallowing my limp arm, the same sensation I felt when Calatin got the jump on me.

I wasn't the only one having problems. In my peripheral, Viora slumped forward, her hands clamped on her knees for support.

Shit. The virus must be starting to work its way into our systems. I started feeling breathless, which was quickly smothered by an eerie calm.

Exactly like when Calatin had already nearly killed me with this damn virus.

Whatever hope I had that Nechtan hadn't noticed died the instant I saw the look on his face.

'So, that explains why you were so foolhardy in drawing me here. You're already dying.' He said, examining us appraisingly.

I snarled, hitting my numb arm a few times until I could feel it again. 'Not fecking yet, we aren't. Listen, it's in as much your interest to stop Calatin as ours right now. I know you're limited in what you can share, but we need more if we're going to nab him before things get unsalvageable. I already know Calatin's planning to use you and some others as agents to deploy this new bioweapon, but what's the actual plan?'

Infuriatingly, Nechtan chose that moment to once again go stone-stiff. 'I'm afraid I've no answer for you.'

Even with my emotions dulled, I was able to muster up enough boiling anger to inch the nails forward ever so slightly. 'Trying my patience, fairy. We're past the point where you can play dumb.'

At the sight of the nails, Nechtan went from statue stiff to frightened prisoner stiff, his handsome face marred with horror. 'No! You misunderstand! There's no plan for my forces to engage with any factions first!'

My first instinct was to keep forcing the nails closer, only I noticed something about his word choice. 'First? So, the plan involves someone else launching the virus, then you and your lot come in afterwards?'

Nechtan half opened his mouth, only to flinch, glowering at the marks on his chest. 'You may speculate however you wish, I can't comment.'

'Who? The Lemurians?'

Nechtan let out a sharp laugh. 'Oh, dear me! In the state they're in after yesterday? Any leader trying to march them into war now would be deposed in a heartbeat!'

My jaw clenched at the unexpected reminder of my rampage.

Still, for better or worse, if the Lemurians had a role in Calatin's original scheme, that role would've definitely changed now that several of them had been killed and their den completely demolished. The only other significant paranormal group in Dublin that could even theoretically serve as the main inciters would have to be–

My stomach twisted violently as I put the pieces together.

'The Seventh Wave?!' I shouted. 'There's no way! They've been your main enemy up to now! Calatin doesn't even have any agents there! Why would they work with your lot now?'

The nails quivered precariously before I remembered to keep focusing on the spell. Between my lungs trying to curl into balls, and the sheer disbelief, losing control was quickly becoming a matter of time.

Even so, I stared daggers into Nechtan, determined to get answers out of him.

Nechtan's eyes drifted to the nails as they shuddered. 'Indeed, the idea that our respective groups could ever join together is preposterous. In fact, I see no way the Seventh Wave would knowingly attempt any hostile action against your organisation or human citizens. That said, if they were somehow tricked into carrying the virus unknowingly....'

'Yes?!' I rasped out, beads of sweat forming on my brow.

Nechtan scratched his chin idly, examining the nails with feigned clinical disinterest. 'An interesting fellow, that simian. What's the word, ah, Vanara. The second in that duo that followed you into the Lemurian nest. If an agent of this greater chaos knew of his presence from the lips on a forced informant, it would be easy to reason that if anything were to happen to you, he'd be one of the first to find your body.'

He looked from the nails to me, smirking. 'On an unrelated

note, did you know many of your kind's most virulent illnesses can be carried by monkeys?'

'That-that can't work. The virus works on sympathetic rules. Only humans should be carriers!' I stammered, thinking back to Dawkes' theory. Our whole plan ran on that assumption, if it was wrong...

Nechtan's brow raised slightly, his expression pleasantly surprised. 'You've proven wiser than you let on. Unfortunately, I feel inclined to note there is already one exception to that rule.'

He cast a meaningful look over to Viora. 'Just as she likely relies on partial human ancestry to share your burden, such a potential mystical contagion could lay dormant in a sufficiently ape-like being, only to pounce once human contact was made. A plague monkey, if you will.'

Distantly, I heard nails and a knife both drop to the ground. Oh, God, Bhajan.

If what Nechtan was saying was true, Calatin had counted on Bhajan coming across me, whether the virus had killed me or not.

I should've guessed. If the virus could be transferred just from a sample on gloves, just having traces of it on his fur would turn Bhajan into a walking biohazard. Hell, if there were any other Vanara in Dublin, traces could end up on them as well.

And, just to top it all off, I'd told him to rally as many as he could to make contact with the Enlightenment, and, knowing Bhajan, any potential meeting would have him there in the front row.

That thought alone made me want to curl up and let the virus take me. On top of stabbing me in the back, Calatin had still managed to play me and those around me. Sure, with how tense things were right now, Bhajan would probably avoid human contact and lay low, but that would only prevent immediate human casualties.

The Sidhe and Lemurians barely need to do anything, just capitalise on whatever chaos would ensue when Enlightenment agents contacted the Wavers, with Bhajan in tow. Worse yet, if any of the resulting violence spilled over into Dublin proper, the same virus could spread aggressively across the city, killing hundreds, even thousands.

The whole thing would look like a concentrated effort by all the paranormals in Dublin to wipe out the Enlightenment, and they would have no choice but to hit back with everything they had.

Through my shocked daze, I spotted Nechtan step over the nails now lying discarded on the ground, passing over them with a sneer.

As he got within a few steps, a few of the nails suddenly lurched up from the ground and shot with bullet-speed past his already cut cheek. Nechtan glowered at a spot to my left.

'Not another step.' Viora stumbled into view, standing over me, hand held out. 'Nails hurt, yes? Not as precise as Enlightenment, but much faster.'

Nechtan glared daggers at her, but he raised his arms in surrender. 'Hold. I've already fulfilled my obligation here. It was made clear to me a few minutes ago that it was imperative that I use all means at my disposal to try and kill you, should I encounter you. I did my best, but alas, in the end, you bested me, using iron to intimidate me into submission. Hardly the first time that's happened, and certainly no-one could claim I didn't exercise my full might to try and end you. Such a shame you won regardless.'

Nechtan spoke casually, but I could see his lips twist.

That's right, Nechtan was working against Calatin as best he could. While that attack was no pantomime, he was interpreting Calatin's instructions as maliciously as possible, hence this whole charade.

I shot Viora a grateful look as I stood up. 'Right. I get it. Shit, this is bad.'

'Clarify?' Viora asked, still focusing intently on Nechtan.

'If Bhajan's carrying the same virus we've got, then we're in deep trouble. All Calatin needs is for him to get just a little too close to any human and it could turn into a death spiral. If the Wavers go on the move for any reason, which they will once Bhajan sounds the alarm, if even a couple of them can carry the virus like he can, they'll become vectors too.'

'Find monkey first. If going to Wavers, just go to where Wavers are and prevent movement. Explain situation.'

'Not that simple.' I replied. 'The Seventh Wave aren't one movement, they're a bunch of different paranormal communities scattered across Dublin.'

Viora stared at me blankly, and I realised I needed to elaborate. 'It's part of why they're called a wave. They band together and wash over any outside threats and keep to their own affairs otherwise. I've no idea who Bhajan could approach first, and just being in those communities will risk the virus spreading to local humans.'

'Call Monkey on cellular device?' Viora asked again.

I blinked. Huh. Amazing the things you forget under stress. 'Good idea. Need to get out of the Shroud first.'

Looking back to Nechtan, I fixed him with a stern look. 'So, what now? Guessing you can't just tell us where Calatin might be at right now? Or maybe give us a clue how to fight these bioweapons you two have been throwing around.'

Nechtan shook his head with a quiet laugh. 'My deepest apologies, but as you say, my hands are, in many ways, tied. Still, I can offer a small word of advice.

'Yeah?' I asked.

Nechtan leaned in until I could feel his breath against my ear. 'Any individual so focused on achieving the outbreak of chaos you theorise is happening, and is improvising the plan ad hoc, is not going to be far from the epicentre of the instigating event, if only to make sure events proceed according to their plan.'

I nodded. It was something. I still didn't know exactly what the 'instigating event' might be, but one major idea sprung to mind.

Once Bhajan made contact with the Wavers, he'd try to contact the Enlightenment, exposing several humans to the pathogen. If I could track down where that was going to happen, Calatin would be there. He couldn't afford not to be.

'In that case, the only thing we can do now is bring you into custody. With your testimony implicating Calatin and the hit to Sidhe morale from your capture, we might just turn this around.'

I made to grab Nechtan's arm, only for him to pull back. 'There might be a problem with that, I'm afraid.'

I raised an eyebrow, but before I could ask what he meant, I heard a strange howl in the wind.

Looking around, I saw dark shapes fly through the air, then land, revealing themselves as tall, dark shadows of men dressed in coats and wide hats, gliding towards us.

I could feel a chill run through my body, could see the grass shrivelling and dying as they passed.

'The hell are those?' I shouted over at Nechtan.

'Ah. You recall that I mentioned I was obliged to try and kill you with all means at my disposal, yes?' Nechtan responded.

'Yes?' I replied.

A smug smile rose on Nechtan's lips. 'I'm afraid that included not mentioning that my personal guard have a means of tracking my location if I were ever to go missing. My apologies, I would've mentioned this sooner, but that would have sabotaged our efforts to kill you, which would hardly have been using all means at my disposal. I'd recommend retreat, the Ankou are not known for mercy or restraint.'

That bastard. I should've clocked it.

For all the help he'd given us, Nechtan was still an arrogant Sidhe noble, the kind that rankled at any sort of restriction or binding. He'd worked with us in the hopes of freeing himself, not to get jailed by a third party.

I brandished my athame. 'You son of a-'

My arm yanked back, as Viora came into view, holding me back. 'No time! Flee now!'

I didn't just want to stay, I wanted to put my knife in Nechtan's neck. I swore loudly before swiping my blade in Nechtan's direction.

'This isn't over, Nechtan! Just because Calatin's got his hand up your arse doesn't mean I won't kill you if I have to!'

Nechtan's smirk stayed unmoved. 'Perhaps, perhaps not. Good luck, Arbiter, you'll certainly need it.'

I bolted to the hillfort. Viora at my heels as we scrambled through the door. I slapped the nearest wall with my hand and shouted 'Friotaíocht!', once more feeling the uncomfortable shift as we crossed back to our world.

When reality stopped spinning, I kicked the door open and ran in the direction of the car.

We'd barely made it three steps when I noticed the chill in the air and the sense of dread.

I sprinted across the muddy grass, hopping over the fence separating the field from my parked car.

Half a heartbeat from getting the door open, I heard Viora let out a gasp. My legs disappeared out from under me, that I was flying through the air only registering a second after I'd already hit the filthy ground back in the field. Recognising the tell-tale feeling of her telekinesis, I spun over to glare at Viora, her hand still held out from when she just pulled me back.

She didn't look back, and I noticed that she was looking with naked horror at something in front of us. My heart threatened to explode out of my chest as I turned around.

Inches from where I was standing, a scythe blade stuck out of the ground, a shadowy figure already half-way pulling it loose, whilst, atop the car roof, the other figure loomed, his scythe held casually as his shadow cast long across the grass in front of me.

Under the shadow, the grass shrivelled and wasted away, as if Death itself loomed over them.

Of course. If Nechtan could transport us past the Shroud so easily, why couldn't his elite guard pull a similar trick, following us back to reality?

Neither shadow made even a single sound, as they both moved to stand in front of the car, our one means of escape, and closed in.

Suddenly, all Dawkes' complaints about me being reckless

made a lot more sense.

# Chapter 26

I'd like to say I'd been in worse situations than this one, but I wasn't sure that was true.

The two figures strolled closer, coming up to the fence separating the field from the road. One of them reached out a hand and touched it. I saw the wooden fence rot under it's hand, the decay spreading rapidly.

The figure yanked once, causing the fence to fall apart, leaving enough space for both to walk through. As the two got closer, I tried to remember everything I could about the name Nechtan had given them.

Ankou. Omens of death, living incarnations of it's inevitability, and, from what I'd heard, their presence alone carried the weight of death with it, withering and decaying anything in their presence, or struck by their scythes.

Some weren't all bad, watching over graveyards, guarding the dead there, but others were more...proactive.

Think claiming the life of the first thing to enter any new house in their territory proactive.

Shit.

My hand went to the pocket where I had been keeping the box of nails, feeling for any nails that might be left. I felt four or five graze my fingers. I cursed myself for forgetting to grab any others as we fell back. We needed to flee, fast.

That'd be the plan if they weren't standing right in front of the car. I doubted either me or Viora could outrun them.

As if having two incarnations of death looming ever closer wasn't bad enough, as they got closer, I could feel the unsettling, all too familiar numbness in my limbs, seeping through my muscles and travelling slowly up the bones.

The virus was upping its game, and I'd bet anything that the two death spirits closing in probably had no small hand in that. For all I knew, they didn't need to do anything to kill us, just being in their proximity might be enough to let the pathogen accelerate past our efforts to contain it.

'Viora, can you hear me?' I thought as loudly as I could.

Another voice spoke inside my head. 'Plan?'

'We might still have a chance, but I need you to listen carefully.'

One pretty big benefit I was starting to realise regarding telepathy is that you get a lot more conversation done under pressure.

In the time it'd taken the Ankou to take another couple of long lingering steps towards us, I managed to convey what I wanted Viora to do. She started falling back, while I stood at the ready, facing our assailants head on.

As they approached, I whipped my athame out and barked out 'Tintreach!', sending a coursing volley of electricity out towards the nearest one. The Ankou, not even breaking stride, slashed his scythe through the air, the electricity sputtering as the blade sliced through it.

I had to force myself not to yelp as my spell quite literally died on the Ankou's scythe. I tried to focus that fear into more power. Standing my ground, I slashed the athame back and forth, channelling force from my tattoos into a pair of large, invisible blades of energy, which sped towards their targets. Again, the Ankou swept their scythes, catching the blades, which dissolved into nothingness, the energy dying out.

It was one thing to hear second-hand that even spells died at an Ankou's touch, but it was another to see it in action. I dropped down as my knees gave way under me, fear and the numbness of the virus sapping all strength from them. My breath came out in harsh wheezes as I tried to crawl away, the dark shadows bearing down on me.

This was it. I couldn't stop them. I had just one last shred of a plan. I squirmed and I whimpered, real terror adding to the act. I knew how pathetic it was, but it'd be worth it if the Ankou would just keep looking at me.

They did, the nearest reaching out his rough hand towards my face. At this distance, I dimly recognised the shadowed face of one of the bikers that Nechtan always kept close by. Now I knew why.

But, like so many before them, they forgot about Viora while focusing on me.

As the Ankou's hand was half an inch from my face, it vanished under a tidal wave of grassy mud. His twin had enough time to blink before the same wave swallowed him up as well, the two harbingers of death buried under a mass of sloppy earth torn from the ground, spilling up like a geyser, propelled by Viora's will.

I pulled power from my tattoos, the heat practically the only sensation in my arms as I awkwardly thrust them up, hands clutched shakily around the athame.

'Now!' I shouted, and a moment later, the geyser stopped spilling up, leaving a split second where the two Ankou were now sprawled in a large trench in the ground, splattered with mud. Seizing the brief chance, I bellowed a roar as I swung the athame, bringing down a blade of blue-coloured force with it that struck the trench with the force of a truck, making the trench as deep as I could.

The Ankou, too dazed to counter it, fell deeper into the pit I'd just made, quickly followed by another tidal wave of filth, as Viora siphoned as much loose mud as possible down the trench, until neither of us could see our assailants under their improvised prison.

What followed, once Viora stopped the telekinetic assault, gasping for breath, was a moment of pure dread, as we watched the mound for any sign of the Ankou bursting out. When no such explosion came, I let out a breath, then started hobbling over to the car.

'Right, come on. Hopefully that should keep them busy.' I called over to Viora, keys already in hand.

'What if dirt rot away, like fence?' Viora asked, her gaze not leaving the mound.

'You can't exactly kill dirt, Viora. That won't stop them forever, but with any luck, they'll have to dig their way out, and death spirits or not, that's gonna take time.'

Viora's brow furrowed, but she didn't say anything else as we got into the car. It took a couple of tries to get the key slotted in, my hands still trembling from adrenaline.

My stare was glued to the mirrors as we pulled off, waiting for the second the earth would burst open. Only once we were out of sight of the hillfort did I looked over to Viora. 'How're you feeling?'

'Numb.' She responded, squeezing her arms tightly. 'Not as frightened as before.'

I winced. It wasn't just me after all. 'That's probably the virus. Thing dulls your body and emotions. Calatin claimed it was so anyone infected would have a peaceful death.'

'Or reduce panic. Keep resistance minimal.' Viora murmured, flexing her fingers.

'Probably.' I conceded, with a bit more reluctance than I expected, the thought that Calatin would've been that callous sitting poorly in my gut. Part of me had still nursing its wounds over Calatin's betrayal, I suppose, still flinching at the notion. That was something I'd need to get over fast.

Whether Calatin had planned for things to go this way or not, I'd still been the one to hand him the tools to make this mad scheme happen. If I hadn't dragged Bhajan into this, hadn't revealed him to Nechtan and therefore Calatin, Calatin might not have realised he could use him as a literal plague monkey to poison us.

Because of me, when reinforcements from the Enlightenment almost inevitably tried now to establish contact with the Wavers, who Bhajan was this very minute organising, it was going to turn into a massacre. I had to fix this, before it was too late.

As I tried to figure out what to do next, I started hearing what sounded like galloping behind us, only much faster. I glanced over at Viora, and the puzzled look she gave me was enough to let me know I wasn't just hearing things. Confused, I looked back, then stopped short.

Was that a fecking horse-drawn cart?!

That was certainly what it looked like, except that it, and the horses pulling it, one in the prime of health while the other looked sick and weakly, were all speeding down the road fast enough to gain on the car, wooden wheels clattering loudly as they drew closer.

Seated atop the cart, two all-too familiar cloaked figures, wielding scythes, pulled and yanked the reins, urging their horses onwards with furious bellows.

'Said can't kill dirt!' Viora shouted over.

'Must've found another way out!' I shouted back. I'd known the dirt wouldn't hold them for good, but this was beyond unfair. 'Throw anything you can at them!'

Wrestling my athame loose, I rolled my window down, keeping the oncoming cart in sight of my mirrors. The car shuddered and jolted, jarring my attempt to draw a bead on the target, only for my side-mirror to explode in a shower of glass. I pulled back, shards slicing at my cheek.

I glanced up at the front mirror, only to see that one of the Ankou had produced a revolver, old and worn enough to pass for an antique, but clearly more than functional, loud pings echoing across the car as he continued pumping bullets into us.

'How's finding something to throw back going?!' I barked over at Viora.

'Going by objects too fast! Can't focus!' Came the frantic reply.

I growled, but then I caught sight of the next turn. Along it, there was a small stone wall, separating the turn from the field next to it.

'The wall! Use the wall!'

Viora followed my finger to the incoming wall, ducking as another ping ricocheted off her side of the car. She looked back and gave a firm nod.

'Hold tight!' I said, then locked the wheel and slammed the accelerator, spinning the car into a hard turn round the corner.

Viora made her move halfway through the turn, both hands stretched towards the brickwork. The bricks in the wall started to shake.

I heard a loud crash, and in the mirror, I saw an entire section of the wall rip away from the whole, the bricks tumbling and scattering back down the corner like shrapnel. I heard the distressed whinnying of the horses.

No chance they were going to able to keep pace with us after that. I checked the mirrors, just to be sure the Ankou wouldn't still take a couple of pot-shots-

Oh, you have to be joking.

Not only did the Ankous' cart swing around the corner, horses and riders all clearly battered, but not nearly hard as much as they should've been, but the cart had picked up speed again, ripping across the road and getting closer by the second.

I moaned, glancing about for another wall or fence to fling at them, when another shot to ring out. Immediately, the car lurched slightly to one side, the screeching of a wheel working against a flat tire followed my sudden struggle to keep the car level.

The next few seconds were a whirl of confusion, as I struggled to keep the car moving, Viora yelping as the sudden swerving and shifting send her yanking violently back and forth. A couple more shots, one shattering our back window. Through it, I saw the cart speeding up, the horses almost up our back.

Just as the vehicles got within a stone's throw of each other, the gun-wielding Ankou stood up. Dropping his gun to brace himself against the cart, the Ankou then leapt with a superhuman burst of motion that I only saw as a blur.

In the heat of the moment, I barely heard something land above us with a light thud.

Fucking Christ! He's on the roof!

I heard the metal on the roof start to creak and groan, the weight of the Ankou pushing through the steel, the lining of the ceiling rotting and falling away to reveal rust blooming along the metallic surface.

Viora stared up at the roof in horror, pointing up at it. 'S-steel just iron alloy! Should hurt them!'

'Needs to be pure iron! Out!' I shouted, pushing over Viora to thrust her door open. I shoved her out, then dived out after.

I heard the car roof give way and heavy boots slam onto the seats. Scrambling up, I saw the horses gallop to the side, the cart cutting off the rest of the road, leaving me and Viora stuck, pinning between our assailants.

The Ankou atop the cart let go of the reins, striding onto the ground, a grim smile at his lips, while, just as I stepped back to get a wider view, I saw the other peel himself out of what was left of the car, his expression darkly irritated as he traded a glance with his counterpart, before raising his gun to Viora, the other readying his scythe.

Just like that, we'd been cornered all over again.

Still, there was one last trick I had, and I hardened my heart in preparation.

'Viora.' I mentally called over. 'Do you trust me?'

An agonising half second passed before I heard the telepathic response. 'What's the plan?'

I braced myself, taking a harsh breath through my nose as the Ankou drew closer. 'Hold firm. I'm coming back, I promise.'

The athame came out once again, and I swung it left and right as I peeled back, my body turning transparent, then invisible as I fled the scene.

Viora whipped her head around, her expression shifting to horror as I vanished, leaving her standing alone against the Ankou. I gritted my teeth as I forced myself to keep moving.

From my fallback point, I saw the Ankou both glower with clear disgust at my retreat, before turning their attention back to Viora.

She could've tried to run herself, or maybe beg for mercy, but instead, she flicked one of her hands out, sending the revolver trained on her flying out of its owner's hand.

I ran around the other side of the car, trying my best to ignore Viora screaming, the sound of flying objects and the Ankous' quiet snarls and grunts. My free hand slipped to my pocket as I got in position.

One shot. That was all I had.

I poked my head above the car bonnet as I waited for the moment. Even slowed down by the virus, Viora kept delaying their advance with a series of flung rocks that pummelled them as they got close. But a delay was all it was, and soon enough, the pair had managed to close the distance, Viora already shrinking to the ground as their shadows cast over her, just like when they'd cornered me.

But they'd made the same mistake again. Only this time it was me they'd forgotten about.

The Ankou's attention firmly on Viora, I hopped over the front end of the car to prowl behind the Ankou. Once I got in range, the Ankou barely an inch from Viora, I reared my fist back and punched the closer of the two in the back of the head.

Normally, a blow like that wouldn't have done much. If it

weren't, that is, for the sharp iron nails sticking out between my knuckles.

My fist throbbed from the impact, but the nails met no resistance as they pushed straight into the Sidhe's skull. The effect was instant, the Ankou dropping to the floor, dead. My invisibility wearing off, I planted my shoe on his back and pulled my fist, taking the nails smoothly out of his head.

The other Ankou, seeing his comrade fall, whirled on me, scythe raised to strike, only for Viora to raise her hand, causing it to swing wide, taking his momentum with it as he stumbled.

A second's distraction, more than enough for me.

Nails still in hand, I called out to the force hiding in my tattoos, sending it through my fingers into the waiting nails. Then, with a flick of my wrist, I let go.

The nails, propelled by the energy, darted to the remaining Ankou, three of the nails striking him square in the chest, the other two hitting him in the shoulder.

The Ankou's face went pale, and he let out an agonised scream. Without the mercy of a clear headshot, the nail wounds burned and smoked. Dropping his weapon, the Ankou grabbed futilely at the nails, each attempt only managed to leave horrific burns across his hands as he fell to his knees, still screaming.

I stared at the scene in stunned shock, then stepped forward, yanked a nail loose from his chest and, in the same motion, rammed it straight into the Ankou's head. He went silent and fell without a hint of resistance.

An iron death. Even knowing they were trying to kill us; I couldn't help but feel guilty for resorting to it.

As the body hit the ground, I saw it and it's twin start to

dissolve into mist, the fate of all paras who die outside the Shroud. Without their wills keeping them here, their bodies simply melted away, leaving no evidence of their presence.

A groan from Viora jolted me from my stunned state, and I went over to her, offering a hand up. It took Viora a moment to register my presence, taking gasping gulps of air as she trembled, but her hand latched onto mine tightly as I helped her up.

'Sorry.' I said quietly. 'I know that was a lot to ask.'

Viora's head turned up to me, and for a second, I worried that fear I sensed from her was now being directed at me. Then, she shook her head, and she pulled back gently, running her hands through her hair.

'J-just promise that Enlightenment will be bait next time.' Viora responded, her voice returning to its usual monotone.

'Duly noted.' I replied, even as I wondered why exactly she felt there would be a next time.

As we both tried to compose ourselves, my right leg went out from under me, and I had to grab hold of Viora again to stay upright. Viora went rigid, but held me up, as I tried to massage feeling back into my limb. I should've been getting nervous, but the odd lack of emotion I was feeling was more than clue enough what was happening.

'Not much time.' Viora noted flatly as she led me to the car bonnet, which I leaned against until I could move my leg again.

She wasn't kidding. The virus was only getting worse by the minute. Even with our delaying tactic, eventually we'd probably wind up losing all movement before slowly dying.

'Nope.' I looked over to the now thoroughly wrecked car. 'And I don't see this car going anywhere fast.'

'What now?' Viora asked. From here she looked frail and empty, like her soul had been ripped out of her. Did I look much better?

I threw that train of thought aside and looked about, trying to think of something we could do. Making it to Dublin on foot before succumbing was a pipe dream.

That's when I caught sight of the cart the Ankou had been riding. Unlike their owners, the horses were still here, and seemed relatively calm. It was a punt, but if I could get them to move as fast as they'd been chasing us...

I pointed over the cart, patting Viora on the shoulder. 'That's what's now. Get in.'

'Know how to handle those animals?' Viora sounded uncertain, but followed anyway, pulling herself up onto the cart. She looked uncomfortable, frightened and most of all, exhausted, but she hadn't complained once.

Grabbing hold of the reins, I gathered as much resolve as I could. It didn't matter what'd happen to me, but screwing up now wouldn't just lead to Calatin's plan going off, plunging Dublin into war, it would also mean Viora would die with me.

The burn from my fingers clenching the reins cut through the malaise fogging my mind. Like hell I'd let that happen.

I glanced over. 'Depends. How'd you feel about mind controlling animals?'

# Chapter 27

Luckily, Viora didn't have much objection to using her telepathic influence to get the horses moving.

Thanks to them, we'd be back in Dublin in minutes, even accounting for slowing down once we got in view of mundane drivers.

The bad news, was that this didn't really help with the ticking deadline hanging over our heads.

For one, the fact we were still both infected meant we'd have to avoid contact with any of the one million humans living in Dublin, lest we become the patient zeros Calatin wanted.

Even if we somehow stopped the paranormal forces from ripping each other to pieces; the more I'd thought about it, the more I'd realised we only had one chance of stopping the virus before it killed us.

We'd have to kill Calatin. It was his will that was keeping both the viruses we were dealing with alive. If Calatin was taken out of the picture, the spells would have no will driving them, and any samples of either virus would hopefully dissipate without a trace. Even if I was wrong, and we were doomed no matter what, we might as well take our killer down with us.

Not a happy thought, but it kept me moving. I didn't know

if I could say the same for Viora, but after all she'd done for me so far, I owed it to her to at least try to keep her alive. Even if that meant going toe to toe with an Archdruid while terminally ill.

But hey, at least we got the horses moving.

'Planning to call others?' Viora's voice startled me.

'Huh?' I mumbled back.

Viora frowned slightly. 'Wasn't plan to contact Monkey and other Enlightenment? Warn them about monkey being infected?'

That's right. I'd meant to try and call either Bhajan or Dawkes, but it'd completely slipped my mind. In my defence, I was being chased by two apparitions of death at the time.

I made a vague sound of acknowledgement as I fished my phone out of my pocket. I decided to call Bhajan first. Bhajan needed to know he wasn't safe around humans right now. Especially since, if Nechtan was being straight with us, he was currently Calatin's plan B.

It took longer than I'd have liked before Bhajan picked up, and I liked what I heard on the other end even less.

'Ah, Reilly! What wonderful timing! I have great news!' Bhajan's voice bellowed in my ear.

I flinched as the sound hit my ear, then tried to speak as quickly as I could. 'Bhajan, listen! You need to-'

'Hold, hold, my friend!' Bhajan's loud voice cut me off. 'I'm certain you have something important to say too, but let me speak first! For you see, I've managed to succeed in our joint effort beyond even my own lofty expectations!'

I paused, my spine going rigid. '...What do you mean?'

Not noticing my unease, Bhajan continued. 'Nothing less than that I, the wise and clever Bhajan, have managed to rally some of the most central leadership of the disparate immigrant paranormal communities of Dublin and, with the aid of the audio recording you so kindly provided, impressed upon them the need to take a joint stand against the threat that faces us all!'

I glanced over at Viora, the landscape whizzing by as she stared back, brows knotted together in confusion.

'Oho, but that's not all, my dour, yet courageous friend! For you see, thanks no doubt to the decisive actions of the fair Agent Dawkes as well as myself, our respective groups have already made plans to meet to discuss this menace!'

My face went cold. 'Wait, Bhajan, you can't-'

Bhajan's voice cut in again, only fainter this time.

'Bah, just a moment, you overgrown pest! I'm speaking to a friend!' Bhajan's voice spoke again, now back to its original volume. 'Sincerest apologies, Reilly, but it seems I've run out of time. We're meeting your crew down by the Docklands, by the Point Village. Whatever you have to say, it'll have to wait until we meet there. Safe travels.'

'No! Stop! Bhajan, listen to-'

He'd already hung up.

I stared at the phone in impotent anger, just barely resisting the urge to smash it against the cart seat. I called back about five times in rapid succession, only to get the canned voice on the other end telling me the other phone wasn't available. Fucking typical!

I tried calling Dawkes. The phone barely got two rings before returning to dial tone. Cursing, I tried again, and again and again, only to get the exact same robot. How the hell could Dawkes not be available?! I knew those damn smart glasses could take calls!

Except that, of course, if the Enlightenment were on the move, then of course they'd try to block any communications in or out of Dawkes' unit! I had no way of getting in touch with her.

In one last bid, I tried calling Enlightenment HQ, only to, this time, get a robot telling me that the current number was engaged. Of course, with everything happening right now, HQ must be exploding with reports of paranormal violence across the city. They might get to me eventually if I waited, but it'd already be too late.

This time, I didn't resist the urge. I slammed my phone against the seat repeatedly as I screamed in pure helpless rage.

I threw the remains of my phone off the cart. Viora watched as the phone tumbled away, then slowly turned to me. 'Phone calls unsuccessful?'

'How'd you tell?' I muttered back.

I filled her in on the rest. How the Enlightenment and the Seventh Wave had both sent representatives to meet at the Docklands. Bhajan and Dawkes would both be there, which meant not only was Bhajan in prime position to accidentally infect the task force that arrived to meet him, but also, I couldn't get in touch with Dawkes, since the same force is probably taking precautions to block any electronic signals coming in or out of whatever bubble they've set up.

'Possible to do that?' Viora's eyes widened slightly.

I shrugged back. 'We've kept the paranormal a secret from billions of people with access to smartphones. It'd be impossible to do that if we couldn't interfere with electronic signals.'

Viora looked down; hands clasped tightly together. 'What

now?'

I let out a sigh as I scanned the horizon. We needed to get the Docklands as fast as possible, and we couldn't bring the horses into Dublin.

I glanced over to Viora, trying to keep the uncertainty out of my face. 'Hang on. I'll tell you when we get closer.'

We'd just about managed to roll up to the rough edge of Finglas, stopping at the point where the lonely road we'd been riding down converged with the N2 motorway. The trip had taken longer than I would've liked sticking to the side roads, but I was not going to risk having dozens of witnesses see a horse-drawn cart speeding down the motorway at car speed or exposing anyone to the virus.

I hopped off the cart, nodded to Viora to jump down as well, then starting walking, leaving the cart behind.

'What about horses?' Viora asked as she followed, looking back at the placidly lingering animals.

I waved my hand dismissively. 'No one's going to be looking for them. Once I get a chance, I'll just tell the Enlightenment where they are, and they can send someone to handle them.'

Viora looked back at the horses once more, then shook her head. As she caught up to me, she poked her head into my vision. 'Didn't explain earlier. How get into city?'

That was the question, wasn't it?

Me and Viora were biohazards right now. We couldn't even risk walking down the street without infecting anyone we came across. That didn't leave much options for getting to the Docklands in any kind of reasonable timeframe.

What the hell was I hoping to accomplish here? All this time, I'd been mindlessly pushing myself on and on, but I'd never stopped for so much as a second to consider if I could do anything. With contact with the Enlightenment cut, I was a sick man in the middle of nowhere, slowly dying from something that would kill any other human I came in contact with. Calatin had managed to outmanoeuvre me at every step. What if even my effort to stop him was part of Calatin's plan?

Then, a thought hit me. At first, I discarded it. That'd never work. It was completely stupid. But then, the more I thought, the more I realised I had nothing else.

I let out a groan. Guess we're doing stupid then. 'I have an idea. I'm going to need your help with it.'

Viora, still leaning into my vision, straightened up. 'What is needed?'

'Your telekinesis again. Also, I'm going to need you to steer.'

'Sure this is good idea?' I felt Viora wriggle a bit on my back.

'I ran out of good ideas days ago, Viora!' I responded, trying to properly position my legs. A tall order when you're standing in a muddy field, in the rain, with an alien on your back.

'Considered all possible variables?!' Viora shouted over my shoulder. 'Impacting with ground? Colliding into obstacles?!'

'That's where your other role comes in.' I shouted back. 'As we're making each jump, I want you to use that telekinesis to slow our descent. Between that and reinforcing my legs with magic, I think this should just about work.'

'What about possible sighting?' Viora's voice raised a couple of octaves. 'Jumping through city with supernatural force will likely draw attention!'

'Thought of that, too.' I responded, pulling out my athame and performing the familiar gestures that swiftly rendered the pair of us camouflaged. 'Between this and the rain, any potential onlookers are going to hard pressed to notice anything odd!'

Viora's next response was a low murmur. 'Rain will also make determining direction difficult.'

I rolled my eyes. 'Well, it's either this, or lay down and die, Viora. What's your choice?'

Viora fidgeted uncomfortably, then said something quietly.

'What?'

'Enlightenment will get hurt. Don't want that. Already hurt enough.'

The words left me stunned for a moment. My mouth opened and closed a couple of times. 'Viora, I'm not just doing for myself right now, or even for the Enlightenment. I'm want to stop Calatin for both those reasons, sure, but-'

I forced myself to continue. '-But I'm also trying to save you right now. Me dying would suck, but it'd be a price I'd pay if it meant I could bring Calatin down with me. Thing is, the only reason I'm even here at all is because you've put your life on the line to buy me time. After something like that, there's no way I'm going to let you die from that virus if I can stop it.'

I stood there, my shoes getting wetter and wetter as I waited for Viora to reply.

When she did, it was curt. 'Fine. Better not regret this.'

I let out a breath. Then began bracing myself.

The process was slow, far slower than most spells I'd done up now. Between having to build energy, pulling power from my tattoos and channelling it all into my legs, while also having to channel energy into maintaining our invisibility, and on top of that, having to push through the malaise of the virus weighing down on my mind, it probably took me nearly half an hour to get everything ready, a splitting headache forming above my left eye from holding all of it in place.

'Ready?' I asked at last.

'Ready.' Came Viora's response.

I bend my knees, the muscles in my legs burning so intensely I almost expected steam to start coming off my legs. I fixed my gaze on the city ahead of us, putting all my focus on the need to get there, praying that doing so would lessen the upcoming pain.

Boiling with potential energy, I let that energy loose in one movement.

My vision went white as the explosion went off, my ears ringing from the thunderous crack as I was flung off the ground, feeling only hot agony. Somewhere, under the pain, I thought I must have shattered my legs, reduced them to gory stumps.

As my vision started to clear, I risked looking down. My legs were still there, which was a good sign, only now they were hanging in the air, the fields and roads under them now small and distant as the residue force carried me across them. Wind and rain slapped against my body. I wasn't normally afraid of heights, yet as I looked down, mind steadily registering that we were easily over a hundred feet in the air, my heart started pounding.

Without even thinking about it, I felt myself pull my remaining gathered power into my legs, hardening them against the inevitable drop, as the buildings close to the edge of Dublin starting coming into view. At the same time, I felt my descent slow, whilst also shifting, so what was initially looking to be a rough landing in the middle of the street was redirected into a landing atop a building, Viora playing her role perfectly to keep us from becoming smears on the pavement.

We slammed into the roof. The pain came back with a

vengeance, like I'd kicked a concrete wall.

My knees buckled as I slumped, gasping, just barely able to stand upright. I heard Viora speak, a worried note in her voice. 'Well?'

Hissing a breath through my teeth, I forced myself to stand up straight again. 'Intact, which is about as good as I could hope for. Good idea directing us to a rooftop. Probably saved me having to look for replacement kneecaps.'

'Yes, very much the intention, since Enlightenment did not consider possibility.' Viora muttered irritably. 'Second jump from here should clear more ground at once. Landing area will be very important, to prevent Enlightenment from crippling self.'

I stared out at the city before us. That's going to be quite a few jumps. 'Guess I'll leave the landing up to you then. Gimmie a moment and we'll go again.'

The next few minutes were an exercise in sheer pain endurance. Each jump like steadily shredding myself piece by piece. Every leap, an explosion that threatened to paste my lower body, every landing, a thunderous crack that seemed to pulverise my bones.

Ironically, the weather was actually a help, as the rain sent pure, numbing cold down my body, not enough to smother the pain, but taking the edge off. The experience was hellish, yet as I landed each time, and I felt Viora's weight press against my back, I reminded myself why I was doing this, why I had to keep going.

It'd been a mixed blessing, being able to see Dublin from relatively high up. Viora had taken full advantage of it to better direct our mad flight, pushing us to ensure the landings were, at least, tolerable. However, a few times, through the thick haze of rain, I caught more than a couple of sights of how far things had gone.

On the streets, while most people were rushing for cover or the safety of the bus or luas, some were simply on the move, and even if I ignored the way none of these were in groups of less than twelve, and all seemed to carry any number of tool or random object repurposed as a weapon, my magical senses told another story.

Each time I spotted a group, I could feel the heady mix of violent and aggressive energies in the air around them, a boiling pot of power, waiting and ready for the chance to explode on what sorry target they had in mind. I'd no way of telling if any of them were Sidhe, Wavers or even Lemurians out for payback, but it was clear things were coming to a head. If we didn't stop this war from kicking off, the damage would be immediate, and total.

Then, on what I think was the fourth or fifth leap, I landed once more on a rooftop, not even bothering to stifle the wounded howl that slipped out of my mouth. I dropped to my knees, gasping deep mouthfuls of air as I felt Viora clamber off my back, then make her way to the edge.

'Arrived.' She remarked.

'You sure? I replied, stumbling over to the edge to see for myself.

True enough, the building we'd landed on overlooked the Point Village, a collection of businesses and shops all centred around the 3Arena. In other words, we were right next to one of the biggest and most successful amphitheatres in Europe, definitely not where you'd think two secretive groups would meet up to discuss alliances, but as I mentioned before, oftentimes the best place to hide was in plain sight.

Now we just needed to find out where our allies were.

My first impulse was to look for the closest exit, only to quickly realise this rooftop didn't have any way of getting down from it. I chewed on the issue for a moment, then looked over at Viora. The barrage of rain we'd been dealing with for the last hour had left her looking miserable, the baggy clothing I'd given her now clinging to her in a way that emphasised how skinny she was.

More concerning, was the way her arms hung limply at her sides, while her shoulders were tensed up, as if she was struggling just to stay standing. I hated that I'd have to ask more of her.

'Viora, can you levitate us down to ground level? Sorry, but I can't see another way down.'

Wordlessly, Viora raised an arm, the movement slow and jerky, and I felt my feet slightly raise off the ground. She walked to the edge, me floating softly alongside, then stepped off, taking me with her as we fell off the roof. The fall was slow, though a couple of times during the descent, I saw Viora abruptly fall a few feet faster, letting out a quiet gasp before catching herself. I suffered no similar problem, which only made my guilt worse.

We touched down a stone's throw from the main plaza, my feet clapping against the pavement as gravity rushed to claim me again. Viora, having landed only seconds prior, let out a whimper as she slumped to the path.

Oh shit.

I bolted over, trying to catch her, missing by a hair as she collapsed. Frantically, I knelt down, reaching to check her pulse. She let out a nasty sounding cough.

'How're you holding up?' I asked, as I gingerly lifted her

up.

Viora let out another couple of gasping wheezes, gripping my shoulder tightly as she stood. 'Exhausted.'

'Just get under some cover, out of the rain. You've done all you can. I'll take it from here.' I reached into one of my pockets, producing the last of the potions I had on me. 'Here, if you have any wounds, pour that on it. Hell, you can chug it if you want. That can help with tiredness.'

Viora looked from the potion up at me, her face barely conveying worry behind a dense layer of exhaustion.

Slowly, and with great effort, she pulled herself from me and shambled over in the direction of a couple of shops, the canopies shielding the entrances from the downpour. Once I was sure she was heading to relative safety, I turned around and began walking to the plaza. Viora had given me far more than I should've asked. My turn to return the favour.

I pushed forward across the square, the chill from the rain becoming nothing more than background against the ever-pressing numbness. More than ever, it felt like it was sinking deep inside me.

Viora wasn't the only one short on time.

I squinted, trying to make out any figures in the rain. At this point, my hopes of killing Calatin to save myself and Viora were pretty thin, but if I could even just find Bhajan or Dawkes and warn them, maybe they could put him down before this virus killed us. And if they couldn't, at least I would have managed to throw one last wrench in his plans.

As I got closer, I made out the rough shape of a group in the distance. There were maybe nine or ten of them, standing in the centre of the plaza, packed close together, obscured by a mist that'd settled over them, but I could tell they were tense.

I broke into a jog, praying that I was about to find either the Enlightenment or the Wavers and not one of the violent bands I'd spotted jumping over here.

I felt a thrill of triumph as I clapped eyes on Bhajan in his human guise, his back turned as he surveyed the area. Alongside him, I could see the other figures were largely human in appearance, but I could tell from the way my teeth tingled as I got closer that they must've been other members of the Seventh Wave. Likely important ones too, assuming Bhajan's boasting earlier was anything to go by. I picked up the pace, ready to call out, only to see something that knocked all the regained strength out of me.

Maybe a kilometre away, another group, similar in size was coming in the direction of the Wavers. Again, the rain kept me from making out any details. But I didn't need that to recognise the rolling combat formation of armed troops, arranged in a circle around three other figures. The rain wasn't falling on them, the three seemingly occupying a bubble of dryness. I didn't even need to see the dark suits of my fellow agents to tell that they were the ones leading the troops.

Shit, shit shit! The Enlightenment's here already!? I forced my way up to a wobbly sprint. Instinctively reached out to Bhajan.

Then, something collided with me, the pavement hitting me in a way that forced the air out of me. I tried to thrash loose, kicking and squirming against the mass atop me as I opened my mouth again, only for a fist to slam against the side of my head. I tasted blood as I went limp.

What was happening?

That question got its answer when I made out the rough

shape on top of me. A large man, balding with a red nose, had pulled me into a grapple, while another, younger with a green jumper under his raincoat, retreated from having just punched me, revealing another, between the others in age, greying hair hidden under a flat cap, tapping a crowbar against his hand.

Maybe it was the impending concussion, but all I could focus on was that I recognised all three faces. From the Silver Arm pub.

With that, the third, Domhnall, I think, leaned forward, a grin splitting his face as he let the crowbar scrape against the road.

'Well?' He said, blocking my view of both the Wavers and the Enlightenment. 'Did you see that one coming, Enlighten-ment boy?'

# Chapter 28

I probably should've started panicking.

Not only was I dying and trapped, at the mercy of three men who didn't have much to spare, but if I couldn't find a way out of their grasp in a couple of minutes, the Seventh Wave and Enlightenment would make contact.

Once that happened, Bhajan would unwittingly unleash Calatin's bioweapon on Enlightenment agents at a truce, and all but seal the fate of every para in Dublin.

Yet, even with all that weighing on me, I was struggling to muster up any emotion. The space inside my head turned grey as I watched myself get dragged out of sight of the two groups. Ah, probably near the final stages, then. It was supposed to sap any motivation out of me before killing me.

I ought to be angry about that.

The only thing I had any sort of opinion on was just how annoying it was that of all the people to stop me at the final hurdle, it was some gobshite who tried to start something with me a couple of days ago, and his two buddies.

He was saying something to me, his tone slurred and smug as he tapped the crowbar meaningfully against my leg, the other two chuckle brothers chiming in here and there, but I couldn't tell you what they going on about. Probably something about how I was going to regret lording over them just because I was Enlightenment or something. The real mercy, I mused, was that Calatin's virus had stripped me of any ability to care.

It was getting hard to think about much at all. As the grey continued to creep in, I wondered if the men attacking me knew I had an infectious disease. Would Calatin have told them, or done something to protect them?

Come to think of it, how'd they know to find me? I only knew I'd be here a bit over an hour ago. Even if Calatin told them where to go, how'd he know?

'H-how did you k-know I'd be here?'

Domhnall leered down. 'Oh, would you look at that, lads? Not so big he can't talk to us now, is he?!'

The other two laughed tauntingly. Christ, was I really about to die to a pack of overgrown school bullies?

'A-answer the q-question.' I responded; my voice robotic as I tried to care.

Domhnall's grin widened. 'The Hierophant told us you'd be here. Said he'd snuck something on you that let him track you when you tried to kill him. Guess us 'Hedge Witches' aren't as pathetic as you lot think, huh?'

Tried to kill him? Was that the story Calatin sold to the Ciorcal Darach?

No, focus. What could he have put on me that would let him track me? Sure, I was easy pickings for planting pretty much anything on, then. But it didn't add up. Calatin was obviously trying to kill me at the Silver Arm, why waste time with a tracker?

Then it clicked. The thing he used to track me was the same thing killing me.

The virus. Dawkes had even said that she'd thought the virus worked by sympathetic magic. If that were true, then it would be trivial for Calatin to track down anyone infected with his pathogens, just by using the connection they had with him.

'You r-really shouldn't have t-tackled me.' I managed to reply, my mouth feeling like concrete. 'I'm infe-infected. Any phy-physical contact passes i-it on. S-should have j-just hit me w-with the crowbar.'

Domhnall sneered, slapping me upside the head. 'Nice try, shithead, but the Hierophant told us you'd try to pull some shite out your arse about him infecting you with some disease.'

'D-didn't say C-Calatin infected me.'

'You were about to!' One of Domhnall's buddies slurred out.

I'd have rolled my eyes if I had the energy. The only hope I had was to buy time, as I tried to think of a way out.

'Th-that's what you think's going on? What'd you r-reckon that meeting's about? We're trying to keep the peace h-here.'

'Oh sure. Your fucking peace, where you lot are the ones on top, while we get pushed to the sidelines, while all those fuckin' paras you're supposed to protect decent folk from strut around, claiming territory like it's their fuckin' city!'

The crowbar smacked against my thigh. 'It's not! Dublin's ours! And maybe a bit of war's exactly what we need to finally get rid of all the monsters and fascists stomping around our city!'

Getting hard to think now. Train of thought harder to string along. Still had plan. Just needed more time.

'E-even if it means in-innocent people die in the crossfire? Or d-do you actually t-think you wo-wouldn't get caught up in the fighting?'

Domhnall's fist collided with my face again. 'Shut up! I don't wanna hear one more fuckin' word!'

With one last sneer, he gestured to his buddies. 'Hold him still, lads. It's payback time.'

This was it, then? Beaten to death by a pack of idiots, inches from the very people I was trying to save? Should've known I'd die like this. That was the story of my life. Always falling short when needed.

Maybe I deserved this. I'd done so much wrong, hurt so many. It was pathetic to think I could even hope to try and change what I was.

A failure who couldn't even save a single person.

Domhnall brought the crowbar down on my gut. It felt like getting slapped by a pillow. When I didn't cry out, he scowled, bringing it down again, my left leg registering the same empty sensation. At least my death would be painless.

Looking up at the sky, I reflected on those who had trusted me, who I'd let down. Dawkes, who'd pushed me again and again to open up. Bhajan, who'd followed me into hell and back, all for a burger.

Viora, who hadn't even asked to trust me, but was forced to, when everything else in the world turned on her.

I'd tried to warn them, tell them I couldn't be trusted, and they hadn't listened. What was going to happen to them? Could any of them survive what was about to happen next?

No, they wouldn't. Viora was infected too, already inches from death. Once Bhajan got close enough, Dawkes would catch the virus off him. She'd die. Bhajan might be able to make a getaway, but for how long before either the Enlightenment or the Sidhe hunted him down? Not long at all.

My body twitched as the crowbar struck again, paling in comparison to the real pain that hit me. Good people, people who'd seen the ugliest side of me and refused to look away, were going to die. People who'd stuck by me, for reasons I still couldn't understand, were going to die. All of them was about to die, and it was all my fault.

No.

Something shifted inside me, a strange feeling I'd never experienced before. I couldn't explain, but I knew. I might be doomed, but I was not going to drag the people who trusted me down as well.

I started to pull myself up, ignoring the dull slaps of the crowbar. Maybe I deserved to die like this.

But they didn't.

'The fuck?!' Domhnall took a baffled step back, glancing back to his buddies, then forcing on another snarl. 'What some more, do yah?! Think you got some trick that'll weasel you outta this?! Yah don't even have a feckin' weapon!'

'Go-got one t-thing.'

'Yeah?! What?!' Domhnall screamed back, spittle hitting my face.

'M-magic.'

Domhnall's eyes squinted. Then widened as electricity crackled along my arm. Pain wasn't felt, but could smell skin burning. No athame to direct energy safely meant body taking the hit.

Fuck it. Dying anyway.

One tried to pull away. Other started kicking my chest. Both made wrong choice.

'Tintreach' I said quietly. Electricity coursed out of hand, hitting closest attacker. He fell back, screaming, only for electricity to fork off body, striking next. Domhnall realised too late to get away, same chain of lightning hitting him too. All fell to the ground, spasming.

No time left. Need to act now. Reached out hand again, seeing burnt, blistered skin. Used hand to push self over on chest. Called out to remnants of will, coaxed tattoos into life. Pumped hand with kinetic force, giving enough strength to start pulling body along ground.

Started to get hard to see as shadowed figures of groups came into view. Both close now, almost meeting at centre of plaza. Not yet, not allowed to die yet. Repeated thought as hand pulled body. Only one shot.

Let energy out of hand, went limp immediately. Started focusing on legs again. Legs were limp, unmoving, but spell done enough times now repeating was simple. Legs twitched. Power built at toes, readying for last jump.

Pavement cracked as body flew across plaza. Bhajan and leading agent already walking towards each other, both turned, tensed. Body hit pavement, twisting to keep momentum. Rolled across pavement, pain completely absent now. Came to stop flat on back, staring up as rain splattered face.

So tired. Hard to stay awake.

'Reilly?!' Lead agent called out. Now closer, could see it was Hu, Dawkes and another flanking. Looked confused, then angry, glared at Bhajan. 'What's the meaning of this?!'

'How should we know!?' Bhajan shouted back, hands up. 'We're not stupid enough to parade one of your wounded about when talking diplomacy!'

Tried to remember why here. Something important? Worth

staying awake for?

Wait. Yes! Very important!

'N-no closer! G-get a-away from B-bhajan!' Shouted, slapping hand against pavement.

'Why? What's going on here, Reilly?' Dawkes spoke, looked concerned, but took step back. Good.

Hu looked at other agents. 'Will one of you go see to him already?!'

Bad! Very bad!

'No! S-stay a-away!' Used hand to pull away. 'I-infected!'

Dawkes gasped, grabbed Hu's shoulder. 'It's the virus, sir! Reilly's probably still infected!'

'Is that so?' Hu glared at Bhajan. 'Is that why he's trying to keep us apart, 'Master Bhajan'? Do you have some of this bioweapon on you?'

'Y-yes!' Shouted again. 'Carrier!'

'A carrier? What's does that mean?' Hu took step towards Wavers, fists clenched. 'Explain yourselves, Wavers.'

Bhajan tried speak again, interrupted by larger man next to him, bellowing with Russian accent. 'Explain what? One of your agents shows up half-dead and suddenly we're the villains again?! How do we know this isn't just some set-up? Some excuse to cut us down?!'

'Told you they would try something like this!' Another Waver, tall and reedy, shrieked. 'I said, I said that these bastards were just looking for an excuse to kill us! That agent's probably not even sick! The virus only affects us anyway!'

'Friends, please!' Bhajan held up hands, interposing in front of Wavers. 'I'm sure this is a misunderstanding! Let's just let these good fellows see to their comrade, then we shall-

'

'See to him?! If Reilly's telling the truth, we can't even go near him!' Hu barked. 'If I find out I had to watch a good man die without being able to help, and that you're involved somehow-'

Dawkes bolted forward, waving down Enlightenment, even as weapons raise. 'Wait, everyone, don't! That's exactly what Calatin wants! He's probably the one who passed the virus onto Bhajan, too!'

'N-no, I-i did.' Managed to say, finally. All heads turned. 'M-my fault. A-allowed B-Bhajan to be ex-exposed. D-didn't realise he co-could carry it!'

All paused, uncertain. Breathing getting heavy now. 'C-calatin knew you'd be h-here. P-planned this. Wa-wanted fight. Ne-need to-'

Nearby shop exploded outwards, words drowned under fire and flying glass. Groups fell back, reaching for weapons. Mist still surrounding Wavers thrashed and twisted. Area began alive with whoops and battlecries, figures emerging from nearby buildings. Most looked human, only to change on approach, some revealing pointed ears, others becoming inhumanly short and stout. The Sidhe.

But worse. Large group emerged from burning shop. Flames gave way to hopping Fachan legion, one figure standing at front.

No.

Nechtan strode from flaming wreckage, untouched by rain or flames. Sword drawn, he walked towards both groups. Around him, more Sidhe emerged from buildings, dozens filling street.

Soon surrounded by screaming jeering horde.

Time had run out.

# Chapter 29

The air was filled with pure noise from the battlecries of Sidhe now flanking the plaza.

Hard to see either Wavers or Enlightenment as Sidhe crowded around. Could still make out soldiers training weapons on crowd. Bhajan and fellow Wavers closed rank, looking back and forth.

Nechtan lifted a hand, and noise died down.

Waited with breath in throat. Waited for whatever Nechtan would do.

Didn't expect Nechtan spreading arms wide, grinning, eyes on Wavers.

'My fondest thanks, dearest allies! Were it not for the revelation of your meeting place, this opportunity would not has presented itself! With our forces combined, the Enlightenment will stand no chance!'

Confusion filled air between Enlightenment and Wavers. One soldier swore loudly. 'The bastards sold us out!'

'Wait, no! That's not-'

Bhajan didn't get to finish. Glass bottles rained from Sidhe crowd upon the Enlightenment unit, exploding into flames as they hit ground and soldiers. Most of the troops managed to fall back. One, a soldier, from of the protective circle, caught molotov to the chest. Went down screaming. Couple of other troops tried to help, only to be forced back by more flaming bottles.

Nechtan waved hand, prompting larger group into charge. Fachan hopped and bounded, raincoats parting, revealed solitary legs hopping along ground. The unit, recovering from initial shock, started opened fire on Fachan. Cracks of force and fire plumes joined in, magic and bullet slammed into the horde. Many Fachan died in those few seconds.

Many, but not enough.

Over a dozen Fachan made it through wave of death, only to stop short, as Dawkes stepped forward, flicking and jabbing with glove. Walls burst forth from thin air, like mist, but thicker, divided Fachan from the unit. The Fachan screamed, hammered at the wall.

A sigh of relief briefly left lips. Cornered magi are still magi. No slaughter yet.

Turned head to look at Wavers. Group stood close by, looking around, mist lashing and writhing. Then, thin and reedy one spoke, gesturing to others. 'Quick, let's go! We'll be slaughtered if we stick around!'

Group began to turn, only for Bhajan to block path, face set. 'Listen, you fools! Everything that has happened was a scheme by those who wish us harm to drive a wedge between us and the Enlightenment! If we flee now, what do you think the Enlightenment will assume when their men turn up dead? Besides that, if Reilly spoke the truth, I'm carrying one of their viruses right now! If I flee, it could run wild across the city! Each of you might have it too! Nechtan means to make us his instruments of death! Do you honestly believe playing his game will end well for us?!'

Wavers looked between themselves, looking uncertain. Russian was first to reply. 'N-no, bu-'

Bhajan yelled louder. 'We have a choice here! Stand and fight with our true allies, proving we are no friends of the Sidhe. Or leave, and prove ourselves treacherous cowards.'

Bhajan then addressed the mist surrounding them. 'Is that what we came here to achieve, Lord Bǎohùshen?'

Gentle, calm voice emanated from mist. 'It is not. Brothers, the Sidhe have divided us long enough. Let us end this.'

Then, the mist spilled away from the Wavers, flying to block the Sidhe advance, solidifying into a familiar horned, four-legged shape. Bǎohùshen rose, as majestic as back at the restaurant, staring down the legion.

With a whooping battlecry, Bhajan ran forward, the other Wavers pausing before joining the charge. They began colliding with whatever Sidhe were nearest, knocking them aside or hitting them with weapons pulled from jackets or hidden under shirts. Bhajan leapt over a couple of Fachan, kicked aside what may have been a leprechaun, closing distance with Nechtan.

Nechtan watched, then snapped his fingers. A surge of wind rose up striking the Wavers, sending them flying, slamming against walls and through windows. Bǎohùshen dug their hooves in, but was also slowly getting pushed back by the whirlwind.

A heroic effort. But Nechtan was too strong.

He walked closer to me, watching the siege impassively, his whirlwind pinning down all but his minions, who continued trying to tear down Dawkes' walls. Fire from molotovs stuck to surface of the walls as clubs and fists smashed against them.

'So, here we again, then?' Nechtan shook his head. 'A pity, I had high hopes for you, Arbiter. But it seems you just couldn't put the last few pieces together.'

'N-nechtan, p-please.' Could barely move now. Could only plead. 'S-still time. Wh-where's C-calatin?'

Nechtan gazed down, pitying. 'You know full well I can't tell you that. Nor, before you ask, can I leave the field of battle. The die has been cast, Arbiter, all we can do now is play out our assigned roles.'

'P-people w-will die.' No, empathy pointless. Try another method. 'S-still b-be s-slave if don't h-help us.'

Nechtan's jaw clenched at 'slave'. Picked me up by neck. 'There's is frightfully little to say at this point. All the information you needed; I gave. You knew of the plan, the virus, even its sympathetic nature. If you can't come up with something with that knowledge, I'm afraid you're simply beyond hope.'

Something with that knowledge? Must mean something. Nechtan never said anything without deeper meaning. Plan? Virus? Sympathetic? Think, think! What did that mean!? What did that-

Wait.

Calatin used sympathetic link in virus to spread and track infected.

Virus built on sympathetic link.

Sympathetic links can be disrupted. Broken.

If you know how.

Began to raise hand, fingers shaking. Nechtan narrowed eyes as hand waved in air. Please, please find it.

'Beyond words now?' Nechtan's voice distant and faint.

Could sense disappointment. 'Then I suppose I'd best put you out of your misery. At least one of us will be free today.'

Nechtan let go, body collapsed to ground as he readied blade. Hand kept waving, trying to find it. So little time left.

Nechtan stepped forward, blade sliding up leg, settling on chest. Tried to ignore, had to find it. Could feel something. Just had to keep trying.

Nechtan sighed. 'To think, I was just starting to see potential in you.'

Blade began pressing into chest. No pain, but could feel skin parting. Heart would be next.

No time for athame, but athame only tool. Real power always within. Fingers pinched around cord linking virus to self. Squeezed with what tiny strength left.

Cord broke.

Everything come back in a rush. My hand erupted with glorious pain, burns from the electricity screaming their existence to me. My chest and head joined the chorus, telling me of every blow I'd taken in the last few minutes, my bruised ribs, my scalp cut by the crowbar blow. All the punishment my body had taken came down at me at once, almost overwhelming me.

What did overwhelm me, however, were the emotions. Emotions deadened and smothered by Calatin's pathogen clamoured for space in my mind. I felt fear, deep, cold terror as I lay on the ground, a Sidhe Lord about to cut me open as war broke out around me, the lives of those I cared for about to be snuffed out in at any moment. I felt anger, hot, boiling fury at the man who'd tried to pull every paranormal in Ireland into his sick, twisted revenge fantasy.

But more than those, what I felt most was sheer, implacable

determination. I'd given everything I had and more just to get to this point. I'd tapped into a side of myself I'd feared for years to survive. I'd been forced to show that ugly side to the few people who I could call friends, only to them to reach out rather than turn away.

I'd spent the last day with a death sentence over mine and Viora's heads, and rather than accept it, I'd pushed forward, knowing the only way I could survive would be to get here and confront Calatin, putting an end to his insane plan.

I thought I was a failure. But no failure could get this far.

I sat up, pushing Nechtan's sword a few centimetres in, my flesh stinging as it parted. That sensation only added to the onslaught of will and emotion inside me, and, rather than fight it, I grabbed Nechtan's sword, glaring back at him.

'Tintreach!' As the word passed my lips, I felt my will spill out around me. Pure, blue lightning, coursed out in all directions. The raw power scorched my skin for a split second before instinct caused me to pull from my tattoos, encasing my body in a sheath of force.

Nechtan had only a moment to widen his eyes, before the electricity set upon him, carried up the blade, raking and savaging him. He fell back, letting out a shrill cry.

I couldn't register much, but as the explosion dissipated, and I pulled myself into an upright slouch, gasping for breath, I got a good view of what I'd done.

The fighting had paused, as the Sidhe previously advancing on the entrenched position of the Wavers and Enlightenment had frozen, all looking in my direction. Around me, the streetlights were shredded, the air thick with the smell of ozone.

I saw bodies surrounding me. Sidhe who'd stood too close

to me now lay, blackened bodies already dissolving.

In front of me, I saw Nechtan, flat on his back, his marble-like skin and military dress now merging into one black whole, dead eyes in what was once a face staring back at me as Nechtan's corpse, following the lead of all dead Sidhe, began to fade away, melting into nothing.

Did I actually do that?

Judging from the stunned Sidhe around me, they were as shocked. Their champion, killed by a wizard who'd been near death. I froze up as eyes started drifting from Nechtan's fading body to me. I still didn't know how I'd pulled that off. What I did know, was that I was stuck in the middle of a legion of Sidhe, whose shock would only last so long.

Just as I was trying to force my body to move, the deathly silence was broken. With a tremendous roar, Bǎohùshen erupted from their position, form half misty as they slammed into the nearest group of Sidhe to me, sending them flying.

In the same moment, Bhajan leapt over, kicking the nearest Fachan in the face before locking it in a hold and then flinging it into another pair of Fachan. At the Enlightenment barricade, Dawkes' walls shimmered and vanished, replaced by a hail of gunfire, dazzling displays of flaming coronas, bolts of force and Sidhe suddenly spasming and dropping joining the hellish symphony.

I could see the Sidhe ranks buckle, some already fleeing the scene. Most held firm, but the tide had turned, between the Enlightenment fire support and Waver brute force, it was only a matter of time until the Sidhe broke. The war was over before it began, all I needed to do now was find Calatin and make sure his pathogens didn't spread further.

I suddenly remembered Viora. I'd been so sure I was about

to die that I hadn't even considered her surviving. But, if she was hanging on, even just a bit, I could cure her now! She didn't have to die!

I started sprinting, pumping as much will into speeding up as I could. Time slowed to a crawl around me, as I ducked, jumped and pushed past the violence surrounding me.

Getting away from the melee, I bolted to where I'd directed Viora. I got to the shop and jerked around, trying to spot her, when I caught sight of a still form slumped under the canopy.

There she was, her large eyes now shut, her skin the same odd dark tint from when I first found her. Next to her, I saw the potion I'd given her, open and discarded, the remaining liquid pooling out and dispersing in the rain.

No. Not today. I yanked my athame free as I ran over, already going through the familiar motions. Now I knew what to look for, I could feel the thin sliver of the sympathetic link of Calatin's virus, coming from her chest and going off who knows where. The second I got in range, I brought the knife down, slicing the connection, the magic thrashing in the air before spluttering out.

I got down on my knees, checking Viora. Barely breathing, pulse erratic.

No no no.

I pushed her onto her back, getting my athame and placing the flat of the blade against her chest. I channelled my worry, my fear and my refusal to let her die into it. I didn't even really know what I was doing, only that I was not letting this happen.

Reaching deep within myself, I pushed my way back down to the vault in my mind, where I'd kept all the parts of myself I hated. I could feel the power emanating behind the door, yet as I pulled it open once more, a tide of renewed anger and might filling me, I focused that anger, that spite, not at what I could break, but what I could heal.

'Tintreach.' I growled, sending a jolt of electricity through the blade into Viora's body, my will pushing the current down into her erratic heart, trying to jump start it. I put my free hand to her neck. Dammit, still fading.

'Tintreach!' I snarled again, pumping another pulse into the heart, the edges of my body crackling with barely restrained power begging to be let out, which I just barely held back. I checked the pulse again.

No, no no! You're not dying, Viora!

I gripped the blade one more time, building the energy once again as I looked into Viora's still, quiet face. I owed so much to her. I wouldn't even be alive if she hadn't risked herself for me. I can't fail her. I won't fail her.

I don't know when the tears started, yet the grief and pain only became more fuel for the electricity as I readied the last pulse.

'Please!' I cried out, sending the electricity into the whole of Viora's body, gently spreading through, attempting to coax heart, lungs and muscles back to life.

Viora's body jerked. Was that it? Or was it just a spasm? I leaned forward to check again.

Only to get thrown off my feet as something collided with my head.

By the time I'd even registered that, my vision went white as my back slammed into something, the taste of blood lacing my mouth. I hit the ground, tumbling until I hit against something hard.

Dazed, I tried to look up, my vision spinning, until it all came into focus at once.

I was surrounded by shipping containers. Directly ahead of me, I saw a wall with a large hole, the same one I was just knocked through. Something had just punched me straight into the nearby docks, now so far away from the fighting I couldn't even hear it over the rain.

More importantly, I saw a large figure striding over to me. His form wrapped in a heavy robe and clutching an oaken staff. The features were hidden under the hood, but I could still make out the beard and sneering mouth.

Calatin stalked towards me, the top of his staff starting to glow a dark green.

He glared down at me, the light showing just enough of his eyes for me to make out the pure hate in them. 'I've grown weary of your meddling, Reilly.'

# Chapter 30

When I had thought of all the ways I might've wound up facing Calatin, it was with a small legion of Enlightenment agents behind me.

Definitely not alone, injured, just coming off a serious viral infection.

Nevertheless, as Calatin approached, I made an effort to stand up, just about managing to shakily make it up, despite the deep ache in my limbs.

Wonderful, I'd successfully stood up. This fight's turning around already.

Calatin stopped, maybe twenty feet away from me, watching with cold eyes, only made colder by the ghostly glow of his staff. There wasn't a trace of the man who, only a few days ago, had greeted me so gratefully for helping the same people he'd just moments ago set on me like wild dogs.

Then, Calatin spoke, his tone glacial. 'I always wondered what I would say, if I ever found any of the damned souls who'd destroyed everything I loved. I've rehearsed moments like this on many a lonely night, when nothing but a bottle of whiskey could offer me any comfort. When I slept, the same rehearsals would play out in my dreams, though I never had a true face to attach to all the evils done that night.'

I shambled backwards, moving to place one of the large shipping containers between us, but he simply kept pace, breaking neither stride nor speech.

'I've waited a decade to finally have a face I could stare down, to make answer for the wrongs done to me and my blood, and yet, looking at the sad broken creature before me now, I can only wonder if you'd even comprehend the enormity of the wrongs for which you've escaped justice.'

I gripped the container for support, Calatin's words reawakening the old guilt inside me. Still, I braced myself. 'You're wasting your breath, Calatin. We're not in Dingle now. This war of yours is the issue now, and everyone knows your part in it. Your puppet lies dead. The Sidhe he manipulated are falling apart. You're done.'

'Done? Done!?' Calatin's voice raised and he slammed his fist into another container, the metal denting. 'I will never be done! Not until the paranormal taint that corrupts our land is purged, once and for all! The cowards in the Enlightenment may know I created the pathogens, but that won't matter once I start releasing them across Dublin. And as for the Sidhe scum, they might break resolve in this battle, yet once I hand them the same virus that should've killed you, the death that will follow will finally force the hands of humanity to rise up and destroy them!'

I managed a harsh laugh. 'Sure, we can stop all the paranormal threats in Ireland, all for the low-low cost of a couple million lives! You certain you've got the math right on that one?'

Calatin gestured furiously with his staff. 'You've no right to speak of morality! Not after what you did! Not after your cursed cabal took everything from me!'

'Exactly!' I shouted back, stumbling further behind the container. 'I'm the one you want, Calatin! Paranormals had nothing to do with what happened to your family! It was humans! Human warlocks who stole your life!'

Calatin surged around the corner, the sinister light of his staff making him look like a vengeful ghost. 'Spare me, you filth! Even if cabalists were the ones pulling the strings, were it not for the existence of monsters like the Sidhe, born for the sole purpose of tormenting mankind, my family, and countless others throughout history would have lived! How many more? How many more broken lives and pointless destruction must humanity suffer before we put these demons down for good? I say no more! Let them all burn! Them and the despicable wretches like you who sold their souls to these monsters!'

'So what then, Calatin!?' My throat burned from the shouting. 'What happens when everyone and everything burns down!? Will that bring your family back!? Will it avenge them!? How many have to die until you're satisfied!?'

Calatin froze in place, his face locked in a rictus of pained fury. He then lowered his head, eyes still staring me down, one twitching slightly. 'However many it takes. However many until I fina–'

Calatin flew back as the bolt from my athame struck him, propelled by the kinetic force I'd mixed into the bolt in the hopes of it punching straight through him, his body collapsing to the ground. Not exactly sporting, but the absolute last thing I wanted was a straight fight with someone stronger than me.

When Calatin landed, he didn't move. The smell of burnt flesh filled the air as I slowly lowered my athame, taking a couple of steps towards him. Was that it?

As I closed, I could see the massive burnt wound taking up Calatin's chest, the cauterisation doing little to hide how deep it was. Magi or not, he was only human. Maybe the element of surprise had been enough.

Then, I noticed the wound starting to close up.

It was surreal and disgusting. New, fresh meat grew, replacing the old mutilated flesh, and in practically the blink of an eye, the devasting wound I'd dealt was gone, the only casualty left being Calatin's now scorched shirt, giving me a view of the glowing ogham tattoos reforming on his chest that seemed to be doing the work repairing him.

Calatin opened his eyes with a harsh gasp, before jumping to his feet in one motion, rising up to his full height, glowering down at me.

'I suppose I shouldn't have expected any sort of honour from the likes of you.'

I spat at the ground. 'Needed to shut you up somehow.'

Calatin's red face got a couple shades darker. He let out a roar, slamming his staff into the ground, cracking the pavement. I began pulling back in the same instant.

I might as well not have bothered.

Where the staff struck the pavement, the earth split open. A dozen thick vines, each the width of a boa constrictor, spilled forth from the pavement, whizzing towards me.

Two vines wrapped around my legs, tripping me up as another was already snaking its way around my left arm, curling in anticipation of crushing me.

I called on the latent power in my own tattoos, flooding my body with kinetic force. Gripping my athame, I brought it down in a wide slash at the vine wrapping around my arm, the force giving my slice enough strength to cut through the vine.

But I wasn't quick enough to stop the vines around my legs, and I paid for it. My legs lit with pain, the vines squeezing so hard I could swear they would crush my very bones into gristle.

I began forming another spell in my mind, only for the vines to rear up, taking me with them, as they slammed into the shipping container I'd been gripping moments ago. The taste of blood filled my mouth again as my athame tumbled out of my numbed fingers. The pain came shortly after, so powerful I couldn't even focus long enough to think of a plan, let alone cast a spell.

It was hopeless. Calatin was a master compared to me. All I could do was scream in anguish, as the vines slowly squeezed the life out of me.

Calatin cackled as he closed the distance between us. 'Feel that, Reilly? I only wished it hurt more, but we can fix that soon enough!'

I limply attempted a swing at Calatin, only for his fist to slam into my face. A few more punches followed, barely noticed next to the crushing of the vines and the massive back trauma. I was brought back to reality as my neck began to clench shut, kicking in the air as Calatin dropped his staff, one hand strangling me and the other held at the ready.

To my horror, I saw the free hand distort, growing as the nails changed into blades, each the length of my forearm.

'Goodbye, Reilly.' Calatin spat in my face. 'I hope you see your old cabal mates in whatever hell you wind up in.'

Calatin reared his clawed hand back, talons readied to stab right through my skull. My instincts screamed for me to close my eyes, but I fixed my stare on Calatin, trying to muster as much contempt as possible. I was not going to die a coward.

Calatin then thrust his hand forward, only to stop mid-motion. His face twisted in anger and confusion as his shoulder flexed, trying to urge the arm on, only for it to remain stuck in the air.

As if...as if it was being held in place.

The mutated arm twisted back, bones breaking as Calatin let out an agonised scream. He thrashed and pushed against the invisible presence, then stopped as his eyes fell on something behind me, wide with shock. With what little freedom I had, I twisted my own head around to look.

Behind me, Viora stood, leaning heavily against the hole in the wall separating us from the plaza. One hand was stretched out, fingers clenched. The rain obscured her features, except the huge, black eyes, which glared at Calatin with haunting intensity.

'Leave. Him. Alone.' Her voice echoed out, harsh and coarse.

I could barely comprehend the sheer mix of emotions that hit me. Surprise was chief, but I was also grateful that she'd come, yet afraid Viora would get hurt. Finally, there was confusion, why was she here? Why hadn't she run?

Calatin was not so overwrought. I could see his face shift into a hateful scowl, his previous fury at me seemingly forgotten.

'Cursed alien freak!' He swore, still trying to pull his arm out of Viora's psychic grip. 'I should've known Reilly had been harbouring the likes of you! Too weak to fight your own battles, then?! Had to cower behind a traitor to the human race just to get a shot in?!'

'Have been hiding for some time. Terrified of death, so was happy to hide, be protected by another.' Viora's voice replied, her normal monotone replaced with a harsh growl. 'Time to repay it.'

With that, she flicked her wrist, and Calatin's arm ripped clean off his shoulder, flying across the dock as blood sprayed. Calatin howled, clutching the stump. The vines loosened, then were ripped free from me entirely as Viora swung her hand again, their debris flying over the containers, followed by a splash as they landed in the water.

Taking only a scant moment to relish the fresh air, I lunged for my athame. Grabbing hold of it, I spun towards Calatin to finish the job, only for his remaining fist to slam into my head.

My vision blurred as my face caved to the blow, my body greeting the wet ground again as I tumbled, the next few seconds hazy as I lay there.

Once my senses returned, I heard something crash in the distance. Looking up, I saw Calatin bounce with meaty thuds against several containers, only to catch himself, digging a clawed hand into the ground while he screamed at Viora. 'You think these parlour tricks will stop me, you corpse-skinned bitch?! Once I get my hands on you, I will rend that skin and feed it to you in strips!'

Viora paused, her arm trembling. That second of hesitation was all Calatin needed. He let out a grunt, and, to my complete disbelief, the flesh at his stump start to grow and flex, and in a few seconds, a new arm replaced the old as if it'd never been torn off.

What the hell was this? How were we supposed to fight a guy who could heal anything we did to him?

Calatin thrust his regrown arm into his robes, pulling out a pair of small, cylindrical objects. With a cry, he threw them into Viora's direction, giving me enough time to notice, with no small confusion, that he'd thrown a pair of small corn cobs at her.

The moment the cobs left his hand though, Calatin snapped his fingers. Still in mid-air, the cobs started making a strange buzzing sound, and kernels started flying out by the dozens, speeding ahead of the cobs before they fell to the ground.

Only, as my eyes adapted to the new sight, I saw they weren't kernels at all, but large, buzzing hornets, flying on newfound wings straight to Viora.

Viora let out a shriek as the hornets descended. I couldn't see clearly what was happening to her in the distance, but the screams were all that was needed to send a jolt of white-hot fury up my spine.

I sprinted over as fast as I could, still trying to keep an eye on Calatin even while Viora's panicked screams stabbed into me like daggers. I wanted to focus entirely on her, but I knew turning my back on Calatin would be suicide.

As if to validate that thought, Calatin flung another corn cob over to me, a mocking laugh reverbing out from him, more hornets spilling out of the cob.

I kicked the ground hard, sending a pulse of kinetic force out that shot me a few metres in the air, the resulting pulse hitting the hornets and exploding them like eggs thrown at a wall. Calatin grunted irritably, then reached for his robes again, only this time pulling them off and throwing them aside.

Before I could see what he was planning, I landed with a stumble, now close enough that the buzzing of the swarm attacking Viora roared in my ears. Viora had fallen through the hole in the wall, hands over her head as dozens of vicious hornets stung her, her arms covered in angry welts.

I brandished my athame. The swarm might've caught Viora by enough surprise that she was helpless, but I already knew what to do.

Shame it was really gonna hurt.

I dived into the swarm, the hornets wasting no time in savaging me. No individual sting hurt that much, but the sheer mass of them was excruciating. I bit down on my own scream as I grabbed hold of Viora, pulling her towards me as the swarm converged.

That done, I slammed down the athame on the ground, unleashing a burst of magic, the kinetic force lashing out in an invisible dome that ripped the hornets out of the air, shredding them.

I let out a wheezing gasp as another lance of pain shot up my spine. I didn't know how much more I had.

I pushed that worry aside to check on Viora. The hornets had left their marks, large patches of her skin now bearing several vicious stings.

'You alright?' I asked, not quite stilling the worried quaver in my voice.

Viora shakily nodded as she pulled out of my grasp. 'T-thank y-you.'

I scoffed. 'Don't mention it, you came for me first, anyw-.'

A furious cry split through the air. Whipping around, I saw Calatin splay his arms out, his dark outline put into focus by the rain as a pair of wings ripped their way out of his back, large and membraned, like a bat.

Calatin flapped the wings once and disappeared up into the air, invisible against the darkness and storm.

'Is he gone?' I asked Viora after a moment, not quite believing it myself.

'No. Still sense mind. Circling area, probably for another attack.'

Figures. Calatin had said himself he'd waited years to kill anyone he could blame for Dingle. He definitely wasn't going to leave when he had the upper hand. Hell, he might not leave at all until he killed me, given my role in that whole mess.

Which was good. This was probably the best shot anyone had at killing him before Calatin planned another bioterrorist attack.

Shame it was just me and Viora tackling him now. Between the rain, the distance and the bloodbath going down by the 3arena, no-one would notice us, and trying to get help would just give Calatin a chance to pick us both off. If we tried to run, he'd pounce.

I glanced back at Viora. 'Can you sense his general location?'

'Yes.' She responded.

'Alright, here's what we do.'

As always, mind-to-mind communication proved far faster than talking, and the plan came together in about three seconds. Excellent timing, as that was roughly the same time I heard the sound of buzzing, as another swarm of hornets descended from the black sky.

We bolted in separate directions, as the swarm came into sight, then split into two as they got to ground level. As my half got closer, I shot out another pulse of force to kill them. A bolt of green light struck close to me, unleashing another blooming array of furious vines, spinning towards me.

Fortunately, this time we were prepared.

Viora shouted out 'Now!', and I felt my body shoot up into the air, rain stinging my face like tiny needles as I flew blindly through the downpour. It was a basic idea, using Viora's telepathy to pinpoint Calatin's location, then having her fling me in his direction, but it worked, as I quickly collided with something solid, which swore loudly as I grabbed hold.

Everything became a blur, as me and Calatin wrestled for an upper-hand. He thrashed and squirmed, trying to knock me off, while I wrapped an arm around his neck, legs locking around his torso to hold me in place. I took a few scratches and bumps, yet despite Calatin's strength, both magically and physically, I had the leverage, too close to even risk a spell at point blank range, and I held on long enough to pull out my athame.

The head. That was the key. Calatin was powerful, but his regeneration was like any other spell, it needed a conscious mind to maintain it. If I could just get my knife between his eyes...

The blade came down, only for a sudden jerk to knock it off course, stabbing deep into Calatin's exposed chest. We both grunted as I pulled the blade loose, already trying to find the right angle again. I saw a shot and took it, and this time Calatin managed to move his head just so that I lodged the blade in his right shoulder.

Rather than yank the blade loose again, I channelled force along it, the energy taking its own edge as it shot forth from the blade, plunging deeper into Calatin. I heard something exploding loose from Calatin's left thigh as he bellowed in bestial agony.

I yanked the blade free, hoping I'd thrown him enough to get a shot at his damn head, only for my vision to go black as something wrapped tightly around my head.

Multiple stabbing pains cascaded along my skull as claws dug deep into the flesh, the pressure getting tighter by the moment. I screamed, and as I did, I stabbed the athame into the clawed fist crushing me, sending a volley of electricity through it, the blue light seeping through the gaps in the fist's fingers.

I heard a pained splutter, and then suddenly I was flying across the air, the weightlessness only a brief reprieve before I smashed into something hard, my back going numb as I tumbled a few more metres, hitting the ground face first.

'You little fucker!' Calatin's voice screamed out.

As I managed to sit up, I saw him slam into the ground too, his descent more controlled, despite the blood streaming out of the large hole on his thigh, and the burns along his arm and wings. Calatin's glare stayed dead on me, his breath coming out in hot, visible plumes.

Then, Calatin flexed, and all the damage I'd just done started healing over, right back to square one.

I tried not to panic, but it was hopeless. Calatin didn't even need to overpower me, all he really had to do was wear me down, which wasn't going to take much longer.

As Calatin began to advance toward me, there was a glint of something metallic in the air behind him, and like a shot, one of the smaller shipping containers launched from the rain and slamming down on Calatin's lower body, catching his legs and pinning him in place with a fleshy squelch. Calatin cursed as he struggled against it, but was stuck fast under over two tonnes of metal.

'Enlightenment falling back down not part of plan.' Viora said behind me, her tone oddly wry.

'Plans change. You still got the shot off.' I replied. I'd hoped Viora'd be able to get his head under the box, but at least this gave me a better shot at his head, which I wasn't going to waste now.

Apparently however, being squashed under a shipping container wasn't enough to shut Calatin up. 'S-so arrogant. So sure of yourselves. Pathetic. The enemy used you so thoroughly, weaponised you, wrecked your life and still you run to them for help, Reilly. It's sickening.'

The jab didn't faze me this time. Whatever I was now, Calatin didn't know a damn thing about me. 'Think whatever you want. It's over.'

'You're right. I've wasted enough time toying with you.' Calatin sneered, not betraying even a hint of pain even under two tonnes of metal. 'Relish these final moments, whelps. I'll make sure they hurt.'

Calatin's flesh began bubbling. I was already sprinting forward, athame at the ready to plunge straight into his skull, but it was too late.

Calatin reared his head back and let out an unearthly roar, his clothes and large chunks of his body erupted forth, things sprouting from his body. I skidded in place, trying to change direction, but was too slow to dodge one of the things extending from Calatin's back and speeding towards me, revealing a large pincer, like that of a crab.

The pincer clamped hard against my torso, pushing the air from my lungs. The ground dropped away as I was lifted up. More of the limbs were already coming, growing out of Calatin's back as claws, talons and thick hands.

Distantly, I heard Viora's all-too familiar cry of distress, as more limbs flew off to the side, a raptor claw lifting her into view. Below us, Calatin, still held in place by the container, looked up at us, eyes gleaming with violence. A feral grin spread across his lips, a new arm and two pale legs already wrapping around the container pinning him, as if to lift it up.

Even dazed, I could still feel my senses ringing as the same, wide presence of Calatin's magic seemed to flicker and twitch, like a mad web. That's when I realised with utter fear, that Calatin had surrendered control.

Just like I'd done back at Lumintech, he was deliberately letting his power run wild, lashing out at whatever was close, heedless of anything but breaking what had enraged him. Surrendering all self-control to his inner demons.

Perhaps the irony would've sat better if it hadn't been about to kill me.

Even still half pinned, Calatin managed a glare that chilled my blood. 'I've lost everything because of you, Reilly. My home, my family, even my plan lies in tatters because of you. So, I'm going to make you watch me break this alien whore before I rip you apart. Piece. By. Piece.'

Desperately, I started looking around, for something, anything I could use to escape this, when I caught sight of something strange. Behind Calatin, just lurking behind the container, the air shimmered for a moment, revealing two figures closing in.

I started to laugh, a series of wheezed chuckles that scraped unpleasantly against my ribs. Of course, of course: broken, bound, and desperate, after giving everything I had to this fight, after getting into it alone without involving them, I'd given those two the perfect chance, hadn't I? I was never going to hear the end of this one.

Calatin's wild eyes went even wider. 'Why are you laughing?! Why are you fucking laughing?!'

I stopped laughing, it was getting too sore anyway, and fixed him with the most defiant glare I could muster. 'Should've flown away when you had the chance.’

# Chapter 31

Even under the feral malice, I could still make out confusion in Calatin's eyes.

His new limbs started spasming, the ones working on the container went stiff, then smashed themselves repeatedly into the ground. Calatin yelled in alarm, only for the space behind him to shimmer again, a fist emerging from the space, colliding with the side of his face.

As the spell concealing them gave out, Dawkes and Bhajan emerged from the dark, Dawkes falling back, fingers working as she directed Calatin's limbs to turn against their owner, while Bhajan pummelled his main body, fists flying so fast I could only see the blur.

While Bhajan hammered Calatin, Dawkes ran towards me and Viora, waving a hand at the extremities still holding us. The pincer that had me pinned loosened its grip, sending me collapsing to the ground. Air sped back into my lungs in heaving gasps. As I recovered, I saw Dawkes' face, somewhere between anger and relief.

'I can't leave you alone for two seconds, can I?!'

'How'd you know we were here?'

'Easy. I just followed the two lunatics putting on an electric light show in the sky!' Dawkes tapped at her invisible keyboard again. A few of the stray limbs sped towards Calatin, smacking into him as he tried to track Bhajan. Unperturbed, Dawkes walked over to Viora, also gasping, and extended her a hand.

'I expected better from you, Viora! It's bad enough having to take care of him without you trying to get killed as well!'

Viora stared at the hand blankly, then took it.

'Sorry.' She responded, then pointed at me. 'Bad influence.'

Dawkes smirked. 'No kidding.'

I stared back. Dawkes and Bhajan would've had to have been looking for me to notice that. With how much they'd done for me already, maybe that shouldn't have shocked me, but it did.

Bhajan's voice cried out. 'If you good fellows are done catching up, how's about some help putting this pile of meat down?'

Calatin's eyes focused on him with an ugly glint. He slammed his fist into the ground. I'd expected vines again. What rose up instead, I could only describe as a spiralling pillar of plant matter. It roared up from the earth, coming down on Bhajan like a snake.

Bhajan backflipped away from the pillar, yet when it hit the ground, the mere impact was enough to knock him on his side with a pained cough, rolling out of my sight.

Dawkes was already at her smart screen again, but that didn't stop the pillar from heading towards toward us, all a hundred feet of it. Behind it, the assorted hands and claws Dawkes had managed to take control of, darted to intercept it. Calatin spat at the sight, then flexed his torso, the limbs suddenly tearing themselves loose from his back, flopping uselessly to the ground, rapidly dissolving.

'Hold on!' Viora cried out as she grabbed at both Dawkes

and I. My body went weightless as her telekinesis took hold. We were all flung to the side, the pillar eviscerating the spot where we'd stood as it charged past us, reducing the pavement to a crater of dust and rubble.

We landed in a heap, barely managing to pull ourselves up as the pillar's front rose up, ready for another pass. Back on the other end of the dock, Calatin was already growing new limbs, his staff glowing with a painfully bright light.

I swallowed, then flicked my gaze in Dawkes' direction. 'Don't suppose the rest of the Enlightenment task force's going to jump in any time soon?'

Dawkes winced. 'Our team's still fighting off the rest of the Sidhe, same with the Wavers. Maybe if we last another few minutes, help'll show up.'

We looked back at the two monsters, Calatin and the serpentine pillar facing us. Calatin had lifted the container off his legs; his crushed lower body disgustingly reinflating like a balloon as he began to rise. Already his flesh was warping again, this time into some form of carapace, his skin blackening and hardening as he strode forward, the pillar snaking around him protectively.

'Help arriving in time seems unlikely.' Viora said.

With another rising cackle, Calatin began towards us on now-healed legs. The mass of tentacles, claws and hands, carrying the shipping container, easily the size of a large car, suddenly reared up and flung the damn thing at us.

My arms were already around both Dawkes and Viora's waists in preparation to jump clear, when a shape spun out of the rain.

It collided with the container mid-air, and knocking it back towards Calatin, who flinched back. His plant pillar bolted in front of the incoming container, blocking the blow for Calatin. The container crashed into the pillar with an organic ripping sound, leaving a large tear in the pillar's midsection.

The dark shape hung in the air for a second, then spun in our direction, as Bhajan emerged, fur soaked from the rainfall. He grinned a large monkey grin and shook himself.

'Ah, Reilly! Viora! Good to see you're both still alive. Don't suppose you've figured out how to take down this crazy sonuvabitch yet?'

It took a moment for me get my voice back. Judging from the complete silence around us, I wasn't the only one. 'It's his head. If we could get to that...'

'Sounds good. How?' Dawkes cut in.

'Just throw everything you can at him. I have an idea.'

Calatin stood across the dock, barely recognisable under the black, smooth carapace he had now grown, grasping limbs snaking from his sides and the pillar of vines beside him readying to strike. Yet, as I stood opposite, the only people who'd ever accepted the worst part of me at my sides, I felt oddly calm.

I shouldn't have. Calatin had shrugged off everything we'd hit him with, and if we didn't kill him, he'd kill us, then continue his crusade against all things paranormal.

The stakes couldn't be higher, but despite all that, as I glanced over at Bhajan, cocky grin still on his face as he put his fists up, Dawkes, staring Calatin down cooly and Viora, who, despite nervous gasping breaths, held her ground, I felt like we actually had a shot.

Maybe it was just the adrenaline making me giddy, or just plain denial. But, maybe, it was the fact I finally had people I wanted to fight for, and who'd fight for me. Whatever it was, it was enough to convince me that this was possible.

Calatin was the first to act, swinging his staff with a shout, urging the pillar into another charge. Behind it, I saw wings extend from the druid's back again. He bolted into the sky. I glued my eyes to him as he merged with the dark. The pillar, as dangerous as it was, was only a distraction.

We all split up, knowing we were forcing the pillar to pick a target. It didn't need to think for long.

It charged straight at Viora, who had ducked behind one of the containers.

I was already aiming my athame at the pillar when it stopped, slamming straight into a misty wall. Standing off to the side, Dawkes shook the tension out of her hand. She let out a laugh.

'How'd you like that, you damn weed?!' She jeered, before glancing in Viora's direction, a smirk on her face. 'Hey, Space-Girl! You planning on just watching?'

I couldn't see what response Viora had for that, but I did see the container she was hiding behind suddenly fly up, soaring, then smashing down on the pillar as it attempted to reorient itself. The thing squirmed and thrashed, only to slam into another misty wall emerging in it's path, conjured by Dawkes, as the same container lifted up for another assault.

Bhajan clapped a hairy hand on my shoulder. 'Looks like the ladies have the plant covered! How about we handle the main event?'

I nodded, then pointed up. 'We need to get him down.'

'Say no more!' Bhajan's hand retreated, his body already curling into a stance. 'Watch closely, my friend. You're about to see a master at work.'

Bhajan leapt into the air, putting himself between me and

the mass of Calatin's appendages descending down from the sky, like the tendrils of some unholy jellyfish. As they rushed down, Bhajan grappled the closest limb, a large talon, and swung on it, into the middle of rest of the oncoming mass.

Then, locking his legs around the talon, Bhajan readied his fists to intercept the mass of extremities, now all bearing down on him. I rushed forward, intent on helping, only for the limbs to start flying back, bent and warped.

As each limb came, Bhajan punched, crushed or ripped. I almost thought Bhajan had grown extra arms himself, only to realise he was simply punching so fast his fists seemed to be in several places at once.

Somewhere up in the darkness and rain, Calatin was trying to overwhelm Bhajan, and with the constant appearance of more and more body parts, he might've done. If he hadn't just indirectly revealed his position to me.

Moments ago, the limbs seemed to be lunging down from every direction, but now, their movements stopped by Bhajan, I could see the central point they had all originated from.

I thrust my athame up, sending a lance of force straight into the rough centre of the limbs. The force struck something hard, and I might've even heard a grunt somewhere in the cacophony.

I yanked the athame down to the ground, and felt the force pull something down from the sky. I saw the dozens of pale skinned limbs drop as Calatin fell, smashing on top of another of the containers, the metal roof denting in as he slammed into it. Before the force flickered out completely, I shouted 'Tintreach!', sending a cascade of electricity up the lance, into Calatin once again.

In an instant, the limbs that Bhajan had been battling

back collapsed, twitching. Behind us, I heard the sound of something shredding, and, looking back, I saw the pillar, trapped between walls of hardened air, as the container smashed repeatedly down on it, give out another few death squirms before going still. Dawkes and Viora stood, staring down the mass as they killed it with efficient coldness.

Bhajan dropped to the ground beside me, then smiled. 'Think that got hi-'

A furious scream cut through the air.

A beaten, smouldering mass pulled itself out of the container I'd slammed Calatin into. The black-carapaced thing, barely visible against the black sky, yelled garbled obscenities before slamming it's hands into the roof of the container, sending out a pulse that almost sent me reeling.

With superhuman speed, vines pulled themselves out of every corner of the ground, grabbing and wrapping around me so fast I couldn't react. Bhajan cursed and spat, tearing into the vines, only to get pulled down too.

As I hit the ground, or rather the vines now below my feet, I saw they'd spread across the dock. I saw Dawkes and Viora both brought down, yet as I tried to free myself to help, the vines covering me constricted, my vision blackening as my body screamed.

I tried to reach for another spell, only for the vines to crush around my hand. My hand exploded in agony, and I felt it's grip on my athame slip, the blade tumbling into the vines.

The ground cracked around us, and Calatin let out a laugh.

'Monsters! Monsters and traitors all!' Calatin's voice became deeper, more garbled, less human as he howled. 'Die! All of you will die! Enlightenment and monsters alike! Suffer for what you've taken from me!'

As I kicked and fought, Calatin's words sent a rush of anger through me. The bastard was going to kill me, then my friends, then every other paranormal in Dublin and it still wouldn't be enough. He was nothing more than a rabid dog, a living weapon.

The surge came slowly, only this time, I wasn't letting out the fury and resentment I'd felt before. What I called on this time was something so deeply buried I hadn't even realised myself that it was there.

As I looked at my comrades, still struggling and fighting, even as the vines spilled across their forms, burying them. I felt every moment I'd spent with these three over the last week, every argument and every setback, but also every time we'd supported each other.

I was still scared of losing control, still scared of the monster I knew I could become. But I was far more afraid of seeing them, these strange people who could stand being around me, die.

And perhaps that's what made the difference.

With my remaining free hand, I pushed past the vines pulling me. I yanked at one already trying to force itself through one of my eyes. My tattoos glowed hot once more.

Just like that, the world stopped, then, with energy coursing through my body, I sent down a burst of force, a dome erupting and ripping away the vines under and around me.

Freed, I bolted up and fixed eyes on Calatin. As much as I wanted to help the others, he was the source. Killing him would save them.

I ran across the ruined ground, dirt and concrete crumbling under my feet. I heard the air crack behind me. Each step fried another vine. Electricity, pulled by my will, came crackling down from the street lights, leaving the dock in pitch blackness, save for the electric blue that began dancing around me.

From his vantage point, Calatin turned, my new sense of time slowing his movement to a crawl, yet one that rapidly sped up, as the air around him started to burn with power. Now Calatin sped up to match my own pace, spinning in place to meet me, clawed arms spread wide.

I slammed my feet on the ground, shooting myself up once more, rocketing towards Calatin like a missile.

Calatin saw it coming. As I reached the top of the container, a claw launched out, the talons slicing right through my shoulder, impaling me.

Before the pain could hit, I thrust forward, only for Calatin to shake me back and forth. My body spasmed, reducing my punch to a limp slap against his face.

But I knew I didn't need to hit back. All I needed to do was touch him, and I managed it. I focused with everything I had, reaching out to whatever will I could draw on.

Above us, the sky began to rumble.

Calatin stared at me wide-eyed, I think some part of him realising what was about to happen. In that moment, I saw myself reflected in his eyes, a grim figure, not too different from the one I was facing now. Both twisted by the same event in our pasts, defining us to our cores.

I looked into the demented eyes in front of me, eyes that could've been mine. 'I'm sorry I had to do this.'

Calatin screamed in blind fury, one last expression of rage and grief before I cried out one last time. 'Tintreach!'

The sky opened, and a crackling branch of pure light struck down, illuminating the dark sky. The bolt struck my hand,

and Calatin's forehead, and my whole world became agony. No athame meant nothing to channel the power.

Electricity coursed through me. In that instant, all I could feel was pain, my throat going raw from screaming. Miles away, I might've heard Calatin's scream mix with mine.

Just as quickly as my world became white, it turned dark, as I felt myself fall through the air, then slamming against the ground, bones cracking on the pavement.

My vision faded in and out. I could make out Calatin's large form next to me, a bloody stump all that was left of his head, the lights from distant torches as faint figures approached the pier.

And I saw three more, close to me, Viora shouting something to me I couldn't hear, while Bhajan gently turned me over, looking grave. A little further away, Dawkes was yelling something to the other figures, waving them down.

I would've speculated more on what was happening, but I was tired, and sore, and only wanted to rest.

So, I closed my eyes.

# Chapter 32

I didn't awake all at once.

Sounds and lights that my brain wasn't cognisant enough to comprehend assaulted my battered senses, leaving me disoriented as my mind tried to pull itself back together.

Eventually, I was able to open my eyes, wincing as an intense light sliced into my eyeballs, making me close them again, my hand clapping shakily over my face as I let out a moan.

'Don't be a baby. It's just sunlight.' A familiar voice spoke up.

'D-dawkes?' I moaned, cracking my eyes open as little as possible. Sure enough, there she was, leaning slightly over me. 'W-where are-'

I tried to pull myself upright, only for Dawkes to gently push me back down. 'Hey, easy, easy. You're in a hospital. Got you down here as soon as we were able to peel you off the pavement.'

I was indeed in a hospital room, the bright cream walls doing little to help with the open window next to me, letting in more of that bloody sunlight, almost obscuring the chair Dawkes had just risen from. The bed I was lying on was damn stiff, and I could tell immediately the sheet was as thin as paper. But there and then, damn if it didn't feel like the most comfortable thing I'd ever lay down on.

Which was just as well, as when Dawkes pushed me down, several aches and pains took the chance to alert me of their presence. Loudly.

'Good boy. Best get used to that bed now, you're going to here for a bit.' Dawkes said, my eyes now able to see her properly. Her suit was rumpled and creased, and her face bore the tell-tale dullness of fatigue, but she still smiled as I stared blearily up at her. 'Between the multiple bruised ribs, muscle trauma and, oh right, the several third degree burns from when you turned yourself into a living lightning rod, that bed's going to be your best friend for at least the next couple of weeks.'

I blinked at that, lifting up one arm to look at it. Between the gaps in the bandages wrapping around it, I could make out some redness and blistering. Not pleasant, but actually far better than what Dawkes' had just described.

'Don't look like third degree burns.' I muttered.

'Well, it's amazing what they can do with military-grade magic these days. Turned years of healing into a few weeks.' Dawkes responded with a sigh, before leaning over and poking me on the forehead, her expression turning stern.

'Not that it's any excuse. Do you have any idea how close you got to actually killing yourself out there, Reilly? If it weren't for literal magic, you'd been crippled for life!'

'Not as close as when the virus was killing me, I think.' I murmured back, already bracing myself for what was coming.

Sure enough, Dawkes let out a dramatic groan as she slumped down on the chair next to me, her hand clapping against her face, while still conveniently leaving gaps to glare at me though.

'Oh, don't get me started on that! When you told me you were just going to try and get something out of Nechtan, I assumed you were planning to spy on him! Not conjure him in the middle of a field!'

'Ah, I'm guessing Viora told you that, then?' I said, feeling embarrassed.

'Among other things!' Dawkes shouted, slapping her hand down on her leg as she loomed over me. 'The poor thing's been in bits since you went down, by the way! You ever had to explain to a hysterical alien that, yes, we do know what bacteria is, and yes, the place we're keeping you has been properly sterilised?!'

The thought of Viora sent a wave of memories through me, as I remembered the complete mayhem of the last few moments before I passed out. 'I-is she alright? Is Bhajan alright? Wh-how long has it been?'

Something in my questions made Dawkes' face soften, the tiredness seemed to return to her. 'Three days. It's still too early to tell, but it's looking like that fight down by the 3Arena and losing Nechtan broke the Sidhe Army. No-one's heard a thing from them since, and word is most of the Sidhe in Dublin have mostly been trying to keep their heads down.'

'Have there been any more viral outbreaks?' I pulled myself up a bit, ignoring the throbs and stings.

Dawkes shook her head. 'Nope. Seems once Calatin bit it, any samples still out there fell apart. I think one field agent found what was supposed to be a stockpile of them, but there was nothing in the test tubes aside from a mish-mash of bacteria. Bhajan came back clean from whatever he was carrying, too.'

I sat there, completely still as I took it in. 'T-then...is it done?'

Dawkes let out a laugh as her head dropped back again. 'Done? God no. That whole fiasco at the 3Arena's going to take the rest of the month to cover up, between repairing the worst of the damage, fabricating gas leaks amid a gang war and all the usual. Things with the Wavers and us are still tense and the reinforcements we called are annoyed that they got sucked into the coverup that night turned into once you lit the fuse on it, rather than the military op they'd been expecting. There's still a lot to deal with before this is anywhere near 'done'!'

I relaxed a bit, letting the realities of our jobs comfort me. It wasn't good, but it was familiar. 'Fair enough. But the virus is gone? Viora and Bhajan, they're ok?'

Dawkes glanced back me, then smiled, putting a hand on my shoulder. 'Yeah, Reills. The virus is gone. Everyone's' alright. And you'll be too, providing you actually get some rest for a change.'

I snorted a bit, long past having the energy to argue with Dawkes' fussing. Then, something else occurred. 'Calatin's dead, then?'

'Most people wind up that way when you blow their head up.' Dawkes replied, with a slight chuckle, only to drop the smile as she looked at my face. 'You ok?'

'I-I don't know. Calatin wasn't going to stop, I'm sure of that.' I caught myself off guard as I immediately responded, even more so when I kept going.

'At the same time, he only became that way because of something I was complicit in. Maybe it doesn't matter, maybe Bodhmall and the rest of her cabal would've unleashed hell on Dingle either way, but I was there. I played a role in creating the monster we had to kill back there.'

Dawkes didn't respond right away, her hand rubbing my shoulder in silence.

When Dawkes did reply, her tone was slow and considered. 'Reilly, whatever happened in Dingle, Calatin made his own choices after that. Tragedy's no excuse for genocide, and you did the right thing by stopping him before he could set that in motion.'

I looked over at her. 'I know. All the same, seeing what Dingle had done to him, leaving him with nothing and no one...it was unnerving.'

Dawkes nodded deliberately, glancing off to the side. 'That's what happens, I guess. When something traumatising happens, and you don't have anyone to help you, your mind can go to some dark places.'

Dawkes' hand suddenly moved up, ruffling my hair.

'Makes you appreciate the people in your life, you know?' She said, smirking as her hand bobbed my head back and forth.

I growled as I batted her hand away, glowering as Dawkes continued to smirk at me.

'Subtle.'

'Tell you what. You stop being so dense and maybe I won't need to hammer the point in quite so much.' Dawkes shot back, looking a bit too satisfied with herself before she took on a more serious expression.

'Look, I wasn't there, so I can't tell you how you should feel about the whole Dingle mess. What I can say is that, from where I'm standing, you and Calatin have one big difference.'

My rising indignation lost it's steam. 'What's that?'

'Neither you or Calatin had a say in what happened in Dingle, but you were both able to choose how to respond to it. Calatin chose to blame everything around him for what happened. You tried to change yourself for the better. Sure, you've gone about it in a bit of a weird way, but whatever monster you think you were back then, that's not the person I'm looking at now. You understand what I'm getting at?'

'I...I think I do.' I responded after a moment of thought. The strangest part was that I meant it.

Dingle and my part in it still lingered in the back of my mind, but it was different now. The weight no longer felt quite so personal. Dawkes had told me a few days ago that I was a victim too, some poor kid that Bodhmall had manipulated into going along with setting the events there in motion, and while I knew I was far from innocent back then, that much at least wasn't my fault.

I didn't think that I could ever forget what happened that night, nor that I should, the horrors of that one night needed to be remembered by someone. More importantly, what I was certain of now, was that I would never let something like Dingle happen again, not if I could stop it.

'Glad to hear it.' Dawkes got up. 'Anyway, I should probably get the others. They'll want to know you're up.'

I glanced up at her, my previous musings forgotten. 'The others? You mean Bhajan and-'

'And there he is, the man of the hour!' The door to the room exploded open as Bhajan strode into the room with a flourish, arms spread out as another tall, familiar figure lingered just outside the door. 'My most heartfelt congratulations, my dear friend! Not many can say they killed a magical terrorist and lived to tell the tale! Though I hope any tellers don't forget our small role in that, as well!'

Me and Dawkes each stared at Bhajan for a moment, nonplussed by his convenient entrance.

'Thanks, Bhajan.' I replied. 'How long were you waiting out there for one of us to mention you?'

Bhajan's pose seemed to deflate a bit. 'Last five minutes. Couldn't just barge in without a proper cue-'

Just then, he was abruptly pushed aside, stumbling and cursing as Viora sprinted over.

Before I could get a word in, I was interrupted as a pair of long spindly arms wrapping around my torso. More than a few wounds throbbed at that, which didn't concern me nearly as much as the trembling, sniffling alien now hanging off me, her thin arms squeezing with more pressure than I thought possible for such spindly limbs.

'Viora?' I managed to croak out.

'T-thought would die. So many burns, so much blood.' Viora's voice broke as she buried her head into my shoulder. 'B-but safe. A-alive.'

I sat there, stunned for a moment as I tried to figure what I was supposed to do. Eventually, I settled on reaching over and patting Viora on the back. 'Um, yeah, I guess I am. Wonders of modern magic, right? How've you two been holding up?'

'Ha! Listen to this one! Moments after awakening from a coma, and he's asking us how we're doing!' Bhajan spoke up again, grabbing the chair and spinning it to sit backwards.

Dawkes grunted irritably as he reached past her, stepping back as Bhajan sat down. 'Quite well, it must be said! Don't misunderstand, your condition certainly put a pallor on some of the celebrations, but my fellow immigrants have been more than happy to no longer be afraid of deadly viruses or nationalistic fairies! On that note, I hope you don't mind, but I may have made a few embellishments in the retelling of Calatin's defeat. Not enough to reduce your role in it, of course!'

I rolled my eyes, just about managing to hide my relief at seeing Bhajan whole. 'Sure, whatever. Have you gotten much trouble from any lingering fanatics?'

'Nothing of the sort! The remaining Sidhe under Nechtan's banner have scurried back to their hovels and dens.' Bhajan replied with another laugh, spreading his arm in a grand gesture.

After a second however, the somewhat fixed smile dropped as Bhajan then sagged into the chair. 'Though, in complete honesty, matters between us and your Enlightenment are still fraught. Took some convincing on Dawkes' part to even let us in here.'

'Fraught? Why?' I leaned forward in concern, only stopped by Viora's continued stranglehold.

Dawkes rubbed the back of her head. 'Like I said earlier, when High Command agreed to send reinforcements our way, they were expecting to fight off a paranormal assault from all fronts. While I can't talk for Bhajan or the Wavers, honestly, I think a fair few people on our side of things were frustrated things turned out the way they did.'

Bhajan nodded as he pointed at Dawkes. 'Indeed. While many of our own are celebrating the end of the Sidhe Army, several are already refocusing towards the threat the Enlightenment represents to our autonomy. No doubt soon some will start to question if we should have aided you at all against Nechtan.'

I felt the blood leave my face. 'D-did they want a war to break out?'

Bhajan let out a long breath as he looked up at the ceiling.

'Nothing as direct, my friend. No, it is less a desire for war so much as it is the simple nature of politics. When one threat goes down, another must take its place. Alliances forged yesterday are easily forgotten today, when the danger that created them has passed.'

Rubbing his chin, he continued. 'Not to mention, while I doubt this 'High Command' of yours or its troops explicitly wanted a war, they would not have shied away from the chance to curb rabble-rousing paranormals, regardless of the faction.'

Dawkes leaned against the wall, her body almost shrinking from fatigue. 'More or less. Hate to say it, but it's probably best you keep your head down, Reilly. While everything turned out as good as it could, we stretched more than a couple of rules to do it. Captain Hu's covering for us as best he can, but we still probably shouldn't give the higher ups any reason to poke their noses in.'

I wanted to protest, tell them the Enlightenment wouldn't be so quick to condemn one of it's own, only I couldn't. While Calatin might've been an extremist, I couldn't deny the Enlightenment's view of the paranormal was far from rosy.

As much as I didn't want to concede it, I could easily see some of our number getting frustrated at being denied a chance to crackdown on them. And why they might have a dim view of the agents who denied them that opportunity.

Even though it felt like bile in my mouth, I replied. 'I... understand. I won't make any waves, then.'

Eager to change the topic, I then looked down to Viora, who'd stopped sobbing, and was now just clinging on silently. 'And you, Viora, how've things been for you?'

Viora glanced up, sniffing as she pulled back from me, regaining some of her usual composure. 'Strange. First time since arriving on planet that life hasn't been in constant danger. Gave time to think. Thought Lemurians could provide way to contact other ships. Return home. Was wrong. Stuck planetside.'

Damn, I'd forgotten all about that. Without anyway of contacting other Visitors, Viora was stranded. 'Where've you been staying?'

'She's been staying in your apartment still, but that can't last.' Dawkes said, prising herself reluctantly from the wall.

She'd hit the issue on the head. The higher-ups might've been willing to turn a blind eye to me housing a paranormal telepath when it was necessary for the mission. Now that the mission was done though, Viora's presence in my apartment wouldn't be tolerated. Her being my familiar would mitigate some suspicion, but not all of it. Many magi had made deals with paras that'd gone sour in the end.

Just ask Calatin.

In fairness, while I trusted her not to, Hu or any of my other superiors would have no reason to assume I wasn't susceptible to her mind control.

I nodded. 'I know. Still, that doesn't mean we can't come up with something for Viora. You guys have any ideas?'

'Not to worry, Reilly! Your wise and cunning friend Bhajan is already hot on a solution to our little grey girl's homeless issue!' Bhajan popped up from his seat, his usual energy back as he thrust a finger upward.

'Word has travelled far in the last few days, you understand, and more than a few of my fellows in the immigrant community are aware of her part in saving us from mass slaughter. I'm confident I can scratch a few backs, pluck a few heartstrings, and find a place for her.'

Bhajan then reached over, patting Viora's head. 'Who knows, maybe we can even find some way for Viora here to take part in human society. Learn to blend in as we have!'

Viora grimaced at Bhajan's touch, swatting half-heartedly at him. 'Knew of this offer already. Wished to wait until awakening for answer.'

Viora knitted her hands together, her voice taking on an uncertain note. 'Good idea?'

The question threw me. Why Viora cared so much about my opinion that she waited this long for an answer, I had no idea. Still, I felt obliged to consider the issue, so I did.

Despite all that, though, when I answered, it was the first response that had come to mind. 'I can't make that decision for you, Viora. I don't think it's a bad idea, but only if you're comfortable with it. All I can say for sure is that you can't stay with me. Neither of us have a say there.'

Viora fidgeted, reminding me starkly of the frightened girl she been when we first met.

Then, she looked back to me, even while her hands picked at themselves, her face half hidden with her hair. 'Will...Reilly... visit?'

My heart skipped a beat as my name passed Viora's lips. I didn't exactly what it meant for her, but I could tell it meant something.

I gestured at the bed, feeling a small smile twitch along my mouth. 'Probably gonna be stuck in this bed a while longer. After that? Sure.'

A weight seemed to lift off Viora, as she reached up to pull the hair from her face. She didn't smile back, but her posture and demeanour brightened. 'Good.'

As the tension left the air, Dawkes stepped back into my view, smiling at Viora as she spoke. 'Don't worry about a thing, Viora. We're all on the same side here. Whatever happens, we'll handle it as a team.'

'Oh? A team are we now? Perhaps I might be allowed to visit your home, in that case?' Bhajan waggled his eyebrows.

Dawkes immediately shot back with some sharp retort, as she and Bhajan fell into their now typical banter. The rest of our conversation was, honestly, rather senseless, drifting aimlessly from topic to topic. I didn't speak much, simply lying back as the conversation washed over me.

Despite that, there wasn't any awkwardness and their talk was relaxing, not the usual trial conversation was for me. And when they eventually left, I felt oddly empty.

After that, the next week and a half went by at a snail's pace. For what was possibly the only time in my whole life, I had nothing to do, confined to a small room as my injuries healed. Whatever magic the Enlightenment medics had worked on me while I was out had healed the worst of the damage, but I still could barely move from the bed without my legs giving out.

However, that unpleasantness was nothing next to the boredom. I'd spent practically every waking moment of the last ten years either doing something or planning to do something, only now unable to do anything. Worst of all was knowing it was almost certainly a way to force me to keep my head down, while, if Dawkes was telling me the truth, everyone in Dublin was still at each other's throats.

The only thing that kept me sane during that time were the regular visits from Dawkes, Bhajan and Viora, whom I pumped for anything they could tell me about current events. It took three days to realise I was looking forward to their visits.

Aside from them, I had other visitors. Captain Hu dropped by at one point, taking the chance to gently, but persistently grill me for my side of the story, finishing up with some laconic well-wishes and firm instructions to stay until I was fully healed. I even had a short visit from Boyle, healed from his own injuries and cheerfully informing me he would handle my responsibilities until I was well.

That probably would've been more reassuring if I didn't now have to worry I was being kept out of the way. I held my tongue regardless. Throwing a fit wouldn't help, and maybe if I did keep my head down, I'd avoid whatever political hell was being raged outside.

The most concerning visitor however, came during the night.

I don't know what woke me up, but I woke with a start. As I scanned the room, breathing deeply, I tried to calm the pounding in my chest, the darkness leaving me in pitch black.

As my eyes adjusted, I made out a tall figure standing in the corner. They were wearing a dark suit, so dark the edges of it seemed to blur into the natural darkness.

What wasn't indistinct however, was the burnished gold hair that framed sharp emerald eyes, gazing into my soul from a marble-pale face.

Nechtan's lips quirked up in a smile, revealing slightly too sharp teeth. 'Ah, you've awoken. Good to see sleep doesn't dampen your instincts, Arbiter.'

I froze. 'I-I killed you. I saw you fade.'

'Yes, yes you did. As did all those gathered there. And

such a decisive blow it was. A blast like that would surely kill anyone, so there'd be no need to ponder the possibility of say, a convincing illusion of a fading corpse.'

Nechtan spoke softly as he stepped closer, giving me the chance to notice the scars marring his face. Black lines, spread out like tree branches, now covered his cheeks and forehead. I quickly realised they might even extend further, perhaps across his whole body.

As he came closer, I pulled back, which provoked a small laugh from the Sidhe. 'Not to denigrate your efforts, mind. No-one's come so close to slaying me in centuries. The illusion was as much an escape from your wrath as it was from Calatin's shackles.'

While Nechtan talked, all I could think of was how vulnerable I was, stuck in bed, completely defenceless.

All I had was my voice. 'T-that's what this was all about, wasn't it? The whole time, you were looking for a way out of his geas. You didn't care how any of this went down, so long as you got out from under Calatin's thumb.'

'Naturally. The sheer arrogance of that man, to think he had the right to bind me was simply repulsive.' Nechtan's lip curled in a brief sneer, quickly replaced with an irreverent smile. 'Now, however, with him dead, I'm finally free. No geas to bind me, no upstart wizard to order me. You have my gratitude for that, dear Arbiter.'

'Then why are you here?' I asked.

Nechtan stepped around to the side of the bed. 'Is it not obvious? With the identity of Lord Nechtan firmly dead, I shall have to move on, adopt a new persona and way of life. Something I can hardly do with loose ends still hanging.'

I forced my face to stay neutral. 'And that's me, then? The

last loose end?'

As he came up to my side, Nechtan held a hand up. 'Calm yourself, Arbiter, I've not come to kill you. Even if I were so inclined, killing you would not be conducive to letting me disappear peacefully. No, I'm here to repay my debt.'

'What debt?' I relaxed slightly, but only slightly.

Lifting his hand up to examine his nails, Nechtan continued. 'Knowingly or not, you've performed a great service to me, Arbiter. By killing Calatin, and facilitating my own 'death', you've given me the chance to regain freedom on my own terms. That means I owe you a debt, and I have no intention of letting such a thing hang over me.'

Nechtan drew his other hand out of his pocket, revealing a flash of gold. He stepped forward, and pressed the object into my hand. I looked down, and saw it was a large golden ring, large enough to fit around a neck, made of thick strands of gold, weaved together like rope, terminating at each end with holed terminals.

'Consider this precious torc a return of the favour owed. You'll find the qualities it provides you more than sufficient recompense.'

I stared down at the shining torc, my curiosity piqued despite myself. 'Qualities? Does this thing have powers?'

Nechtan let out a huff in reply, looking strangely put out. 'How common. I hand you a centuries-old relic of great personal value, and you want to know if it'll let you spit fire or sprout wings. To answer, I suppose you may find it a useful tool for enchanting. I never did it myself, but its construction is more than suited for bearing some manner of enchantment. More to the point however, should you find yourself ever below the mounds where my fellows while away their immortalities, I strongly recommend taking that with you. The benefits will make themselves quite apparent then.'

I narrowed my eyes. 'Why so vague? Why not just tell me them now?'

Nechtan gestured dismissively. 'Because such things are always best experienced, rather than explained. Rest assured, on the day you need it, it's use will become very apparent.'

'Fine.' I muttered, rubbing the torc with my fingers. 'Since you're here, I had something I wanted to clear up. Now I've had a few days in hospital to think about what happened, something's occurred to me that I need to know.'

Nechtan looked from his nails back to me, eyebrow raised. 'Indeed? Well, I suppose I can indulge you. Speak your question.'

Too late to turn back now. 'Calatin couldn't have just summoned you up with nothing. He'd have needed to at least know your name first. Which means the two of you met before he bound you with his geas.'

Nechtan nodded in response, his expression wryly amused.

'On top of that, you yourself just said you were looking to see more of the world before that happened, so odds are good any opportunity to run loose in our world, you would've taken.'

After Nechtan offered no contradiction, I pressed on. 'Calatin lost his wife and child when a legion of beings from the Shroud were called into our world, the two apparently killed by a Sidhe in their own home.'

Nechtan was no longer nodding along. In fact, he had stopped moving at all. I didn't even think he was breathing.

I stared him down. 'It was you, wasn't it? You killed Calatin's family.'

The room fell into silence, save the faint rattle of rain

against the window. I took deep breathes, trying to still the pounding in my chest as Nechtan continued to stand perfectly still.

Nechtan's eyes moved, fixing on me as he began to speak, his voice flat. 'There are very few things in this world that truly inspire anger in me. I've learned over the centuries to take the slings and arrows the world has to offer without letting emotion take hold and distract me.'

There was a blur of movement, and suddenly Nechtan was directly in front of me, his cold emerald eyes blazed with barely hidden fury. 'The one thing, the only thing I cannot forgive, is disrespect. When I came into your world, all I wanted was some milk and bread to whet my palate, before I set about seeing what the world had become. So, I went to the door of one whom I sensed power from, someone who knew the old obligations. Yet, do you know what happened when the druid Calatin opened his door and I made my request?'

Nechtan stepped back, teeth bared. 'He scorned me. Claimed he had nothing to offer and nothing to fear from me, then demanded I leave his home. In doing so, Calatin offered an unforgivable insult, so sure in his power that he thought I had no ability to harm him. I proved him wrong.'

'You killed an innocent woman and her child over some milk and bread?' I spluttered out, instantly regretting it.

Nechtan's brow furrowed. 'No. I killed that family for failing to meet obligations long laid down between my kind and your druids, those who were meant to commune between us and humanity. Were it not for the druid himself fleeing after his family were slain, he would've joined them then.'

As quickly as the fury took him, it left Nechtan. His voice immediately calmed. 'Alas, I failed in properly exercising punishment, and paid the price for it. Only two years later, the scum conjured me in a ring of iron and branded me with the geas marks. Suffice to say, I'll make sure the next ones to disrespect me are not dealt with in half measures.'

I shifted back from Nechtan. I'd seen plenty of inhumanity among paranormal beings, enough that I thought I had a handle on understanding where these beings differed from humans.

Nechtan was something else. He wasn't trying to make excuses. There wasn't so much as a shadow of guilt on his face. He didn't just not feel guilty for murdering two innocent people, if anything his tone was vindicated. The only type of person or being who could understand that mindset was a psychopath.

In that moment, I was very glad the rest of the Daoine Sidhe were happy to hide away in their mounds.

'I see.' I managed to gasp out. 'Well, what do you plan to do now, then?'

Nechtan pursed his lips. 'Now? Now I return to Lumintech. Nechtan may be dead, but Thoun lives. The Lemurians of Ireland need a strong leader to bring them out of their squalor, and I believe I'll be more than up to the task. The Lemurians might not have the strength of my fellow Sidhe, but they are wily and clever enough that I can make something of them.'

'You realise the Enlightenment will know about your split identity, right? I haven't told them yet, but I'm sure my partner has already spilled the beans.' I replied cautiously, idling hoping maybe this would scare Nechtan into disappearing outright.

Nechtan nodded. 'Yes, I suppose they most likely will. Perhaps your organisation could unmask me, reveal that the great revolutionary, Lord Nechtan, survived his gruesome injuries, thus forcing me to take flight once more.'

He looked back at me, a knowing smile on his face. 'They could certainly do that, but will they? Does your Order stand to gain from angering me so soon?'

Would they? The Enlightenment had just managed to evade a war, and however the higher ups may feel about that, no-one would want to risk things burning out of control so soon after they've calmed down.

But the whole reason the Sidhe Army had fallen apart was because they didn't have Nechtan as a figurehead.

If he was exposed, what was stopping him from raising another army and repeating the whole damn process all over again, only this time without someone else holding his reins?

Nechtan let out a quiet chuckle that made me stiffen up. 'Ah, I see I don't need to explain any further. I suppose I'd best take my leave. You still have a great deal of recovery ahead and I have no shortage of work myself. This certainly wasn't what my fantasies of seeing the mortal world promised, but I'd be lying if I said the experience wasn't stimulating.'

I slumped back, only for Nechtan to abruptly lean over. I tensed, ready for a fight, only for him to grasp the side of my head and pull me forward, planting a kiss on my forehead, then pulling back to look me straight in the eyes, Nechtan's own glowing in the dim light.

'Rest well, noble warrior. No doubt a man like you will find himself pulled into many more trials in the future. I for one look forward to seeing how that shapes you.'

I was speechless as Nechtan, with one last smirk, stepped back into the darkness, melting into the long shadows, before disappearing.

Strangely, it wasn't the realisation then that Nechtan could seemingly appear in front of me at any time that left me unsettled. No. What disturbed me was the weight of the torc in my hand.

Lifting the thing in front of my face, I squinted at it as if it held any answers. Did Nechtan know something I didn't? Some secret about these 'trials' he was talking about? Or was it just empty talk, a way to get under my skin?

And if any of those were the case, what was the torc's role here, beyond just a quick way for him to get out of his debt to me?

Questions about my suddenly uncertain future danced in my head as I gazed into the glimmering metal. The torc offered no answers, and eventually I lowered it and closed my eyes.

It has been said that human imagination is both our best friend and worst enemy. Certainly, as I lay there, drifting into dark and foreboding dreams, I felt I'd only just scratched the surface of how true that was.

Printed in Dunstable, United Kingdom

67349374R00241

**SOME HISTORIES DON'T WANT TO BE BURIED. THEY WANT REVENGE.**

Agent Reilly is used to dead ends. But when an alien ship is found drifting over Dublin – its entire crew twisted by a plague that leaves no trace – the mission that follows will throw up more questions than it answers. As factions turn on each other and forgotten powers stir beneath the streets, Reilly must track a bioweapon that defies science, confront a killer driven by grief and madness, and wrestle with the question that's haunted him for years: can a man shaped by trauma hold the line between worlds without becoming the very thing he fears? Step into a darkly spellbound Dublin, where magic mutates, monsters remember, and nothing stays buried for long.

ISBN 9781036925918

9 781036 925918 900

CONORRENNICK.COM

Cover design by designforwriters.com